Romance, adventure, and double-dealing sail aboard the Mayflower!

Out of the pages of THE PLYMOUTH ADVENTURE swaggers a venal, sly, and fearful man of destiny, Captain Jones of the *Mayflower*.

Never suspecting that he had been bribed to land at Cape Cod instead of the Hudson River, the little band of men and women he tricked and bullied found, not paradise, but a wintry hell at the end of the voyage. Here is the novel that makes you a partner in the Plymouth adventure, a witness to the triumph over one little-known historical double-cross.

●　　●　　●

"Admirable, authentic, fascinating reading."
—Edward Stanley, *Saturday Review*

"Thoughtful, racy and entertaining . . ."
—Charles Poore, *N.Y. Times*

"THE PLYMOUTH ADVENTURE can't miss! . . . Good story, real people and plenty of action."
—Francis Ludlow

The Plymouth
Adventure

A CHRONICLE NOVEL
OF THE VOYAGE OF
THE MAYFLOWER

BY ERNEST GÉBLER

PERMABOOKS
Garden City, New York

PERMABOOKS EDITION 1952,
BY SPECIAL ARRANGEMENT WITH
DOUBLEDAY & COMPANY, INC.

There is nothing that can be invented by the imagination concerning human conduct, about a man, a personality, a course of action, saints or devils incarnate, mass madness or absolute courage, that has not been surpassed somewhere, at some time, in real life. The plain recorded history of men, their motives and deeds, can present drama of such a nature that the inexperienced reader is at first glance hard put to it not to believe it something contrived out of imagination for dramatic purposes.

When the boatload of refugee weavers, hatters, homeless men all, ground on the desolate beach of Cape Cod from the *Mayflower,* in search of land whereon to build the first North American settlement, they were not met in any obviously dramatic way by hordes of screaming savages, although that was quite possible. Instead, they saw their first Indian in so subtly and magnificently dramatic a way that this reader of history, for one, was hard put to it not to believe the whole episode something deliberately furbished up for its dramatic value. The plain recorded history of the *Mayflower* settlers is overflowing with such incidents.

The story of the *Mayflower* stands in its own right as a piece of superb drama; which may indeed be the reason why it has been fought shy of by historical romancers: certain men have put such an imprint on their history that as long as the world shall last it will resist anything the imagination can do to better it or twist it to another shape.

But that is no good reason why an epic, so closely woven into the fabric of our civilization, as is the beginnings of the New World made at New Plymouth, should lie in closed books, yel-

5

low tracts and the letters and transactions of historical societies. THE PLYMOUTH ADVENTURE is an attempt to illuminate and interpret the conduct of the men and women who sailed out on the *Mayflower*, while leaving the stiff framework of known events to speak for itself. When the Captain deliberately, as it seems, runs into shoal water, that is as it happened in reality; when the Captain has a revelation concerning his own baseness, that is history as it could well have been; but herein imagination has tried to walk with fact without pushing fact out of the way for its convenience.

The sequence of events, particularly in the explorations, are followed out faithfully, step by step, as told by the accounts and journals of the men themselves, without juggling or altering for the sake of the "story."

What has resulted from this treatment of history is a form of documentary chronicle rather than a historical novel; which may prove not altogether happy for those who would have only an account of passions and actions without purpose (the log cabin defended to the last bullet but one), and care nothing about the relation of a story to actuality or what brought it into being; happily, these shameless ones are in a very, very small minority.

But in the long run it matters little who tells or how; the fact remains that the men and women who ventured out on the *Mayflower did* do that incredible thing, and that is all that does matter.

Consequently, there is no character in this story who was not a living person engaged in the events dealt with, though their personalities have been almost wholly dreamt up from clues and inferences; and a list of all the people who sailed on the *Mayflower* is given at the end in an Appendix, with some notes on their subsequent history which, while not coming within the period covered by the voyage of the *Mayflower*, may be of interest to the reader, and a useful guide to who each person is and how they are concerned in the story. This list of *dramatis personae* will be found on page 410.

Book One

THE VOYAGE

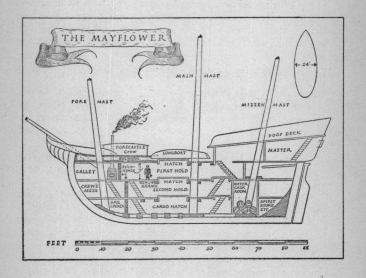

THE MAYFLOWER

MAIN MAST

FORE MAST

MIZZEN MAST

24'

POOP DECK

FORECASTLE
Crew
BULWARK
LONGBOAT
MASTER

HATCH
FIRST HOLD

BULK-
HEADS

GALLEY

HATCH
SECOND HOLD
WATER
CASK
ROOM

CREW'S
MESS
BEAMS

SAIL
LOCKER
CARGO HATCH
SPIRIT
STORE
ETC.

FEET

0   10   20   30   40   50   60   70   80   88

1   Fifty paces up from the quays of Southampton, the ancient walled town on the Test and Itchen rivers of England, stood the mapmaker's shop where the gilt and varnished sign, grimy and blistered, hung out above the buckled doorway, announcing:

RICHARD OSBOURNE. GEOGRAPHER.

The cobbled street carried a single open gutter to drain household slops and rain water to the harbour below; in summer it stank, in winter it ran like a mountain stream; summer and winter depressed hens wandered about in the shadows cast by the overhanging, timbered shops, dwellings and warehouses.

Here Richard Osbourne had dispensed through book, chart, globe and word of mouth for longer than fifty years both accurate knowledge and splendid imagination.

In the summer of sixteen hundred and twenty the old man finally completed his turning out of the back room. He had carried armful by armful, up the murderous stairs to his apartments above, a fifty years' hoarded accumulation of dust-blackened, gnawed sea charts, maps, spoiled globes, blank globes, globes faded blind, papers, books, mousetraps, mad compasses, collections of trout and salmon flies, broken astrolabes, ship models, dirty platters, empty wine bottles, a good ship's trumpet that had conquered by fright many a sea monster, an old long coat that had turned from black to green and which now hung in the yard to air with a view to further service; and a mound of other mouldering and forgotten objects.

He had surveyed, contemplated, planned, shaking his greasy yellow dome in at that dark back room, for years. On Wednesday, the second day in August, he stood triumphant within in the musty gloom, accompanied by a young carpenter.

9

"Most are sound," the geographer said. "You will not have to make good many—well . . . not as many as might be thought by looking at the place." He banged his fist on the rotten panelling "See, boy, stout—no need to pour out money——" Again he banged, but the weight of his thin hand split the panel apart and a little cascade of wood dust fell into his sleeve.

John Alden, the carpenter and barrel maker, treated the old man with a friendly, awkward patience; willing also to be entertained by the alarming expressions of cross temper the geographer could in an instant ruck up upon his pointed face. "Dry rot, Mr. Osbourne," shaking his head seriously. "The worms are in it something awful. I'll have to pull your house down wholesale, Lord help us . . ."

"Dry rot, Mr. Carpenter! Don't you spread tales of dry rot in my house, John boy . . . or off with your ears. Get out your rule. Measure over for your wood—I'll enter it down on paper for you."

"I'll enter it down myself," the young man said impudently. "I wants to make a few shillings, not end the job owing you."

"Ah, it slips my memory I'm dealing with a learned scholar," the old man said mockingly.

"My hand can be read—more as can be said for some half the time . . ." John replied promptly.

"No impudence, boy!"

The young carpenter wiped the windows to let in some light, and began to measure the panels; the mapmaker craned his neck to see the rule and examine the first jotting.

Outside, the street door creaked open, and in entered a strait-laced gentleman with a confident air, followed respectfully by a tall girl breathing obedience; both had the resembling features of longness of face and proud, injured airs; but where the father's face was blemished and inclined to creases, the daughter's was soft in its young womanhood, white-skinned, faintly freckled, and barely pretty.

The geographer looked out; the man was a stranger, and not a seafarer. But after a second viewing with his good long sight he decided that the customer looked stupid, and showed money by his dress, so he hurried forth. Alden, the carpenter, continued to measure and poke at the panels with his knife, keeping his ears inquisitively alive to the voices outside.

The good weather would continue, Mr. Osbourne said. People usually asked him about the weather. Once a countryman had offered him a shilling to make it rain in certain parts; so he invariably told that joke while running an eye over a fresh customer. Good cloth here, in a sober suit of dark russet. Lately shaved. Offensively clean-looking.

Mr. William Mullins, taking off his black felt and holding it in his hand, as he had observed many men of high breeding do, said, "I am, by name, William Mullins. I have heard that you keep engravings for sale of those places across the Atlantic seas?"

The Western World, the New World, there were many names for it. Fine woollen stockings Mr. Mullins wore; and cleanly oiled leather shoes—a substantial merchant; a pretty girl.

"Yes, the New World," Mr. Mullins said, simply, reverently, and after a deep breath.

"Sir? Whose New World? Grönlande? Brasillia? Virginia?" He glanced up keenly at Mr. Mullins' sober merchant's short bob. Then at his plain band, a simple collar of white linen worn turned down out over his coat. But here was no shopkeeper dressed up in his Sunday best. He had asked about Virginia? They were from the ship—but *they* . . . had no money, it was said, at least of their own, more the pity.

"They are said to be from true likenesses, made by a man who visited the coasts there," Mr. Mullins said calmly. "I know nothing of the place myself. But many have heard of these pictures, yet never have seen them. They treat of the country, and the savages that dwell there, of the plants that grow, of animals . . ."

In the back room John leaned against the wall, folded his arms and listened.

"I should be most grateful if you would allow me to see these engravings," Mr. Mullins said. "I . . . I'm interested in trade with the heathen people."

"You sound like a Londoner," the geographer commented, irrelevantly.

"Well? You don't show your pictures to Londoners?"

"And you're on the *Mayflower*—for Virginia?"

The girl, standing behind her father, ceased her glancing about and became still and expressionless.

"We have taken a passage here," Mr. Mullins said, after a moment's hesitation, "but on what ship, and where it sails . . ." His eyebrows lifted slightly to indicate that the rest concerned only himself.

Old Osbourne clamped his gums together and cocked his scraggy beard up at the taller man almost insultingly; he joined his hands behind his humped back and walked up and down the uneven boards a few steps each way, a schoolteacher in the act of exposing a boy's lie. "Come, sir," he said kindly, "few ships leave the port of Southampton without my knowing where they hope to throw down their anchor. Ships are our business; you have come to Richard Osbourne the geographer; on my charts very likely your course will be plotted. Your Master on the *Mayflower*, Mr. Jones, came yesterday for a new copy of Smith's coast discoveries—having spilt his dinner on the one he had."

"Everyone in Southampton knows where the *Mayflower* is intended on her voyage?" Mr. Mullins asked stiffly.

"Everyone harbouring a whit of interest in where ships go— such as I, myself, know where she goes and what about. But have no fear! If the Government desires to stop the ship, and *can*, mind you, dear sir, stop the ship, why they will do so."

"Why should the Government want to stop the ship?" Mr. Mullins' colour had deepened.

"You possibly know that just as well as I do, Mr.——?"

"Mullins. But this ship, and her sister, sail under the orders of the Council for Virginia."

"The Virginia Company, Mr. Mullins, are a band of merchants set upon making money. As for these they call 'troublemakers'—well, you are right in your strength not to let yourself be beaten from pillar to post."

The young man listening could make nothing of this; Mr. Osbourne had never before, to his knowledge, tried to put anyone off the idea of Virginia. It was not what he said, but his tone. Here at last a ship was setting out from Southampton with settlers who would live in the new country and the old man's tone of voice showed disapproval.

"But make no mistake about it," Mr. Osbourne continued, "the Government merely think it cheaper, that you sink and are destroyed in unknown seas, than that they keep you in the Clink on crusts and Thames water till you relieve them of your troublesome presences by dying."

"Really, Mr. Osbourne! I have never been in a gaol—nor would ever be if I remained in England."

"Really, Mr. Mullins! Well, well . . . your book of De Bry's pictures of the savages . . ." He wandered to the shelves and laid hands on a stepladder to draw it into position.

"I am going . . . to set up in trade there," Mr. Mullins said loudly, "and carry knowledge of Christian things among the heathen. There is also much trade to be done among these savages; and so it appears that someone has to begin by living and planting themselves in this New World."

"And so I have been saying for forty years," the geographer said, and laid his elbows comfortably on the top of the stepladder. But this pompy, self-important Mullins and his tightfaced, silent daughter were not in the wind, nor near it. "And you are not afraid, even with your women, to be cut off in the wilderness, thousands of leagues from any Christian man, the whole black Sea of Darkness between you and England?" He pursed his lips for a moment, chin thrust out, looking again at the girl. She was pretty, in truth, the poor thing, but all tightened up in fear for her ass of a father. Mullins was certainly a puritan—of the more objectionable type—for there was no mistaking that loose-skinned, seamed, righteous face; happily, they were not all of his ilk and manner.

"Your daughter goes with you, you said?"

"My wife and daughter go with me, God willing."

John took his weight from the wall in the back room and moved across to where he could look out and have a view of the wayfarers. He stared at the girl, examining her with a slow, speculative interest.

13

He was conscious of her tallness first, and reassured himself that she was not too thin. She struck his eye as trim and neat, in a dress of fine dark purple-blue; bodice hooked and eyed from waistband to throat; orange collar and cuffs; skirt falling fully from high waist to above ankles, in length neither the floor-sweeping hem of quality nor the just below knee of the commonalty, but somewhere in between. About her shoulders she wore a walking-out kerchief of linen in French green; on her head and tied under her chin a similar kerchief.

She would wish, then, to appear well bred. But, he thought, even he could have told her that hooks and eyes were not worn by ladies, nor every one done up under the chin on a summer day.

Anyhow, her brown hair had a fresh sheen, her skin was pure, pink and white, and her teeth could not yet be black; and her hands seemed soft and unworked. Such cleanness of face, hair and hands in an unclean world was hardly distinguishable by him from beauty.

Her father did not bother him, but he would not seek the eye of a gentlewoman stockingless and in his greasy working breeches. So he stood very still, ready to step back should she turn around. Her face from the side was to him cleanly cut and pleasing to look at.

The geographer harangued the pair gently from the rostrum of his stepladder. "The change of air, diet, and having to drink all water—for your beer will soon run out—must infect bodies with sore sicknesses and grievous diseases. Such prospects must be faced up to boldly, and accepted, before setting a foot on the way. You have not heard of Jamestown? Those who shall escape or overcome all other difficulties will yet be in continual danger of the savage people—ah! who are cruel, barbarous, treacherous——"

"Nonsense, sir!" Mr. Mullins said stubbornly. "Those who have seen them closely in their daily lives know them to be children—if heathens. All children are answerable to stern management."

"They are most treacherous, sir," insisted the geographer, "being most furious in their rage, and merciless when they overcome, not being content only to kill and take away life, but delight to torment men in the most bloody manner, flaying some alive with the shells of fishes, cutting off the members and parts of others by piecemeal."

"Have some regard for my daughter's presence, Mr. Osbourne."

"And taking the flesh from their enemies while they still live, they broil it on the coals and eat the collops in their very sight, with other cruelties, Mr. Mullins, too horrible to relate without moving our very bowels to grate within us. I should think twice, myself, before throwing my wife and daughter among such fiends, in a distant and desolate land."

"My father has to go," the girl said suddenly.

"No man has to," the geographer corrected her, and gave her down a thin, eager smile.

"If the savages kill us God wills it so, not my father." She compressed her lips together and looked down at the toes of her shoes.

Her father cleared his throat. "Tell me, Mr. Osbourne, is the passage through these seas . . . is it a fair and possible thing of accomplishment in such a ship, shall we say, as the *Mayflower*? Is it not true that such ships pass daily without being swallowed up?"

"They have gone out of this port in barrels of fifty tons and circled the world."

"There, girl." Mr. Mullins smiled for a moment upon his daughter and patted her arm. "Our ship is three times fifty tons."

"You must have seen many monsters of the deep, sir?" the girl asked.

John inclined his ear attentively in the back room; her voice was somewhat sharp, a little high, perhaps, but pleasant, if youthfully overdetermined.

"The beasts?" whispered the old man, dramatically staring down at her from his perch on the stepladder. "Ah! . . . I will tell you a story—of a sea captain out of this port of Southampton, who went to fish and salt cod on the far capes. Out west did they sail for ten weeks and had no sight but the mountains and valleys of the grey sea. A storm came out of the night and blew

15

their poor sail to rags and tatters. So then it fell away into a still calm; when they were left riding under bare poles; so wearied they were all asleep without a watch—where, in the stillness of the calm sea, the timbers of the ship began to rattle like a bundle of old bones in a bag, and a most fearful roaring sounded from the sea hard by. There was light enough in the heavens to see the beast, and the Captain saw it to be a physeter. He had seen such a beast before—and come back to tell the tale. But here, in the vast sea, they had no sail upon the yards to fly from him. He had a trumpet, this Captain, if all else failed—a trumpet may drive the physeter off, but it may atimes drive him into madness, and in his lashings he will destroy the ship. Therefore, being a provident man, he had thrown out tubs of butter and meal to the beast, which he carried on the deck against such occasions. These did seem for a little while to put the beast in a better humour, while they tried to get up some sail and away from him, betimes he was busy devouring the food. He lay by the side of the ship cracking the tubs in his jaws like cobnuts—but I won't weary you with his descriptions, which every man knows."

Mr. Mullins cleared his throat again nervously, nudged his daughter, and whispered sharply, "Close your mouth, girl." To the geographer, he said, "No doubt it is an offence in your eyes never to have been to sea, sir, but I must admit to it, and to having no knowledge of these sea creatures. . . . It would be charitable of you to give me some signs for their recognition. . . ."

"You will see, as my Captain saw and all his men, a creature two hundred cubits long, wallowing on the top of the water, cracking the tubs of meal in his ravenous jaws, which are set in a monstrous square head, his mouth all set about with prickles, girdling his neck long, sharp, crooked horns growing out of the skin—which have made men liken him to some huge tree torn up by the roots."

"Bigger in size than a ship?" Mr. Mullins asked.

"Many times bigger, sir. In colour he was all black, which made his eyes shine out like beacon fires in the dark. Over the rest of his body he was covered with bristly hairs like a hog; his forked tail by fifteen or twenty foot broad. The sailormen knew that when he had eaten what they had thrown to him he would come upon them in anger, and if he did not flood the ship with water—from the great spouts on his forehead—crunkle it in pieces with a snatch of his teeth, because they would not have the sails up in time to get away. The poor sailors cried out to the Captain, 'Oh, sir, what are you going for to do? We are destroyed!' The physeter was rubbing against them with rumblings and gushes of steam. Then it was the Captain lifted the ship's trumpet to his lips and blew a blast such as he had once split an iceberg with at Grönlande. All the sea heaved in a fury. The physeter sounded, plunging under the ship to the bottom of the ocean, in a fright." Mr. Osbourne clapped his hands together loudly; the girl started and gripped her father's arm.

John, drawn unwittingly to the door, smiled, shook his head and scratched his cheek doubtfully.

"But, please, sir, ships come back . . ." the girl said, out of a dry mouth.

"Yes . . . yes, maybe. Many will go, some will come back. Take rue," he looked down solemnly, "called by some the Herb of Grace; thrown to sea creatures, it is said to make them drunk and faint, and your ship may escape."

"Our prayers, girl, are all the magic we take," Mr. Mullins said, regaining himself. "The engravings, Mr. Osbourne, I would see them, without further delay."

"Humph," the old man said, "see them then—but be warned, if you are frightened I'll take no blame on it."

Swinging herself a little about, twisting her fingers together and frowning against thoughts of sea beasts, the girl glanced back and saw the young carpenter leaning against the doorjamb and rubbing his jaw. Once seen by the full gaze of her eyes, he remained where he was. Her gaze was quick, frank, proud, and departed without apparent interest.

She saw a rough-looking young man who had not shaved for three or four days, with a strong face, large, clear features. Thick dirty fair hair curled behind his ears and upon the nape of his neck and was sun-bleached to the colour of straw over his forehead. She saw that his skin was flushed from sun and wind, except where it shewed through a tear in his shirt, that he stood over six feet, so proportioned, dressed for fair weather in an unbleached shirt of coarse linen, soft-skin working breeches blackened down his thigh fronts from hard wear and uncaught below the knees. He wore no stockings, his feet happy in half-laced, split-open boots.

She turned away without expression and without any particular feeling of interest; the geographer looked a bad old man and would therefore have bad-minded, cheeky servants.

One of the geographer's stockings at that moment finally descended about his skinny ankle, as he came down off the stepladder, carrying an armful of books.

"These are the most lovely copper plates of Master de Bry," the old man gloated, "John White his pictures, the first ever made in Virginia, the New World."

Mr. Mullins turned the pages and looked down at the books with his head on one side, as a man will who looks in deep ignorance at a strange object and desires to appear familiar and expert.

Priscilla Mullins leaned over by his side and, in another book that the geographer had laid open on the table, saw an engraving of the classically beautiful, and mostly naked, figures of the Virginian Saturiba walking forth in the evening with his Queen, her maidens and attendants. Priscilla's mouth fell open, her colour deepened and her lids forgot to blink. By the Chief's side walked young men carrying great fans, said the text, while behind him followed another, wearing gold and silver balls hanging from a little belt around his hips, who held up his train.

From another book Mr. Mullins was reading in a hissing, breathless voice: " 'Clothes they wear little, and never for modesty; which are for the most part of finely worked leather, for brave arrays or protection against winter weather. I found them all about there to be upright and well proportioned in body. Their colour of skin is a rosy brown. They are neither a flat-nosed or a big-lipped people, but much as we are, though rounder and fuller in the face, and have sad, unabashed eyes. To me they shewed kindness and dignity—however they treat their enemies—while to all children they are very tender and loving——' " At which point Mr. Mullins noticed his daughter out of the corner of his eye and turned upon her sharply. "These are not for you to see." He began closing the books. "Have you no shame?"

She stepped back from the table, reddening completely and looking at her fingers.

The geographer laughed out loud: when she got there, if ever she did, she was likely to see that the artist had put more clothes on these people than they even had in fact; for they were as unashamed as Adam before the fall, and wore as little.

"They will not be allowed the environs of our habitations until . . . Your price for this book, Mr. Osbourne?"

John grinned at the old man's hoots and whinnies of laughter; he had also heard sailors' tales of the children of Paradise.

"How much do you ask for this book of John White?" Mr. Mullins asked, sternly.

The thought of losing a book cut short the old man's enjoyment instantly. "Twenty shillings," he snapped.

Mr. Mullins winced; he haggled with dignity for a further minute but in the end had to pay the full price. Osbourne followed him to the street door, sourly telling over a list of disasters at sea. "And Francis Blackwell you have heard of . . . who went forth for Virginia with one hundred and eighty to set up in freedom——"

"I know, I know," Mr. Mullins said, grinding his teeth and prodding his daughter before him.

What in the name of the Lord did this toothless scrivener expect him to do at this hour of the day? "I curse your impudence. Shall I drag my wife and children back, be whipped as a beggar in the streets of London where once I was respected? All my property is sold and vested in this venture; I cannot get it back —nor if I could would I ruin the enterprise of a hundred poor people for my own cowardice." He wrenched himself out, clasping the book in his trembling fist, and strode away over the cobbles with long, ungainly steps, the girl running by his side.

"The good God help them indeed," the old man shouted, "if they have many more ignorant and foolish men like that on their ship."

"I never did think I'd live to hear Mr. Osbourne putting people off America," John said awkwardly.

"I am particular who I let plant their feet in my country! I it is gave it them, made charts of its waters and harbours since I could hold a pen, watched and hoarded the knowledge of it from loss, saw fine ships go out and never come back, followed captains day and night till I'd sucked them dry. That man has no passion for a new world, but only for himself. He is not the right kind of man for it."

"Would you say now as I was your right kind of man?" John Alden asked.

The old man stopped dead in the act of slapping dust from his thigh.

"For of a sudden I've a mind to go and see it," the young carpenter said.

"To see it! That's all over. This is sixteen hundred and twenty. The days of Ponce de Leon searching for the fountain of youth are gone also; when we go discovering now we go to seize and settle." The ancient geographer padded back and forth over the creaking, worn boards, his beard-tufted chin on his chest, his hands clasped behind him. "And here comes this— this smug thing, half righteous ape, half petty man—oh, I take his kind in with one glance! What new world can he build? Hard engrained with our dirty habits: meanness, pride, ignorance, arrogance. He must make my country into but a bad copy of this old world. Give that man but six months there and he will have a law made to cut off the savages' heads for eating of the grapes that grow in the woods. But God be thanked, if he never had a dream, there are others to go that have. And as for you! . . ." He came to a halt and wagged his bony finger under John's nose. His face had become markedly purple; his other hand he held over his heart. "What dreams have you? Pah! Meat and bone. No dream like Raleigh's will ever carry you to the ends of the earth."

"Dreams?" John said with heat. "They go as in they're treason subjects, Mr. Osbourne. The King proclaims them, I've heard. They'd go to the gaols if they was to stay on England soil."

"Hah!" the old man said passionately, waving his hands as if dispelling a cloud of insects from before his face. There below was a shipload of people, he said, and if their only hope was one day to rise out of the mud and escape cold and want and daylong toil, then they would succeed, and in the same day, fail; for this thing also needed men gripped by the throat by their own dreams.

John sat on the floor with his chin on his knees and stared at him; but he said nothing for fear Osbourne would remember the work to be done in the other room and stop talking; and so the day drew on towards noon, and the old man's silences grew longer and more frequent; until finally he asked him:

"When do they sail, Mr. Osbourne?"

"Tomorrow. The day after. Whenever they are trimmed—and as near one mind as needs be. Why so, John boy? What is it to you?"

What it meant to John Alden he could not put into words at that moment. But while he had been sitting there a warm, inexpressible desire had gathered in him, a restlessness, a conviction that something immensely important to himself was happening or about to happen almost beneath his nose, here in the town, below at the quays; that the ships going out to the New World were somehow his ships, his concern—and but for the grace of God they had all but sailed without him! Yet, once stirred, his slow imagination worked up and on till he found himself possessed of a firm purpose. Receiving no answer, the old man again forgot about him, and rambled on.

"Then they are off, boy, off, chasing their muddy dreams across the great Atlantic Stream, out across the Sea of Darkness —a-looking for the world in its first innocence, in as it was when Adam came out and first beheld it, before cities and spires or the greedy man learnt to crush the simple man. I'm a poet, boy. Poets see too much." The tired eyes sunk in the small bony face turned to the young man, brightening.

"And some do have the secret shameful dream," he said pipingly, "of gentle brown people, of kings and queens weighed down with gold chains, who wait, in their innocence . . ." He cackled. "The which are to give their gold and their bodies to the stranger, when he does come with a cheap trinket. Have you such a dream, is that it?"

The young man's expression of interest sharpened, but he suppressed his eager and knowing smile just in time.

Osbourne looked at him shrewdly. "Are you aware that here on these ships, for the first time in my knowledge, are some who are unnatural men to the rest of the world, men mad, men of fierce and terrible will, who have put aside the dream of poor men to be kings and instead would be contented shepherds? For them it is to be a stern, clean land. You will perhaps get no free gold or women with *them.* . . ."

John shrugged.

"They burn their boats," the old man continued, "they go forth into the darkness." His voice was grown hoarse and weary; he closed his eyes. "And I, I am too old."

The young carpenter rose to his feet at last, and was passing out into the street when the old man seemed to awaken.

"Young man!—you steal away? Have you the canker too? What's to do with my panelling? Now it will never be done. . . . God take me for a romancing old fool."

"God will take you for a good man, sir. But it is time for me to go for my dinner."

"See their ship's Governor, a Mr. Martin," the old man said, and, rising, came across the floor and slammed the door after him.

2   It was known generally among the people of Southampton where the adventurers intended to set sail, and it was rumoured that the company included dissenting subjects, rebels against the established ways of English life. But little else. No one from the ships concerned would give any more detailed information, certainly not to the casually curious. Groups of sightseers usually gathered in the evenings, gossiping and staring

out at the anchored ships; and returned as wise as they had come. Shopmen fared no better with the occasional customer from the *Mayflower* or *Speedwell*.

But John Alden, by his several visits to the geographer's shop, found himself slightly better informed. He knew that the larger vessel had been there over a week, fitting out and stocking provisions, and that she had come from London with roughly forty men, women and children; families drawn principally from the South, but also from the Midlands and North of England. According to Osbourne, they were some sort of rebellers against the bishops and the King, though not supposed extreme or unlucky enough to have as yet suffered imprisonment or chastisement.

The settlers had kept to their ships during the ten days they had been anchored out in the Water; their gaffers, or Governors as they call them, coming ashore for the purpose of provisioning and like matters; some of the women had visited the shops now and then, or on a rare occasion such an important person as Mr Mullins went ashore to make a purchase.

Four days previously the smaller *Speedwell* had come in, to drop anchor alongside the *Mayflower*. Of this second ship not much was known either, even by the geographer, except that she had come from Holland and probably brought a further forty or fifty men, women and children; who were thought by Osbourne to be some of those English subjects lately living in Holland as refugees, having fled England as members of the separatist congregations known as Brownists—from Robert Brown, a preacher. Their leaders were thought to have come originally from Scrooby, in Yorkshire.

Of what the Brownists wanted or believed the carpenter had no clear idea; but he did know very clearly, as even the most ignorant were forced to, that to live in England without at least outwardly conforming to the social and church laws was as much as a man's life was worth. And, like the majority of Englishmen who neither knew nor cared what such groups of people's ideas and aims were, having a healthy fear for his own safety of person, he had the normal fear and resentment for them.

They were still ferrying food and goods from the smaller ship to the larger. It was said that an exchange of passengers had also taken place in preparation for the long voyage. Both ships were to attempt to cross the Atlantic Ocean.

That much John Alden knew, at midday, on August the second, as he went down to the quays.

The young carpenter passed under the West Gate and walked on to the quays as the bells began to strike midday, sauntering with one hand in his pocket and the other holding his canvas jacket slung over his shoulder. It was a busy port, and his way was beset both by the goods carried on the sea, the spars and tackle of ships being refitted, and by the many oddly different kinds of men concerned with seafaring; but he progressed determinedly, though his gait did not suggest a set purpose, only now and then pausing to view the better some particular vessel among the shipping alongside or anchored in the fairway; until he came to a point opposite the 60-ton pinnace *Speedwell* and the 180-ton *Mayflower*.

Both ships rode off the north end of the West Quay, looking somewhat set apart in the Water, as if they meant to keep their distance from the rest of the shipping. They were anchored about a hundred yards out. And there, plainly to be seen, were the women and children. He had stood so before and looked out at the *Mayflower*, but this surely was as if he saw the scene for the first time. On the decks of both ships were women and children—women who intended to cross the vast oceans and had no intention of coming back. Seeing them now, hearing the children's thin voices across the water, it was incredible. They were such very plain little ships, to attempt such a thing! . . . He scratched his head and stared hard.

The big ship itself—one could not count the little one, the *Speedwell*—was the most commonplace of weather-beaten old tubs. By the miniature *Speedwell* the *Mayflower* might well look quite large; but compared with any one of the score of oceangoing ships, of six and seven hundred tons, anchored in Southampton Water, she was a dowdy, scrubbed, cut-down little barrel of a ship. But to give her her due, he admitted, she looked a good, solid, young ship, if heavily laden and sitting low in the green water.

He judged the *Mayflower* to be not more than eighty feet

long; and being a typical apple-cheeked boat, about twenty-five feet across in the beam—only a little over three times as long as she was broad. She would have a crew of twenty. And, low in the waist, would certainly be a wet ship. Carrying the usual three masts, the fore and main were square-rigged in the simplest manner, while the short mizzenmast behind on the poop was rigged to fly a lateen sail. Built across the foredeck was a roomy forecastle, like a small house that had been forcibly jammed forward. Her stepped-up poop deck slanted back and up over the stern, suggesting for all her rotundity and squatness the folded wings of a gull at rest on the water. Between the forecastle and poop was the low waist deck, where the settlers leaned about and sunned themselves. So much he took in in a few glances; such ships he saw every day of his life.

There were forty or more people crowding about the narrow limits of the middle decks of each ship, continually coming and going below, emptying slops, talking, jostling about aimlessly, stitching clothes, hanging washing to dry, happy in the fresh air and warm sun. The chimney of the galley fire, sticking up out of the *Mayflower's* forecastle, spouted smoke. A figure came into the bows from the forecastle hatch and shot a bucket of refuse overboard, bringing the gulls swooping and screaming down over the glinting water.

He stared hard but could see no one who looked like Miss Priscilla Mullins; and seated himself on a hot stone. After a while two canvas-trousered young seamen came along the quays and squatted down near by on their roped bundles.

"Going aboard?" he asked, with a jerk of his head towards the *Mayflower*. He was answered without hesitation, very soon told that they were hired for a year to go abroad into the New World with the settlers, there to teach them to sail their coasting and fishing shallop, a small boat carried in sections in the hold of the larger ship. Their names were Robert Ellis and William Trevore. Across the ocean they were to serve under Thomas English, another mariner hired by the merchants, whom they had not yet met. A Mr. Thomas Weston had signed them on in London, and they were going aboard today for the first time. Ellis did most of the talking; he came from Woolwich, on the Thames.

The other spoke Somerset and had the silent repose of a well-rooted tree.

"This Master Weston is a merchant, who 'as put up the money," the first sailor said. "'As all to do with the ships. You sit 'ere long enough you'll be bound to see 'im. There's likely a way of buying in, to be a settler and get land, if a man had a piece of money."

John shook his head; he had no money. Then he might indent himself as a servant for seven years; some on board were taking men that way, men who were neither sailors nor farm hands nor useful in any particular way, passage paid, all found, in return for seven years' labour.

"I'm a carpenter," John said, "and I wouldn't go as a servant."

"You wouldn't 'ave to—you'd be a useful boy. Their ship's Governor said he was on the lookout for a cooper—Martin is his name, man with a red face."

John saw that a young woman had come to the quayside and was sitting on a broken bollard some twenty yards away. She had a green kerchief round her head, and was sitting bent forward, her hand to her face. He got up and went towards her, pushing his hair back tidily behind his ears. But when by her side and about to speak he saw that she was not the girl who had visited the mapmaker's shop that morning. And she was crying, silently; a pale young woman with a small, girlish face; she was plain-looking now, when serious, but would be pretty when she smiled. She had the kind of face that a man might think plain at first, and find it to be very beautiful when he came to know it well. She looked up through her tears, yet with the beginnings of a smile.

"Beg pardon, mam," he said, "I mistook you . . ." He was turning back, when he suddenly thought of a way in which he might get out to the *Mayflower*. "If you'd go aboard, mam—I could get a boat, I'm sure, for to row you out? . . ."

"Thank you for your kindness," she said, "but they'll send for us in a little while"; wiping her eyes with a corner of her kerchief.

"I hopes no one has handled you roughly, mam?"

"Ah, Southampton has, your town—these very stones offend

26

me, because they remain behind." She shrugged, smiled, as if waiting in a child's fashion for him to join her in smiling. "I won't see England never no more, never no more. . . . Won't never set foot on it again, once we sail from this quayside! So I remember that—I don't often find tears in my eyes. . . ." She had the trick of appearing half the time to be talking to herself. "Very foolish of me, because I haven't been in England since I was very small. But first we left——" She stopped short, frowning. "But when we left the other place, to come to Southampton, to come to England, it was like coming home at last. Now we have to go away again, away to the other far place, because they all want to go, far, far away—and I have a toothache!"

John sat down beside her. There was no need to call her "miss" or "mam"; she was plain and poorly dressed. "But the amazement of it over there," he said, "don't you think on that?" He wanted to pat her reassuringly. "The sun shining from morning till night like a brass plate, every bird and animal in the world, grapes growing in the woods—pick grapes when you like!"

"Grapes?" the girl said, smoothing her hard serge skirt over her knees. "A woman has little time for picking grapes, wherever she is. And the ships . . ." She shaded her eyes to look out at them. "How can a little ship like that sail from one side of the world to the other, without stopping? A man told me there were great waves in the sea as big as——" She broke off, absently gazing at her string bag, resetting the hank of thick wool, cards of pins and hooks and eyes she had bought in the town.

"All the seas have waves, mam—miss." But of course she was simple in her mind.

"A scholar in Leyden told me the waves out beyond are as high as mountains." She looked around into his face, drawing down the corners of her mouth in mock seriousness, leant a little closer and said confidingly, "I ought not to be talking to you, ought I? My husband, Mr. Bradford, will be coming from the wineshop and . . ." She looked round and about slyly, and smiled her little smile of invitation again, as if to join her in some joke.

He stood up instantly, not understanding that her dim moments of humour were a part of her nature and not directed at him particularly. "Would I be allowed on the ship for to see Mr. Weston, or Mr. Martin, mam?"

"Why, Mr. Bradford has gone to speak to Mr. Weston, in the wineshop, where they sit at tables." She turned sideways on the bollard to point across the stretch of cobblestones at the line of lodgings, wineshops, chandlers', and the hostelry. "There he is, my husband. Ask him anything; he is the kindest man in the world for answering questions."

John moved back a pace from her. The young woman looked towards her husband as she might were she seeing her child come to her; while she pushed a bit of her brown hair back under her kerchief—from where the lock escaped again a moment later and fell into its old position by her right cheek. The man came onwards with a vigorous, careful carriage, wiry, thin in the leg, just noticeably narrow across the shoulders; he held his head up and back straight as if it were a strain for him to do so but something he thought necessary. His clothes were ill-fitting, coarse and strong; black Irish stockings, brown breeches and short jacket, and a dark orange shirt open at the throat.

"Look at his shirt," she whispered. "I dyed it myself, for the long journey—a colour keeps cleaner. He didn't like it at first but he's quite proud of it now."

Few in Mr. Bradford's presence would have been aware of his clothes; his face claimed too much attention. It was an irregular face, long in the upper lip, whipped pink by sun and wind, though but a week before it had held a smooth pallor. He came up to them with a deliberate sturdiness, a sandy man, hair cut short, unsmiling, looking upon them forthrightly with deeply set, light blue eyes; it was a northern face, hard, intense, and aged in appearance beyond his thirty-one years. A boat pulled out from behind the *Mayflower* as he came to a standstill before them, and he nodded satisfaction at this to his wife, standing with his hands behind his back, looking across the water then.

"Here is a young man seeking Mr. Weston, William," she said in her very soft voice.

Bradford looked at John, examining him.

"Mr. Weston is in the wineshop which is called the Red

Bottle," he said, pointing briefly. He spoke carefully, in a strong but thin voice, with a Yorkshire accent. "Did someone send you here?" he asked, a little sharply.

"No one sent me. I'm a cooper," John said confidently. "I'd have my chance to go for Virginia."

"But who told you to come to Weston?"

"I live here. Mr. Osbourne is my friend. Mr. Osbourne said I should seek out a Mr. Martin." He was not going to like this uncomfortable Bradford, John felt. "I heard it said as there was a chance for a cooper, or maybe a carpenter, to go."

Mr. Bradford said nothing for a few moments, frowning and looking down at the stones. A touch of quick anger warmed the carpenter. The other was after all not so many years older, still a young man, despite his air of resoluteness—and not, from any signs that John could see, any better off in the world than John Alden. If Bradford would have himself accepted as a man of affairs he ought to dress like one. John immediately took his reserve for offensiveness.

"I thought you might have travelled a long ways here," Bradford said. "Sent. Understand? Most here have come from afar, after long waiting to go. Whether you can be taken on at the snap of a finger . . ." He shook his head doubtfully.

"I have said I am a stranger. Do your masters fear strangers?"

"We are all strangers on our ships—were and will be for many a day yet to come——"

"And them that's come out of the Low-countries," John persisted, "strangers to each other?"

"Low-countries?" the young man in the orange shirt repeated stiffly.

"That's what is said."

"It's said also that there's a man in the moon," Bradford said uncomfortably.

The boat bumped against the steps below and Bradford took his wife's arm and descended. The sailors, Trevore and Ellis, came along the quay and followed them down the steps. John slung his jacket over his shoulder and set off towards the wine-shop, now fully determined to get on the ship at all costs.

3   Under a clear sky the water stretched a half a mile to the opposite bank, blue and sparkling, when John appeared on the quay at eight o'clock the following morning, ready to go aboard and be assigned quarters. The shipping rose and sank gently on the soft swells. About the *Mayflower* and her little sister ship, the *Speedwell,* scavenging gulls swooped and screamed, and he could see many people out and about on the decks of both vessels. The mainmast of the smaller ship had been stripped for retrimming.

The young carpenter seated himself, and mused over the water. Now he would take his chance, as all on the two ships were prepared to take theirs. For no one could tell where it would end. One man's opinion was as good as another's, and his own as good as anybody's. . . . The less he worried over his own ignorance of the whole business on that bright summer morning, the better. For there he sat dressed as if for a holiday and feeling as if the day was a holiday. Thinking on this problem or that, he told himself, only addled the brain of a man and left him unable to cope with things as they came. It was a time in the world for young men to go forth into oceans where none had been before; he who would not seize on such a heaven-sent chance was a fool, and so on.

Nevertheless he began to ponder on the events of the day before, frowning as though in great effort; for though his wits were nimble enough if faced with the necessity for quick physical action, his mind had had no training in reasoning or spelling out cause and effect.

He had left Mr. William Bradford (in orange shirt), leading his wife down the quay steps, and gone off determinedly to the wineshop. There, he had sought out and found, in a quiet corner, Mr. Thomas Weston, a fussy little London merchant; and Mr. Christopher Martin, a large, red-faced man and the "Governor" of the *Mayflower.*

Mr. *Mayflower*-Governor Martin was self-important, pugnacious, fat, breathless, and seemed to be all red face and soup-stained shirt front. Mr. Weston was clean, small, white of face and like a bird, very sharp in his ways and gave himself airs in a silk-braided doublet and black ribbon bows beneath the knees.

Long the pair had argued, haggling over his wage of a shilling a day, but in the end had signed him on as a barreller for a year and a day, all found except for his kit of clothing, the which he must provide himself. For the law, the gentlemen had learned or remembered to their consternation but a few days before, required that, where over a certain number of barrels were to be carried out of the Kingdom and not returned, a cooper of the trade must be aboard to cut barrel staves to the same number for shipment home again. Which law he could now thank for the chance to go beyond the world's rim and see such wonders as no man had beheld since the Creation.

With a sudden glow almost of astonishment he remembered the other inducement that had been quietly held out to him in return for so risking his life. Land. If he cared to stay after his time was out, then he might know that miracle, to own land. They were going to build houses and stay there! He and his might dig gold in his own back garden; he and his that had been allowed to own nothing since the beginning of the world, as he thought. His hand had shaken fit to split the pen when he had signed the paper. "I, John Alden . . . Twenty-one years . . ." "I am an orphan, sir."

Then he had mumbled on how he hoped he would not be got at to say his prayers any other way than how he had always been taught was right. . . . Were there not odd things being said about the people setting forth? And the merchant from London had stared at him with a cold eye indeed. He was no Minister of the Crown, said he, he was a merchant. It was, true, in part his ship and his money. But he had no power to command a body of men to leave off saying their prayers whilst standing on their heads (when they got to the other side of the world), if that was the way they would say their prayers, or die for it. "Blockhead. You go to mind barrels. Leave politics to your betters." What had he meant? Time would tell. John gazed out at the *Mayflower* steadily. Soon he would walk on her decks, see the girl with the long, eager face who had come to the geographer's. They were taking their women and children. They must know what they were doing.

Among them he would be as good as any, decked out in his plum-coloured jacket, breeches to match, all in hardy, sensible cloth, new stockings and clean shoes—he had forgotten, however, to wash his face and hands on rising or, for that matter, any other part of his person; but it did not trouble him, he had given himself a good wiping over face and neck the Sunday before, which was after all only three days past.

He took up his bundle and from it half withdrew the stock of a silver-mounted wheel-lock pistol, his sole possession with any pretension to grandeur; it had been left to him by that uncle who had also taught him to read and write. His father had been humble; but his uncle was in the law, and thus, he often thought, he had a right to dream of bettering his lot. In those far places a man might escape his birth, gain a seat, sit upon his own horse and direct large affairs. Others going there might have better airs, but he went among them no pauper. Slowly and with deep satisfaction he told over his possessions in the bundle of his dunnage: one hat costing three shillings; one quite expensive shirt at two and six; one waistcoat costing two and six; one suit of working frieze, nineteen and sixpence; one jacket lined in oilskin against the rain, thirty shillings; three pairs of Irish stockings, five shillings; one pair of strongest shoes, eight shillings; and a long, lined coat of thick, soft, dyed canvas. With such a fortune in kit alone who would be afraid to set out into the New World?

'Good morning, cooper," said the little merchant, Mr. Weston, behind him. "You are out eager and early. Every man will need to be eager on this business if he is to prove his worth."

He turned and saw that Weston was accompanied by another gentleman—or perhaps not a gentleman, it was hard to tell with these people.

"Mr. Gilbert Winslow," Weston said. "Sailing for Virginia." He hinted in intonation at perhaps some slight disapproval.

Mr. Winslow was a young man, something over thirty, long, thin, pale, clean-shaven, with bobbed brown hair and large dark eyes; he had a graceful shabbiness even with his new leather working breeches. He smiled readily, inclining his head, while dumping down a rolled sleeping palliasse, canvas sheeting and grey blankets. Mr. Weston was fussily waving his handkerchief at the ship.

While waiting for the dinghy to come in for them Mr. Gilbert Winslow hummed to himself or addressed odd, self-sufficient questions to Alden, in a quiet, absent-minded way. Weston walked up and down.

"You belong to this town of Southampton?" Gilbert Winslow asked, looked away, took a few steps along the stones and returned. He had come down yesterday from London himself, he said, to join the ships—had slept ashore though, liked a little comfort while still possible. An elder brother was on board the *Speedwell,* who had, well . . . been trading in Holland and with whom he was now going out to Virginia. A moment later, seated on his bedding, he was poking at a hole in the sole of his shoe. "Have to mend that. It might rain in America!"

The dinghy was putting in, a sailor rowing, Mr. Martin sitting in the stern. He came up the steps, puffing. "Lord, the things there's to do and no time, no time. Stocks are nowhere full enough, Mr. Weston. Complaints that they'll all starve."

Weston took him aside. Alden and Winslow descended the steps and seated themselves in the boat. After a few minutes' delay the diminutive merchant came down and climbed into the prow and they started out towards the larger ship. A line of faces watched their approach from behind the bulwark of the waist deck.

From nearer on the ship looked sounder than John had expected; her upper works were seamed and well seasoned by salt water and sun, but the tar on her hull, coming up to well above the water line, clung unbrokenly and tightly to the grey oak. A set of steps were rigged on the flat down the sloping side, which the outswelling curve of the ship caused to stand out from her several feet at the bottom. He became aware suddenly of the sound of feet and muffled voices, a child's cry, of all the sounds made by people about their business of living.

A glance at the man with the hole in his shoe, who sat in the stern by his side, proved a suspicion that he was being observed with open interest.

"You don't know anyone aboard, I take it?" Mr. Winslow smiled.

"You stay along with me and I'll direct you to the right man there," Mr. Weston called from the other end of the boat.

They touched, and the little merchant went up first, awkwardly and carefully, like some black inelegant spider. John Alden followed, holding his bundle over his shoulder with his left hand. He swung over the low bulwark and stepped down onto the deck: those on the deck had drawn away to allow their entry aboard; they seemed to examine him covertly, but amongst themselves said little; there were many children, some quite young. Mr. Weston had crossed the waist deck and was going up the poop steps to the high deck aft. In some embarrassment the young carpenter followed, without thinking of what he was doing. The high deck aft was for officers only.

At the side of the poop deck by the mizzenmast was an encased hatchway, down which the little merchant eased himself backwards, after a rap with his knuckles and a call of, "Jones, Master Jones." A deep voice within shouted back for him to come down. Greetings passed in the Captain's cabin; the Captain seemed to be at breakfast. Mr. Weston was not aware that John had followed him up to the poop deck.

John sat down near by with his back against the mast, to make himself less conspicuous; a fresh breeze hummed in the rigging and it was good to feel the gentle movement of the ship; to be upon a ship was to be upon something known yet exciting in its possibilities. A man came up from the sailors' quarters in the forecastle forward and pitched a bucket of potato peelings over the side, making the gulls dive and scream in a whirling mass. Tarring of a replaced section of ratline was going on and two younkers were up on the mainmast yards supposed to be working, but John could see that they were lazing and talking.

He became aware that some of the conversation going on in the Captain's cabin was plainly audible when the wind dropped.

He heard Mr. Weston's voice say: "The information about this harbour comes from a Captain Thomas Dermer of the New-

34

foundland Company, no later than yesterday!" And the other voice, presumably the Captain's, answer: "That Cape, Mr. Weston, is well above the forty-first parallel. . . ."

"Our territory," Mr. Weston's voice continued, "the territory of the London Virginia Company, only extends to the forty-first, good. Let us have it clearly: you make landfall *above* the Cape. The sum, we have already agreed—it shall be . . . You can find excuse from wind and tide to make that point."

"Slower, slower, Mr. Weston!" the other voice said. "First, nothing in writing at any time to pass between us on this matter. And should question ever arise, I will call you liar in your face, as you have leave to do me. Let us at all costs have a gentleman's agreement." A laugh, as if in a barrel, followed. The voices were not distinct on every word, but clear enough to catch some sense here and there.

Mr. Weston: ". . . a quarter . . . the rest on your return."

"But I would like your drift of this clearer, Mr. Weston," the Captain's voice said, "how can you make more by putting them outside legal territory . . . than by planting them within? If I go north of the Cape . . . Without sense to me, for if this settlement takes root and lives your Virginia Company must, in the long run, make great profits. . . . Is it not true that Gorges' Plymouth Company has rights north of the Cape?"

"Let us say that it is a matter of state and let it so lie until— until you return, Mr. Jones."

"Matters of state are none of yours, Mr. Weston, money is. This other company of merchants, the Plymouth Company, have wasted their money—for how many years?—to get a settlement on their own territory. None would go!"

"Granted, Mr. Jones, but let me say——"

"And now the chief manager of the London Virginia Company would make a free present of a settlement, provided for, shipped, outfitted, to the Plymouth merchants' company." The same laugh; but this part of the conversation came not at all clearly to John; even had his wits been sharper and the increasing warmth of the sun less inclined to make him drowse, he would have had difficulty in absorbing it. He still did not understand that the words he heard were fragments of a conversation of vital importance. He shook his head sharply to wake himself up, and stared forward at the middle deck. The children began to play tag, rushing madly about squealing and screaming; a woman clapped her hands and attempted to stop them, and found herself being used as a maypole.

John tried to return the attention of his hearing to the hatch near by; in the tones of the two voices below there was something that rubbed at his mind for understanding, apart from what meaning the words might have. There was wrongdoing in their voices, he thought. Did he only know sufficient of the whole enterprise he might make some sense of it—later, at any rate, when he could puzzle at it without having to take in bits of a conversation at the same time.

"The Plymouth merchants have failed up to this day, Mr. Weston, never having found a true body of earnest people, they who would stick together through thick and thin. But here, let us say, they see a party bound together by their common dissent to the laws of England. They never even had a thought there could be a body of settlers so well bound together as this lot, good or bad. To get such delivered free, with the other company paying the piper . . . There's big money there, Mr. Weston. Sir Ferdinando Gorges and the Earl of Warwick's Plymouth merchants stand to control a whole new world . . . make fortunes never before heard of . . . and you offer me a pittance!"

"They may all perish!" Mr. Weston's voice shrilled faintly.

"Whether they do or not, how much do you make before they even set foot upon the way?"

A babel of noise rose from the children playing in the waist; John inclined his ear deliberately towards the hatch.

"Upon my oath, Mr. Jones, neither the London Company nor the Plymouth Company know of our agreement."

"Then why turn out your pockets to make a settlement outside . . ."

"I am still the London Company. I am here now on their business . . ."

"Then there is no sense in you, or in your arrangements to go north of the Cape. Am I to think you raving mad, cutting your own nose off to spite your face? As well give me a cargo of your goods and tell me to sink them in the middle of the ocean to make money for you."

Robert Coppin, the second mate, came out from the forecastle, where he had been below in the galley mess having breakfast, and stood for a moment in the sun with half-closed eyes, while he wiped his mouth with the back of his hand. The two sailors above on the yards saw him immediately, but he did not look up at them; his gaze settled towards John on the poop and remained upon him as he crossed the waist deck.

By good chance John was not at that moment inclining his ear very conspicuously towards the hatch; the second mate's face appeared above deck level, stared for a moment, and then the whole man heaved up and sprang upon the boards; John saw a huge figure attired in dirty leathers; a young man in his twenties, shaven only roughly about the mouth and cheeks, dark-complexioned and with red-rimmed eyes.

"Off this deck with you. Passengers between decks or on the waist only."

John wiped his eyelids with his fingers, smiled, but did not rise to his feet. "I'm signed on as cooper, hired by the Governor of this ship for a year."

"Governor! Martin, you mean? There's only one Governor on this ship, and that's the Master, Mr. Jones. You're not hired by the ship, you're hired by the passengers, hired out to a company of ragpickers!"

The young carpenter shook his head slowly.

"That's what they are," the sailor said, "ragpickers. English folk chosen rather to be fustian makers in Holland than abide in their own country. With the airs and graces of selecting themselves Governors. Now lift yourself off the Captain's deck or I'll lift you."

John got to his feet.

"You'll be glad to say your prayers after the right fashion before you're through this trip," Robert Coppin said.

Gilbert Winslow came up from below and stood a moment by the poop ladder. The second mate unexpectedly gripped John's bundle and pitched it forward along the deck; it shot off the end, dropped towards the waist deck and was caught by Winslow.

John would a moment later have attempted to take the second mate by his loose leathers and pitch him after, but Winslow called up, "Carpenter, you can stow your stuff in my encampment below until you have your own corner. One mustn't bandy it with mates."

John walked past the second mate without hurry and descended the ladder. "Anybody's dunnage left on decks'll get heaved over," the second mate said. He leant on the rail picking at his teeth and spitting into the water.

Down in the first hold Gilbert Winslow had put his bedding in a portion of the shallop. Many were using the segments of the fishing boat stored below decks for the same purpose. To prevent the portions rocking or shifting they had been roped to rings in the ship's timbers.

The air inside was pleasant, holding a settled, aged tang of turpentine and salt fish; for the gunports were opened up wide and, no guns being carried, though they let in little daylight, draughts of fresh air swept back and forth. So far the two buckets, canvas-screened at the end of the hold, had not been used here, Winslow carefully pointed out; and there was a law against their use, unless the weather at sea should absolutely forbid anyone going on deck. This ruling had not been made by the ship's officers, but by the people themselves; so it was all the more important to keep it; a remark the young carpenter did not understand. Otherwise ordinary necessity was served by buckets behind firmly lashed canvas screens up on the waist deck, each person emptying over the side and swilling by aid of an attached rope. This arrangement was against the port bulwark, hardly higher than the bulwark itself, to escape wind pressure, and was a concession the passengers had insisted upon.

Winslow's pallet was laid on the deck near a gunport; he sat down, gazed out at the water idly, spoke intermittently. "This the sailors call a deck also, but we call it the first hold, and the one beneath the second hold."

John, with his thumbs stuck in his belt, rested his back against a beam. Had the second mate not come just when he did he would surely have heard more, perhaps the few words that would have brought sense to what of the conversation he had picked up. Which had spoken of the Cape? But they had not named the Cape. He did not even know if the spindly-shanked little money-lender had won his point in the end, or what his desire had been. Here was a strange state of affairs if they were arguing at such a late date about where landfall should be made.

When he had signed his paper to serve a year, he had done so explicitly to go to a place named Hudson's river, in Virginia; where the boats would cruise about up the reaches and look for a favourable site for settlement. And any waterfront man that kept his ears open knew that there need be nothing haphazard about finding the right river once the coast was struck; what they might find when they landed was another matter. The positions of all the bigger rivers and prominent capes on the coasts of Virginia were well, if roughly, known; fishing boats, traders, mappers, whalers, adventurers, had been striking those self-same coasts, and charting them, on and off, since John and Sebastian Cabot sighted Newfoundland in fourteen hundred and ninety-seven and took possession in the name of the Crown of England.

The tone of voice used by the Captain had suggested that Mr. Weston desired him to do something, connected with the landing, that was not to be generally known. But, John thought, he himself had been hired by Weston; so why should he speak to strangers of a mere suspicion, snatches of a conversation he did not understand and should not have listened to, and perhaps land in such trouble that he lost his position and was turned back? Nor, now that he came to think of it, could he speak out to Weston on such a point, when Winslow's elder brother was apparently a declared separatist, a dangerous fanatic who had been living in exile in Holland. Better he watched and waited and found his footing more securely.

So far the settlers had not by all appearances taken much notice of him. They were quiet in their manner—perhaps watchful—poor, soberly dressed, clean. He raised his chin from his chest, began looking about the hold, and listening carefully to Winslow's remarks.

The first hold ran without division of bulkhead the full length of the centre of the ship, from the galley bulkhead forward to the tiller-room door. Through the middle of this long, low chamber, the mainmast base passed from ceiling to floor, as it did below again in passing down through the second hold, and so through to the main hold in the bottom of the ship and onto the keel timbers.

Less than a dozen rough box bunks, with partial partitioning at each side, had been fixed to the decking; there were also four tiny cabins in the poop allotted to the passengers. Otherwise, Mr. Winslow said, one just put one's bed down where one could or where told. Christopher Martin was "Governor," having been elected by the "English" party before the arrival of the *Speedwell*. To him had been given the power of allotting all accommodation so that there might be no argument. He was also Treasurer of the "English" section's money invested in the enterprise and had been given power to conclude the provisioning with the help of Cushman and others.

Here the hold was free of gear except for the fishing boat carried in sections; each family or single man had their own few square feet of deck space to camp upon. The passengers in the second hold below were not so comfortable; there, spars, rigging, cable and some of the lighter cargo was stowed, the only ventilation being by way of the hatchway to the first hold. Most of the pallets and bundles were corded or roped in some fashion to bolts and rings in preparation for the high seas.

Winslow suggested that John find himself a corner and settle down.

"No, sir, I'll see what comfort there is down in the cargo hold first."

"Ah, I forgot you were not a poor terrified passenger. You won't mind being in the bottom of a watery pit, as it were. But you'll not find any room down there. Please yourself. I wish I'd more lonely quarters myself."

Some forty men, women and children were set out about the hold, which looked like a nomadic encampment. The Mullinses were not present. John later learned that they were among the few who had secured one of the tiny cabins aft.

The people sat on their palliasses, most of whom had two or three laid one upon another, or sat upon the decking. Meals were to be eaten here, food a community affair and distributed from the community stores by orderlies; there were different orderlies for each day, so that each passenger took his turn.

A limited quantity of food might be prepared on a brazier of charcoal, which was slung above a section of iron plating and a sandbox hearth in the centre of the hold. Any food that had to be cooked was cooked all together at one time and must do for several days, dished out cold and sparingly.

"Many bellies will be clapped in," Winslow said, "after a few months afloat here."

John pushed back his thick, fair hair uneasily and asked, after pondering a few moments, "You mean, sir, that we are going to be on short stores? What about the merchants, and Mr. Weston, and the money they're said to have put up? And don't these people have money in it too?"

"Merchants and their money?" Winslow said sadly. "They've called in the settlers' halfpence into the pool, every mite—but the business of merchants, John, is to comb into their pockets as much money as they can, while letting the smallest amounts out again. And our Governor, Mr. Martin, it seems, has spent up the grant of provisioning money here, but leaves everyone unsatisfied. I don't think you'll starve though—not altogether. . . ."

Gilbert Winslow impressed him deeply as a calm, observant man, knowledgeable without being weighty; and someone who might be fairly relied upon to give a straight answer. He looked like a person of some parts and means who had come down in the world, but he showed no distantness or stand-to-the-down-wind-of-me-sir; he had a voice of education and fair breeding, and while a humble cooper should tread warily with all such persons, John's hesitations with him were passing. It was not that Gilbert Winslow had gone out of his way to show kindness or helpfulness; his manner suggested that he treated all people more or less in the same way, if spoken to answering civilly, if left alone, just as pleased.

"You might tell me, sir, about this Mr. Martin—there's things I do not see . . ."

"What do you not see?"

"Mr. Weston's Company charters the ships, puts up the most of the moneys, all what is needed, food—but it passes me how they expect to get their money back, and a profit."

"The secret, John, is that a man can sell his labour years before he performs that labour; as we all have here, as I have, heaven help me—excepting you and one or two other aristocrats of labour who incur no debt and can come and go consequently when they like. We have sold the labour of five days in every week of our life for the next seven years. Every cod we dry, every skin we get, every plank of wood we hew from Monday to Friday, will be called for and collected by the merchants' ships for the next seven years—will that not show profit in a vast country running wild with fur and trees and herbs and oilfish and every other product of nature's bountiful mercy? On the other two days of the week we plant and grow to support our bodies. But we can own nothing there for seven years, until the debt to the merchants is worked off."

John wiped the sweat from his face. "Every man, woman and child a bond servant?"

"Not exactly."

"But you said . . ." He stood stiffly in surprise.

"Yes, I know. Well, I suppose it is bond servitude in a way—but we don't like to think of it like that. . . . There's the boat out again." He rolled over and went forward on his hands and knees until his head was through the gunport, ducked back in and scrambled up. "Coming ashore? Might as well while there's the chance, you'll be battened down here long enough."

John followed him towards the hatch steps aft, along the free centre of the deck.

"I think to lay in a little private store of nuts and biscuit," Winslow said, wagging his finger, "for hard times."

"So too, sir, I'll acquaint my lodgings she'll have an empty bed comes the sailing day."

They leaned over the side and Winslow called down, "Boat going ashore?" The boat was.

Out from under the poop came the little merchant, Mr. Thomas Weston, wilfully shaking a fistful of papers, his face an angry pink. Following behind him were William Bradford, John Carver and Robert Cushman.

Weston almost ran to the side; with one leg over he waved the papers and cried, "Let it be your last word, my masters—last words do not cost anything. Stand on your own feet from this out; see how long you'll remain upright." He brought his other leg over the side and backed down to the waiting boat.

William Bradford remained by the poop door, silent, with a set, stubborn face. Cushman, a small man like Weston, worried and ill-looking, followed to the bulwark, calling out, "Let us talk about it more, Mr. Weston, you cannot expect acceptance of so drastic a change on a moment——"

Carver, the third man who had followed Weston up on deck, looked serious but not worried; an old man in sound, well-to-do dress, of great physical ease, bearded, bald, benign. He strolled after Cushman, his hands behind his back, his eyes on the deck, excusing himself and smiling when he bumped into a woman who was standing by, whispering to her friend.

"Look lively," Gilbert Winslow said to Alden, "or we'll be left." He swung over the bulwark and down the ladder after Weston; John followed with difficulty, excusing himself past Mr. Cushman.

"Enough, Mr. Cushman," Weston shouted, stumbling in the dinghy and flopping down. "If you refuse, you refuse. I can do no more. I wish the Lord I'd washed my hands of the whole business earlier."

The boat pushed off, John and Winslow again in the stern.

For ten or twelve strokes of the oars no one spoke. The boatman was whistling; but as he began to need his breath more, he ceased.

"I pray we are not going to be held up further?" Winslow said gently to the little merchant.

For a moment Weston did not answer; then he spoke down into the stern sheets in a small bitter voice. "I have worked day and night for over a year to help them, so that they might set themselves up in freedom from interference and persecution. Now, when I ask them to concede a point—*no!* Mr. Cushman treats me as if it were *my* demand and not the instructions of the whole Company's council."

"Will this difference hold up sailing?" Winslow asked.

"Every penny of my own personal fortune has gone towards this enterprise," the merchant answered, "and as the Lord is my witness they are welcome to it if thereby . . ." He fell silent, shook his head, clasped his hands and stared with martyred expression across the waters; he would say no more. The boat touched the landing steps; he stood up, climbed the steps and hurried away.

On the quayside, John said, "Is all put off?"

"I shouldn't think so. I proceed forthwith to complete my little arrangements as if nothing had happened. Quarrels have been springing up and dying down over this affair for something near ten years now. Our little ironmonger there, for all his writing of pious letters—for which I believe he has a fine facility—will not wash his hands of his investments whatever else he does. Well, we'll see tomorrow."

They went across the quays, John to his lodgings, Winslow to the inn where he was staying. . . .

4   Shortly after dawn John was out of bed. There was not much he had to do, having few friends, and no family; his possessions were so slight and of so little value that what he could not take he rid himself of by simply abandoning in his lodging room. The things he intended to take included, of course, his eating knife, normally carried on the person in a sheath, a wooden drinking cup and platter, a waterproof canvas bed sheet, two strong and thick, if lumpy, blankets, a well-padded and quilted waistcoat for cold nights, and a small sack of powder and lead for his pistol. There would be powder and lead in the general store but it might prove useful to have some in his private possession. His clothes and the pistol he had left aboard with

Winslow's kit the previous day. All he had to do now was buy a couple of pallets, and say farewell to the old geographer, Mr. Osbourne.

At nine o'clock he knocked on the geographer's door. A neighbouring woman, who at odd times cleaned and cooked for the old man, opened it and peeped out.

"Can I see the old man?" he asked.

She nodded, knowing him by sight, and brought him in, but shut the door and bolted it again. She went ahead up the stairs, silent and gloomy. At the door of Osbourne's bedchamber she turned and held up her hand. "No, you'd best wait till he's laid out decently. You can wait below with me in the kitchen; they won't be much longer."

"Is he sick?"

Her face loosened in surprise, the expression lengthening, while she clapped a hand to her cheek in a silly way. "You didn't know he was dead?"

"I was busy about things . . ." Then he realised it.

"He died early in the evening, after a stroke. He was let but never opened his eyes again. The surgeon said the stroke must have split his brainpan inside, for he never opened his eyes again after being found on the floor. Such a state, papers all round him, one of his new charts clasped tight in his fist."

"I'd see him now—I may be sailing . . . He was kind to me. I knew him well . . ." Not knowing what he was saying, he pushed past her into the room and went to the head of the bed. The old man had died with his gums clamped tightly together, so his face was unbound. The face was so very, very small, skin on bone, the colour of dirty candle grease, the pores imbedded with dirt. John stared down at him for almost a minute, turned abruptly without speaking, and descended the stairs to let himself out. But at the foot of the stairs he stopped, looking in at the empty back room that the old man had engaged him to repanel in his spare time. And, as if in a dream, he walked in and towards the window, wet the side of his hand and wiped his pencilled figures from the panel, the lengths and widths of boarding he had measured the day before. Then he let himself out, closing the street door after him gently.

Straight away he bought two straw pallets, returned to his lodgings, collected the rest of his stuff under his other arm, and proceeded down to the West Quay.

The regret he felt was centred not on any person, but on the old geographer's house and his own lodging room. What male companions he knew had increasingly annoyed him even by their presence as a willing audience for self-vaunting, and no help towards any bettering of his lot could come from them; for while he had little knowledge himself, his being able to read and write simple English inclined him to impatience and overbearance, with, at the same time, a sense of powerlessness not becoming his unusual physical strength.

From early morning till nearly sundown his days had been spent at the barrelmaking yards in hard work, while his few free hours in the evenings he had usually put in before his hearth, dozing, reading any old tract or bit of printed English he came by, or carving rough models of carts, windmills and ships. He had never read a full book, nor ever had one in his possession; nor did he own a copy of the translated Scriptures, no more than other artisans. They were too dear, or so he thought, and he had never had an inclination to possess the Book.

Behind him he now left the geographer, dead; and behind him he left his own bare-boarded room, empty, scattered with the bits and pieces, the refuse of his past life. Blindly he had come to what he was, and he felt no uneasiness about going blindly out across the ocean; only a healthy regret and a pleasant excitement.

Knowing now how to wave from the quay for a boat, he soon got taken out, and found the little deck jammed so tightly with men and women that he had to push his way through to the hatch with his stuff, piece by piece. He was told that the settlers would hold a meeting shortly, and went below—as another six men came aboard from the smaller ship, the *Speedwell*. Gilbert Winslow was not in the first hold, nor was any other male. The women were nearly all below by then; there was no room for them on the deck above when all the men were up there; they now appeared to be anxious, and even furtive, pressing towards the hatch stairs and talking in low voices, at times hushing each other to hear what was going on above.

John saw amongst them the Mullins girl whom he had first seen in the geographer's shop; although not apparently housed in the first hold, she had stepped down with the rest, to listen.

The shuffling on the deck above suddenly quietened and John, without stopping to think whether he might be welcome or not, but so that he might authoritatively push past her, went back up the stairs. She folded herself back into the crowd without noticing him.

Most of the male settlers from both ships were on deck; thirty men. Mr. Mullins, the girl's father, stood at the back of the meeting, tall, impassive, his hands locked in a swing before him. Bradford, Carver, Cushman and Edward Winslow, Gilbert Winslow's elder brother, were at that moment climbing up onto the poop deck, where they stood at the edge, looking down at the meeting. Mr. Jones, the Captain, with the first mate, John Clarke, and the second mate, Robert Coppin, were leaning on the rail at the very back of the poop.

The old man, John Carver, spoke; he wore a grey, trimmed beard; and his voice was low and pleasant, determined, and coloured by the North Country.

"You know," he said, "that we must get upon our way from this port with all haste. *Not* for reasons connected only with those of us who have come to join you from Holland. For every day we stay here we endanger ourselves in many other ways— the wind may change around and not allow us to get out at will, we consume our scanty stores that are for our upkeeping in the new land, and our debts mount——"

Voices on the middle deck put up questions about the delay, the provisioning, the remasting of the *Speedwell*, the spending of money. Mr. Martin, the chosen Governor, standing in the press on the waist deck, shouted for silence, refused to answer questions, although he had not been asked, so that no one voice could be heard clearly.

Carver raised his hands and they gradually quietened.

"Hear this out," he said, "we have no time to argue back and forth. We are here together because a decision must be made, which can only be made by the agreement of every man. We can get out of the port by selling some of our stores to pay harbour dues, putting ourselves still more in the risk of starving——"

"Where is the merchant, Thomas Weston, that should pay such dues?" someone shouted.

"Mr. Weston has presented new terms, which we have not been able to sign without the consent of you or of our people who remain in Holland——"

"What have your people in Holland to do with us?" Mr. Martin said. "What about the people who have been brought here by the merchants from London and other parts——"

"There was no time given either to consult the people here gathered in by the merchants, or anyone else."

Martin tried to speak again, but now a solid body of voices called him hush. "Hush," they said, "hush, speak in turn, you are not bawling at children." Attention moved for a moment to two fighting gulls that swooped by the waist bulwarks, screaming.

"The merchants have at last faced us point-blank with their threatened new agreement," the old man, Carver, on the high deck, continued. "Some say that this has been done at the eleventh hour that we must be forced to sign it or return home penniless and broken. That is apart. Whether or not Master Cushman, here employed quietly in England for some time on our business with the merchants, had knowledge that new conditions were to be imposed, or whether he knew not, is apart also."

The worried Cushman, standing behind Carver, took a half a step forward, anxiously.

"We know he worked only for our good," Carver said. "But that is not what we have to decide, nor whether Mr. Martin, chosen by the half of you who have come directly out of England to this venture to order your affairs, has spent wisely here in provisioning——"

"I protest that you mention my name so," the red-faced Mr. Martin shouted.

"In the old agreement with the merchants," Carver said quickly and more loudly, "that signed agreement under which we all came upon these ships, we were to hold in the New World two free days a week to work for ourselves. Also that the homes we builded with our own hands, vegetable plots and flower gardens, should be ours from the beginning—*not* subject to being valued and divided with the merchants after the seven years."

Everyone agreed, nodding their heads up at him.

"Well, yesterday, as many of you have since learned, Mr. Weston, speaking for the merchants in London, came aboard here with a new document—a very long one, as long as my arm—and demanded that those certain of us who had before signed in surety for you all do again put our names to it. In this new agreement we were not to have those two days for ourselves free from work for the merchants. We were asked instead to work seven days a week, everything produced, bartered, grown or made in the New World, in any way, even be it gold we find in our back gardens, besides even our homes and the tables and chairs we make for them, were to be held only in trust. Which would mean that if they were not satisfied after seven years—that they had their moneys back and enough profit—they might send out to lawfully seize every stick and stone we had laboured to raise."

The men on the waist deck shouted in protest, except John, who had been moving slowly along the bulwarks towards the poop, looking curiously at the would-be settlers. North Country accents predominated among the "English from Holland." Most were poor, workers to judge by their clothes and faces. There were two distinct kinds of face: the red, roughened, swelled features of the outdoor worker, and the pale and generally pinched face of the indoor wool carder, shoddy maker, tailor or baize maker. Those who had come from Holland, it seemed, had worked indoors; they were also thinner and more bent than those who had come directly out of England to the ship. They were pitifully ill fitted to cross unknown oceans and cut out a new and more glorious England in a distant and unknown land. The carpenter's forehead wrinkled in distrust and disappointment.

Mr. Carver had continued: "But we answered that we could not, nor had the power without full meeting to be had with every man concerned both here and in other places inaccessible, sign this new agreement and put every life—that had trusted in us to lead them—into a bond slavery fitter for thieves than honest men. Some of us with the means had got servants to come with us in bond; but if we are to have no day that is our own, our servants serve only the merchants. Thereupon, as you saw, Mr. Weston departed in a great temper, leaving us without as much as a halfpenny to pay our harbour dues."

He paused, looked from one face to another; all were silent.

"Don't be cast down. We are brothers in more than just this venturing across the ocean. For if we have the will we may sail out tomorrow. . . . And here is a course Mr. Winslow suggests as to how we may do it, which we have talked back and forth amongst us and agree is the best."

Edward Winslow now stood beside Carver. Between Carver, Cushman and Bradford, down to the poorest of the Holland exiles, there was a relationship to be seen clearly, even in the manner in which they carried their clothes; plain jackets and breeches and woollen stockings; they had the air of being members of a closely knit and sober family.

The elder Winslow, alone, had a bold air of distinction. He wore his hair falling in waves almost to his collar, hanging down freely against his cheeks. Few others present allowed themselves such obvious adornment—heads were cut closely and roughly with a most definite defiance of convention. He was a man in his early thirties, with a smooth, good-natured and handsome face, a straight nose and dark eyes, carrying a neatly trimmed down of hair on upper lip and chin. A fine lawn collar turned out from his throat, tied beneath with silk, red-tasseled cord; his coat fastened down the centre with a row of more than twenty silver buttons. Altogether not a man to be suspected of voluntarily exiling himself in Holland for the sake of a religious or political belief.

After glances of agreement between himself and Carver, Edward Winslow addressed the meeting.

"What Thomas Weston means to do now, we cannot tell. Whether he expects us to remain here until he gets back from speaking with his associates in London . . ." He shrugged, threw up his hands smilingly and moved his tongue around behind his full lips; his speech was easy, musical and very nearly accentless. The faces of the Holland Englishmen showed that they knew him well, and perhaps admired him, despite his drawl and brushed hair.

"Captain Jones for his part says he got no order to delay sailing," Edward Winslow continued. "The which may have been an oversight of Mr. Weston in his fury, but is God's mercy on us! Therefore, if we can but raise the money to pay our dues out of this harbour, we may leave in the morning. And then, as Weston said, we stand on our own legs—not forgetting that our merchants have looked for big profits from us, and will not at all be eager to abandon their investments."

"Are we to be planted among savages a thousand leagues the other side of the oceans, and left forgotten?" a nervous voice asked.

"That is our risk. We go on, or go home. But there's the rub—for the first time in our lives we may rightly feel thankful for the covetousness of man's nature." He smiled broadly and encouragingly. "For see how privileged we are in owing all this money! We need but remember, if seeking comfort, that a man is rarely abandoned by him to whom he owes large sums of money, or by he that hopes still to make a profit from him."

"And if we're written off as a sea loss?" Martin asked, in the tones of a man who loved to hear the sound of his own voice.

"If they write us off . . . we have neither the motives of profit behind us, or of King and country——"

"But we are with God—and we have our strength!" William Bradford, the man in the orange shirt, burst out, from behind him.

"The merchant made no mention to me of such new conditions," Martin shouted. "I had no money for provisioning on *those* conditions, so we are not beholden to them, in justice, for a pin. Let them rot, they are bloodsuckers!"

"He knew long since they would make stricter condition," broke in Robert Cushman, the middle-aged, worried little man, the fourth of those who stood on the poop facing the meeting. "I admit it, why does he not? I told him long ago, and others I told, that the merchants would try to put new conditions on us, to bind us further. But Mr. Martin was content, while he could go about lording it and laying out money for this and that. Now he goes about to bluster us down, has cried out into my face that I have betrayed all into slavery in making our arrangements with the merchants. Lord save us!"

"Friends," Carver cried, "we will never make a plantation this way. Peace, Mr. Martin, we will have time and enough to go over all this on the long way. . . . Where is the meek and humble spirit that re-edified the state of Israel?"

"Not walking abroad with Mr. Martin—from whom is not the sound of Rehoboam's brags heard daily amongst us?" Mr. Cushman said tremblingly, and at a look from Carver compressed his lips and bowed his head.

"There is a way that we can get money to clear us from the harbour," Edward Winslow resumed, in a sudden bellow that drowned even Martin's bull voice. "A merchant here in the town offers to buy our butter. This butter may be the staple of our nourishment that our children will hunger for. . . . Well, sirs? It is your butter lies in the hold—little enough of it—sixty firkins. But with it we may pay our harbour dues and sail."

The men nodded doubtfully, talked a little; there were resentful and frightened looks.

"It has to be settled by everyone," Winslow said. "Let us put up our hands who do agree."

After a moment hands began to go up, until finally about three quarters of the men hesitatingly put up their hands; the others could not make up their minds.

Shortly after the meeting the quartermaster unwedged the battens of the cargo hatch in the middle of the waist deck; and in the decking of the first hold below, and the second hold directly below that again, lifted large double traps in the planking. And John helped the settlers haul up out of the cargo hold fifteen three-firkin casks of butter, which was little short of their whole store of that food. No one knew how long it would be until they saw a cow again.

Later, a longboat was set to ferry the casks ashore, and a merchant's waggon came and took them away. The merchants paid sixty pounds for the butter, two thirds of its value. It was just enough to pay the harbour dues and settle a few other small debts.

52

John approached Christopher Martin that afternoon, as the Governor was going ashore, thinking it to be about time he was told where his quarters were.

"You 'aven't any. Don't bother me now, lad, else I'll never get done by nightfall—we sail in the morning!" But he turned back from the bulwark for a moment, on second thoughts. "Here, the gentlemen from the *Speedwell* who were aboard, they told you Mr. Martin is of no importance? Well, they will, you mark it. You've been got at!"

Martin thrust his face close, large, coarse, rigid in challenge; John saw minutely the sweaty black in his pockmarks. Dare contradict him, said his face, dare at your peril. John grinned, stepping back from him. "I been told nothing—but that it was you had charge. The ship's men say it is none of their business where I set down. I don't fancy wandering round like an orphan child."

"You're raw to this. Stay on the right side—on my side. Keep the rats out of the meal and the crew's fingers out of the stores. Take orders from none but the Governor—that's me—and you'll do well. Find a hole or corner where you can." He slung his fat body over the side and backed down the ladder to the dinghy.

John descended into the main hold in the bottom of the ship. It was completely dark, but by groping around he found where the lanterns hung on hooks by the hatchway stairs. He took one above and went forward to light the candle from the galley fire, rather than spend five or six minutes trying to strike a light from his tinderbox. The lantern was unhorned, a square box of heavy tin, vented, with a handle hooped over the top, two sides perforated with pinholes to allow the light out.

The crew's cook, a gnome with a hump between his shoulders, a little creature with greasy hair, face and clothes, was baking bread in the circular brick oven. He gave a light cheerfully, and an invitation to come in and see him when they got under way. For there he'd be, he said, in the eye of the ship, thrusting across the belting seas with the Captain's daily bread in the oven leading the way. His name was Tandy Fall.

Returning below and opening the door of his lantern, John began to look over the cargo hold. Sternmost, under the tiller room, was a small spirit store, well and strongly padlocked. Next came

53

the bread room, packed tight with barrels of biscuit-bread. Then the water store, extending up for the height of two decks, wedged solidly with casks; little leakage, he noted, fair condition. Further forward, but still behind the base of the mainmast, was the settlers' gunpowder, lead, ironmongery, tool chests, an assortment of agricultural implements, all interspersed with ballast sacks of sand to keep everything in place. He poked about, looking into boxes of trading goods; knives, bracelets of bead and copper, rings, scissors, copper chains, blue and red trading cloth, cheap glass trinkets for the ears, small mirrors, shoddy blankets, hatchets, nails, hoe heads, rusty fishhooks too large to catch anything but shark or porpoise, netting and balls of twine.

She was a dry enough ship below, in fair condition; there was a little ooze here and there in patches, nothing unusual. The main hold ran forward, packed with boxes and barrels. Most of the settlers' food was contained in tubs and barrels, the smoked beef and dried tongue in sacks. The barrels were in two layers, lashed to the timbers, a gangway down the centre.

As he moved about, testing the soundness of the barrels with taps from the side of his boot, he lifted a lid where he could and sniffed the contents. There was salt pork, peas, oats, dried salt cod; a little bacon, onions and turnips; much smoked herring, flour, unmilled wheat, and more biscuit-bread. There was also a great many barrels of watery light beer, more than seemed necessary for such a voyage; perhaps a provision against the drinking water of the New World being no more reliable or healthful than that of the old world.

Now he began to feel of some considerable importance. Until landfall was made every cask, tub and barrel was his responsibility. He must see to it that none were squeezed, weakened and made leaky by the rolling of the ship; and where that did happen, as it usually did at sea, repair the damage immediately. Almost a hundred men, women and children would have to depend on the food store for not less than two months on the open sea, but probably longer, and for a further two or three months after landing.

He now came to the forward end of the cargo hold, and directed his light upon the door of the sail locker; here then was the very place to make himself at home, if the crew raised no objection! He pulled the door open.

Roomy, clean, narrowing roundly to the cutwater timber of the prow, and stacked with canvases, he could ask nothing better. His bed should be high and dry, sprung on fifty folds of sail. He turned to leave, and start bringing his pallets and bundles down, but paused, seeing as his light swung around a slight movement under an unfolded, loosely thrown piece of sailcloth. Rats could be uncomfortable bed companions. He side-stepped silently and, as there was nothing to hand for a weapon, prepared to kick its life out. With a jerk he tore the sailcloth away and thrust it behind him. An old man sat crouched among the canvases, screwing up his bearded, knobby face and blinking in the candle-light.

The stranger let out his breath with a hiss. "Be not alarmed," he said, "I—I thought to have a quiet hour here. It's hard to get an hour's peace to your soul in a beehive, eh?"

The man was holding a lantern himself between his knees, unlit. Here was an odd occasion: the man spoke exceedingly well —but he looked like a homely, if clean, clerk, was somewhere between fifty and sixty, had an open volume between his feet and spectacles on his nose; his beard was full, streaked with white, his hair bobbed short and going grey.

"Your pardon, sir. . . . I thought to lay my bed within 'ere, but seeing as . . ."

"Oh, but take no notice on me, lad! Do as you will. Take it that I am not here, I'll be going above, well, shortly, let us say."

John observed that the old man eyed him anxiously as if trying quickly to discover something about him from his face and clothes. He ventured to ask if the stranger intended to take up his quarters in the sail locker; and the man answered, laughing, that he had no such intention, very quickly regaining his ease. He fancied quarters with more air and light; and besides, the rats were always ferreting about down there; and it did bring on a fearsome feeling being below the level of the water. But why in Christ's holy name did he thus hide away there? The old man paused, and then asked frankly if John was a member of the crew. Being returned a shake of the head and the information

55

that the young man was sailing with the settlers for Virginia as a carpenter, he put a further question: Did he ever say his prayers? Morning, noon and night, John answered glibly. Then he should know, the stranger continued, that it was very necessary at times to be alone with one's soul. For what? To say one's prayers, the gentleman laughed, calling him a blockhead.

"Oh, ah," John said good-humouredly, "that's what you was about, sir, saying your prayers? With your head, sir, under a sheet? . . ."

"Why not? But to tell the truth, lad—I hid on hearing you approach. For I liked not the idea of being rooted out of my earth. And these sailors, mark you, are most terrifying swearers and scoffers. Whilst above there the children scream and dance the livelong day, the wife grumbles at her lot, and they all talk and talk from morning till night. So I hide away and read my Scripture."

With a straw from his pocket John relit the other's lantern candle for him and, as he bent over, screwed around and looked at the open volume. He remarked that the gentleman seemed to read strange Scriptures.

"Oh, Lord, here is a cunning lad, I see. A lad to read books too. Most excellent. But I would not have said that you looked like a fellow for books? . . . Books, now, are they not rare things to the common man? But then, as you come for your conscience' sake you will no doubt be a man well able to read and expound."

John shook his head. He did not know anything about expounding on a text—but he knew very well how to read, let him make no mistake! And anyhow books were far too dear for his like, and if they weren't rigmaroles on religion they were rigmaroles on politics, and a man grew quickly as tired of one as the other. Books were not for the man who sawed and hammered. But by his faith they could be for everyone, the old man said warmly, were it not that true knowledge lay so heavily suppressed. There were hardly more than a dozen presses allowed the King's permission to print in the whole of England, Scotland and Ireland! He picked up his volume, fingering it lovingly. It was entitled *Advancement of Learning* and was written, he said, by a certain gentleman named Francis Bacon, who had lately been made, God save his soul, a Lord Chancellor. He had brought packed in his scrine to the voyage a number of books and if the young man so desired he could borrow when he chose.

The gentleman had not given his own name, so perhaps he did not want to state it. . . . But as he had no objection to him he would bring his stuff down. "But let me have it clear, sir," John said, "—do I admit to your honour being here in this sail locker, if I hear a cry raised for your whereabouts?"

"You do not. Or rather, I do entreat you not to make mention of it, most especially before the crew."

"What of the other gentlemen who go to be settlers?"

The other got up, came across and looked him squarely and smilingly in the face. "No one is a-going to ask you questions about an old man saying his prayers in the locker—unless you speak out on it first. You are a settlers' man; we must learn to hold together against the crew. But should you run into Mr. Bradford or Mr. Winslow, say that I'm got mighty hungry. But other than that . . ." He put his finger upon his lips and shook his head.

John tugged his forelock, smiling in mock ceremony, and went out and along the hold. His stuff was all dumped beside Gilbert Winslow's pallet in the first hold; if he brought it down then he could prepare his bed and leave it ready for the night. The stranger most certainly was someone of importance; and while he might be a fanatic, as was called any man that held neither to the King's church nor the Pope's, there was no sign of horns on his lined forehead.

Gilbert Winslow lay on his back with his head in the open gunport, enjoying the sunshine on face and breast. "Ah, hello," he said to John, but immediately closed his eyes again.

"The gent in the sail locker would like his dinner," John whispered.

"Go away. You're too old to be playing japes, a big lump like you."

"It is what I been told to say, to Mr. Bradford or Winslow—from the gent is hid below in the sail locker," John said, and winked.

Gilbert sat up with a jerk. "By God, he meant the brother of mine, my important brother, Edward. Well, stretch me, is that where they have him put! What are his features?" John described the old man as having a madman's beard, apple cheeks and a bulb on his nose. "What a place to hide him . . ." Gilbert whispered. "But don't the crew go there about their business?"

John said he didn't think so, not when the sails were new-stitched and ready on the yards for the beginning of the voyage; so whoever had put the old man there knew what they were about. "He bears the port of a right good gentleman. . . . You do know him?"

"I have a fair notion of who he might be," Gilbert said cautiously, rubbing his knee through his new leather breeches, the reflected light from the water without rippling on the side of his face. He remained silent, uneasy.

"He give me warning to keep my tongue still," John said. "You may have no fear I'm going to shout from the masthead."

"I had no thought you would, friend. But don't take it lightly; it may turn out a dangerous business for you."

"How may it for me? I did not put him into hiding, if he is a wanted man."

"No, but you know he is there now, as I do, since you've told me. Should anything happen to him and it became known we both knew of him we might find ourselves in the cold sea one dark night. The most that go here are men well used to fighting for their lives, and they value this man like a king should be valued. That's fair warning, friend John. Myself I am no very favoured person here, you should know that too. I am not one of them, but am come as a sort of poor relation in spirit of my brother Edward's. No doubt it is hoped I will behold the true light from the examples of the good people. Anyhow, I dare say he'll be out of there and come into the open when we get to sea. We will keep our mouths shut, and if anything happens—we don't know nothing."

"But what danger stands he in?" John persisted.

"The ships have been searched before, I believe; they may be again. William Brewster is accounted some importance by the State."

"William Brewster is the gentleman's name?"

"What! Did he not tell you?"

"I don't recall it; perhaps he did." John sat down on the end of the pallet.

Gilbert Winslow's immediate instinct was to go on and tell the carpenter all he knew himself about the settlers' leader who lay hidden in the sail locker. Alden had nothing to gain by making trouble. He already knew the old man was in hiding, waiting for the ship to sail; and he must already know that the majority of the persons on board were in danger of being run into gaol. He, Gilbert, knew John better than anyone else on the ship so it was perhaps his duty to stay him. He had not felt it prudent saying even as much as he had, but as the fair-haired young carpenter had shown himself so stupidly persistent he felt that a point had been reached where, if he did not pretend to treat him with complete confidence, he might well take offence and turn ready to inform; that he should even hold a resentment was dangerous, should he be questioned by constables or busybodies on the quays about a certain William Brewster. But if he appeared to make him party to a piece of dangerous business his obvious simple good nature should come to the top.

He went on to explain, with a hand on John's shoulder, to give comfortable assurance of brotherhood, that whatever one might think in general about fanatics, as all reformers were termed, the gentleman in the hold was according to his lights the most well-meaning, the kindliest gentleman imaginable. Of all those who had revolted against the penal laws forcing attendance at State worship, against submission to the doctrine that kings had a divine right to throw their subjects in prison and execute them without trial, this man was of any the most humane, courageous, and least dogmatical of them all. An educated gentleman of some means and preferment in the world, well set upon the way to Government position, he had thrown all up, returned to his Yorkshire village of Scrooby and gathered the common people into a free fellowship; hoping to attain with them to some spiritual worth, away from the inquisitional and corrupt tool of Government, the Established Church.

Naturally, they had been beset and watched and persecuted,

as much by the local gentry as by the bishops; for many people feared that the great numbers in England who were still Catholic in sympathy would one day rise in rebellion, and looked upon all separatist reformers as madmen, and a danger to their own growing ascendency.

So that they had been virtually hunted out. But rather than submit they escaped to Holland and there gathered themselves together into a body and tried to live as they desired. This man who lay in hiding in the hold had led them with gentle admonition, courage and faithfulness. He had used up his own money for them in all ways; with Edward Winslow and others, he had set the type and made books with his own hands, which were smuggled into England, so infuriating the King that he had forced the Netherlands Government to confiscate the printing press and hunt out this man. On the run for the past year, if he was taken by the English he'd certainly be hanged, as had many others of his kind.

To venture into the New World and live the desired life there had been the idea of this man and his companions; but they had no money. Thus came the merchants, signed away their lives for seven years and gathered up in England another fifty men, women and children to make a full-sized effort and an economic proposition. The little *Speedwell* alongside had brought the Brownists back from Holland, and probably the Elder had been smuggled onto the *Mayflower* amongst a crowd, it being less likely to be searched.

"And if we get out in the morning with him, the Captain will not be for turning back—when he sees him?"

"There's some likelihood, but I suppose they have to take the chance. You go up and tell Mr. Bradford his Elder wants his dinner—the sea air makes a man hungry. But be careful." Nevertheless Winslow did not intend to allow his own laziness to prevent him from following and observing the carpenter's actions. The suggestion that John go to Bradford should prove him definitely one way or the other. If he went for the side or to the Captain's cabin, then an attempt would have to be made to take him below, with regrettable force, and hide him too, until they made the seas.

"I'll do that; I'll have a word with Mr. Bradford," John grinned, knowingly. A chance to discomfort Mr. Bradford was very welcome.

"Don't be barked up a tree by Bradford," Winslow smiled, sensing something. "He's Elder Brewster's favourite boy, comes from Scrooby too, but they've all had a hard time of it and feel pretty bitter."

Bradford was not on deck. He and his wife, John learned, had their quarters in the dark and cluttered second hold; coming from Holland on the *Speedwell* after quarters on the *Mayflower* had been allotted to the merchants' gathering of "strangers," they had had to take the only space left.

The wan young woman whom he had first met weeping on the quayside two days before told him that her husband was certainly about the ship somewhere, but where she could not say; she sat on the tarpaulin-covered hatch in the waist, sewing and casting up amused glances from her lowered face at the children who were playing there. He tried to count the children on the deck, surprised that there were so many, and counted seventeen, all between six and twelve years. And there was certainly above another dozen on the *Speedwell*. . . . It was then he stopped to think of the large numbers that were here engaging their lives in the adventure to make homes on the far coast of America—certainly over a hundred!

John went on under the poop in search of Bradford, eager for the pleasure of shocking the dogged and self-sufficient young man in the orange shirt. Under the poop there were four small cabins which accommodated Mrs. Brewster and children, the Mullinses, the Martins and the Hopkins family. One of the cabins he knocked upon was the Mullinses', wherein was that same gentleman he had first seen in the geographer's shop; there also was his daughter, his wife, and young son Joseph, cramped like rabbits in a box. Mr. Mullins knew nothing of Bradford's whereabouts either; of the girl John had barely a glimpse. A cold wench, he feared, but there was plenty of time ahead in which to show her a few tricks.

Going back through the first hold, he found that a mush of peas, meal and bits of salt pork was being handed round by the women. John got his wooden bowl out to receive a share, and, taking up one of his bundles, went down into the cargo hold again. William Bradford met him between the barrels, a lantern in his hand. John grinned. A watchdog on guard; out at the sound of his boots to head him off.

"Hope you brought the gentleman his dinner," John said, pushing past him.

"Wait!" Bradford held him by the slack of his sleeve. "Are you the man who was down here a little time ago?"

"Yes, sir, John Alden, to nurse the tubs. And leave me go." He was let go, marched on to the locker and pushed the door open. Elder William Brewster sat on his throne of canvas, a lump of meat held in a napkin in his left hand, an eating knife in his right and a bowl of mush between his knees. Bradford followed John in and carefully closed the door.

Gilbert Winslow stole away from the top of the hold stairs, smiling; Bradford could look to this large and inquisitive fellow now.

"Brought you down some food," John said. "But I see you're took care of. I'll have it myself."

"Shall you be coming up and down here often, this evening?" Bradford asked. He stood with head tensed forward, his back to the door.

"Not if I'm annoying of Mr. Brewster, I can lay down to sleep above."

"Come, I asked you to put no seem on my being here," Brewster said. "I thought we understood matters. By four o'clock in the morning we'll be going down the Water, and I'll leave you in undisturbed possession."

"It's no bother, sir, having your voice for company—most of them aboard are a bit stiff in the tongue." He had placed his lantern down where the light shone out towards Bradford and had not missed the apprehensive twitch of lip when he mentioned Brewster's name so casually, then sat back to his biscuit and mush.

"Look here," Bradford began determinedly, "Mr. Brewster has

62

some very important letters to write, and wished not to be disturbed. If you come up and down time and again it may attract the crew . . ."

"Don't prick at the lad, William!" Brewster protested through a mouthful. "Mr.——"

"John," Alden said.

"John and I have an understanding."

"You saw him for the first time in your life less than a half an hour ago," Bradford said coldly. "And I, for my part——" He broke off and looked away; the old man was on the point of speaking sharply.

"I'm to be your carpenter and make houses in Virginia," John said to the older man, with the confiding simplicity, half guile and part nature, that smoothed out his face and made it at times large and square and young. "You're right not to fear I'd want to see you hanged." He bent over his bowl, spooning food into his mouth.

The Elder's beard jerked up and swept over his mush; his chewing ceased abruptly, his lips apart; he turned and looked up at Bradford's startled face, and shook his head very slightly to tell him to keep silent. "Lord, man," he said softly, after a moment, "don't mention such things." His chewing began again, slowly, the dark skin under his eyes crinkling up as if he were attempting to see against the sun, his knobbly face warm and red. "Do you mind me asking, what gave you such a fearful thought?"

"I thought I smelt a kind of fear," John mumbled unhappily, "among all the poor people."

"Ah," Brewster laughed, "it's Bradford's smell. But let me thank you for the assurance."

"Who told you such scandalous things?" Bradford came forward, his nails gripped in his palms; his brow was damp and glistening.

"I'm no fool, Mr. Bradford, but you will go to treat me as if I was." Then on the spur of the moment, wanting somehow to pacify him, he remembered how he had tried to listen on the poop deck while the little merchant Thomas Weston sat in Jones's cabin, forgetting his resolution to keep his mouth shut until he should know who was the greater power on board, the Captain or the settlers. "There's more things than one I could tell you—if you wasn't so waspish with me—maybe something of what passes between Mr. Weston and the Captain when they was alone together."

"Never mind Mr. Weston," Bradford said, his voice almost a whisper. "Who on the ship did you hear speak of Mr. Brewster?"

"Take no offence at his anxiety, lad, take no offence," old Brewster intervened.

"I didn't hear nobody say a word, Mr. Brewster—it's . . . imaginings. I swear it, sir."

"Good. I can see an honest man on the spot, I wish poor William could. Do go above, William, and get your food—it's your empty belly makes you anxious. Go on, lad, go on!"

William Bradford took up his lantern, turned about sharply and went. The gleam of light and his orange shirt disappeared into the darkness of the hold outside. John pushed the door to with his boot.

"What's this about Weston?" the old man said, wiping his beard down with his napkin.

It was difficult to explain; now he did not want to make it appear more than it seemed; and on the face of it there really was so little to tell. The voices of Jones and Weston had been the voices of men about bargaining, that was the main thing. "The rigging was humming like a whole beehive, sir, and what with the children and the noise I couldn't hear it at all plain." The merchant Weston wanted the landing to be made north of some cape, that much was definite; and the name of Gorges he remembered. Mr. Brewster's face showed keen interest.

"Sir Ferdinando Gorges? I know that name well!"

"Then Mr. Weston said that neither one company nor the other company was to know, or did know, about him wanting the Captain to make landfall above this Cape. They did not say the name of the Cape. The Captain talked about his share, or maybe his shares."

"He may have bought shares in Weston's Company, there's nothing amiss with that."

John told him everything else he could remember of what he

had been able to hear. "But they have a plot, sir, certain sure, to put ashore somewhere . . . somewhere where's not . . ."

But to his surprise, the old man nodded. "What can we do?" he said. "Nothing. Our greatest fear is that Captain Jones will not continue in his willingness to sail in the morning, or that Mr. Weston will come back and forbid it. . . . If a word is spoken against the Captain he may refuse to sail, and all our hopes be dashed to ruin, our people destroyed—they have no homes to return to now. We must wait and see. If the merchants are fighting for us, we must try to see that they cut their own throats without cutting ours. Yet, God willing, and with the help of honest and upright young men," he bowed a little in compliment, "we may hoist Mr. Weston or Sir Ferdinando Gorges, with their own petards. My dear lad, you can do me a great service, if you would?"

"Willingly, sir."

"Do you know by sight the constables and such people, in this town?"

"I am from London when a boy, but lived here many, many years, I ought to—everyone that has importance."

"Well, Mr. Bradford does not, nor does anyone else of our people. So if you have a while to do nothing in, put it in with your eyes turned to the town. Any party, with military, or a justice, or constables, or suchlike men coming for the ship that you recognise to be a danger, come below and give me warning, eh?"

John agreed willingly, gave him his candle, and went above. Mr. Brewster picked up his volume, but did not read.

He sat staring with the muscles of his face tightened and the skin puckered up under his eyes; the ship suddenly still of feet and voices, the sound of the water lapping against the hull reaching within to the sail room; his face was then the face of a prophet seeing his vision of burning cities or unattainable beauties. He relaxed slowly, tension softening, scratched his knee through his breeches and slumped back, a benign, leather-faced old man, aged before his time, with an air of being ripe with plain, practical wisdom; a tolerant Moses at last faced with a real physical desert, not smiling, but determined to lead with good cheer.

Because of his hunger to be faithful, to someone or something, John Alden watched the quays all afternoon and evening; not because he knew what he was doing, or who these men were, or what they meant. A week ago, if asked by authority, he would have said obediently that all such should be whipped or hanged.

Gilbert Winslow came and leaned by his side for a few minutes, as the sun was going down, and said, "What's your mind's eye on with such intent, my golden lad? A little apprentice boy, William Button, has just told me he is going to be a king."

"Better than having no notions at all, Mr. Winslow."

"Oh, I wish to have pretty notions too, but I can never hold them up. Perhaps we'll all be rich—but I can't keep any belief or hope going. Rather do I see it that I'll make meat for the fishes. But there you are, go we must, to see with our own eyes if it really is a whole new world or just the backside of the old one." He shook his head clownishly down at the water. "I must look upon the quaint coloured people, see the fabulous animals, see the palms and the warm sands and the mighty rivers—and get bitten to my death by the snake that crawls in every Eden."

5   *But now we are all, in all places, strangers and pilgrims, travellers and sojourners. . . .*

The rent-taker lives on sweet morsels; but the rent-payer eats a dry crust often with watery eyes. . . . Many there are who get their living with bearing burdens; but more are fain to burden the land with their whole bodies. Multitudes get their means of life by prating; and so do numbers more by begging. Neither come these straits upon men always through intemperancy, ill husbandry and indiscretion, as some think, but even the most wise, sober and discreet of men go often to the wall, when they have done their best. . . . Each man is fain to pluck his means, as it were, out of his neighbour's throat. There is such pressing and oppressing, in town and country, about farms, trades, traffic,

&c; so as a man can hardly anywhere set up a trade, but he shall pull down two of his neighbours.

Let us not thus oppress, straighten, and afflict one another! But seeing there is a spacious land, the way to which is through the sea, we will end this difference in a day!

> ROBERT CUSHMAN, *Reasons And Considerations Touching The Lawfulness of Removing Out Of England Into The Parts of America.*

*   *   *   *

The first crashing thud awakened most of the sleepers; half-awake men and women cried out questioningly, voices wailing and booming hollowly in the dark hold. Men rose up in their sleep and stumbled about, falling over screaming women or running into the ship's beams.

But with the third and fourth rattle of chains and slamming bang, reassuring voices called to each other, and the hold quietened. The heavy square doors of the ports, held up by chains from the outside, were being dropped; they had been open day and night since anchoring in Southampton. One after another they thudded down, until complete blackness filled the first hold. The settlers began to hear feet scraping and pounding on the decks above, and the creakings and rustlings of ropes and canvas.

Christopher Martin ran out onto the waist deck in his shirt and trousers, shouting, "What is this? Are we moving?" stumbled forward, around sailors pulling on the mainsail halyards, to where he could see back onto the poop, and called up to Mr. Jones, "Do you not acquaint us, sir? What treatment is this? I am these people's Governor, and I will be consulted——"

"Get off the deck," Mr. Jones called down, in a bellow.

"I demand to see you in your cabin," Martin answered.

"And I will have no further meddling from you, not from any man of you—we are now under sail, my good fellow, the which makes you subject of the laws of the sea!"

"You will do as you're bid, sir, for he that pays your wage," Mr. Martin cried passionately, thumping his breast.

"Put that fellow below deck," Captain Jones roared down between his hands.

Mr. Coppin, the second mate, sprang willingly to this pleasant duty, took Martin by the back of his shirt, heavy man though he was, and propelled him, stumbling and protesting, to the poop door, where he kicked him in.

In the chill before daybreak the sailors worked silently; but the voices of the mates, bosun and quartermasters could be heard below.

"Let fall your main," the bosun sang.

"Bring your cable to the capstan and break out anchor," Mr. Coppin followed, with harsh volume.

After the last of the port traps had been dropped a quartermaster came down the hatchway carrying a lantern and a mallet. He made his round, slapping up the iron locking bars and driving in wedges to secure them firmly, going about it with scant courtesy, stepping upon the pallets and even on the legs of those lying on them. To the many questions put to him he replied but shortly and with sleepy bad temper. No passenger was to dare go on deck until all sails were set and the ship was free of the narrow Water; the decks must be kept clear for the crew. The wind was fresh and favourable, and if they did not get out with it there and then they might languish in Southampton Water another week before it came back on the point of the tide. And from that moment onward, until the ship again anchored in a calm harbour, the ports must remain tightly wedged or they'd all be drowned with the high seas and a good end to them!

In the sail locker John was roused from a heavy sleep by Mr. Brewster shaking him and saying, "John, lad, we're putting out to sea." He slipped on his boots in the thick darkness, as the anchor cable began to rasp and groan overhead, to the creaking of the 'tween-deck capstans.

"Ask William Bradford to give me wind of it before we are off the land entirely," Brewster said, "if you would be so good—so I may see the last of our birthright, our dear land of England."

John felt his way along between the barrels and up through the hatch. In the first hold the men were pressed closely around the poop hatch and stood on the stairs, those at the top looking up and out at the rigging and the grey sky and reporting back what they saw. Both anchors were soon up and they guessed by the filling sail, the bottom of which was to be seen, that the ship was standing out down towards the Solent and the Channel.

"Younkers!" sang the bosun. "Let fall your topsail."

Six sweating sailors, young, savage-looking men in breeches, shirts open to the waist, and bare feet, trooped back through the hold, after working the 'tween-deck capstan to lift the forward anchor; the stairway was cleared for them to pass above and John, falling in behind, managed to get to the top, poke his head out and look along the waist deck. Light was blooming in the white clouds, which were high and motionless. Following the sailors and turning off, he took up a stand against the port bulwarks, under the poop.

Mr. Coppin, passing back, paused to eye him; John returned his gaze quietly and warily, with an expression of tolerant patience, intertwining and flexing his thick strong fingers like a wrestler preparing for a bout. He looked immense, healthy, strong. Mr. Coppin decided wisely that that was not just the right moment for trials of strength, and passed on.

The fore and main topsails were flown, as were the two big square sails and the lateen sail on the poop; she was moving slowly out and down the Water, rising and falling no more than at anchor. Like a great black fish the upturned longboat was lashed down over the waist cargo hatch; the jollyboat was aboard on the back of the poop. The town of Southampton had diminished into the distance, a sharp black outline of rooftops against a cold sky. Following behind, the little *Speedwell* edged out, a toy boat on an immense grey pond.

Alone on the poop deck, above and behind John and out of sight, Mr. Clarke, the first mate, stood by the mizzenmast, now and then shouting down to the steersman at the whipstaff, "Put her down a breath"; or, "Put her up a breath"; a voice answering from the blind steerage hole below the deck, "She is on it, sir."

Jones came up frequently, stamped about, surveyed the rigging, looked back to see how the *Speedwell* kept up, bawled once down into the waist at the bosun over a lose trimming rope to the foresail yard, descending again heavily to his cabin.

The summer day proved bright and fresh and shed warmth upon the ship as it sailed gently before the wind, leaving far behind the platform of cannon on the tip of Southampton's tongue and into the broads, where the water stretched a mile to land on either side. The other male passengers then began to take courage and come up, and finally the women, but they did not stay, for a meal of biscuit-bread, a slice of smoked bacon and a mug of beer was being served in the first hold, by candlelight.

Shortly, John was again the only passenger on the waist; and he was on the point of going down for food when a procession came slowly on deck. Mr. Brewster, whom John had not forgotten, for they had over twenty miles of land-bound water yet to divide before emerging into the Channel from behind the Isle of Wight, stepped out into the sunlight; on his arm leaned his wife, a comfortable, gentle-looking woman, past middle age; by the hand he led a little boy of no more than six years, while his wife led another, some years older. Bradford preceded them, his thin face actually happy and softened by a kind of filial veneration, his eyes constantly returning to the face of the older man. Behind them followed Samuel Fuller, say maker and spare-time physician, a lanky, long-nosed man with a crop of warts upon his face.

Brewster looked around and up at the sky, and inhaled deeply. The ship was beginning to catch the breeze better, but starting to rise and fall and lean from the wind when it shifted, softly creaking and flapping.

He would wish him to know his good wife, Brewster said to the young carpenter, and his two children. They were between nine and twelve years; his youngest; and the only two of his children to sail with him. His wife would under no circumstances let him sail out alone; and he for his part could not see her parted from these two; so there they were. The smaller was named Wrastle, who hid in his mother's skirts, and the elder one was named Love. John nodded to the woman, and thanked God that no one had burdened him with such a fool's cap of a name.

The wind had turned appreciably more variable by the afternoon but kept constant enough for the two ships to continue on a straight course down the middle of Southampton Water. The

Mayflower rode with the satisfyingly steady motions of a heavy ship on an inland sea. Thus, they did not seem to move, yet Calshot Castle came by and passed into the distance behind and they turned into the Solent, the ten-mile stretch of water between the coast and the Isle of Wight. By evening they should leave the Solent, roll and creak past the outjutting spit of land where stood Hurst Castle, and into the English Channel.

Later in the afternoon Priscilla Mullins and her father and mother came out and walked arm in arm about the waist deck. The young carpenter did not see her, but he thought of her long pale face as he went earnestly around the cargo hold below with his lantern, tapping at the beer pegs and tightening faulty barrel irons. Tandy Fall, the crew's cook, had given him a piece of fresh-baked soda bread, saying, "For I'as taken a liking to *you*, see. This crew, love me, is a dirty lot—you mind 'em—I keep 'em aht here wi' the carwing knife." Which gesture had pleased the stranger mightily.

Now heeling more, beginning to plough up and down at the bow, on and on; while Fall prepared the officers' dinner; while the passengers fell more into silence, dazed by the growing motion and the never ceasing creaking and rustling of the rigging.

On a ship for the first time in her life, Priscilla Mullins lay on her plank bunk in their tiny cabin turning from hot to cold and hot again, not caring if she lived or died, while her mother wiped up the mess and Mr. Mullins spoke firmly—and held a crock near in fear she'd do it again. Then Mrs. Mullins took faint and had to lie down, and Father wiped up the mess himself. The girls between fourteen and twenty took sick first; moans came from other daughters, sitting or lying on their pallets around the first and second holds; but for the most the landspeople were only beginning to feel the sea.

Dorothy Bradford had been sick over the bulwarks, and stubbornly refused to leave the waist deck and lie in the stuffy darkness of the second hold amongst spars and gear; William Bradford stood by her as she gripped the side, her body rigid, her face chalk-white. She'd felt the same crossing from Holland. Silently she rejected the support of William's arm—which shrugging little bad-tempered action hurt him exceedingly—because she was filled with a blind need, in her illness, for utter solitude, yet could not give it tongue.

At seven o'clock in the evening all who were able came up to see the passing of Hurst Castle; perhaps their last near sight of England, should their course take them out into mid-Channel and Start Point and Lands End be passed in the distance. They viewed the arm of land across less than half a mile of lively, sparkling sea.

But with the sun's disappearance the wind changed, bringing the duty watch running to haul in the port tacks, cursing the passengers out of their way. The first mate, John Clarke, shouted the altered course down to the steerage hole; and the settlers flocked below. Then the ship wore around to catch the wind again, flapping canvas ballooning out, heading into the open and the first real swells.

Below, mute-faced, enveloped in the gloom of the holds and frightened by all the new sounds of the straining structure, the settlers to the New World waited anxiously for each monotonously sickening swing up, and swing down. Prayers moved lips in faces of stone, a woman chattered hysterically, another slapped her child, an infant cried fretfully, a man snored. In the candlelight their eyes avoided each other; for now it was done, at last they were out on the open sea, to live or die. From that day their lives were cut off, they faced the incalculable breadth of a mighty, lonely ocean, and the distant vastness of an unexplored wilderness. No ships would pass their two sails, day or night, for thousands upon thousands of miles.

And now the whole ship had come terrifyingly alive, filled with the hollow echoes of slapping, vicious water, with a multitude of sounds from the taut sails, moaning timbers, creaking yards, as the bulk of cord, canvas and oak thrust against the open sea. Down in the main hatch the cargo clanked and bumped wherever the lashings were not strained to the utmost. The *Mayflower* was five points off her course by nightfall, but sailing well, with the little *Speedwell* wallowing at her heels.

Of all the passengers only John slept without break throughout the night, now alone in his locker deep in the bows. In both the first and second holds those who were not sick were awakened constantly by the wailing of children, rattling of cans and agonized groans on every side, as the ships beat down the Channel cautiously under reduced sail.

By nine o'clock the next morning a baffling wind had set in, and Mr. Jones, sitting alone in his Great Cabin, ate his breakfast of porridge and boiled eggs in an exceedingly bad temper; a head wind had come dead against them and while it lasted they must beat back and forth, hauling about and wearing the clumsy ships a weary zigzag course.

Amongst the settlers on the *Mayflower* who had come straight from their homes in England, there were seven adults of Brewster's exiled group from Holland. They had been transferred from the *Speedwell* at Southampton to the larger vessel. They were Mr. John Carver and his wife, Catherine; Mr. William Brewster, felon, and his wife, Mary; young Mr. William Bradford and his wife, Dorothy; and Sam Fuller. The other nine families from Dutch exile travelled on in the *Speedwell*.*

It being Sunday, the Holland exiles thought it proper and pleasant if, as at home in Leyden, Mr. Brewster read out from the Book and lifted up their spirits with good words. The other passengers on board, being collected up separately by the merchants to make a full complement, were some of the King's church and some purifying dissenters of varying degrees. Freed of the fear of being hauled before a court for listening to unauthorized reading, they were not disinclined to take comfort where they found it. Thus, on the first Sunday morning at sea, Mr. Brewster came into the first hold and sat himself down by the tiller-room door, and all those free of the seasickness sat about him on the deck to listen.

On the big table in the Great Cabin Captain Jones placed his traverse board on one side of him and his personal compass on the other, swallowed a tot of gin, munched an apple, and read his log entry for the previous day.

*A list of the Mayflower passengers will be found in the Appendix at the back of the book.

73

MAYFLOWER: of Harwich: Christopher Jones Master.
Contract Voyage to Virginia in the Western World: For
London Virginia Company: Mr. Thomas Weston: With
seventy-two persons men women and children.

SATURDAY, AUGUST 5TH, *Anno Domini Sixteen Hundred
and Twenty*: Sail from the Port of Southampton.

He uncorked the ink, wet his pen, and holding firm against
the ship's pitching, laboriously began the day's entry.

LOG: AUGUST 6TH: Beating out Channel. Sea rising fresh.
All sound. Wind constant, veering awhile. No losses or
disorder. Coming up the Portland Raz.

Then, biting his knuckle, the Master fell to thinking of the
merchant Thomas Weston. Since his last conversation with
Weston at Southampton the problem had constantly been in his
mind: How much did Weston stand to make out of this secret
arrangement with the Captain of the *Mayflower?* Thomas
Weston, a shareholder of the London Virginia Company and
handling its affairs, had paid him a hundred pounds to land the
settlers to the north on a rival company's territory. (Little
enough, less than a pound per head.) On the face of it, a man
gone clean out of his wits. But not so! Mr. Jones had begun to
see the shape of the land ahead, as the saying was. He had put
the sum together and now he had the answer.

Weston and the London Virginia Company had chartered and
outfitted the *Mayflower* and *Speedwell,* and put the settlers under bond for seven years, to make a permanent, profit-producing
settlement within the stretch of territory assigned to the London
Virginia Company by Royal Charter.

But north of the London Virginia Company's territory a certain Sir Ferdinando Gorges and Company, called the Plymouth
Company, held all rights to another unexplored tract of country.
The other, Plymouth Company, had never succeeded in persuading or gathering together a group of honest, sober and hard-
working people to make a permanent settlement, never mind
transporting them safely across the oceans and proving that the
land could be settled and lived on, so that others would follow.

Weston, therefore, with the London Virginia Company's venture under way, had staked his fortune on a somewhat involved gamble. Shares in the unsuccessful Plymouth Company were to be bought cheaply. Weston, then, secretly disposed of his shares in the London Virginia Company at a profit, while still its active agent, and probably under another name bought up cheap Plymouth Company shares. It then remained for him to bribe the Captain of the *Mayflower* to transport the settlers to the wrong territory, to land them above the forty-first parallel, where the Plymouth Company held all rights of settlement. Lastly, Weston had forced a quarrel on the settlers in the name of the London Virginia Company and at the last moment, that they would be the more ready to agree to being landed to the cold north when they reached the New World, thinking to escape from Weston's harsh terms.

The Plymouth Company would then have a settlement made for them without a penny's cost, with nothing more to do than send a ship out regularly to collect produce and taxes; consequently the profits for Weston would be ten times as great.

Once an accomplished fact, the unfortunate London Virginia Company merchants would have no alternative but to sell out their rights and investments in the enterprise for whatever the Plymouth Company offered.

The motives behind Weston's at the time apparently insane proposition and bribe of one hundred pounds were now very clear—occasioning Mr. Jones considerable smarting as they began to be so. He had been a fool, he thought, in accepting, in the dark, a mere hundred pounds from Weston. But, if once brought off, another reckoning could always be had with Mr. Weston. . . . Could he but accomplish it without total disaster. . . .

John, ascending into the first hold and hearing Brewster's voice speaking out strongly, squatted on the hatch steps awhile to listen and look and see what he could learn from the faces of the madmen who were going out into the blind ocean. Dorothy Bradford, wan and serious, was picking at threads in her dress, but she gave the young carpenter a little smile of recognition.

"Why, it is as if a man escaped from prison," Mr. Brewster said, raising his hands and bringing them together before his chest with a clap, "where he was forever gagged and bound and beaten, for the sin of using the mind God gave him; as if he escaped from this prison into a fair garden—as we pray it may be—so far away that his enemies could not pursue him, and where he might dig, and grow, and order his daily life with love and understanding.

"Thus, it is a wonder that amazes me every time I think of it. . . . Why then would we not risk everything, dare the horrible and vast oceans, winds, storms, famine and nakedness, savages and, yes!—ten wildernesses, if we might cross over at last into our Promised Land of Canaan? For God has looked upon the land again, and, behold, it is corrupt and filled with violence."

Stroking his beard, he read again from his Bible. " 'The earth also was corrupt before God: for the earth was filled with cruelty. Then God looked upon the earth, and behold, it was corrupt: for all flesh had corrupted his way upon the earth. And God said unto Noah, An end of all flesh is come before me: for the earth is filled with cruelty through them: and behold, I will destroy them with the earth. Make thee an Ark of pine trees: thou shalt make cabins in the Ark, and thou shalt pitch it within and without with pitch.' "

And there was one man there, listening as if in a trance; one who could have stood forth, above all the rest, as a living example, to shew the power exercised over unlettered men by those who had the art of reading and expounding. Edward Thompson's passage had been paid by the White family; in return he had signed a bond to work for Master White—in his "free" time —as labourer and servingman, for seven years. He was an undersized, dried-up man, of an erratic but vivid imagination. To him reading was a form of magic; and he listened, it seemed, as if in a dream, with locked hands and tensed body.

A man looked at a thing called a book, at pages whereon were lines of meaningless black marks; and by so peering at the wonder he could repeat the stories of man and God, all day if need be, and the next day, and the next, every story different, without hesitation, without the use of memory; repeat a story and the words were exactly as spoken before; each performance was a fresh miracle. The power to read was held by the few, and for

Edward Thompson they assumed by virtue of that wonder some of the nature and power of God Himself.

The world was very full of Edward Thompsons. For to ten out of twelve men the personal message of God, the source and knowledge of right and wrong, came through the mouth of some other, through the mouths of the powerful on earth and the privileged with God. The man who laboured was not encouraged to learn how to read.

The immense power of the printed word, as King and Government were well aware, could be either a prop of the State or a lever to its destruction. Those who would not conform were silenced by imprisonment, or death, or fled the country. Every man who could read was a potential revolutionary.

Finding that Miss Mullins was not present, although her father and mother were—both looking attentive and extremely well disposed towards the Brownist Elder—John went onto the waist deck. But she was not there either; only Gilbert Winslow, walking around and around the deck, with head bent. He went back down to listen to Mr. Brewster.

Contrary winds continued to blow throughout the rest of the day, the sky patched with high, thin clouds, warm but brisk. An air of awe had settled on the passengers, their voices low and wandering, their conversation fallen to the bare necessities. The greater number had never been on the sea before, and if not racked sick, were now, inlanders, thoroughly dazed by the rich sea air, by a completely strange world to both ears and eyes; staring at the mesmerizing sea, while their heads rang, without ever a moment's respite, with the continuous groaning and humming of the rigging; their first day on the open ocean.

The great width of the *Mayflower* to her length made her attempt to waltz at every change of wind, which now and then brought a thunderous flapping of canvas, and bellowing curses from the mates and bosun; she sailed somewhat the way a dog trots, a little diagonally across the dead line of progress.

Below deck the enclosed air was soured by the sick, although the women kept the spruce deal planking swabbed clean with salt water around their nomadic-like encampments of bedding, bundles, crocks and pots. Hot drinks of black currant preserves,

77

possets of spiced milk and such they would have had at home in sickness; the doled-out water on the *Mayflower* was flat and tepid.

Mr. Brewster spent as much of his time on the open waist deck as he could, since the only light in his tiny cabin was that from a candle, and the days were mild and warm. Here, on Monday, their third day out, a grinning sailor came to him about midday with a request to present himself to the Master, and led him aft under the poop, down the passage and into the Captain's Great Cabin. Alone in his comfortable quarters, Mr. Jones sat back in a padded chair, bathed in a green light coming through two glass windows in the stern.

"I know your name, sir—Mr. Wright," the Master said, leaving the old man to stand at the far end of the table. "Which is since learned by my officers, though none can account your coming aboard. But we are engaged to move you by tonnage, as it were. One here or there makes no odds—if you would but bide yourself in patience!"

It was the first time they had seen each other at close quarters. Mr. Jones felt that he saw a man of some intrinsic importance, before ever he heard his voice; so that an unexpected misgiving stiffened him further in prejudice. Brewster's unobtrusive, settled assurance and ease of bearing he immediately desired to shut out by loud words and measured pronouncements.

Christopher Jones was a solid, tightly built man, though neat and short, in his early thirties. Here indeed lived a crass fellow, Brewster had thought as he entered, the smell of his feet an abomination. . . . A dirty man shewed out what he was within. For the extreme reformers, which the Brownists were, cleanliness was a part of Godliness.

"I have to give you a command. I cannot allow any fanatical preaching on my ship. You understand that clearly?"

"Speaking English, I could hardly fail to."

"Fair enough. It is not that I would make any man of you to suffer discomfort. Though I transport felons, I would be just with them. I am a just man!"

"I am sure you wish no one discomfort, sir, though you cause it extremely."

78

"Cause it, cause it?" Mr. Jones said loudly, pouting his red lips vexedly. He had a wet mouth, shaved above and below the lip. "I see you put up to be of a better cut than the most of the bobtail on board. How do I cause discomfort?"

"Sir, it is unwitting. Your feet are somewhat high. If you suffer with your feet we have a man, by name Samuel Fuller, a clever man to make ointments and remedies."

"My feet are in good trim," Mr. Jones said brusquely, "and my stockings are washed in my pot. There is a tip for you; on the sea, where water is scarce, the cleanest washing's done in your night can." His pale eyes half closed suddenly; this man no doubt thought to lead him off his course. "You heard me on the matter of this fanatical treason preaching? Why break you this order yesterday?"

"Sir, we had singing. It was Sunday."

"You spoke against the King!"

"Not against the King, Captain Jones."

"You deny me authority. On this ship I am the King's agent. I am thereby the sole government——"

"Whist, sir—who has denied you your position?"

"You, when you preach treason. You preach it therefore against me. What of my crew?"

"What I speak to my companions, Mr. Jones, is the private affair of our conscience."

"I am the Master. It is my affair. Every soul 'board ship stands under the Master."

"Their souls also, sir?"

"Yes. They are set to my protection. Let you know, my fine sir, that I am in full knowledge about you. That I know of those certain of you now aboard my ship who fled trial in England and lived at Leyden in Holland. I know also of the other class of man—such as Mullins and Martin. They escape out of England on my ship! With the prison chains not far behind. Deny it not to be so! I know of your kind of man. And I will not have any least one of you do your work here. You shall not be about to stir up the innocent people. They are strangers to you from Holland. You are no longer Englishmen. You would bedevil all with wicked thoughts, against church and King. These poor people were not gathered up in England for such. I am charged for their care. I must answer for them on my return."

"How then have you no qualms of sailing away from Virginia, Mr. Jones, and leaving them to our fanatical and untender mercies?"

Mr. Jones paused uncomfortably. "Then my duty is past. But you will not preach treason on my ship!" Virginia, indeed, they'd get a sharp awakening on that score.

"Accusing treason is not to be done lightly, Mr. Jones, these days. However, we are already in a freer air. And I am very sensible of how much rests with you in this venture, sir. As no doubt you are yourself. . . . I take it most fully into account. So that rather than quarrel with you, I will take my leave." The older man turned away from the table.

"I said I was a just man. By God I will prove it!" Forgetting that he was the sole government aboard, Mr. Jones kicked back his chair and stamped around the other side of the table to the door, his voice running surprisingly high.

The sailor who had fetched Brewster to the poop cabin was outside in the steerage with the steersman. The Captain called him in, a gangling, tangle-headed young seaman, whose expression when he grinned was always near something of embarrassed enjoyment of obscene conduct. Like the other sailors, he wore only breeches, a filthy shirt and a short leathern jacket, and could be smelt like a wet dog before a fire at several yards.

"Here is Richard Salterne," Jones said, as if he were shouting at a meeting and trying to work up some passion. "Sailing under me since a boy! He doesn't lie. Below here in the tiller room there is a judas with a shutter on it in the door, whereby can be seen the main deck. Yesterday, going down from the steerage, he heard you preaching in the main close by the door." Mr. Jones turned the puffy stare of his pale blue watery eyes upon the sailor. "What did you hear preached in my ship?"

"I be mazed in this boot, Master, to hear mun preach against the King," Salterne said eagerly.

"Against the King?" Brewster said. "You heard me speak of the King?"

"And of being escaped the Government," Salterne added.

"There is an honest witness," Mr. Jones said. "You can go forward." The sailor padded out, grinning and nodding.

Twisting a little horn into the end of his beard, Mr. Brewster said sadly, "Such honesty cannot be questioned. But, Mr. Jones, would you have me deny them when they ask to meet together on the Sabbath? Who else can read Scripture if we do not? Would you allow Mr. Martin?—he is not one of us from Holland."

"He's a meddling fool enough then! I'll allow him a rope to be hanged with."

"We are to be confined together, Mr. Jones, for many a long month, and we'll be but poor creatures if we cannot find some middle path of understanding. What would you have us do?"

"I forbid you, or any of the others who have been in Holland, to speak or preach treasonably with the words of religion to those other settlers on my ship who are but innocent strangers both to you and your ways."

"And among ourselves? We are not to meet on a Sunday or in the evenings?"

"I cannot well stop you talking unless I gag you."

"Ah, Mr. Jones, dear sir! There is the rub. Yesterday I prophesied, as we say, read and spoke on the text—but how prevent a comfortless soul creeping up and listening?"

"You have heard my mind, sir, and what I order."

"I have heard your mind, Mr. Jones, indeed. Good day."

"We are forbid to meet any of the others together and expound," Mr. Brewster told Bradford, after coming from the Captain's cabin. "He is an ordering, interfering man—we can only hope to win his good will in time."

"They shall all come to our way, in time," William Bradford said angrily, "if we were beset by a thousand such men."

Mr. Brewster returned to his seat on the cargo hatch, and leaned back against the upturned longboat. The shouts and laughter of the children playing in the waist resounded all about, mingling with the crying of the wind and the hissing water beating along the lee side. The sea air, he noted with pleasure, was agreeing with the children, whose faces were turning brown, or pink and red, and who apparently were already quite at home on

81

the ship, running about with abounding vitality from morning till night, so that the young women orderlies set to watch them on the deck had their hands full seeing to it that no one got up on the side and fell overboard or climbed into the rigging.

"Give over your worrying," the old man said to Bradford, "and enjoy these happy children."

6   Log: August 10th. Wind continues contrary. Set all sails. Beating out Channel. *Speedwell* continues close. She lags and we let her come up. About seven in the evening she flies distress, when we hove to. Mr. Coppin put off to her and brings report from the Master, Mr. Reynolds, that his ship is strained beyond a safe point in her masting, that she has in this straining sprung a-leaking. So we turn aside to make Dartmouth, a good safe port and the nearest for our need, there to see how she can be trimmed.

Log: August 11th: Friday: On course for Dartmouth since last evening. *Speedwell* making slow way. My ship runs splendidly, as ever, though we are heavy in the water. It may well be God's especial grace to us that this leaking came before we had left the coasts of England.

Log: August 12th: Made the port of Dartmouth in the afternoon. Longboats out and hauled *Speedwell* up to town quays. The settlers' "governor" on the *Mayflower*, Christopher Martin, and the "governor" on the *Speedwell*, a Mr. Cushman, held a manner of conference with other of the gentlemen who have taken it on themselves to direct this venture now Mr. Weston is left behind. I will arrange repairs to be done, on credit for the London Virginia Company.

Log: August 13th: Sunday: At anchor in Dart River. I think it worth some pains to set down, for a record, my

command of these people. So that should I at some time be
called to account or otherwise be accused of favouring
them or leaning towards their desires or opinions, I may
have this evidence. On last Sunday an old man amongst
the passengers held a meeting in the main. He came on
board at Southampton from the *Speedwell,* to ease her
overcrowding. His name has been given as William
Wright. Yet he may be the King of Spain for all I can
know, they have had so much of this business confined in
their own hands. (I could wish I had known more of my
cargo at London and Southampton, where I might have
made enquiries both into the lawfulness of these Englishmen from Holland going, and if I have been directed into
an error by Mr. Weston. Yet, if events prove in the
meanest to work against me, I swear now before God that
I acted in all innocence.) Thus, ever diligent and just to
my command, I had this man to me. I said to him: "You
have been overheard to speak out to all against the Governing of England and against its Church." He answered
a denial. Whereupon I had brought to me my informer,
Richard Salterne, who is my sailor. Thus, by my witness
I confounded the guilty man, who could say nothing further than that he had erred in the heat of the moment.
Then I ordered it that while on my ship none should
speak unlawfully: that as no ordained minister was on
board with us, no man to take it upon himself to preach:
for if unlicenced preachers speaking out unto assembled
people be against the law in England it is against the law
on an English ship. And if any man did, I said, I would
confine him and return him back to Authority to answer
for it. In this wise I dismissed William Wright, my duty
done. For I know so little of these people, who they are
and in truth what they mean, that I will take no chances
of unlawful proceedings.

Log: August 17th: The *Speedwell* adjudged fit and
good for the voyage by the shipwrights that mend her. We
prepare again to put to sea.

Log: August 18th: Weighed anchor. Wind fair. Course west-southwest.

As they passed the Scilly Isles, Dorothy Bradford took leave of England. She had not, before Southampton, been in England since a child, yet, at its mention, she had always felt sad, even homesick; perhaps because the exiles in Holland had talked so much of it, like men of a lost race that pined in their very blood to return to the land of their birth.

" 'Fair, fair England, where the birds do sing . . .' " she said, and thought, how could she cry for what she had never known?

But there were women on the ship of less restrain; they waved handkerchiefs at the distant rocky isles, cried and sobbed and held up their children for a last look.

Here, out past Lands End, the ships began to meet the real Atlantic swells and the powerful ocean winds. Spray flew up at the bows and often drenched the waist deck. The last sea gull turned back to land.

Log: August 19th: Ran on course west-southwest till out of sight of land. Then west by south.

Log: August 21st: We run before a strong wind. Course west by south. *Speedwell* close by. Today one hundred leagues west by south of Lands End. Took observation: We incline to be in the Latitude of forty-eight north. The *Speedwell* lags, so that we constantly shorten sail both by day and night, and keep the wicks burning brightly for her guidance.

The sea, the sea! The never-ending, tossing, white-flecked face of the ocean lay wherever the eye turned, from horizon to horizon. Since running out of Dartmouth, with repairs completed on the *Speedwell,* the sun had shone every day for four days without a cloud in the sky; so that while not as yet steady on their legs, the eyes of the settlers were clear again, their minds beginning to move, their stomachs tight but easier. Then, a bare three hundred miles out, on a day of bright sunshine and sparkling blue sea, catastrophe again overtook them. The smaller *Speedwell* flew distress signals and hove to.

Mr. Reynolds, the *Speedwell's* Captain, refused to go on. He complained that his ship was again opening in her seams and leaking badly. He had manned the pumps but it was as much as he could do to keep her free of water, and the stores she carried were being ruined. The women and children were terrified; the ship must go back.

Mr. Clarke, the *Mayflower's* first mate, who had put off to the *Speedwell* in the jollyboat, also brought back the news that the Master of the *Speedwell* desired the *Mayflower* to accompany him back to a safe anchorage; for if the *Speedwell* foundered alone on the high seas her passengers must all drown, there being room in her longboat for the crew only.

The affair put Mr. Jones in a foul humour; but back he must go also; for if the smaller ship sank alone, on the way back, he knew he need not ever shew his face again in an English port.

At the same time he spoke against any hope being entertained of further overloading the *Mayflower* with settlers and goods from the disabled ship.

But already there were on both ships would-be settlers ready to return to England at all costs; they were the few fortunate ones who had some homes or friends to go to. The faint-hearts were mostly amongst those gathered up in England by Weston and his moneylending merchants; although Cushman, one of the true "fanatics," growing iller day by day, now decided that he would remain behind—if the little ship ever got back to port. In harbour they might effect some exchange of passengers, and send the returning settlers back to London in the *Speedwell* when she was patched up.

This major mishap, Mr. Jones reminded them, would cause the landing to be made in America in dead of winter; he would have them remember that the responsibility for anything which might result therefrom would not be his.

The mystery of the *Speedwell's* recurrent leaks was talked over by the distressed leaders on the *Mayflower* with John and the hired sailors. And the latter's opinion was that the cunning Master of the *Speedwell*, taking advantage of the fact that his little ship was overmasted, had consistently sailed her under every sheet he could fly and with the rigging slacked off. This would strain her timbers in the wrong places and cause her seams to open. It was an old trick but an effective one.

The Master of the *Speedwell* had demanded, and secured, a third of his wage for the voyage before setting sail from Holland with the exiles. It was not possible to ascertain whether he had changed his mind since seeing how his ship behaved on the open Atlantic or whether he had intended from the very first to default. But certain it was then that he would not go on in the ship under any circumstances. If they gave him a new ship, yes —but that was out of the question.

It had been intended that the *Speedwell* should remain with the settlers in the New World. Without it they would be bound to whatever part of the American coast they were left upon. The small fishing shallop, carried in pieces in the holds of the *Mayflower*, undecked and no more than twenty-five feet in length, was only a fair-weather coasting boat. From the poop Mr. Jones stared across the water at the ploughing *Speedwell*, as they turned on a course back for England and Lands End, and wondered how much its defection had cost the wily moneylender, Mr. Thomas Weston.

While old Mr. Brewster, after being told by the obliging hired sailors just how a cunning Captain might make his ship to leak under certain circumstances, wrung his hands and, with his knobbly face crimson, cried, "Villains! Villains! Oh, Lord save us, they are all villains." And William Bradford prayed behind his tight-closed lips, "God, God, we beseech You, do not sunder our loved ones from us, stopt on the perilous ocean; do not let us be betrayed even again by evil men or unhappy chance."

And now the days were flying fast and their inadequate provisions eaten up in wasted sailing back and forth on the English coast, unhappy and fearful under a morose and suspicious Captain, thousands of miles on the wrong side of the ocean.

Log: August 28th: Came into Plymouth Harbour in Devon this evening, Monday, in company with *Speedwell*, without further mishap. The weather, by God's grace, very fine, and a good wind in. For this harbour is an open and shallow water to come over in bad weather.

We ran right in and anchored in the roadstead, or, as they call it here, the Catwater, to anchor here in the open water being dangerous, where a good wind brings the swells up and may bounce a ship off the bottom and wreck her. Thus may a ship be brought through unsuspected hazards by good seamanship and a wise knowledge of all ports.

7   The ship was astir with the rising of the sun. A meeting of the settlers from both vessels was to be held on the *Mayflower*. The ships had come to anchor within shouting distance of the town of Plymouth, where they lay snugly in placid water; and the passengers, in crumpled clothes and with nervous faces, dirty and dogged by their own odours, crowded to the sides to gaze over in longing at the little town. Out of its narrow streets people came onto the quays and stared at the ships that were carrying men, women and children out to the fabulous New World.

Here was ordered living, neat houses, fresh-baked bread, milk, and unlimited fresh water to wash dirty linens. How like hard chalk did the musty ship's biscuit-bread taste! Few had ever thought to see an English town again. There in Plymouth people slept in solid beds . . . in unmoving quiet; not shut in an airless hold, on a tipping deck that ceaselessly altered its slant, packed in a black, creaking hold with everyone's chattels rattling and banging and your neighbour scratching and moaning.

John Alden, the cooper from Southampton, listened to the pilgrims and travellers with close attention. Fourteen men, the "dangerous fanatics" from Holland, came aboard from the disabled *Speedwell* for the meeting. And they were as different somehow from the merchant's gathering on the *Mayflower* as to appear almost another breed of men. They created an impression of being in some way more alive and intense, people who held their opinions doggedly but passionately, while being able to act

87

in their general affairs as a close-knit body; though they obviously loved argument of any kind for its own sake. And they were all old friends. Mr. Brewster's group of Holland exiles kept among themselves the feeling of a family; they had formed a separate church in name, but in effect it was a small social commonwealth.

The women were quiet, depressed; yet they did not complain that the seamen cursed and laughed at them, or of the hard decks they had to sleep upon while certain privileged persons had bunks and cabins, or of the monotonous, cold, tough food or the already unbearably heavy smell of the holds—but merely that they had not been allowed fresh water to wash either themselves, their clothes or their children.

The meeting went on for hours, principally because the waverers could not make up their minds whether to risk all and go on out in the *Mayflower* over the Sea of Darkness, or stay either in hospitable Plymouth and try and begin a new life there or go back to London with the leaky *Speedwell*. Lists were made, altered, torn up; families went into corners, changed their minds again and again until, finally, a frail and fevered-looking Mr. Cushman went aft with Christopher Martin, the Governor, and the completed lists, to interview the Captain.

John sat down beside Gilbert Winslow on the cargo hatch. Gilbert, with a bottle of ink hanging on a chain around his neck, had been making notes in a pocket book. Near by, four little girls between eight and ten had found a space to sit on the deck in the sunlight and were singing, "Nick-nack, pally-wack, give a dog a bone, this old man came rolling home."

"Ah, friend," Gilbert smiled. "I am here engaged as of old—clerking it," he said after a moment and without being asked. "Brother Edward thinks to write an account of our adventure . . . someday; for the unwilling ears of the world. He would have us all keep dates and names and events."

John said that by the look of him he thought Gilbert had been sitting there muttering prayers.

"Prayers! I'm saying over the names of heroes setting forth for the Golden Land, names to become legends. Moses Fletcher, a smith; Isaac Allerton, a tailor; Samuel Fuller, master of all trades; William Button, a boy in bond; Miles Standish, a man to wave the sword; Tom Tinker, a wood sayer; Degory Priest, a hatter; John Alden, a cooper."

"And Mr. Gilbert Winslow," John added.

"And Mr. Gilbert Winslow, a tutor out of employment, a man of many parts but of little success. But now we are all and every one heroes, in our patched breeches."

"Are these the true names?" John asked. "Is Standish a true name?"

Gilbert pointed out a small, red-haired and red-bearded man in buskin boots. "As true as he stands there alive, though it be the name of a man out of a play. Degory Priest, Tom Tinker, John Alden, all names out of a play—but we don't know how the play ends."

"Thus, we are in a dire plight," Cushman told Mr. Jones. "For even could we raise more money, or credit, to repair the *Speedwell*, Captain Reynolds says his crew refuse to make the voyage in her."

"So you'd have me take the *Speedwell's* passengers aboard here!" the Captain jumped to the point, frowning. "I am overladen. That's an end of it."

"It would be no more than a readjusting," Mr. Cushman argued. "Two of our *Mayflower* families would go back home. Their children sicken. I have a list . . ."

Christopher Martin handed the list forward. His time would come, he thought bitterly, and he would be proved right in the end. If Brewster and his had not wasted money in Holland on such an old hulk as the *Speedwell*, fitting her out, lading her with goods, now all spoiled, they would not be going out into the wilderness with hardly enough provisions to keep them alive a month—with not a piece of leather to mend a shoe! But they dared to accuse him of squandering in provisioning the *Mayflower*. . . .

The Master examined the list with an angry, judicial frown. "Thirty-four men, nineteen women, five hired hands and sailors, eleven men going under bond, one woman servant, six orphans. What are these orphans?"

The "orphans," Mr. Cushman explained, were homeless waifs from the streets of London. A leading merchant of the London Virginia Company had been induced by the Mayor to ship them off to the New World at a cheap rate. Thus they had been apportioned amongst the settlers' families. It was a great act of charity and they certainly could not be left behind.

"How old are these little servants?"

"They are between seven years and twelve years, and are much more adopted children than they are servants."

"It is surely a new thing for wool carders and your like to have servants! But I'm sure, as you say, it is a most charitable act —especially when you get them so cheaply. . . ." He looked up, waiting to see if either would answer his sneer, but they held their tongues. "You have not made a total here."

"We would be seventy-six, all told," Mr. Carver said—not mentioning the settlers' own twenty-six children. There was just a chance that the Master might not notice their omission from the list, which omission made their full number look so much less.

"Very well," Mr. Jones said. "But let it be understood that should you be in want of food I will leave you down or ship you back, but wherever you are, coming or going, on sea or land, your feeding is always your own concern. That is the terms of my contract. On my return I shall have to answer for the lives of my men. So should you starve on the wide ocean I can do nothing, for my own stores will provide only sufficient for the crew. Let us therefore see all our conditions clearly and let you bring only what numbers you can feed."

Mr. Cushman might have said that it had been hard enough persuading the returning members to go back as it was, so that the expedition might go on at all costs; or tried to explain that few had any employments or even homes to go back to; or that those who would go forward feared starving on the sea no more than they did starving in England or lying in prison. But no argument would serve any purpose with such a blown-up toad as Mr. Jones; Robert Cushman, thin and bent, felt very weary.

Mr. Jones continued, "For were there ever a suggestion of these people of yours having any of the crew's victuals I'd have a mutiny raised against me. You will recall that fact to your other leaders' thoughts. Nor can you have any more space on board than you are already provided with. And my final rule on these matters is this: on any complaints or trouble from you or yours over this new placement I perforce will about and return to Southampton. So as our understanding be complete no cry of unjust dealing may be brought against me."

Martin and Cushman returned to the waist deck and gave the news out that the interview had passed off successfully. But Cushman declared that he now felt too weak in health to go on across the ocean; with the other families turning back he would return to London in the *Speedwell*. It then being agreed who was to go back and who go on, attention turned again upon the civil Governor of the *Mayflower*, Christopher Martin.

The Holland exiles from the *Speedwell* said that as they were now to travel on the *Mayflower* a new Governor and assistants should be elected to organize and oversee the well-being of all for the period of the voyage, as they had had no part in the original election of Mr. Martin.

The men only were allowed to vote. But Martin's fall from power was assured by the seventeen votes of the Holland Brownists from the *Speedwell*. The number of male settlers direct from England was also seventeen. Mr. Mullins, one of the latter, raised the question of Mr. Martin rendering up account of all money spent by him on provisioning at Southampton. But Mr. Martin said he had not yet had time to put the accounts in order, and lost his temper.

He had checked the stores himself, Mullins said, and the position was dismal in the extreme. As far as he could see the whole body of them would have to support themselves in some fashion or other directly off the country two or three months after landing. The original scheme had worked out that they must have a year's supply of food, or enough to cover them to a first harvest of corn. But all reports spoke of it being an abundant and plenteous country and they trusted in God. He suggested Mr. Carver be made Governor for the trip. And Mr. Carver suggested Mr. Mullins. Mr. Carver was elected. He had a kind face, gentle voice, and a beautiful gentlemanly beard; attributes which neither Christopher Martin nor William Mullins possessed.

Throughout the showing of hands for and against the three of them, Martin kept his sullen silence and hot defiant expression. Then swung round and stamped aft under the poop.

The new Governor, Mr. Carver, had already given the women, and anyone who wished, permission to go ashore; with the advice that they conduct themselves in such a manner that when they left they would take their leave here from friends. For, unlike Southampton or London, no man had anything to fear in the little town of Plymouth from the Government gentry or bishops' agents.

Then tomorrow they would have all the baggage and unspoilt goods transferred to the *Mayflower;* when the crew of the *Speedwell* would patch up their vessel, take on board the settlers whose courage had failed them and make round to London.

The day following they ought to be ready to leave Plymouth themselves and turn out into the Western Ocean.

8   The pilgrims and travellers found a welcome far beyond expectation in the town of Plymouth. More ships had gone out seeking across the Western Ocean from Plymouth than perhaps from any other town of its size in the Kingdom.

Things took longer than had been anticipated, and it was Saturday before the *Speedwell* was ready to sail for London. Bitter tears rose to William Bradford's eyes as they watched her pass out, sailing splendidly. . . .

On Monday the *Mayflower* should have sailed, but some of

the passengers had been taken out to a farm for the week end and could not be located in time. Most of the crew were allowed ashore again that day; and John and the hired sailors went walking in the lanes behind the town. That afternoon the ship was almost deserted; the pitch between the upper-deck planking being so hot that it oozed up and stuck to shoe soles; few felt like wasting such a summer day on board. But William Bradford's impatience had brought him back to the ship at midday, leaving Dorothy washing clothes at the brook with most of the other women and all the children. The Mullinses were also aboard, Mrs. Mullins lying down with a fainting headache and Mr. Mullins fanning her. Jones had gone on shore early in a bad temper because sailing had been delayed again.

Priscilla Mullins came out and discovered herself alone on the waist deck for the first time in her experience. She looked down at the bright waters and at the sun gleaming in the fair hairs on the back of her hand; and it was dreamlike having the ship so still, the cordage silent, no voices echoing in the holds, no children's cries, no feet sounding on the decks.

A man sang, thickly, in low snatches, near by; then it came nearer, on the other side, and she heard the creak of oarlocks. She crossed the deck to look over the bulwark.

It was Mr. Jones returning, rowed by one of the townsmen in an ancient jollyboat; Mr. Jones seemed to be the singer, sprawled in the stern sheets, dabbling his fingers in the sparkling water. After one glance she moved back quickly out of sight, turning to hurry below. But she stood still the next moment; she would not be driven from the deck by the mere fact that the Master might pass close by on his way to the poop. She remembered uneasily that he had several times given her queer covert glances; and that was perhaps all the more reason why she should shew no concern and stand her ground. He came up the side with sagging heaves, got his arms over the bulwark and rested, panting, his face puffy and his hair standing on end. Only then she realized with a shock that he was drunk.

"Dearie-O, Pretty-O, lend a hand." There was a watery gurgle in his voice. "Lend a hand to your Master," he gurgled louder, "or I'll lock you up. Heave 'em over, Lord love us . . . ." His dark

93

face shone sweatily in the bright sunshine, looking fuller, and relaxed.

She continued to stare across the water, as if unaware that she was no longer alone, but seeing him out of the corner of her eye. Some stubborn thing between fear and pride prevented her from turning on her heel and going in; it never occurred to her that the way to deal with the situation was to pull him on board and laugh at him.

The voice of the townsman came from below the side; he had come up the ladder and was pushing at the Master. Mr. Jones lifted himself, then, with apparent ease, swung over and thudded down onto the deck.

"My good young woman," he said, "you hadn't ought to stand there insulting the Master—not to be insulting the Master with your silence and your scorning looks! You are all the same if I as much as move near you—silence and scorning." A metallic breath of brandy and gin blew upon her; his thick, small hand slapped the bulwark by her elbow.

The jollyboat put off; he dug out a shilling quickly and threw it down into the sternsheets, while she edged away a few paces, seemingly unconcerned.

"I am sure I mean you no insult, sir," Priscilla said, still staring out unmovingly across the water, as he turned back to ... "Nor do anyone on the ship. People are not forward in speaking . . ."

"Ah," he said, looking at her through half-closed eyes, with his head thrown back. "Give to all men love, as your preachers say, eh?"

"Love is from God," she said, not knowing quite what she was saying.

"And you are not frightened of me? There is nothing in me to frighten you. Let me tell you," he said, very near, "that I have love in my heart too. I am a Master, a Master of a ship—but I have no more ease of speaking than . . . than a boy. But I break out! The brandy frees me, I am another man—— They can laugh behind my back, at the small little man. . . . But I speak command to them, and then they know that I can pick them up with one hand."

94

His panting breath blew in her ear; he swayed, and gripped the bulwark with one ingrained hand; the animal smell of his leather and body enfolded her and caught her somewhere in the throat so that her lips parted, trembling.

"Your neck is white," he whispered, near her ear. "I've watched you walk the deck, my deck. We used to haul timber and wine and skins—but now people, my ship full of people . . . I'll learn to master them. And if you come to my cabin—I have olives, fruits, sugared cherries. I have things . . . We were in the Italian Sea . . ." His breath splashed on her cheek, his weight tilted against her.

She pushed from him, gasping; but his left arm clamped round her waist, his right hand gripping the bulwark and holding him steady. "I'll call," she cried, having to look down a shade into his face, "I'll call out——"

Mullins and Bradford, sitting in the coolth of the first hold where a mild breeze blew upon their faces from the open gunport, heard her.

"Oh, leave off your grip of me," she cried, banging the point of her elbow into his ribs.

"Give in to me, give in to me," he gasped, beginning to run into little bursts of slobbering laughter, "or I'll keep you clapt to me till Doomsday."

"Leave go. You are the Devil! Leave go," she cried, over and over again, while the point of her elbow continued to jerk back and forth at his chest and wind him.

"I have you," Mr. Jones spluttered, choking from her fierce elbow but bubbling over into wheezing laughter. "Swig ho, the merry cup——" She was dragging him along by the bulwark; he held on blindly, putting all his weight on her.

Mr. Mullins staggered out on deck into the dazzling sunlight, his heart thumping after his run along the hold and up the stairs, his pouchy face drained white. Inarticulate, he ran with ungainly steps, stiff-jointed, arms flung out before him with open clutching hand. "Beast of the Apocalypse!" Mr. Mullins moaned, getting his trembling hands between them.

Jones suddenly let go the bulwark with his right hand and got it around the girl also, shaking with wheezing, wet laughter.

Bradford gripped the Captain by the arms from behind and pulled at him. They staggered across the deck, tripped against the cargo hatch and all fell upon it in a heap, Mr. Jones underneath.

The girl struggled free and ran back wildly to her cabin. Mullins and Bradford got upon their feet and looked down at the sprawling, panting Captain. "This was my fear," Mr. Mullins shouted. "Oh, that I should see my nightmare walk in the daylight. Shame!—to lay your profane hands on a Christian woman like she were your taproom thing. I will hear your penitential sorrow when you've recovered your senses." Grinding his knuckles together before him, he went after his daughter to their cabin.

Mr. Jones's eyes suddenly overflowed and the tears ran down his face. He raised his hand towards Bradford, for help to rise. The young man gazed down at him with white, controlled ferocity.

"She was like that daughter denied me," Mr. Jones said weakly, wiping his eye, sitting up.

"These are good people, who walk with God," William Bradford said, his voice high with excitement. "Who touches one touches us all, as you will one day discover. There are no taproom wenches among us. So you may go back ashore for that."

Mr. Jones stood upright slowly and straightened, swaying. "Upstarts, ragpickers!" He blundered forward a step and pushed Bradford with all his force in the chest, so that William sprawled backwards and sat down against the bulwark. Cursing and blowing through his lips, he swayed down the deck and in under the poop. "You'll sit in this harbour till you acknowledge your Master." The door of his cabin slammed resoundingly.

By nightfall all the settlers were aboard again and ready to sail in the morning. Mr. Jones kept to his Great Cabin; Miss Mullins walked on the waist deck in straight-backed defiance, though her father brought her in to their cabin time and time again. News of her misadventure had quickly spread through the ship; the passengers were very quiet, keeping off the upper deck, the sailors noisy and full of quips. In the night those in the little cabins aft heard the Captain shouting in his sleep.

John learnt of the affair that night, in the company of Gilbert and the hired sailors, English, Trevore and Ellis, and his first reaction was to go up into the poop and beat Mr. Jones soundly; but Gilbert, smiling at his red face a little mockingly, soon recalled him to his senses, and in the end he laughed at himself. For after all, the girl was nothing to him, in fact, as yet, whatever she might be in imagination. He was a hired man. And no one would thank him for such unwise interference, least of all the girl herself. The certain outcome of such rashness, Gilbert pointed out, even in no more than speech, would be that Jones would have him thrown off the ship and left behind.

In the grey light of morning a crowd of Plymouth people gathered on the quay to wave them good-bye. The tide rose full, and began to drop, but no sail was unbent. An hour passed; the copper glow spread in the east, and the red glare of the sun burned upon the horizon.

The male passengers gathered on the waist deck, waiting anxiously. The heads of the families, Isaac Allerton, Edward Winslow, Christopher Martin, William Mullins, William White, Stephen Hopkins, John Billington, Edward Tilley, John Tilley, Thomas Tinker, James Chilton, John Turner, Francis Eaton with Brewster, Bradford, Carver and Fuller, stood quietly together, talking in low voices.

Two small coasters, each rowed by a score of Plymouthmen and youths, came off from the quays to help tow the *Mayflower* out into the Sound. They waited alongside for nearly an hour, before Mr. Jones appeared on the high deck aft.

His black figure climbed out of the poop hatch, and turned abruptly before the mizzenmast; with his hands on his hips he looked down over the ship. He could not have hoped to create a better effect, both on the settlers and on the sailors sitting on the forecastle roof, were he a demon shot up out of a trap door. Everyone stood stock-still, staring back at him. His face was as near paleness as it could be; he had washed carefully, a rare event enough, and shaved all above his jaw-liner of curly black hair; the stiff hair of his head was also plastered down with water, so that his haggard face was framed neatly. He had on his best cloth doublet and a clean white shirt. When he had stood, rocklike, for perhaps a minute, he suddenly put his hands to his mouth and sent his voice bellowing down the length of the ship.

"Mr. Clarke, Mr. Coppin, Mr. Duff!" Duff was the bosun. "In Christ's name break out the anchor. We can sit here no longer. We get under way. Who's not aboard can stay where he finds himself."

The sailors sitting on the forecastle scrambled down; from the forecastle door Mr. Coppin appeared, chewing, followed by the bosun and quartermaster. Knowing that some sail would be unfurled even as they were being towed out, the settlers went below into the darkness of the first hold.

"And it's perhaps better we keep as much to ourselves and out of all the crew's way as we can," Mr. Carver advised. "At least till his sore head has cured itself. Which is a pity: this is our real and true farewell; a farewell from England taken from friends, though we can't wave as much as one handkerchief to them." But comforting, they heard the men in the boats ahead singing as they pulled the oars,

> *"Tom o' Lyn and his wife and wife's mother,*
> *They went over the bridge all three together;*
> *The bridge was broken, her mam fell in.*
> *'The Devil go with you,' quoth Tom o' Lyn."*

Thus, on the morning of Tuesday, the fifth of September, under a partly clouded sky and with a small east-northeast gale blowing up, the *Mayflower* was cast off from tow by the Plymouth boats, and came round, trimmed, into the wind, so that a sudden gust filled the mainsail out with a resounding slam.

The unexpected gale wind held, and when the ship had cleared the Sound and was set on its course west-southwest, it had a strong following wind; they ran before it for Lizard Point, keeping the land in sight to starboard, ploughing through a kind, sweet sea, till they passed out and the Scilly Isles dropped away into the waste of waters behind. Then the *Mayflower's* blunt cutwater rose and fell heavily, smashing through the dark frills of water, the ship fully alive, straining, creaking and heaving;

and the sickness again gripped those afflicted with that weakness.

But others, like the Winslows and the young carpenter, lived those days almost wholly on the upper waist deck, savouring the miracle of a ship sailing in summer through the beating open ocean. Dorothy Bradford also stayed much on deck; she was less afraid there, than below, that the shuddering, groaning edifice of scoured wood and bleached canvas would break up about her ears any moment and be scattered over the tossing desert of water.

They drove on without a moment's drop in the powerful wind or its altering a point, until, as the days passed, all the passengers began to come up on deck for airings, cautious, but happier, becoming used to the ocean winds, which at first had seemed so terrifyingly persistent, threatening and destructive.

By then the children had made themselves free of the ship from end to end, the Great Cabin only being one of the few places they dared not enter. Tandy Fall, the cook, early succumbed, and groups of children were always to be found hanging about the galley door at the end of the first hold, each hoping to become one of the privileged and be allowed to remain within, "helping" the cook and picking up snacks; those lucky ones were nearly all little girls, the favourite being Ellen Moore, a London street waif of nine years, now adopted by the elder Winslow and his wife. Ellen and Tandy from the beginning recognized each other as brothers-in-arms against the world. And very soon the crew gave up shouting at them when they played in and out of their quarters forward; and the most horny-handed villain of them all began carving whistles. . . .

By Sunday morning, September the tenth, the first Sunday on the sea after Plymouth, the *Mayflower* was again one hundred leagues beyond Lands End, and Mr. Clarke kindly told the settlers that the time lost by having to put back to Plymouth had almost been regained.

The steady good weather had so raised Mr. Brewster's spirits that he did not even think of asking Jones's permission to call a thanksgiving gathering in the upper hold. There the whole body of settlers, children and servants in bond, gathered, sitting on the decking close together, said prayers common to all, listened to Edward Winslow read from the Breeches Bible and Mr. Brewster speak hearteningly on their coming new life and the virtues and rewards of unselfish love of man for man.

Then the people dispersed and William Brewster set his foot on the stairs to ascend up onto the waist deck and into the sunshine. Close behind him stepped Bradford, elated, in one of his infrequent garrulous moods.

"Why, sir, we have every reason in the world to thank God," Bradford said loudly. "We might not have you with us. John Robinson stays in no danger in Holland, but you, Mr. Brewster, you to be in England was to walk with death——"

They both looked up at the same moment; Mr. Jones stood blocking the hatch opening. He rarely came down from the poop deck, or out from his quarters onto the waist, but there he stood, looking down at Brewster with an expression of mingled surprise and cunning.

"Your name is Brewster?"

The Elder glanced back at Bradford, whose face had become a mask of anguish at the realization of his betrayal. "My name is Brewster, William Brewster."

"It was not so the last time we met, you remember? . . . Nor on the proper lists of this ship is there a William Brewster."

"Mr. Brewster took another's place," Bradford said instantly, in a whisper.

"That is very true," the old man said, coming up the remaining steps, firmly brushing past Mr. Jones and walking out onto the deck so that the Captain had to follow; here Mr. Jones could not dominate from a higher point, but must look up into the face of the tall Elder. "Let us not dissemble in any way at all to the Captain," Brewster continued, "so that our future relations may be the better. I took the place of a friend, by name William Wright. My name is Brewster, and you would have known shortly, in any event."

"Who led his people into Holland," Mr. Jones added with an unpleasant smile, beginning to remember scraps of conversation with Thomas Weston concerning the missing leader.

Brewster inclined his head slowly in unconcealed agreement. "If you would put it that way."

"Why hid you yourself in Southampton—if no one else on the ships had need of hiding?"

"For certain private reasons, which I am sure you will respect."

"For the good and simple reason that you were in danger of arrest!" Mr. Jones guessed.

"Nevertheless, no matter what you think, Mr. Jones, you cannot well turn back *now*."

"I may turn about any time I please," Mr. Jones flared, stubbornly. "Yet, why should I turn back for one man, when I can lock a dozen up and bring them back in the long run?"

Bradford's words escaped him in a torrent, against his very will. "You forget that we are more now! You forget that we are more in number than you and yours, that we will not always accept the command of those who ought to serve us—that we cherish each other's lives more than our own, and this man's far above any——"

"Are you making threats?" Mr. Jones snapped in his face.

"Not at all," Brewster said, "the young man is testy."

"I do not like your attitude!"

"Nor we perhaps yours," the old man answered promptly, but courteously, "so let us all alter our attitude and come to a happier state."

Mr. Jones laughed outright, savagely.

"Why are you so set against us?" Bradford asked humbly, to try and make amends by pacifying Jones at all costs; he had betrayed his most revered benefactor into the man's hands.

"I know that tactic," Mr. Jones said, "accuse another first, to hide your own fault."

"But you have shown in some ways," Brewster said gently, "that you are set, a little, against us. Has any man of us ever done hurt to you or any of yours? Give us but our just due, Mr. Jones, sir, that is all we ask—give us . . . your blessing, with your help. If we build any new world your name must then be part forever of the good of it."

The settlers on deck had crowded around now and encircled the three closely.

"I resent your accusation. I am not set against the success of this endeavour, for that is what you mean, or against you and yours, without just cause——" As the ship rolled someone leaned against the Captain's back. In a sudden fear Mr. Jones pushed out from amongst them, saying, "We will have this out shortly, Mr. Brewster!"

He strode back under the poop, now angered as much by his own cowardly moment of panic as by the Elder's disregard of his ruling against preaching and publicly addressing. But any group of men close about him, let alone a hostile gathering, caused him extreme uneasiness and a sheer discomfort occasioned by his sensitivity to his smallness of stature; in a crowd he stood out as a small man. High on the poop, alone, he could forget that, and believe that others forgot it also. He had come to the head of the hatch stairs to hear with his own ears what these men "preached" and see just how they conducted their forbidden meetings. Well, he thought later, there were other ways of dealing with them. . . .

"Don't be afeared," the old man comforted Bradford, "he knows nothing of me." A sea captain would hardly know that a certain obscure North of England man, William Brewster, who had been in exile in Holland for over ten years, if caught in England would more likely than not be hanged or starved to death by order of the Anglican Court of High Commission for preaching that congregations should have the power of electing their own teachers. But Jones did know something, Bradford argued, as his remark about Brewster leading his people into Holland proved.

"There, lad," the old man said, "the man is a fool, but not such a fool that he would turn his ship back in the middle of the ocean on a suspicion. The merchants know who we are; their Captain should also know."

Mr. Jones wrote in the log:

A man, whose name I had thought to be William Wright,
an old man whom I writ here of for the 13th of August,

on my having him before me for unlawful religious speaking to some assembled, says now he is another man, that he took another's place, and that his real and true name is William Brewster—whoever *he* may be when he is at home. That is all I could learn of him. They are forever arguing religion amongst them, that much I know, which is most offensive.

If there was a price in reward money to be had for him, he thought, then it would be a different story; he'd be worth bringing all the way back from the other side of the world. But they were all such small men, of such insignificant worth, they merited not a pound's payment on their heads—but what was paid for their passage in shipping them out of the way.

Every third day a charcoal fire was lighted over the sand on an iron hearth, a cauldron of porridge made from soaked oats and another cauldron of stew; the porridge was eaten hot every third morning, cold every other two. Fumes from the bad charcoal made them cough, but this was thought a small inconvenience in return for a steaming bowl of food. The porridge was eaten for breakfast with a lump of biscuit-bread and a cup of beer or water, everyone sitting down around the hold with their bowls on their knees. The midday meal was usually cold stew and mush, or biscuit-bread with a slice of smoked bacon or smoked beef.

In the evening their frugal meal was again mainly of biscuit-bread, with which they could have a small portion either of cheese, heavily smoked and salted sausage meat, soaked peas, raw onion, finnan haddie, kippered herring, or dried tongue, and a mug of beer.

Delicacies, apples, prunes, raisins and pickled eggs, of which the store was small, were given only to the children, the sick and the pregnant. All food was carefully rationed out by the orderlies. Meals took a long time; the food was small in bulk but tough in substance. Most of the meat had to be chewed at great length, and even then was hardly digestible. They were always hungry, but it lay in their own hands: they could eat well now, if they chose, while idle, and starve later on when perhaps they would have heavy labour to perform; the majority did not so choose.

The younger men brought in by the merchants played cards; the men from Dutch exile slept, talked endlessly, walked around and around the waist deck; or sat with their hands clasped and a gaze of meditation, doing absolutely nothing, day after day, for the first time in their lives. Brewster, Bradford, Carver or Winslow the elder sometimes read aloud to groups from various dull books. Puritanism as a painful rule of unrelaxing behaviour was not yet known amongst them.

They could not wash daily; the ship barely carried enough beers and drinking water to tide them over two or three months' ocean voyage. When it rained, the sailors said, they might lay out rags to catch it and wash themselves that way, but if they took their advice they would forget about soap and water till they trod land again—one's skin kept best in the salt winds with a dry wipe now and then, when in a sweat. The majority believed they would come out in running sores if they washed in sea water; and their soap made no lather in salt water, in which greasy clothes went into a stiff lump. But no rain came down on the ship, although black clouds sat low over other parts of the near ocean. Dirty shirts and shifts were trailed in the sea and hung out on the waist deck to be freshened in the winds, which the crew found entertaining in more ways than one.

But tempers were kept in check and a workable order of good manners and discipline of a sort took shape.

Mr. Jones stayed the next few days almost wholly in his own quarters. John Alden put himself in the way of Miss Mullins and smiled at her; but she still kept her steady gaze elsewhere and went about her business without giving him a word. Gilbert Winslow and Dorothy Bradford began a casual conversation as if they had known each other the better part of their lives. The voice of Edward Thompson was to be heard ceaselessly, talking amongst his cronies of the gold to be found in the earth of the New World, fruits falling from trees into their hands, of the paradise of monkeys and fabulous beasts waiting for them up the river of Hudson; firmly and soberly corrected repeatedly by Mr. Mullins, holding his book in one hand but never lending it out, an authority on conditions in the New World.

Many eyes sought a glimpse of a sea monster or a mighty fish, but the sea gave no sign of the mysterious and terrible life going on in its depths.

It began to be cold in the holds at night.

9   Log: SEPTEMBER 13TH: The East-Northeast wind continues constant at our back, so that we keep on our straight course west by south. The ship stays in good trim and we move fast though we are so laden, now eight days out on the Great Sea from Plymouth. The settlers will have musket lessons for their men tomorrow morning on the waist deck (which from all accounts they need, being better trained to thread needles than fire off balls). It grows cool, but still has not rained where we have passed.

The women were instructed to keep the children, and themselves, below, while the first class, of twenty men, received their preliminary lesson in the use of firearms.

The small military Captain with the red hair came up the hatchway and marched out and across the deck; he was followed by John Alden, carrying four matchlocks in his arms. The guns were old, oiled but rusted, with great heavy downward-curving stocks.

"Miles Standish has served in the wars, until he was a captain, in the Netherlands," Governor Carver said to the men. They were muffled up against the hard wind, while the new Governor wore his felt hat tied down over his ears with a neckcloth.

"We hope never to have to use weapons against men," Mr. Carver said, "but we must know their use. This country we are going to for our home is one running wild with all manner of animals. We had not means to get a gun for every man, but there are enough for the majority of us, and some others have their own. To our military Captain, Mr. Standish, we must all learn to give obedience in military matters. Few of us know a thing about these weapons," he touched the stock of one of the matchlocks distastefully, "but our lives may come to hang on them. And Captain Standish has agreed to begin our instruction as we were raw recruits—which we are!"

The men seated themselves on the deck, sheltered by the poop and bulwarks: Standish faced them, holding a matchlock. He was a small, sinewy man with bright red hair, a florid complexion and a wiry, auburn, pointed beard. He wore stiff knee boots, which he had waxed and polished for the occasion, seasoned leather breeches, and a leather-lined jacket belted and buckled; set straight upon his ears was a black felt hat with a round crown, a wide brim and a crimson band.

"A gun," he said, holding one up, unsmiling, pugnacious.

"Gar, that ain't no gun, man," John Billington called out, from the back row, "that's for poking the fire." He looked from side to side clownishly; a couple of guffaws rewarded him.

A hard gust of wind slid across the sea, smoothing the choppy points flat, and, whistling and groaning, shouldered the following wind out of the sails; the ship heeled over, the sails flapping frantically, before the east-northeast slapped them out again with booming sounds.

Standish, his feet apart in a steady, balanced stance, continued, shouting above the rustling, smacking sea and the creaking and whistling rigging; some hoped to see him stagger, but he kept his balance.

"This is a gun," he repeated harshly, "which is the most simple made; and called a matchlock because we touch it off with a smouldering wick or match cord—some call it a slow match. It has no wheels, flints or steel to misfire. And like a good simple man, it will not leave you in the lurch if treated honestly."

"We are the simpletons, God help us," Stephen Hopkins said to William White, poking him with his elbow, "to have our moneys laid out for us on rusty pieces of iron."

The most of them had looked forward to some amusement from this lesson, either from the novelty of first handling guns or ruffling the usually silent, spruce little Standish. The young men nudged and whispered, eager for something to laugh at; they had had little enough to laugh over since coming on board the *Mayflower*. Sitting at the front, still managing to look incongruously well apparelled, Edward Winslow glanced around, smiled handsomely and shook his head at them. Hopkins repeated his standing joke: "Have to get your hair cut now, Edward—you will not be getting enough to eat to keep that lot growing." Gilbert, sitting next to Edward, smiled at him and nodded. The other leaders continued to ignore the interruptions.

"The first law," Standish said crisply, "is to carry your length of wick in your left hand, your gun under your right arm, or on your right shoulder. You will then never touch your weapon off by accident going through woods or in such places. For when you go armed you will carry your wick glowing—this is it—ready to be screwed in the clasp on your gunlock, which clasp we call the serpentine; where, when you pull the trigger, it is released down onto the primed flashpan. Then the powder lights from your glowing wick, runs through the touchhole, explodes the powder in your barrel, and your ball flies forth."

Standish gave detailed instructions, determinedly, without humour, on how to wash out the barrel with boiling water, how to keep powder dry in rainy weather, form lead into shot with a ball mould, measure a charge, and the use of the ram, with dire warnings on the danger of putting home second and third lots of powder on top of previous, unexploded charges and the risk to life and limb occasioned by carrying gunpowder carelessly about the person or near fire; and continued the lesson with a practical demonstration.

John went below for a light and set the end of a slow match glowing. Standish poured a charge of powder down the muzzle of a gun, slid in the ramrod and patted it gently, dropped in a ball and with the rod saw that it was fully home. He shook a few grains of the mealy black powder over the touchhole, put some more in the flashpan by its side, and slid over the flashpan cover while he screwed the glowing end of the slow match into the movable arm, which would jerk it down and dab the spark in the primed pan.

"It's like waiting for one's execution," Hopkins said. "We can only pray there'll be no damage done."

"Face the wind," Billington called, "face the wind, your lordship."

Standish turned his back to the wind, holding the gun above his right hip and pointing upwards, to port. Deftly he cupped his powder-blackened hand around the flashpan, protecting the powder from the wind, as he slid back the cover; and all in one movement changed his position, gripped the gun with both hands and squeezed the trigger. The serpentine and wick jabbed down, a little puffing explosion of muffled fire and black smoke hissed up out of the flashpan, followed by a red belch of flame and sooty smoke from the muzzle. The heavy weapon bucked back under his arm alarmingly. Acrid sulphur fumes and specks of soot blew across the faces of the class in the back-surge breezes from the mainsail.

Claps and appreciative voices acclaimed his steady handling of the miracle. One of the settlers might now step out and repeat the performance under his guidance. John Billington sprang up, pushing his way forward, his sharp, city face anticipatory of some devilment. Standish handed him the gun.

"Take this for your own, keep it, and be responsible for it."

"Hold hard, Captain—there's a split here. Can't I have a better relic than this?" Billington winked at the others.

"You have seen me fire it. It is in good order."

"In good order!" He faced the settlers with the gun in his hands. "I've seen a gun before, I can tell you what's a fifteen-shilling musket. I could 'ave 'ad these 'ere in Petticoat Lane at a bob a dozen——"

"Oh, give over your gabbing, man," Mr. Carver said, "and let's get on. A very little of your taproom humour goes a long way."

"Well, I don't know as I'll risk my natural letting this relic off under my oxter," the joker continued, pretending to shake his head very seriously.

"Get back in line," Standish shouted up into his face, laying hands on the gun to take it from him. "I've stood here and listened to enough guff from you for one day."

"And my poor wife and children," Billington said mockingly, "who will care for my orphans, Captain, sir?"

The Captain wrenched the musket from him, his cheeks glowing brick-red. "Get from my way, or I'll boot you out of it—if you are to serve under me I'll teach you to wag your tongue to a different tune." He threw down the gun on the hatch, spread his legs apart even wider and began to unbuckle his belt, as Carver and Winslow scrambled to their feet.

"Here," Billington said, retreating backwards amongst the others, "we're free men—this is no army." He returned, muttering, to his place on the deck.

Standish rebuckled his belt and continued with their first lesson on how to meet the New World.

The same day, sometime after noon, when the passengers were seated around the upper hold ready to begin their midday meal, John Alden at last spoke to Priscilla Mullins. He passed out onto the deck and saw her straining in over the side at a bucket rope. Richard Salterne, the sailor who attended Mr. Jones, held the end of the rope, as if he had only that moment come up to her; the girl seemed to be ignoring him. A couple of sailors watched from the forecastle doorway, joking and shouting suggestive advice.

"Let me give you a hand there," John said.

"Lay off—I'm giving her a hand," the sailor said, trying to push her to one side without being rough about it. "Lay off it, girl."

"Lay off it, you, man." John gripped the rope firmly. "You meddle too much with the passengers. Get out of the way."

Salterne held onto the bucket rope, so that all three had a hold of it; the girl silent, resentful.

"Get away, lad—else I'll lift you over the side." John spoke pleasantly, butting the sailor in the thigh with his knee. "Get away to hell or I'll break your neck."

"Oh, leave me alone, both of you," the girl said fiercely.

"I did have her first," Salterne said, angrily bumping back at John with his hip.

The sailor was as tall as John, but not as heavy; a gangling, loose-limbed young man. And John, with a certain amount of carefulness, noted that in the moments just before he released the rope, stepped back and caught Salterne by his jacket collar and breeches belt. He wrenched him away from the bulwark, and as he stumbled past kicked him with the side of his boot.

The sailor, light on his bare feet, regained his balance instantly, swung around and leapt back. John caught him luckily by the wrists and they strained against each other, chest to chest.

"Salterne," Mr. Clarke roared, coming forward from the back of the poop above and seeing them, "get you forward from your dancing!"

They stepped apart; the sailor, without a word, going into the forecastle. Priscilla had hauled up her rope and was lifting a bucket of sea water in over the side. John took it from her and lowered it to the deck.

"Thank you kindly," she said formally, without looking at him.

The wind pasted her hair across her face; her hair had grown dull in colour, and rather straight; her complexion, though a little pink now from the breezes, was sallow and wan from confinement in the box cabin; her hands ingrained with faint tracings of dirt. She was wearing an old, faded, green woollen dress; and there was a soup stain on her bosom. He smiled, looking at her from head to toe.

She bent over the bucket to untie the rope.

"Your poor mother's been sick again!"

"It's to wash me, if you wish to know."

"There's a sign for you that you've never been on the sea before—you can't wash with the sea, young miss."

"That's a sailorman's superstition. Your fashion is to wait till the dirt is thick enough to scrape off; we are different." She looked deliberately at his neck, her head on one side, wrinkling her nose.

"Well, you can't wash in the sea water, that's all. And if you don't see for why not it's because it won't take soap, and you'll begin to look like raw meat. It will crack your skin all open in no time, and the winds will finish the job for you."

"I don't care. If we are not to have fresh water, even to wash our hands . . ."

"I'll catch you water when it rains, enough to swim in, and nice soft water." He took up the bucket and slung the water over the side.

"It's never, never going to rain," Miss Mullins said, stamping her foot. "We're eight days without it—and you all smell like pigs!"

"I don't smell you," he said earnestly.

"How would you! . . . if you can't smell yourself. Fill the bucket—you threw it out. Well? Fill it—that's what you're hired for."

"Well, tell me, do you smell me now, standing here? . . ."

She covered her nose with her hand and made a slight face. "I pray God I'll not have to smell you after another month—and the sailors! . . ."

"Then I must always stand away down-wind from you," he said, laughing, and puzzled. He altered his position, glowing with the pleasure of her presence. Her seriousness was very putting-off; this talk of smells and washing ought to be spoken in jest; she did it in a distant voice and with a straight face. So it were best perhaps in the long run to keep solemn with her and not frighten her off at the first step. "Now it is I that smells *you* somewhat," he said, sniffing, serious. "But you're not high, you're sweet to the nose. I was always told a strong man's smell was good. We're not royalty, to bath in tubs of rose water, like they say some do."

"Cleanliness," the girl said pertly, "is next to Godliness. Were you never told that?"

"I have heard as how you make it part of religion these times; and I'll wash me when it rains—as the most of us will, I'm sure. So I beg your pardon to smell in your nostrils."

"Oh, you are not too bad," she said hastily, "not like the filthy sailors, abandoned men."

"But you think me a better man not to smell at all?"

She pretended suddenly to recollect who she was talking to, and looked at him a little blankly. "Good people, as my father says, are more times clean people than dirty. Now, will you get my bucket full?"

"Wash in sea water you cannot, and there's an end of it."

"I have done it before!" But though she looked at him resentfully she did not go.

John rubbed his bristly chin. As if she could not spit on a bit of rag and wipe her hands, if all that particular. Well . . . he must do her a worth-while service; put her in his debt; that was the way. (In the new country he might save her old man from lions but that was a long ways away yet.) Suppose, he said, she got a jug and drew some water from the drinking butt on deck, took it to her father's cabin, as she ordinarily would, and there just plainly and simply washed herself, who would know the difference?

Her face tightened, deepening in colour with indignation. "Shame on you. The sooner you learn that we are not common licentious people on this ship, the better for you. You should have stayed in fallen England."

"I'll get you a jug from the cask room," he said awkwardly. "I have a barrel to my own use."

"You have your own water?"

"Yes, mam," he lied, "but don't make mention of it."

In the upper hold the Brewster children fell into a bout of pushing and laughing, which quickly ended in their falling over Edward Thompson's legs and upsetting his bowl.

"You be good boys and keep patient," he said. "There'll be warm rivers for you to paddle in soon—and you can have a little monkey for your own, each—eh? No more being down in the dark like mice. Why, the sun shines there from dawn to dusk, and you can wander up and down picking fat sweet grapes." And as he spoke his tired eyes widened, his thin hand, gesturing at them, trembled.

The women smiled and nodded at each other. But Mr. Mullins put down his eating bowl with a bang, saying, "One would think we were all going just to sit about in our heavenly reward and be spoon-fed by the angels."

"Let us have our hopes, Will," Brewster said. "They can do us no harm."

After eating John went forward, on an impulse, to see the

ship's cook. "Look," he began, stretching his neck and turning his head sideways for inspection, "would you call me dirty?"

"You ain't dirty," the galley slave laughed, "nor you ain't lily-white." What would a gent do? Rub himself with an unction. "Butter is best for to clean up with. Goose fat's better. A lady? Well, so . . . I'll give yer a knob of goose fat; make 'er lips soft."

John came away with a generous knob of goose fat stuck on a chip of wood. He had rubbed some on his face and neck and wiped it off in the tail of his shirt. A present of the remainder should please Miss Mullins.

Her ewer of water had become a soapy soup, diminished in volume; her father, mother and young brother had also washed their faces and hands; Mr. Mullins' conscience being lulled by her reply that it was not drinking water but the dirty end of a cask, given her by the cooper; which she believed, as John had told her that.

The wind had fallen for the moment as she went out on deck to empty the dirty water; but as she pitched it over a whistling gust struck the side on which she stood and splashed her soapy water back over her head and sprayed the face and clothes of the second mate, who was walking aft to the poop and happened to be passing behind her.

Mr. Coppin wiped his face on his sleeve, muttering "slut" at her, tasting and smelling the soap at the instant. She ran past him, in confusion. He followed her into the passage beneath, there halting her by taking her by the sleeve.

"You been washing clothes?"

She shook her head.

"Water from the sea don't make lather like that," he grinned. "I'd better tell you what's the laws on this ship."

"I know those laws, sir. Take your hand from me," she said quietly.

He ceased smiling abruptly, and for a moment, without releasing her, folded his lower lip up upon his upper in an ugly expression. "You better come see Mr. Jones. . . . We've remarked on your gathering up of petticoats, when you pass us poor dirty sailormen."

The door of Jones's quarters was only a few yards away; at the end of the same passage was the door of her father's box cabin. She was pulled along, but kept silent; Coppin threw open the door of the Great Cabin, pushed her in, and said, with a wink of his red-rimmed eye, " 'Ere's a lady what's washing in our drinking water—she looks like she had a bath when she was at it. Not hard to see now how some of them 'ave kept their faces holy bright."

Mr. Jones sat having his midday meal, a stew of pickled pork and onions, and lumps of floating bread. He looked up, with swelled cheeks, and frowned at Coppin.

"Get back to your watch—and knock on the latch when you'd enter here!" He waved Coppin out; the mate went, closing the door swiftly but quietly, smiling. Mr. Jones continued to chew, uncomfortably, looking down at his dish. He had not spoken to Miss Mullins since the incident at Plymouth.

"This, girl, I could punish you for," he burst out, pointing at her with one hand as he sat back and wiped his mouth. "Water isn't as the food—it's common to the ship. If it runs dry we all go thirsty. A rule's a rule . . ."

Priscilla stood with the ewer behind her back, her feet apart to keep her balance, and stared at the top of his head. "If I have done wrong I'm sure punishment is none of your part," and added pointedly, "sir!"

He prodded between his front teeth with his fingernail, sucked to dislodge a fibre of meat, while frowning at her boots. She was an insolent miss, a very difficult kind of fanatic. . . . Now certainly was the golden opportunity to clear up the unpleasantness remaining from their encounter at Plymouth—if only she had the grace to do so. How difficult it always was with women to say anything but formal little speeches. . . . For, as a weak man, he found himself bullying first and thinking on it otherwise later.

"What is wrong with you folk, that you cannot be civil or agreeable?" he asked suddenly and loudly. "The poor sailormen are not used to the sight of girls walking the deck. Good. We admit it. Don't blame them then if they blow lusty at such sights. But we are not dogs. I am a man by my own means, and of learning." He stood up, waving a hand at the volumes in his open lockers. Then he didn't know what to say. "Let me offer you an apple?" he shouted. He took one from the table and came around towards her. "And you can take a seat on my couch," he added, in the same embarrassed bellow. "There's little comfort on a ship, outside the Captain's quarters."

He could surely do no more, he thought, to show her that he bore her no ill will. But all was offered with such rough loudness, in his determination to overcome his own feeling of discomfort, that she only winced, and edged back from him. As she hesitated, he lifted her arm and pressed the apple into her palm.

"Take it," he blustered, "and if you prove an agreeable girl—why, there are many such dainties I keep here. Apples, crystal cherries, prunes, olives, brandy."

He still held her wrist. When he smiled, nervously and determinedly, he revealed his neat, brown teeth. She had heard her father telling her mother that the settlers had agreed to do everything possible not to further estrange themselves from this difficult man; and she might have found it possible to speak to him now, but the contact of his warm, damp hand on her wrist caused a shiver to run up her back. She turned to run from his rich breath and the somehow frightening odours of his cabin, jerking her wrist free and fumbling at the latch of the door with the hand in which she held the apple, tensed and awkward.

She paused. "Thank you kindly," she said hysterically, and swished out, drawing the door to with a bang. Mr. Jones went back to his meal biting his finger. Outside she stood still, her face against the latch, listening; rather than have him follow her out and make a scene she'd perhaps go in again and try speaking to him fearlessly.

John entered the passage, holding his goose grease. He took a quiet step up behind her and said, "Would you be pleased, mam, to accept a small lump of goose grease?"

She swung around, startled, lost her balance with the ship's movement, dropped her pewter ewer, and fell against him.

"Oh, pardon!" Miss Mullins gasped, staggered back, and stood smoothing her dress down guiltily. Her eyes raised to his face;

"Oh, Lor'!" she said and, about to titter, clapped her hand to her mouth.

John's present of goose grease was sticking to his chin. He scraped it off slowly and seriously. "I had a thought you might like it, to put on your face. Goose grease—a good guard against the wind. It cleans the dirt off."

"Well . . ." Priscilla picked up her ewer, and held out her hand, holding the apple, to receive the grease.

"It's to rub on your face," he said. "Then you wipe it off. That's what ladies call an unction."

"I know that—where do you think I was reared? I wish I'd brought a lot myself." For a moment she had nothing further to say. "You have my apple then. The Captain gave it me."

"The Captain gave it you . . ." He looked down into her face forbiddingly. "That's a new side to your conduct, miss!" And quickly grinned and winked together.

"Do not dare to speak to me like that! It was your water set them about my ears. That Coppin creature, seeing me throw out suds, dragged me along . . ."

She looked down at her apple, her lower lip pouted, as if near tears. John patted her arm, and looked stern.

"I'll care for Mr. Coppin," he said meaningly.

"You will mind your own business. You were not brought into it by as much as a word."

He shrugged, silently, and put the chip holding the grease between her fingers, but without taking the apple. The door of the cabin next her father's opened and Mrs. Stephen Hopkins came out and down the passage; the woman walked carefully, being over seven months pregnant, keeping her hands to the partitions on either side of her, as if walking a tightrope. She manoeuvred past fussily, but not without giving Priscilla a sharp glance and a reproving little shake of her scarf-wrapped head.

"There!" the girl said, as Mrs. Hopkins reached the deck. "Everyone will report to my father of seeing us together."

"Yes, mam, what odds if they do?"

"That he is an angry man, and very easily raised in his temper, over his family."

He shook his head, in puzzled exasperation. Miss Mullins

nodded curtly, ran on her toes up the slanting passage, and disappeared into her cabin.

The young man cursed as he went out on deck. Here was a whole boatload of pleasant-mannered people, with neither the reasons of position nor apparently any inclinations towards airs and graces, and the very girl he had a fancy for had to belong to the one stiff-necked family on board; so he spoke to himself, standing and glaring up at the poop deck, while a warm indignation pulsed in his breast.

Mr. Coppin came forward and answered his stare with a like stare. They stood, the one looking up, the other looking down, back braced against the wind.

"You," Coppin called, "do you wish speech with me?"

"I'll speak with you one of these days, don't fear—the kind of speech you won't welcome!"

"What?" Coppin shouted, although only a few yards separated them; he put his hand behind his ear, not having heard clearly.

John made a short, silent grimace up at the second mate, which resembled a dog drawing its lips back over its teeth and growling, and went below.

Mr. Coppin spat after him, and resumed his short pacing back and forth.

10   LOG: SEPTEMBER 16TH: Course by compass. Wind hard, shifting, east-northeast. We remain all sound and making our straight course west by south. It blew a wet squall in the night gone past, but cleared by daylight.

The oil wicks in Mr. Jones's cabin usually burned late, glowing through the stern windows, two yellow eyes rising out of and disappearing into the black ocean. He was often to be heard speaking to himself; he slept at odd hours of the day and night; and the settlers innocently supposed him either to be tormented by the Devil or so distraught and anxious for the safety of his ship and its successfully making landfall that he could hardly bear to go to bed.

Sometimes at night he tried to read; but did not often succeed in doing so for very long. Reading was too like listening to someone else talk; and he had never learnt how to listen. His attempts at reading usually ended in his holding imagined polemical dialogues between himself and an adversary—who was always roundly outtalked, if not outwitted.

Because he held power with a feeling of insecurity and personal inadequacy he allowed the officers no common comradeship with him. When he sat alone in his Great Cabin in the evenings he often heard the voices and laughter of the sailors below in the tiller room, as they talked, sang or diced. To such sounds he listened at times with the sentimental eagerness of a father who had sent his children to bed unjustly, but who was too weak and proud to go to them and set matters right.

Not even from Coppin, with whom he was on better terms than with any other member of the crew, would he brook the least intimacy. He knew too well by experience how companionship lessened his sense of personal wholeness, of commanding by virtue of being a better and a stronger man than any around him.

This course had stood him well in short voyages about the Mediterranean and the coasts of Europe, but as day after day of fair weather came and passed on the lonely and monotonous Atlantic Ocean Mr. Jones became increasingly weary of his self-imposed constraint. For he had reached a state in which he considered himself to be word-perfect in certain arguments, ready somehow to vindicate himself and his conduct; with Christopher Jones it was in great measure his conscience which made of him a bully.

He would call the settlers to him, he thought, and in his usual way, as he imagined, utterly demolish and cow the men of beliefs and principles. Then, when he brought them to the coast of the New World, God's grace permitting, they would be more manageable. . . . For he had to remember that if they fought him openly, standing upon their rights to be landed within the mouth of Hudson's river and nowhere else, they outnumbered him and his crew two to one; and they had their three hired sailors, English, Trevore and Ellis, with whose help, at a pinch, they might make shift to sail the ship themselves. His object then, as he saw it, was to knock them down well before the event, cow them and hold them down, and thereafter keep their spirits and health as low as possible. Cow them, he thought, dominate them.

On the evening of the twelfth day out from Plymouth, as the grey sea was beginning to soak up the darkness of the approaching night, Tandy Fall carried to the Captain's quarters a huge, steaming dish; and a few moments later Mr. Brewster, William Bradford, John Carver, Edward Winslow and William Mullins came up from where they had gathered in the first hold, entered under the poop and trooped into the Great Cabin. They, only, had been invited.

"Come," he said, welcoming them, "sit. Let us have no false manners over the food—you should enjoy a hot supper after all your cold fare and hardtack."

They had agreed to be cautious and reasonable, but not to allow themselves to be browbeaten. Perhaps after all the Master had suffered a change of heart; but it was more likely that he intended to deal some blow in a softened glove; whatever it was, the opportunity of free speech with him was welcome, and the hot food doubly so.

For the first few awkward minutes Edward Winslow and John Carver smoothly threw out a sufficiency of formal conversation, while Mr. Jones applied himself greedily to the meat and gravy with so much vigour that he had little breath for talking. They learnt how to keep their elbows on the table edge and prevent the dishes sliding off.

It was so mild a night, though with a steady wind, that the passengers were able to come and go at will on the waist deck, talking and walking about in fair comfort. But everyone had been warned that there was to be no loitering in or about the poop passage to try and overhear what went on in the Great Cabin, the delicacy of the situation demanding the utmost circumspection on the settlers' side.

These were the last days of summer; tomorrow or the next day, the full force and misery of a North Atlantic winter would be upon them. Dorothy Bradford stood under the shelter of the poop, a rug about her head and shoulders and her elbows on the lee side bulwark. Circuiting the deck, with little Ellen Moore by the hand, Gilbert Winslow paused and looked at her profile; in the half-light it appeared pale and smooth, sad, but at ease. He moved along and leaned on the bulwark by her side. She was taken by a short spasm of coughing, and turned her head away.

He said, in his quiet, slow voice, as if resuming a conversation, "Too far out to turn back now. Your early discomforts are passed?"

She smiled at his question, without looking at him. "They will never turn back," she said.

"You and yours from Holland, no—but the rest might. . . ."

"We are all gone in too deep now, Mr. Winslow. Of homes, nothing is left but some tubs of meal and hoes and spades. Ellen should go down and be put to bed," she added, patting the child's head.

"Ellen don't want to go down to bed, mam," the child said in her high, thin voice. "Uncle Gilbert he's walking me out."

"You like your uncle Gilbert, don't you?"

"Oh yes, mam, and my other new uncle, my uncle Edward. My uncle Edward is married to my aunt Eliza. I'm their children now, how it is they 'ave no children belonging to them of their own. And I'm a-going to live with them in a house——"

"And if your uncle Gilbert asked you to go down to your aunt Eliza out of the cold, wouldn't you go?" Gilbert asked, wanting to talk to Dorothy.

"I would, sir," she said, smiling a thin, gracious smile and hopping off across the deck.

"You sounded sorry that you had come," Dorothy said.

"I have listened to our friends and their plans, and begin to see clearly that little else but a very hard labour, from dawn to dusk, waits for us at the end of this Atlantic Stream. Building a new world, when you stop talking, and where nothing is before but wild savagery, is going to be all a business of spades and tears—

work, I confess, I have of little experience. The things men take upon themselves!"

The peaks of the darkening water were capped every now and again by small lacy frills. She answered him after a few moments. "If they did that alone—it is the things they take on in the name of others, without as much as a by-your-leave."

He could not decide if it were a bitter, personal comment, or a feeling about things in general; it was spoken in a deceptively lazy tone of resignation.

"We learn by the falls we take," he said, "as long as we stay alive. I say to myself, I can always go back in a few years . . ."

"As long as you stay alive! You may go back—if you have a roof to go to and are in no danger. But what of the poor men that have spent a score of years closed up in small weaving rooms, in attics, picking shoddy, saving their pennies? Them that would be hanged for not praying to the King?" She coughed again.

"Is this not better for them?"

"Better? To cast themselves out, from their mouseholes, into the raw elements?"

"You are thinking of all the coughs and red noses, you are thinking that we will all die. What a melancholy way to travel towards the Fountain of Youth."

"Fountains of youth!" She turned her face towards him and smiled reprovingly. "Then you believe this little boat will see land again, Mr. Winslow?"

"I shall be most annoyed if it does not! You look to be very cold, Mrs. Bradford."

"I am used to the cold. Tell me truly, Mr. Winslow, is not this little boat going to break in two, break up all to pieces on the back of a wave? Look at it, so old and worn . . ."

"That is the scouring of the seas and winds."

"Such an old, worn little ship," she said sadly.

"Madame, this is a very large fine ship!"

"But listen to the way it moans, and creaks, and complains. No. Mr. Winslow, the wind presses the poor thing, with so much power. . . . Someday it will give up the struggle, as we all will, the masts fall down, the old bleached sails blow away, and all crack up into pieces."

"Stuff and nonsense; she is strong locked oak beneath. Do you not rather worry about real issues—what they are saying in the Captain's cabin?"

"It is poor Mr. Jones you would pity, if you knew William Bradford—I was going to say also, Edward Winslow, but if you do not know your brother who would?"

They listened, hearing faintly the Captain's booming, forceful voice, intermingled with the rhythmic creaking of the ship, the slash of water heaving against the prow and gurgling along the sides, and the hundred complaining voices of the wind straining in the rigging.

John had come on deck, and with his hands under his armpits was wandering up and down.

"The wall near our mattress is wet," she said softly.

"That is always so on a ship," Gilbert said. "It means nothing."

Again they lapsed, voiceless, as if resting amidst the swarming noises of the ship and sea.

"Is it not strange," she began, "that men like Mr. Brewster, your brother Edward, John Carver, William . . ."

"Their lives and endeavours?"

"Yes, yes, that is what I mean. They could have been high in position, called into the councils of their country—isn't that what you say? And they prefer to be penniless, driven like cattle, going where no man lives, into a wilderness, like—like the old men in the Bible. Why, Mr. Winslow, why?" She waited, looking into his femininely large, dark eyes, while he framed an answer.

"It is that men are not as—as good at living in the world as women," he said.

"Not as good? . . . Will you explain that to me?"

"They will not compromise, as a sensible woman will. I give way here and you give way there."

"That is the very truth of the matter," she said, nodding wisely.

"You didn't want to come, Dorothy, did you?"

His low tones barely penetrated the rug around her head, but she looked about to see if he could have been overheard, a shadow of distress breaking through her set, melancholy expression. "Want?" she echoed him, and smiled faintly at the word. "Want? What right has a woman to want? She grows to being a woman by laws like the fixed seasons. *You* will never open your eyes from a dream, and discover that you have had children, that you have a husband by your side for all eternity——" She stopped suddenly. One did not talk like that, even to your husband. "I beg your pardon. I suppose it is everything being so strange . . . being cooped up day after day. But you draw me out, make me say . . . You never came to Holland?"

"No. I am not an active reformer of other people's lives. It's my cowardly nature. But I believe Brother Edward and the others got on quite well there, squabbling and disputing on the state of man and the world to their heart's content. Had the Spaniards not ended the truce I suppose they'd all have drifted back to England sooner or later."

"The truce, Mr. Winslow?" she said quickly. "This mad voyage was planned long, long ago, before ever anyone knew the truce would end and the Spaniards come back into Holland to carry on the war. It was planned because more from England would not come out to us in Holland, but may come to us in the New World——"

"Yes, I know, my brother wrote to me every other week. I suppose you have a right to be bitter."

"It is true that they all thought they'd go back to England when the King, or the Government, changed towards them. But as time went on . . . there was less money to be earned, less of us English to hold together."

"We understood in England that there was work for everyone in the great trading cities of Holland."

"Did your brother say how hard even the little children had to work?"

"We heard the children, too, did some work."

"Some work! A man's letter will be full of arguments, and policy, and principle, but not of the small things that make up a woman's life. Our very children slaved at the looms all day, at ragpicking, at whatsoever a hand could be put to keep bread in our mouths. The most noble intentions are nothing when you are harried, and harrishing, and worked from morning till night."

Her mature bitterness moved him so that his slight sense of discomfort at being close in her company when her husband was otherwise engaged vanished. She was so very young to be a wise, married woman. "It was very hard?"

"It was very hard, Mr. Winslow. To get the better-paid work we would have had to belong to the guilds. But you could not join the guilds until you were a Dutch citizen. And men like Elder Brewster, and my husband, they never would be anything but Englishmen. Neither would they get used to working in places such as Stinck Steeg—Stench Lane—working like the labourers of the field, without hope of being free one day in England, men who had come from houses and lands of their own."

"And thus they desire to make a strong, rich church and a government of their own," he could not help adding, "able to support its preachers."

"Is that wrong?" she asked, half mockingly.

He shrugged. "They are going to have a cold awakening, if they think Englishmen will leave their comfort and flock to them in the New World."

"They do think more will come. And there too they think the children will not escape, cannot become little Dutchmen, as they did in Holland."

"The young are not usually willing to suffer for their parents' principles, if they can escape it."

Priscilla halted in the poop door, seeing them in the corner with their heads so close together. She stood and looked until she was sure who they were. Mr. Gilbert Winslow had not shown any eagerness to speak to *her,* but here he was engaging a married woman in this scandalous manner before the eyes of everyone. When John approached she spoke to him without hesitation.

"There was more than principles engaged, as you call them," Dorothy said. "You have not heard my husband on the licentiousness of the young Dutch in the great cities? Of the temptations, evil examples, of all those who ran away to sea, or became soldiers?"

"I saw it must be hard to keep together there."

"And all the time there was much crying out against loose women—like me," she said, with an expression of being mockingly shocking.

"So Edward spoke in his letters. They saw, he said, their posterities in danger to degenerate and be corrupted." Gilbert laughed, shaking his head. "As indeed they were, by all accounts. But who in their sanity would believe the air of Holland cleaner than England!"

"They thought they'd be free to live and think as they thought fit, and to speak. But so did every other man, so that there was always someone at them; preaching, arguing, printing tracts. Why, you could not go outside the door but someone took you by the sleeve and shouted contrary in your ear, with curses for you as a corrupter of the Scriptures. Men from every country came there to be free, or so they called freedom. It became such a madhouse I would put my fingers in my ears." She paused, laughing ironically under her breath. "And I watched it all, playing the child, and none knew what I thought. . . ."

"Then you do escape, going over this ocean—you escape Holland."

"I? In Holland I worked the livelong day, and kept my silence. And if we reach the far shores, I will work the livelong day again, and keep my silence. We women are kindly allowed to have a soul to save, but beyond that we are reckoned with the horses. We keep a proper silence, we do not move the great and important affairs of men. Perhaps you can tell me what escape there is for a woman at this journey's end, Mr. Winslow, that is not the final and great escape? Or are you shocked, to hear such things from a mere woman?"

"We understand each other uncommonly well, as you're quite aware, Dorothy. Men are beyond all bounds selfish, that is the answer."

"We'll be better off—all buried in the sea. Clean it is, and endless . . ."

"That's the kind of thought makes you so pale," he said, surprised at his own quick anxiety for her. "Then you will begin to believe it, and put your face down towards the sea."

"I'm not afraid of the sea any more. Looking at it when it's kind makes you pleased and easy in your heart."

They looked at the grey, heaving mass, in silence.

After the main course had been eaten, and Mr. Jones had drunk enough brandy to give him ease and freedom of speech, he began the serious business of the evening with a blunt assertion:

"I know right well, gentlemen, I am accused of disliking my task. It is accused that I am full of contempt for my passengers beyond all reason. Oh, faith, I know it—and I know them to think me blackly ignorant of who and what they are. . . . I had hoped for you to come to me, submit your argument, what plans you had, to put trust in me. But still I wait——"

"My dear sir," old Mr. Carver interrupted, "on the contrary, it is most held against us that we do not keep silence about ourselves! Let us merely say, then, that we have not understood each other. So we are grateful for your inviting us here tonight. We, considering ourselves wronged men, have been raw and touchy. Now, by your good act, we may mend it all and travel on like angels."

Mr. Jones looked around the table for a moment in silence, tapping with the pads of his fingers. He forced himself to speak smoothly and agreeably, holding himself in check. "But, tell me truly, *is it so that you repudiate the King?*"

Edward Winslow and Mr. Carver exchanged quick glances; Bradford looked into his beer, his mouth tightening, while Mullins' expression struggled between denial and fright; Brewster turned his head and nodded to the others.

"That the King should be head of the Church," Winslow answered, "we do object—amongst other things. Any reasonable man must certainly object to the notion that there can be any divine man born since Christ. A church is a combination of men for spiritual ends. Grant a Pope or King divine rights outside the common law and he very soon begins to burn or hang whosoever

126

he divinely thinks fit to be burned or hanged." He sipped his brandy, smiling. The others were drinking beer.

Captain Jones waved his hands, crisscross, before his own face. "These stories of hangings are always thrown up."

"And I can assure you, from my own experience," Elder Brewster said, "that they are not stories, as any man living in the Kingdom knows very well, by the evidence of his own eyes."

"Rogues and robbers and pullers down of governments are hanged, and why not?" Mr. Jones said loudly.

"Many years ago there were with me at Cambridge," the old man continued, "two schoolfellows, by name, John Greenwood and Henry Barrow. They were hanged for holding a simple and innocent opinion. Another you may have heard of was young John Penry. That was the first I began to know of it. The list of them now, who have been murdered, is too long to count. There must, Mr. Jones, be some good cause in this, don't you see, that men will lay down their lives?"

Bradford, with a deep breath, said hurriedly, as if in fear of being stopped by such looks as he had already had from the elder men, "Flung into prison, to rot, or be hanged, for believing the evidence of their senses and the written word of the Scriptures—there's the cause, there's the heart of it."

"And did you not desire control of the Church, and thereby the Government?" Jones asked him directly, and a little too eagerly. It was fantastic that these men should sit there and calmly condemn themselves out of their own mouths, when he had expected to have to incense and infuriate them into such admissions. "Did not you puritans hope to gain such control that the King and Government would be left powerless to govern the country?"

"No!" Bradford contradicted him. "No, sir——" And a wooden dinner plate escaped from the table by his side and bounced on the floor.

"We never did, at any time," Winslow declared calmly, "nor do now, wish to leave England or the church of our fathers, but to cleanse it back to its true primitive state. Our separation from our homes and our country has been forced upon us."

"All these avowals of cleansing England—I have heard them before," Mr. Jones said. He sat forward in his chair at the head of the table, tense and excited, holding his brandy mug tightly with both hands, a dribble of gravy still clinging to the fringe of black hair around his chin. "But what is meant by it?—pardon me for an ignorant man! Isn't it first the gaining of control of the King's church, and through that means the control of men? Power—all men want power."

Mr. Carver raised his hand, and before anyone could speak launched a long, flowing sentence, with hardly a pause for interruption, to give them all time to cool down. "All bodies of people gathered together for the purpose of instruction and example in good and right living," he said, "and for the satisfaction of that common aspiration in man to learn and know something of God, and to find peace by praying to him, and strength in the fellowship of other men, do always tend to go wrong and corrupt the simple truth; truly, some men love power over others, it being in the nature of the vain and corrupt heart of fallen man to do so; and so we come to a time when men must go back to the simple source and fountain of the Scriptures themselves. When it is you have that division between the men who claim that a king rules by divine and absolute right—a claim of kings and governments to every man's life as well as his soul—and the men who claim the right to the governing of their own souls——"

"That's all a preacher's rigmarole," Mr. Jones exploded. "No one is meant to understand it; you don't understand it yourself. And so I see you do not, or cannot, answer me in what this 'cleansing' means—if it doesn't mean pulling down those at the top and putting yourself in their place!" He raised his mug with both hands and gulped.

"Read your Scriptures," Bradford cried angrily. "And you will see that there is no mention of Pope, whether he be James or the one in Rome, or the other in the East, nor of a hierarchy of tax collectors imposed from above on us, or of this ceremony, or that practice, of copes or indulgences——"

"But how do you clean?" Jones shouted stupidly. "How do you clean, my friend, if you do not put yourself in any position of power?"

"Read the Scriptures!" Bradford shouted back; and another dish slid off his side of the table.

"I have sat here trying to hold my peace, because it was enjoined of me and agreed by us all," Mr. Mullins burst out, "but these violent speeches of William Bradford's are beyond a saint's forbearance. And I would wish to make it clear to you, Mr. Jones, that *I* . . . am not of these radical opinions—not wholly——"

The others turned in surprise, having almost forgotten his presence at the end of the table.

"Then keep your mouth shut," Mr. Jones roared, "if you have nothing to add."

William Mullins rose to his feet with deliberate, slow dignity, his face rigid with suppressed indignation. "No apology came for your former breach at Plymouth: I expect none for this," he said, and left the cabin. But his words were hardly heard, for Mr. Jones's shouting, and his departure quickly forgotten. Without, on the waist deck, he mopped his forehead, and was nearly knocked down by Priscilla and John, who were trying to walk as fast as they could around the centre hatch and keep their balance.

"Come in, girl," Mr. Mullins snorted, "and say your prayers."

"You cry 'Scriptures, Scriptures,' at me," the Captain shouted back at Bradford, with his mouth wet and his face shining with sweat, "but you do not answer plainly, straightly, on these counterfeiting claims to cleanse us all."

"William Brewster is a ruler and a government to us," Bradford cried, before anyone else could answer, "and yet we do not fear, or believe that he, our Elder, will take power to our hurt—for the simple reason that what rule he exercises he does so by our will."

Such disputations had been a daily part of their lives; and they forgot for the moment that they had come, not only with the intention of being frank and clearing up matters with Mr. Jones, but also of winning a more favourable opinion of themselves from him.

"As to rulers, Mr. Jones," Winslow said politely, if loudly, "I think the whole point of difference here is this: that we would have our rulers elected by us, our church officers particularly—who are those who make or mar ours and our children's lives by their teaching and commands—and subject *to us,* not us to them by absolute will; we would have them freely deposable by vote if we do not find them fit, instead of being forced upon us from above——"

"So that any common fellow can be 'elected,' as you call it, to teach the rest!" Mr. Jones interrupted violently, pounding the table with his fist. "I know that argument. Shall my common cattle of sailors not also have that right?—to set *me* to the rigging, sweep my knowledge, my ability away, while *they* 'elect' one of themselves into my place?—and run the ship on the rocks!"

Bradford stood up furiously. "Is it not different that, for the first time in England, men begin to see it is their very right, the root of the Reformation and all belief in God, that every responsible man has the right of judging for himself, and of holding communion with God according to his own apprehensions?"

"William, you will wreck us all," old Mr. Brewster said. But it was useless trying to make himself heard at that moment. He wiped his knobbly face unhappily, pushing back his chair, and bent to pick up a dish that had fallen from his side of the table. He was uneasy, and inclined to be angry with William, yet Bradford's ringing, hysterical voice, muscular stance and shaking fist gave him a curious satisfaction—for he had taught the young man. "Oh, peace, peace, we cannot continue like brawling schoolboys," John Carver cried, his silver beard seeming to tremble. "Where is our humble desire to win Mr. Jones's understanding?"

"No, my friend," Jones said, in a quieter voice, "if you keep life in you in your new country—should you reach it," he added deliberately, "and should you grow, you will soon see to it, like every other body of men mad with belief in their own ignorance, that only those may live with you who bow to *you* and *your* will." He waved a hand. "Sit down, gentlemen, I am not ended. Why did you leave Holland, if all you desired was this kind of miscalled freedom?" His question was directed to Brewster.

"Because we are Englishmen," the old man said.

130

The others nodded in agreement. Bradford held silent, though only with great difficulty, still standing when the others had re-seated themselves.

"And I will warrant you this," Jones said, continuing with heavy deliberation, "that did I live to come to this New World you would build, in as little as twenty years or less from now—should you not all be devoured by the wilderness—I should find you few rich, and powerful, above the rest. And seated secure in your power, allowing none such nonsense as 'electing' and 'de-electing,' that you in the start offer as bait to the ignorant, that they may work and clear the ground for you. Yes! And as more fools came out to your so-called cleansed church you would shackle them every one, so that you might be rich and powerful, and free of toil, the dream of all men. I have seen every manner of man, and many more countries than you have even heard tell of, and had long hours on the sea to read the written word and form my opinions of men. And I know that no ventures such as this, no perils undertaken such as here, are undertaken for the love of man to man!"

"He is so stupid," Bradford moaned, "he drives me to distraction!" He clattered his way out, stepping on dishes, pushing blindly against the chairs, and banged the door behind him—for he felt that there was some little truth in what Mr. Jones had said, and on top of everything else, and from such an objection-able creature, such a feeling was maddening beyond endurance.

He stood outside on the deck, holding a steadying hand on the timbers and breathing deeply of the harsh salt air. His wife came from the side, swaying in balance, and put her hand on his arm. He hardly noticed Gilbert Winslow walking by her side.

"Have you been shouting, William?" she chided him.

"God, but he is a stupid, wicked man—oh, and well schooled in lies and chicanery." He led her in and handed her down the steep steps into the hold.

As Bradford left the cabin Jones stood up, unsteadily, shouting across the table after him, "You are hypocrites. You are counter-feiting cranks. None but madmen would drag their women and children across this ocean to throw them to the savages."

The rest then stood up, to leave. Mr. Carver said, quavering in his agitation, "You will one day learn that all men are not wholly moved by their own gain."

"Mostly by their belly!" Mr. Jones roared. "Or by their lusting after gold, to be men of power. You think to find gold. So have others. But never did I see men cover that lust with such wiles as I see here. Presumptuous ragmen . . . But while you have dealing with me, I will have you remember how it is: you are in law treason subjects. It is cheaper to let you go to the wilds than subdue you. You have lost the rights, you have lost the privileges of Englishmen. Remember, sirs!"

"Come," Brewster said, "we can only hope to do better when he is sobered." He bowed shortly and left the cabin, followed by John Carver.

Mr. Jones turned to Edward Winslow, and found his single remaining supper guest still seated, apparently in repose and gazing at him with a bland, speculative look. The Master sat down, and poured himself a drink. Now he felt that where the others were simple, passionate men, Winslow was cool, collected, tenacious, without illusions; a dangerous man; and a gentleman; it was his gentlemanliness that was the most disconcerting of all. Mr. Jones felt suddenly rough, aware of the stains on his clothing, his heavy, dirty, leather-coloured hands. He had sensed Winslow's aristocratic essence early, and had not addressed him directly once.

It was not in Mr. Jones's method to allow anyone to weigh his conduct calmly and silently, in his presence. He had stated his case, drained himself in a pleasurable fever; now let them all get out of his sight—if he regretted it later, that was his own business. But Winslow continued to sit, so silently that he might not have been there. And then Christopher Jones discovered that an extraordinary thing was happening to him: by the mere fact of this handsomely dressed man sitting at his table in silence, he began to feel a flutter of panic in his stomach. Winslow had been drinking brandy too, he remembered. He was drunk! He turned his head to look at him.

"How does a man like you become drunk on three tots of spirit?" Edward Winslow asked, in his low, insistent voice.

"Pray what do you mean?" Mr. Jones said stiffly, surprised into controlling his own voice.

"That some of us can get drunk as much by the wish as by what we consume." No emotion touched his voice; his tone was good-humoured, conversational, as if he had that moment wandered up and bid good day. "A man may often sneer at some poor, drab wretch, because he fears he may touch his heart. But should a Master sneer at his poor passengers for the same reason? I am afraid that you have a good heart after all, Mr. Jones."

Mr. Jones lolled back and laughed loudly; his laugh at any time never rang true. He began to laugh in relief; but it was no relief; and he quickly fell silent.

"Oh, I do not cast blame, in that you do not understand your shipful of simple people; why, simple people are the hardest thing in the world to understand—they mean what they say. But surely you should be blamed," Winslow said, "for being afraid to understand or see their hearts; until you do you will never know why men thrust hardship, suffering, exile and wilderness upon themselves, for the sake of an idea. An idea—a thing no man can weigh, measure, hold in his hand, be rich by or own individually—the idea that they must trust the evidence of their own senses, and not be forced to believe or think what men above them in authority and power demand, men to whom they themselves never gave that authority or power."

"Could I run a ship if I was subject to my crew?"

"The world will not run as a ship runs."

"The world is but a larger ship."

"Very well. Perhaps all they have is the idea that they are right, as you say, and others wrong; or the idea that men must be allowed to live after their own fashion—but *that* they have and hold with their very lives——"

"Treason and revolution begin with ideas, I grant you," Mr. Jones said coldly. "Therefore ideas must be curbed by authority."

"Yes, to you it seems the height of presumption and madness that, having merely to say 'yea' or 'nay' and obey the laws of being present in church, the saying or doing of which could not effect, you think, their happiness of body, or make their homes or properties less worth having or keeping, they chose deliberately, for the sake of saying 'Our Father who art in heaven,' instead of 'Our Father who art in the King,' to uproot themselves from their ancient homes and run to the distant ends of the earth. And so it might be, if that were all there was in it. But you know we are men who are also out *to alter the very shape of the earth*."

"Sir, I wish you would leave me, and chatter somewhere else," Mr. Jones said, and gave the table a bang of finality with his mug.

Edward Winslow stood up, a sleek, solid, smooth-faced figure, his hair falling gracefully on either side of his face. "Here and now this shipload of common people are the salt of the earth, and its hope."

Mr. Jones was staring at him with unblinking eyes like veined stones, his lips rubbing and working furiously against each other.

"For the chance to make a better world," Winslow said, stepping towards the door, "that is all it means when you rub off the excuses and the noise and the cries of each that God is on his side—for a chance to make a better world than the one they found themselves born into, they stake their lives, their goods, and their very wives and children. There is the idea behind us, whether they all know it or not. And this great human courage worries at your conscience to be understood."

"Good night," Mr. Jones said through his teeth.

Winslow stood on one leg, his hand on the latch; but still his voice and attitude were anything but offensive, so that the Captain could not just bring himself to the point of pitching his mug at him.

"I plead with you, Captain Jones, that you are in danger of seeing no further than the end of your nose, if you think to despise these men for being drab preachers, without voices to sing, not swaggering in ornament, dressed like peacocks, swearing in loud, rich voices of their nobility, or, if lacking that, of the men's lives they have put an end to. For these poor, ignorant, preaching sinners are the great in time; they move the world and yet make no thunder. Mistake it not, they have the true splendour of God, poor things as they are. I speak of the simple people, not of their leaders."

Mr. Jones heaved himself up onto his feet abruptly. "Good night, sir!"

Winslow pulled the door open. "No matter how a man may think on or believe on God, his greatness has always shown itself best in proportion to the humbleness of the vessel. I hope we may speak together again soon. God give you a good night. The food was welcome. . . ." He passed out and latched the door behind him softly.

The Captain let himself sink loosely back into his chair, enfolding his lower lip with his teeth. "No," he said, "no, no, no! You will never convert me to treason, to return home and be hanged, while you go free. Treason subjects," he cried hoarsely, "without rights or privileges! And your pale daughters, they are watered-down shrews. . . . I'll give them more than apples. . . ."

The remaining dinner dish slid off the table and clattered on the floor.

Gilbert and John were the last to remain on the waist deck.

"The air is softer and sweeter tonight," Gilbert said, "but I'm to bed."

"What is this fighting on religion like cocks?" John said. "What makes them do it?"

"Their constitutions. You may thank God you haven't the spiritual fire that consumes from one end of the day till the next."

"What that is I know neither—but it is a very pretty night." He looked up at the stars.

"What other way nowadays has a man to protest against his lot than through the words of God? I go to bed."

Down in the second hold William Bradford and his wife were going to bed by the light of a dim and smoky lantern that did no more than reveal its own presence. Bradford was standing up, his hands against the side of the ship, his bent head resting on the wood.

"What are you doing, William?" she whispered. "Are you sick?"

"Aye, sick for comfort. Stand up and pray with me."

"But I'll fall down," she complained. "You've always said your prayers sitting down since we've been on the ship. If you insist on not kneeling, then sit. It looks so silly, amongst all these strangers, standing up, holding the wall. . . . Besides, my cough is bad tonight."

"Pride, pride in its worst form," William said. "I don't know what has overcome you since being amongst the people here. Strangers . . . they will all be ours someday, every soul of them. We shall have them, cut off, and they shall be ours . . ."

She listened to the ship as it swung creaking through the slapping water, to a man whispering his prayers at the far end of the hold, bits of conversation, to a child whimpering, rather than to what her husband was saying. Well, he should be used by now to her being an indifferent prayer, and to her persistent cough, laziness, bad eyesight and her being so easily tired. She just could not be the rock that he was and that was all.

William stood by himself and prayed. She heard his hard, firm whisper while she thought of other things; tomorrow she would be apologetic for her inability to be the strong wife walking with God and William Bradford; but now she thought of the English countryside, as she had seen it those weeks before for the first time since childhood; a cow and a field, a house with a lawn and flower beds, and a clean child in a fresh white smock. And there had been a girl humming a song she knew herself, "I'll go down to some lonely waters . . ." They had deprived her of much, these men, from that distant night when her father had set off from Cambridge for Holland, with the family, in the dark. Nevertheless, she loved them all. . . .

"Lord," William prayed firmly, "let a wretched creature come to Thee, for I sweat for grace to love Thy people—captains of ships notwithstanding. Let me, unworthy though I am, and mean in powers, do some good for us all. Lord, though Thou cast me aside let them continue on and find their way, that the name of Christ is glorious in the world of men. And pardon such men as try to trample on us; they are Thy people too; poor crawling things of the earth as we all are. And pardon me my short prayer, for Jesus Christ's sake—and give us a good night's rest, if it be Thy pleasure. Amen."

He lay down on his pallet and clasped his hands over his

stomach. "I have a pain in my stomach," he whispered pettishly. "I'd not be surprised to find him the kind of man would put poisons in our food."

She smoothed his brow with one hand, and went on thinking her own thoughts; while the ship lurched sickeningly, dealt an unlucky buffet by a high swell, shuddered, shaking it off, and groaned and hissed on its way towards the unknown shore.

11   LOG: SEPTEMBER 20TH: Course by compass. The strong wind at our back continues. We are now a fortnight's way over the ocean. Crew in health, weather cold, ship sound. Wind returning constant east-northeast, for which favour thank Christ our Lord. Whilst the rain do be falling the silly passengers mop it up into buckets for to wash themselves and their shifts. But they will not be restrained from this habit, hurtful to their health. However, the amount of scrubbing and washing they get in between them all is very little. I am told that the women complain that the cockroaches come out of the galley and when slaughtered make a fearful smell, as if they all came from palaces where beetles were unknown. The truth is that women have no place on a ship and should never be on a ship.

Continue on course west by south.

The weather had become so cold that few of the settlers re-mained on the open waist deck for pleasure, but only long enough to take a few stamps around at a time and have a look at the sea and sky. The sky seemed to be blacker every day, the sea to move in ever larger sliding and shifting masses about them, as if seeking an opening, a weak spot through which to push and overwhelm its enemy, the ship; and always that desolation of empty water, on which nothing appeared from horizon to horizon.

The settlers stayed in the holds wrapped in blankets and extra clothing, scratching themselves, irritable and nerve-wrought. The crew at least had some heat from the galley flue, which passed up through a scorched hole in the decking of the forecastle, and passed out through another iron-sealed, scorched hole above their heads; while the Captain had his neat charcoal brazier set under an open stern window. But the settlers had heat for an hour only, once every third morning, when they were allowed to cook up their cauldron of porridge and stew on the charcoal brazier in the first hold; at which frugal rate it was estimated that their charcoal would just about last out the voyage. When the fire was lit the children were seated around it, as near as convenient; a special place always being reserved for Sam Fuller's serving boy, William Button, who was daily growing thinner and paler and coughing himself to a shadow, despite the care and remedies of Mr. Fuller.

But the fire did poor William Button little good; after a few minutes the fumes in the enclosed hold would bring on a fit of coughing, forcing him to go below again to the second hold and lie on his cold pallet.

Priscilla thought Gilbert not so fine a looking man as John; nevertheless, he had soft eyes, spoke gently and with an air that made the carpenter appear in contrast a very commonplace fellow. But Gilbert Winslow never did more than smile vaguely from a distance, and half the time did not see her at all. However, one persistent follower was better than none, and perhaps drew attention to the fact that under different circumstances she would be a much sought-after young woman, by the right kind of man. There were the uncaring young fellows and the sailors; but a look from one of them was enough to send her running to her cabin.

Therefore, being seen with John was a protection as much as anything else; and as time went on she came to greet him freely after meals and dally on the hatch steps or in the first hold, though still somewhat condescending and with the air of a nice girl being well mannered and obliging. All which John took for so much more than was meant. He did not speak to her openly if her father or mother was present, but took it for granted that they had a sort of tacit understanding.

It was the middle period of an early winter ocean voyage when, even under the best conditions, the days drag with interminable monotony and the mind, floating on its own empty sea, casts about fretfully for a moment of enlivening diversion; on the *Mayflower* there was the maximum number of people, and the minimum of comfort for mind and body.

That afternoon the younger Mr. Winslow sat on his pallet with shoe last, nails and candle, mending his shoes and telling some ridiculous fairy story to an admiring circle of children. She stood by listening, but Gilbert did not once look at her. So Priscilla allowed John to take her down among the stores to smell the tainted beef.

"There's nobody here!" she said, pretending surprise. "Does no one live down here?"

"No one but me."

"Oh . . . I did not think . . . " She inclined her head to one side gazing at him, her expression nervous and unwittingly arch. Sitting long hours in her family's airless little cabin had put dark marks under her eyes, made her hands inclined to twitch and her limbs ache nervously.

He told her, as they stood steadying themselves in the gangway between the barrels, that he had discovered some of the meat to be tainted and some of the meal wormy. He had led Governor Carver and some of the others down to inspect the stores further; now he would have to look into almost every cask daily, for the rest of the voyage. Parts of the beef had been so bad, being improperly cured, that they had quietly thrown whole sides of it overboard, for fear it would contaminate the rest. She must not speak of it to the other women, to cause unnecessary alarms and outcries. He was taking down notes of the amounts and adding them up, et cetera, to try and see, by his own judging, how long the food would last.

"Can you do that?" she asked incredulously. "Write, add up in ledgers, like a clerk? . . ."

John showed her his bits of paper, with his careful, grotesque handwriting. She looked at him then with a wondering gaze. He put his evidence of superiority away in a pocket, silent, in deep satisfaction, and led her forward towards the sail locker, taking her elbow firmly when the ship lurched.

"Your father don't like you talking with me?" he said.

"He doesn't mind the passing of words—if it is necessary to our crossing over and setting up in the new country."

"But no gadding!" he laughed.

"No gadding," she laughed in return.

"Your father thinks himself a high and mighty man. Who does he reckon he is! . . ."

Mr. Mullins had put hundreds of pounds into the venture, she said proudly, and was therefore the richest man amongst them all. He had been the most respected of honest shopkeepers in their part of London, before he had started refusing to attend church or mingled with those who preferred to say their prayers with a bare altar table in a back room. But now he was not too proud to labour and begin all over again; he had brought a set of strong working clothes, and lots of tools, and was going to work as hard as anyone else building their houses and trading with the savages for skins, and corn, and gold, and soon be in as good a position as he had been in England.

They entered the sail locker and John stuck his candle on a beam. "That's what all the men want—to come to a good position. And *I* may have the same land as another, though I don't have twopence; for I may go, or I may stay, as I choose. What's for one is for another, else few of us would go."

They talked of her father's book of Virginia engravings, and she confessed to remembering how she had seen him that day in the geographer's shop. "Oh, the fright you were—bold-looking as a beggar." She did not seem to want to sit, but stood leaning against the doorpost, swinging gently with the ship, her hands behind her back. Her shawl was loose on her shoulders, her hair almost black in the candlelight, falling by her cheeks; he marvelled at the smooth, unhealthy whiteness of her skin, her mouth young and pink. He saw her as no longer prim and wary, but pert and free with deliberately attracting glances, as a girl eager and excited to provoke.

While in herself she was no more than charmed with a sense of wrongdoing and excited to be alone with a man in the dark bowels of the ship. "Me frightened of you—of course I'm not. You're like a big dog we had; he was always looking to be patted."

This seeming change in her whole attitude so astonished him that he threw all caution to the winds, knowing little or nothing of the disguised forms assumed by hysteria in young women; his sense of pleasure and sudden warm expectation unbalanced him to such an extent that he kept bending his head sideways and foolishly smiling into her face. The back of her head resting against the post of the door, she laughed with him, rolling her head from side to side.

Her eyes closed for a moment. He found himself leaning forward, one hand on the jamb above her shoulder, the other on the bulkhead to her right, and pressing his lips on her mouth.

Priscilla's eyes opened instantly, her mouth tightening against him; she wrenched herself down and ducked under his arm, lurched around in a half circle, and fell forward against the piled canvas. She was up again immediately and turned to face him; he stood blocking the doorway.

"Easy, girl," John said, laughing. "Being kissed is no cause to fly in a temper!"

She was furiously red, the tears gathering in the corners of her eyes. With her hands to her face she suddenly swung about and pressed against the pile of sails. He stood helplessly behind her, trying to think of something to say. She turned from the sails abruptly, refusing to look at him, and fled through the door.

He swept up the candle and, holding it high, followed her along the gangway, puzzled by her strange madness. She reached the hatch steps and ascended quickly and steadily into the second hold. He stood looking up, in bewilderment, until her skirts vanished.

Log: September 24th: We still run free in the wind, by the grace of God. Yet I reckon it will not hold for us much longer. The knuckles of my feet warn me tonight that a change is coming.

I am chastened to have to note again that Richard Sal-terne, the young sailor, who fell ill some days since, is worsened in his condition, and looks as if he may die. He was my most willing fellow, serving me at table, and on the whipstaff. I have satisfied myself that his is no feign-ing to escape duty; I pressed him hard above the groin and his scream was a true scream as ever I heard. He lies in a fever, sometimes crying out, sometimes in another world, clutching his bowels with all the semblance of agony.

Our own Heale is not a patch on his name: he can do nothing for him. For, says he, there is no lumps shewing to draw or lance. The passengers also have amongst them one of these whose pretence it is to heal the sick. This man, whose name is Fuller, a say maker by trade, is said to have some renown amongst his own people; which kind of renown is so easily got amongst the ignorant. He pleaded that he be allowed attend the sick man. I asked him what concern it was of his, or if the sailor be an espe-cial friend of his. He answered me a rigmarole that the ills of the world were all men's, and that every man was every other man's brother &c. Said I, "If that is the manner you intend to take into the sailors' quarters, I cannot allow it, it being my greatest burden to keep the sailors obedient to rule." And that they would more likely than not shout "Meddler!" at him, and pitch him out. But he persisted, in every manner of means he could think of, saying even that the sick man called for him. I weighed the matter up and down. And to shew that I exercised my position favour-ably, that my care is always over all (no man ever yet cried out "Harsh, cruel man!" against me), I saw fit to give him leave, under certain conditions laid down: That he would not speak or do anything but what tended to the sailor's body ill. He should understand that he, Fuller, had no rights in the matter, but that if he should help Salterne I would be the first to call him forth for com-mendation. And that he must give no medicines or such muck, or do nothing otherwise without my full knowl-edge. He sits with him now, putting hot rags on his belly and cold ones on his head. But the sailor grows worse. Fuller's science is no better than I thought. I pray for the lad's recovering, and I miss his prompt attentions.

"Stop! Hold!" Mr. Mullins threw up his right hand, index finger pointing heavenward authoritatively. "A word with you, boy."

In any other place or time John would have smiled; now he halted, affecting a serious look of inquiry. Mr. Mullins, gripping the bulwark unsteadily with one hand, presented an odd appearance—though no odder than the majority of the passengers since the colder weather had set in. He had his cloak clutched around him tightly; a scarf knotted under his chin tied the brim of his hat down over each ear; from under this black bonnet his long face glowered bleakly, putty-coloured, flaccid, stubbled with a week's growth of beard. John crossed the deck, and took hold of the bulwark by his side. A lively sea was running.

"Do you think that because we are thrown together on this ship, that is a licence for you to flaunt your filthy and barbarous habits?" Mr. Mullins said, shouting over the whistle of the wind and the hiss of bouncing water along the side. "That you can attack my daughter at your pleasure?"

"Why, you are mistook, sir. I never attacked no one," John shouted back.

"You did attempt to embrace her, when finding her unprotected. Do you deny that—or have you no fear of being struck down by the Lord's wrath?"

"I took a kiss, and not a thing more. Where's the harm? If a girl beant kissed every while she'll get to thinking she's a very ugly miss."

"Beware how you make a mocking-stock of me!"

"Oh no, sir, you misread me," John said in a friendly and humble tone. "I've took a liking to her . . ."

"Who are you to take a liking, as you call it, to my child, without my leave? An honourable man would have leave from a father, before he spoke to his daughter."

"Please, sir, then give me leave!"

"Leave!" He appeared to shy back from him in a spasm of rage. "Leave, good fellow, for what?"

"Why, to give her attention."

Mr. Mullins regarded the young man's bland, innocently impudent face with an expression almost of loathing. "My son, you take advantages of our strange circumstances to aim above your head—and that, before we are half begun this enterprise. We may be all dead tomorrow, meeting our God."

"More's the reason for taking a hop and a jump while we can," John interrupted him, imprudently.

"Remember that you are a hired man to this company. You have your place, and we have ours, as God appointed. Otherwise we will come to nothing better than a band of tinkers."

"As you will, sir. But I ask your leave to pay attention to your daughter . . ."

"Such leave I would give only to a man of upright and sincere religion," Mr. Mullins thundered hoarsely into his face, "both zealous and constant, giving by his example an incitement and spur unto all to pursue the same steps, and to utter forth by the instruction of his life those virtuous fruits of good living so pleasing both to God and Christian man. You are not. You are without God. I give you *no* leave! Nor are you the class of man fit to pay her attention. That is all." He clamped his mouth shut, sustaining an eye-to-eye stare with his protruding, dark eyes. "Well? Shall she henceforth go in peace, or do you force me to a further action?"

The young man's expression had turned quickly and boyishly stubborn. "I think I will speak if I like. You mayn't have a man up before a justice for looking at a girl."

"May we not, my fine fellow! I know what *you* mean by 'looking.' You wait just till we find our feet in this new country and you'll see some changes."

"Hah! That's for what I wait, till we're all amongst the howling savages and we'll see who's master then!"

"Young man—you credit yourself very large and strong, but there will always be distinctions. Too much freedom in the day here has gone to your head. I am a man of position and respect in England. I did not come to seek my fortune with a hired man's wage. I brought my fortune with me, in the hold of this ship, in solid goods. Like my brothers, I left England in despair of my idolatrous and filthy countrymen—of the very thing you are to me, ignorant and licentious—so as we might worship our God in a clean and free air. You are of that fleering, winking, sodomite world. And if you dare to pursue my daughter further, I will draw you for your conduct before our Governor—if necessary, before the Captain. My advice to you, sir, is to cool your lust with fasting and cold water. The wicked shall be cut off from the earth, and the transgressors shall be rooted out of it."

Mr. Mullins turned from the side with a dismissive downward flap of his hand, and groped his way along by the poop. An upsurge of rage choked the young carpenter; but in a moment he ran across the deck after him, shouting at the top of his lungs.

"Hired I am—honestly hired! Not running across the seas to flee the prison. Nor have I seen any *gentlemen* on this fish barrel. You come from no better than I. Every man jack of you got his bread with his sweat. And you'll dig for it harder than I where we all go." He stood at the poop door, panting, as Mr. Mullins disappeared into his cabin at the farther end of the passage.

Gilbert Winslow was an erratic chronicler; but on that which took his fancy, whether important or not, he spent himself exhaustively, covering page after page of his pocket book with a tiny script hand, intricately looped and decorated with curled tails and flying upstrokes. Under the heading of September twenty-fifth, he wrote:

I write by a candle, at night, my back against a piece of our fishing boat which we carry in the hold, my end on the hard pallet. It is the quietest time, though to call it quiet is to speak of degrees. And because it is by candlelight day or night unless I sit out on the open deck, which is lately not to be done for the piercing of the winds giving me an earache and stiffening up my fingers. (Will I get there by candlelight?) The occasion is that tonight we have had our first death; not one of us, but one who, by all strangeness, was the most insolent and worrying of the crew and a favourite of the Captain; as what must pass with him for favoured.

This was a Devon youth, Richard Salterne, who has lain screaming sick for three-four days of the iliac passion, under the tender attention of his companions, in their straw-infested kennel.

Sam Fuller, with his true Christian pride, besought the Captain that he be allowed attend him. Whereat, Jones, concealing surprise, ordered him out with hypocritical bellowings, becoming all of a sudden very inquisitive and busy about his sailor, where he had not given him a thought before. The way to move this little Captain is to make him think that ill reports of him will somehow get back to England. He is like a man who has murdered his mother and therefore cannot bear to feel anyone thinks him the kind of man would steal a halfpenny. His conceit makes him hold all the world to be aware of his deeds, that every part will be agog, his name on every lip, when he returns.

But Sam Fuller, when his long nose has twitched out *a true* Christian death to be won, is a demon of persistence and persuasion, and wrung out a permission to attend the sick man in the end. This was given, with as many rules and laws laid down as from a judicatory court, after Jones had proved to his own exceedingly rough satisfaction that the poor man was truly sick, and when their own sailor physicker (a man lamentably named: Heale) had admitted to having no remedy.

There proved to be a sort of inflaming poison in the sailor's bowels, very tender on his right side. Sam kept him warm, putting him on clean bedding straw, and did everything he could for his comfort, staying by his side the whole of last night and today. Until the man, after a sudden easement, unaccountably began to sink comatose, and has now died, about midnight.

They will bury him in the sea in a few hours, the sailors superstitiously disliking a dead body to remain long on a ship at sea. So I may as well keep awake till then.

People put so little seem on death that the thought makes me melancholy. A man is bright and hale and full of life, and the next hour is struck down, and gone to the worms. And it is an odd thing that this thought of sudden dying should be the root of that puritan objection to living life with joy.

For so it is. It is as much natural and commonplace nowadays to be of puritan mind as it is to be ready to debauch and be debauched. The young early gain a stark-staring awareness that though life is beautiful it can be very short; that coughs and summer fevers, bloody fluxes and the plague lurk around every corner. Thus a girl is a ready wanton and grasper of body pleasures before the smallpox mark her lovely cheeks or she marry and die of a childbirth. Four of our six children die before they attain a year old; two out of six of our women die of their first childbearing, no count taken of the hazards of their second, third and fourth, etc. Many a young woman hopes she is barren, that she may reach an old age. And if the young get to sixteen they are lucky to get to twenty. At any moment any age may be stricken down and die helpless, but particularly the young.

Thus it is youth is wanton, careless, eager whilst it has its bloom; and middle age trembling or fearful or cankered for its sins and its lost opportunities for sin—*Beauty is but a flower . . . Queens have died young and fair.*

Life, being beautiful but on a frail stem, breeds all cruelties and wickedness and uncaringness. (And this is well known to be because we live unnaturally in the filth of cities.) And all the cruelties and wickednesses, from our lives being uncertain, breed horror again in its turn and a puritan longing for cleanliness of air and body, frugality and nice living. (For how can a man die if he has not lived through all the experiences that change him and make him fit to die?) So we fly to the wilderness. And I begin to understand that one should rebuke those who call out abuse on puritan minds. Everything has its cause and use.

What multitudes of reasons have driven this ship from England!

147

12   Over the eastern horizon came a pale, diffused suggestion of light, which just allowed the group of sailors standing by
the waist rail and the packed body of settlers behind them to see
the expressions of each other's faces. Patiently and silently the
passengers waited, their cheeks and eyeballs chilled by the pushing insistent wind that whistled and sang through the ropes all
about them, in the cold, soft beginnings of light. The wind had
been rising all night. The sea and sky were of a colour like dark
slate, the ship lunging forward before an uncannily steady and
powerful wind. The corpse of the sailor Salterne lay on the deck
by the lee side, wrapped in a piece of hessian, roped to a board,
a bag with ballast sand in it tied to its feet.

The whole crew had assembled on the waist deck by the Captain's order; only the men on the tiller had been excused; and
the first mate Mr. Clarke had gone aft to knock on the door of
the Great Cabin and acquaint Mr. Jones that the body awaited
his benediction and burial. He had found the Master cursing
and rummaging in his lockers for a prayer book.

As many of the male passengers as could comfortably get on
the little deck were present, the rest on the hatch steps and in
the end of the hold at its foot. Apart from the bosun and mates
the crew numbered twenty-five; they seemed surprisingly many
to the settlers, who had never before seen them gathered all
together shoulder to shoulder.

Mr. Jones appeared from under the poop deck, holding to his
chest a ruffled, yellow-leaved Book of Common Prayer, its cover
missing. Seeing the packed deck, he stood for a moment, survey-
ing them with a peevish and contemptuous stare: they would
put their noses in his business, eager to carry out the burial
themselves, if given half a chance, and mouth their "purified"
jargon. Here they would have him think they stood out of their
sense of reverence to God and their dead "brother"; but they

came to see him muddle and stumble through the prayers for the dead, perhaps casting the corpse forth without hope or word, and laugh in their sleeves, thinking it fitter their own preaching Elder did the work—they having sole rights and authority with God! But if they thought the Book of Common Prayer a mere swollen stream of pagan pomp and ritual, then this day they should have their stomachs well and truly full of it. For he'd read it loud into their ears, and read, till they turned black in the face.

A passage was made for him and he advanced to the foot of the corpse. Digging in his thumb, where he held it between the leaves to mark the place, he spread his legs apart and brought the dim pages up under his nose; there was enough light, if he strained at it, by which to read the small, heavy print. He looked around.

"All kneel," Mr. Jones ordered, knowing that the Brownists did not kneel at prayer.

The sailors went down on one knee, to them a surprising order. Mr. Jones waited until the Brownists, led by Mr. Carver, had reluctantly followed the crew's example.

"By the virtue that I am Captain and Commander of this ship on the sea," Mr. Jones began, "I have the authority to perform this office, in so much that we have no ordained priest amongst us"; which he proclaimed loudly and clearly for the sole benefit of the passengers, though not without hesitations. He held up his book, glanced shortly from side to side, and read out, declaiming at the top of his voice: " 'I am the resurrection and the life, saith the Lord: he that believeth in me, though he were dead, yet shall he live: and whosoever liveth and believeth in me shall never die.' "

Long ribbons of scud cloud had begun to race under the black dome of the sky; and now they noticed that these were travelling westward ever faster, while the power of the wind increased; and then they saw the blackness of the sky begin to be tinged with purple and the masts and woodwork about them touched with an orange light. Heads turned to look back, and behind the ship, on the eastern horizon where the sun was rising, masked, a thin cut of glowing red had pierced the clouds.

Mr. Jones threw up his arm dramatically: here was a favourable sign, in some way, to himself. "And though after my skin worms destroy this body . . ." he was shouting, and had to lift his eyes and look for a moment at the sea. For while it was yet dark, the hurrying scud above had turned crimson and the crests of the black water danced with little crimson flames and blood-red spume. "We brought nothing into this world, and it is certain we can carry nothing out. The Lord gave, and the Lord hath taken away . . ." He saw that the bosun at his side was glancing up at the mainsail apprehensively, the sailors shifting and looking about uneasily. He turned a page, skipping his second pencilled passage, and began to read, hurriedly, "Now is Christ risen from the dead . . ."

The sun disappeared as if by the slow drawing of a curtain, and it was so dark that he could barely see the lines of print; he continued, pausing to take deep breaths, missing words and whole lines. For several minutes the wind slackened and no one looked back eastwards, from where a wall of stone-black was travelling and overtaking the ship. The bosun saw it first, cursed under his breath and spoke to the Captain; but Jones did not hear him and he was taking a breath to shout into his ear, when the wind veered savagely with all the unexpectedness of a thunderclap on a clear day.

Every sail slackened, flapped wildly, boomed out deafeningly, sagged and slapped and rattled again frantically, while the ship, released, reeled on her course, rolling sickeningly and throwing every man against another. The bosun clawed and fought his way across the crowded deck to the port tacks, to tighten in, followed by half the duty watch, the other half scrambling to the starboard to loosen off. Those passengers near the poop hatch began to hurry down out of the way.

Mr. Jones shouted orders: Mr. Clarke to get six men aft to the mizzen lateen; Mr. Coppin to go forward and stand ready to order the foresail down; the quartermaster to take his tiller-room men, put the tackle on the tiller and disengage the whipstaff.

Retrimmed, the sails filled out roundly again, and there was the old steady roar of power in the rigging. The heavy black of the false storm from the east began to dissipate itself, the sea and sky everywhere else growing a tone darker. The deck was nearly clear of settlers.

Spray, whipped from the crests, started flying in over the waist; and at the first dull gale howl of wind through the ropes Mr. Jones waved for the watch to go up and lower the mainsail. In a spurt of temper he dashed the prayer book into the scuppers and stamped back and forth across the deck. But quickly, an elation of mastery filled him at the thought of stormy weather, and seeing that all was in readiness should the gale develop, he recovered his prayer book, turned the pages quickly to the end of the Order for the Burial of the Dead, motioned four sailors of the off watch to prop the body on the side, and roared out as much of the conclusion as he could see in the deepening darkness.

" 'Forasmuch as it hath pleased Almighty God of his great mercy . . . we therefore commit his body to the sea——' " He put his hand to the feet of the corpse and pushed, and the sailors heaved it over into the dancing spume. "Earth to earth, ashes to ashes——" and he could see no more.

The mainsail had no sooner been let fall, taking three quarters of the entire crew to hold it down and bundle it for the moment in the lee scuppers, than the gale was well and truly upon them, tearing and whining. The main topsail rent up one side from its boltrope and in a few minutes blew out in rags; it was an old, fair-weather sail; its flying ribbons of torn canvas cracked like gigantic whips.

Half an hour later the ship was beating back and forth before a head wind coming out of the west, like an animal running up and down before an imprisoning hedge. And though the wind had fallen again, allowing some sail to be flown, the daylight advanced to no more than a half dusk. Such semidarkness and violent shifting of the wind was a kind of weather no one on the *Mayflower* had ever experienced before. Throughout the whole of a dim, roaring morning, the ship wore north and south, with the wind at times seeming to gust in at them from all sides at once, stinging like shot sand with rain and spray.

During the lull, which came at noon and lasted until night-fall, Miles Standish staggered up from the second hold in search of Samuel Fuller, his gait stiff and painful, his face flushed and rucked with suffering.

"These boils I mentioned, Mr. Fuller . . ." the military Captain shouted in Sam's ear.

"Ah, bless you!" Fuller's whole expression brightened, the very wart on the tip of his nose seeming to lose its droop. "We'll attend to you. Cast fear away and look to the Lord for salvation —though it's a bit early for sea boils."

"I frequently have boils," Standish explained patiently. "And I would not trouble you but . . . they're where I cannot see. . . ." He touched himself behind tenderly. "And my wife takes sick at such things. I never in my life had them so large and full of pain before——"

"Good, good. Ripeness is all." Fuller collected a small bundle from under his pillow, found his box of ointments and scrambled up. "Where shall we operate, sir?" he bawled.

"If we go below to my bed, I'm sure we shall have no very inquisitive onlookers. My neighbours are the hired sailors, and as for my wife . . ."

His wife, Mrs. Rose Standish, had already discreetly removed herself to a friendly woman's camp within earshot; and Captain Standish unbuckled himself and lay on his face among his goods and chattels; in stern and rigid resignation.

"Large as beets and like flaming suns," Sam commented good-humouredly, exposing the Captain's misery to the light of his candle. The little Captain had a boil on either buttock, one fully ripe, the other nearly so. "And if the good Lord will kindly quiet the sea at the right moment . . ." He leaned over, waxing two candle stumps to a box on the other side of the bed, as some vast ridge of water struck the ship across the prow, almost making her stand on end and throwing him flat upon his patient. But though the little Captain breathed deeply through his wide nostrils, his beard lay jutted out by his shoulder without a tremor.

Regaining his breath, Standish said commandingly, "Do not say when you are about to put in the lance. That's an old rule of war and a good one. Just do it, sir, with no ado and no warning."

"Oh, faith, you will not suffer on that account—it's the squeezing and kneading to clean out the poison that makes 'em yelp." Sam knelt by him, his cloth folder of knife, scissors, soap and clean linen opened out by his right hand. But he made no move to begin. "I had wished we might come closer together in understanding," he commented abruptly, "but you are not an easy man, Captain . . ." He snuffled and wiped his nose. "You have the vice of self-sufficiency. You treat every man as if he were a soldier and must not presume to speak intimately."

"Indeed?" Standish said impatiently. "But this seems hardly the moment to begin singing wassail together, Mr. Fuller!"

"On the contrary, I have found the curing of body ill to mix with God's ministry uncommonly well. The body is a very good mirror of the soul."

Standish frowned; if this was a preparation, an attempt to talk him into forgetfulness that the first stab might be muffled in consternation and surprise, he would prefer to be without such nonsensical mercies; and if it was a probing at his religion, he could do without that too. "My backside grows cold," he said. "The wind is rising again."

"So it is," Fuller said, picking up his lance. "Are you ready to die?" he asked amiably. "By which I mean," he added hastily, "that as we may go to the fishes any hour now we should look to an unexpected coming face to face with the Lord our God."

"I think you know very well, Mr. Fuller, that I was born a Popish idolater, as you call them," Standish answered brusquely and acidly, "and have never seen fit to change. Now if there is anything prevents you plunging your knife in a Popish idolater, say so, and let us be done."

"There, there," Sam said, patting him and chuckling. "Actions are only sometimes better than words, praise the Lord." And he cut the first abscess.

Captain Standish's muscles stiffened to iron, but by an effort of will he made himself relax completely again, without uttering a sound. Fuller began to knead and squeeze; this he did in the healthy flesh all around the inflamed area, and Standish felt surprisingly little pain. Fuller's fingers were competent, firm but gentle.

"Ah, if men would not take the habit of closing their minds at the first touch, like clams," Sam continued. "Have you now, dear good Captain—who will live with us to the hour of our death—ever, honestly, considered the basis of our radicalism?"

"What? Eh?" Standish grunted. "Do you hear that wind rising again? I wonder does our Captain Jones know his business as well as he pretends?"

"Consider Perkins' six principles," Sam said, louder still, that there should be no possible chance of his words getting lost in the ship's creaking and the hollow swish and crash of water from above. "You do admit there is one God the Father," he asked, giving point to the question with an extra hard squeeze, "distinguished into the Father, Son and Holy Ghost?"

"That is my belief," Standish replied bad-temperedly, "as far as I remember. . . . But I would all men were free to believe as they wish!"

"And you believe," Sam squeezed again, so that his prostrate patient grunted, "that all men are wholly corrupted with sin through Adam's fall, and so are become veritable slaves of Satan and deserving of eternal damnation?"

"If that is your Perkins' principle, let us say it is mine too. But for myself, I do not seem to have such a need of strict religion as . . . as . . . well! What I have, sir, will do me till I die—ouch!"

"But the third principle must then follow! That Jesus came for us, and that we may now save ourselves if we will."

"By God," Standish groaned, "I know now what is meant by the Devil having one by the tail . . ."

"And as to Perkins' fifth principle," Sam went on, not hearing, "our faith and salvation is got through the preaching of the word, and through prayer." He wiped, applied his thumbs and forefingers again and gave a final, forceful squeeze, which made his patient hold his breath and grind his teeth together. "You would surely accept that? Then it follows that we may lose our way through pagan rituals, such as image worship, confessionals, indulgences, kneelings and signs of the cross and all other such incrustations on the true feeling of man for God—as practised alike by the Pope's lost children and the King's church. Yes?"

"No!" the patient said stubbornly, raising his head to wipe the cold perspiration from his forehead.

"Well," Sam said, "that's one done. Now we'll cross the river to the other side. Ah, that we might learn to squeeze the poisons out of men's souls as easily, eh? I remarked that you had Judas-coloured hair, when I first saw you!" He sat back on his heels for a moment, with a loud, happy laugh curling and widening his large, carved mouth. "Beware, beware!" He nicked the second abscess.

"I never argue about these things," Standish said, when he had got his breath back, "though the whole world does nothing else. I have spent my life soldiering; thus I find myself here to teach about guns and defence—and begin anew and sink some roots in the land. I come of great landowners, but our branch was cheated of its inheritance——"

Sam breezily ignored the attempt. "Perkins' sixth should agree with your temper: All men shall rise with their own bodies to the last judgment. And think, sir, if you had died therefore before I'd cleansed you, what a pitiable plight you'd have been in. The body houses the soul; of what significance then are poisons in the body!"

"And I was assured I would not be interfered with in matters of religion! . . ."

"If any man does, just let me hear of it! Are we not going over this ocean to escape interference? But we may persuade—nay, it is our duty to persuade." He kneaded and squeezed enthusiastically; and if a growing heavy-handedness happened to beat time, as it were, to his words, it was not done deliberately.

The thin crying of the wind rose over every other sound on the labouring ship. "Am I done?" Standish asked. "If you are so sure we are going to drown, please respect my desire not to be caught with my breeches down."

"Done you are, for the time being. Keep this piece of cloth between you and your breeches. Now we must purge you."

Standish twisted on to his side and raised himself on his elbow, shouting over the increasing gale noise, "By the Almighty, you will not; your tongue is purge enough."

"I attend you; you must be led by me. I have a good purging medicine here, cañafistula."

"I will not be purged, I will not, I will not," Standish barked.

"Look at this poison that has come out of your blood," Sam shouted. "If your blood is bad and thick you need purging."

"I am not bunged up," the Captain insisted hotly, wagging his little red beard from side to side.

"Everyone on this ship, confined in close quarters, is bunged up," Sam roared. "Next you'll tell me my business!"

"I know how to live in health on a ship, God knows—but if you insist on a victim to unstop, go and unstop Mr. Jones; I don't like that fellow."

Sam sat back with a burst of loud laughter, slapping his thigh. Standish peered suspiciously at him for a moment from under his lowered, bushy eyebrows, wondering what the joke could be; and suddenly realizing that all his pain and mortification were practically over, joined him with his own humourless barks of laughter. But he instantly saw in the dim light faces of dumb and stricken expression looking their way reproachfully, as if it was highly improper to laugh with a storm tearing its way over the ship and a watery grave almost staring everyone in the face. The red-headed military man sank into silence, pushing his shirt into his breeches.

"H'mmm," Sam grunted, looking around, "h'mmm . . ." and immediately his own face was again long, but not quite serious.

At nightfall, the wind remounting to gale force, the ship was stripped and set to drift under bare poles, with a few square feet of stout canvas rigged above the poop to keep her head into it. A high breaking sea began to run, and the gale sprang to hurricane force at twelve o'clock. Lifted on great towering seas, the heavily laden ship slid down their feathered sides into apparently vast pits where the water appeared momentarily polished and clean-sliced, rising again on the relentless, smashing sea, pounded and half smothered.

Mr. Jones did not dare the poop deck in such a force of wind; but before dark he clung his way out onto the waist deck in those intervals when it was clear of sloshing sea water, watching his rigging for signs of fraying and loosening, driving on the drenched and shivering duty watch with the toe of his boot, whenever he saw something that needed attention. He gave his orders to mates and crew alike with waves of his arm and pushes, for no voice could be heard in the wearing, never ceasing roar of sea and wind. But finally, even Mr. Jones was driven into his cabin, where he crouched amid his sliding, bumping goods and chattels, holding onto his screwed-down table.

The passengers, left to fend for themselves, hung on the rope handrails running from ring to ring, gripping the children tightly. Francis Eaton, venturing across the first hold, was flung against the timbers and stunned, so that he had to be tied to his pallet until he regained consciousness.

Water ran everywhere, through the hatch covers, under the two doors opening out onto the waist deck and through many loosened seams in the main decking, trickling and seeping down from deck to deck till it reached the bilge in the bottom of the ship. Down there John, with English, Trevore and Ellis, scrambled about in the dim light of their lanterns, tying and wedging the shifting cargo.

As the storm was reaching its peak Mr. Brewster attempted to make himself heard, to send the sound of connected human words down the hold. He clung to his ring iron, speaking words of faith and encouragement; and saw, by the lanterns' yellow gleam, that even those nearest to him could not hear his voice in the sharpening uproar. For as the wind increased in velocity the pitch of the noise rose, every spar and rope in the rigging screaming deafeningly, while the swish and pound of the seas and the grating and creaking of the ship's structure added a thunderous bass accompaniment.

Many, like Dorothy Bradford, managed to get their damp blankets about their heads, the arm of husband or companion around them, and curled in upon themselves, cold and dazed, clinging to their rope. No one heard his neighbour's sob or hysterical cry. "O Lord," prayed Bradford, "do not grind our people and beat them to pieces as food for the beasts of the sea," his head aching, sick and miserable and half believing he had already died and entered some purgatory specially reserved for the sinful drowned at sea. The tumult beat the mind into weary, fantastic imaginings; while the air in the closed holds was foul with the odours of the churned and rising bilge water.

Sometime about midnight there came a moment when the ship spun her head out of the wind and lay broadside on to the crested swells; out of the howling darkness an enormous roller mounted upon her and broke over her entire length. It tore its huge weight of water over the decks and through the lower rigging, snapping cleats and ropes and heeling the ship so far onto her beam-ends that her spars almost entered the water and the men in her hung as on a vertical wall.

Muffled momentarily under a hundred tons of water, the men heard the screams and cries of their women and children clearly for the first time since the storm had climbed to its height; and as the ship lay over on her side under that weight of pouring water, a splintering crack echoed through her dead and stilled body. In the first hold they saw it happen, for a lantern swung from the very timber: a main crossbeam above their heads, buttressing the centre mast as it passed in through the waist decking, cracked in two where it was bolted to the mast, one half sagging down perceptibly at the jagged break.

Utensils, bundles and personal belongings broke loose and skated and clattered down the deck to the lee side. In the few seconds during which the uproar outside was damped under the muffling swamp of the seas, the splintering crack of the main beam was heard in all parts of the ship.

Dorothy Bradford raised her head from out of her damp blankets, looked at the arching wall of seep-wet wood nearest her, and said, "Now our little ship is breaking up. . . ."

Then the shell of oak rolled back and rose out of the boiling sea, cascading water from her on all sides, broken ropes streaming out and a foremast spar loose in a tangle of rigging, but still afloat, her head into the wind, wallowing stern first down into the black valleys between liquid mountains and rising high, dripping and shining, on their rolling ridges.

At one o'clock in the morning, with the hurricane falling away rapidly, the damage to the main beam was surveyed by the light of a dozen lanterns. The bulk of the passengers were packed below into the second hold, crowded upon each other, with their dazed and crying children, so that many could find no space even to sit down.

Mr. Coppin thought that they should make back for England, with the storm winds behind them. It was not just to expect the crew to venture on further with a disabled ship, and then have to bring it all the way back again in the same condition. They would find no repairing yards in the wilderness, and should they be caught by another storm, she must break up and founder. Which opinion was held also by a large minority of the passengers, bruised and frightened after their terrifying experience. But Mr. Jones answered nothing, directing the ship's carpenter to sound the beams and ribs with his mallet.

Forward in the hold, out of the way, the leaders held their own conference. To return to England now meant that the whole venture would have to be abandoned—their supply of food would hardly take them home again—and ruin for every would-be settler on board.

"We must put all our voices to him now," old Mr. Carver said, "we must keep persuading him."

"And pray to God," Bradford said, "pray, pray, instead of wasting so much time——"

"We had better pray in a practical manner," Edward Winslow said, "that they can mend it!"

They began to see clearly that the ship's carpenter, who was no more than a sailor with knowledge of joinery, was at a loss; and in their realization they all spoke loudly at once, and then, in anguish, fell into silence, searching each other's eyes helplessly.

John stood behind Mr. Jones and the second mate, a reckless excitement growing in him; he thought he knew how the broken beam might be forced back into position. "We have an iron careening jack," he suddenly shouted. "It's down with the passengers' goods. If it was to be put so, brace her up on the deck beams——"

"These ship's matters are not to be understood by you," Mr. Jones said. "Get back with the passengers."

"They are understood by me! More by me than your fool with the mallet. I've builded ships in the Southampton yards. I could restave this barrel inside and out in a week."

"What barrel?" Mr. Jones demanded.

"This 'ere leaky fish basket. You let me to her. I'll knock her back to shape."

Mr. Jones held up his lantern and looked around and up into his earnest, inoffensive young face; and uttered an explosive bark of half-angry laughter. "And who the hell are you?"

John tipped his forehead impudently. "Alden, a cooper, sir, hired by Mr. Weston, where I was working on the Water at Southampton."

The second mate suddenly gave him a push from behind. "Lay below, as was the order. Annoying the Master!" Coppin's opinion was that the damage could not be repaired, especially as they were now entering the period of the equinoctial storms.

"Go on deck, Mr. Coppin, and observe the sky," Mr. Jones said coldly, "and get your halyards and tackles mended."

John grinned after Coppin's great square, stiffly resentful back, as it swayed forward towards the hatch. Above, a pump began to creak and thud, taking out the foot of storm water from the lower hold.

"So you are a shipbuilder, boy?" Mr. Jones shouted scoffingly, standing as tall as he could against John's greater height. "A shipbuilder. Well!"

"In and out, sir, on and off."

"And builded ships in Holland?"

"No, sir, out of England, hired by Master Thomas Weston—to mother his barrel staves and shallop. I said what I was——"

"What's this talk of a jack?"

John explained as quickly and as articulately as he could. Francis Eaton, one of the passengers, had been a carpenter and shipwright too, at one time; and in the main hold was a large iron jack, a new thing invented in Holland, so it was said, which Eaton had brought with him for use in the jacking up of boats for repairing and careening. If this jack was placed beneath on the deck of the first hold, where they then stood, and a stout prop cut to reach from it to the broken beam, they might force the beam back into position by screwing up the jack; then it should be possible to bind and spike a splint across the break, and fix a permanent prop under it lashed to the base of the mast. With the upper deck repegged to the beam and strengthened where necessary the frame should take the pressure of the mast under sail without danger. For the beam on the other side of the mast was firm and sound, as was apparently the rest of the ship.

"Well, may it please your impudence to know—*that is the way I had reckoned to do it,*" Mr. Jones said, turning from him abruptly and impatiently. "We'll have this jack up." This plan of the forward fellow looked very workable. He would let him do the repair, using him in such a way that there was no taking from his own authority. He allowed John to bring Francis Eaton up, and directed the repair as if the method of doing it was entirely his own invention.

Soon after the work was begun Edward Winslow and some few others of the passengers slipped up and unobtrusively took a hand. At three o'clock in the morning Captain Jones, working in his shirt sleeves, glanced into Edward Winslow's eyes with a start, remembered exactly who Edward Winslow was, and at the same moment recognized that he, the Master, had been in the stress of the moment all forgetful of his position for quite a time, pushing, shouting, and sweating with everyone else—as, indeed, under such circumstance it was proper for a Master to do.

The self-forgetfulness of engaging in a common task vanished; he stood back from them, and put on his leather jacket. As he did so the staff with which John was straining to screw up the jack a fraction further slipped from its socket and the young carpenter was pitched heavily against the mast. Mr. Jones stretched down no hand to steady him or help him upright, as he would have done unthinkingly a few moments before.

The mast caught the side of John's head and his shoulder was cut and bruised on a spike. When helped to his feet he was dazed and unable to keep his balance on the shifting deck, and was put sitting down out of the way on the lee side. But his interest in making the repair successful drove him up again a half minute later, and he staggered back to the work, leaving his scraped and bleeding shoulder to take care of itself.

By five o'clock in the morning the break was married, firmly wedged and bound. The relief and joy of everyone communicated itself to Mr. Jones to the extent that he issued a half a mug of spirit to all who had been engaged in the work. Few of the settlers had slept a wink, and as soon as the Master's order, "All sound, we make sail to go on," was told them, they swarmed up into the first hold to see with their own eyes how the broken beam had been set back in place. Even the children were allowed to scurry about excitedly, pale and haggard. The fierce hurricane wind had died down, leaving a sea of heavy swells.

The raw spirit quickly went from John's empty stomach to his head; he sat on a bundle, smiling drowsily. There Dorothy came upon him, and with a soft exclamation pushed back his ripped shirt and looked at the congealed abrasion on his upper arm.

She immediately fetched linen of her own from below and borrowed a bowl for water. She had wiped his arm and shoulder clean and was tearing off a strip of cloth, when Priscilla, who had watched from the other side of the hold for some minutes with a reproving and resentful expression, suddenly came over and knelt down, took the linen from her hand without a word and started to wind on the bandage.

The pleasure of such attention took all speech from him and he smiled foolishly from one to the other. Dorothy spoke to the girl good-naturedly, but received little response.

"To bed with you, and sleep the sleep of the just," Dorothy said, finally, "and God bless you!" She rose to her feet and went to her husband, who had been waiting at the other end of the hold to help her down the steps.

"Do you not feel well?" Priscilla asked. "I will get some one of these men to help you to your bed——"

"I am very well," he said, putting his hand on her arm to prevent her rising from his side. And dim though the light was in the low and smoky hold, he saw that her face was strained and tired, and lacking in resistance. She made another move to go. "My head," he groaned quickly, "my poor head—see, here's the lump. Oh, oh, it waxes hot and cold." He begged her to take up the lantern and light him down to the locker herself, as a special favour, and he would trouble her no more. Here they were talking to each other again like proper Christians; allow him to have but five minutes with her alone and undisturbed and all their past differences must be swept away. He was clear enough in the head to realize that if they remained in the crowded first hold her father would very possibly come looking for her there and take her away.

With a small tightening of the mouth, as if in sufferance of an unmanageable child, she took the lantern, stood up, waited for him to get to his feet, and preceded him forward to the hatch. They were going carefully down the steps to the bottom hold when he remembered that he had not thanked her for bandaging his arm.

What had been done for him was no more than his due in all charity, and under the circumstances, Miss Mullins replied promptly; running on to add a further, unexpectedly dampening explanation: "Had she been another I should have left you to her kind attentions—but not to *that woman.*" But he must not think for a moment that she meant slander; it just so happened that Dorothy Bradford seemed to be a little simple in the head, of a ready, talkative turn and not at all mindful of her good name —or she would not go laughing and talking with young men the like of Gilbert Winslow when her husband was otherwise engaged.

At the foot of the steps Miss Mullins halted and held out the lantern to him. She nodded and turned back. "A good night."

"Am I going to get to talk with you tomorrow?"

She paused and looked down at him. "Can't you find some girl of your own kind? I am forbidden to talk to you—did I want to! —after your bad conduct. You were too bold with my father, and made him rage. He abhors the atheist and loose liver, as I do. You will have to learn to be otherwise, or learn to keep your place."

"Atheist? What is atheist?" But with some vague idea of what she meant he protested that he lived as good a Christian life as any man.

"In the King's pagan church," she said pertly, like a clever child repeating a lesson, "you are all atheists," knowing no more of the word's meaning than he did.

"Oh, Lord," he moaned, "what has churches got to do with kissing?"

Holding tightly to the rope rail, she climbed back towards the second hold.

"Oh, I think I know what fancy gent you have an eye to, my miss!" he shouted after her.

"You common great ignorant dolt!" Miss Mullins cried hysterically, and staggered off over the heaving deck to her quarters, pink and trembling with indignation.

13   A little before midday of the morning following the great storm, one of the settlers' wives, Mrs. Stephen Hopkins, gave birth to a living male child.

Later in the day John Carver, in his role of Governor of the settlers, knocked on the door of the Great Cabin and told Mr. Jones that a child had been born that Sunday morning; adding that the people were much distraught, though thankful for their escape from the storm. And he requested that the Brownists be allowed observe the Sabbath and hold a thanksgiving service in accordance with their own beliefs, at which the non-Brownists, so sorely in need of spiritual comfort after their trials, might attend to hear the word of God read and prayers offered.

But Mr. Jones, irritable at being awakened from a sound sleep, still held stubbornly to the rules he had made at the start of the voyage. "By the laws of England a service cannot be held without a minister; and this is an English ship I command, not a Dutchman. You have heard my ruling on this before."

"Mr. Robinson, the minister so called of our community," Mr. Carver said gently, "was not able to come with us. But even he has no more power to teach than what we as a body have given him. We do not accept ministers from without, or from above, we elect them ourselves, as well you know."

"Treason and blasphemy, sir."

Mr. Carver thought that this persistently stupid attitude was carrying the Captain to the point of madness. "You know that we are withdrawn from the Church of England. Why you will not, *now,* admit to this fact, that exists whether you like it or not——"

"Very easily said, when you think yourself beyond the hand of authority, but there is still no other lawful church in England than the King's church. And I have no wish to be made by you a treasonable subject. What a simpleton you think me! Without a lawful minister you are not a church—while you tread the planks of my ship."

Mr. Carver left in silence, and stayed a moment out on the wild waist deck in a state of musing distraction, watching the shifting mountain ranges of the sea and the sailors clinging about the lee side cutting away tatters of sodden, split rope, preparing to replace the hoisting halyards for the mainsail. Then he returned under the shelter of the poop and descended the hatch, to tell the others what the Master had said; and the Master lay down on his bed to resume his short sleep, and in a few minutes was again snoring.

For many days after the storm poor William Bradford's stomach was so nervously upset that he had to take to his bed in the darkness of the second hold and refuse all salt meat and ship's bread. Even at its best he hated the sea and was continually miserable on it. Now his illness so weakened him that he could not leave his pallet for a week.

Dorothy did everything she could for him, but at times she had to creep away to other parts of the ship to be alone; for even when he lay in still, heroic silence, which he did often for hours at a stretch, his tensed physical presence alone was enough to prevent her resting herself.

It was difficult to find any corner where she might sit absolutely alone, but not impossible. One evening John found her sitting in the pitch dark at the foot of the cargo-hold steps; and something in her face made him pass on and leave her undisturbed. Then, during the days of her husband's illness, she discovered the comfort of the galley fire, and quickly graced her way beneath the cook's bad temper, until he begged her to come when she would, and sit by the oven; a privilege that before had only been extended to John, and Tandy's favoured children. And by that circumstance the curious relationship between herself and Gilbert Winslow began to be recognized by them both, though neither she nor Gilbert ever spoke of it openly to each other; but when they passed in the hold or were near during mealtimes their eyes sought out each other and met in quiet, sad glances of recognition and pity.

For Gilbert, caught by that interest in her which he held against his reason, and almost against his will, had one day followed her into the galley with the excuse of getting a light, and stayed to sit and talk, being allowed to because she asked the cook if he might.

"How is your husband?" Gilbert asked.

"I hope he will be well again shortly. His illness is as much a thing—a thing of the soul with him, as of the stomach. We're all getting sick in the stomach. He and his friends are such men of burning hopes; their desires help to make them sick, like naughty children wanting too much—they want to do so much in the world. . . . I often wish it were possible for you and he to be friends. What good you would do him! You're so calming and quiet. . . ."

The crippled cook enjoyed listening to them talk, because after a while he knew that they forgot his presence, and that he was, as it were, a privileged eavesdropper.

"I fear your husband and I would be like men speaking a different language," Gilbert laughed. "You and I most fortunately speak the same language, but that's a mystery."

"I think you speak any man's language, if you'd speak more and they would listen. Why, you talk to strangers as if they'd been your friends all your life! No? Well, you do to me—a welcome change! But think how badly wicked and damned the good folk would think me, to see me talking to strange men when I have a husband. They'd hold a meeting and sentence me to be thrown overboard."

"But we are not strangers," Gilbert said.

"No, we are not strangers," she repeated seriously.

"Though I was never to Holland to see you there," he said, "I know a great deal about you all from my brother Edward, who used to write to me in London every week. Good letters, about everyone, who they were, what they did. Perhaps one day I even said to myself, 'How dull it must be for poor Dorothy May, a child amongst the wrangling philosophers.'"

"What could your brother have to write of Dorothy May?"

"Words written by him on William Bradford's getting married, which I have never forgotten, though it must be over five years since—because of an odd word used by him at the end. See now if I can still remember: 'Yesterday William Bradford married Dorothy May. She is a young girl of our English community here, pale and slight and exceedingly pretty. She is but sixteen, of very childish airs, speaks rarely and looks, as it were, *haunted*.' Was not that an odd word to use, *'haunted'*?"

She bowed her head and he saw that her eyes were all of a sudden wet. "Please, please—I cry easily. Tell me some more of what your clever brother said about us, about William."

"He said first, of course, that he was a young man; that he was come of good family of Yorkshire, I think, from near Mr. Brewster at Scrooby. That he early came under the tutorship and influence of Mr. Brewster, and fled with him and others to Holland, for the freedom of his opinions, and so on. And that, for such a young man, he held himself most sternly and was almost bowed down with the weight of his knowledge and reading. He thought that one day he would be a very able man, for his aptness to take in and learn. I think too that he said your William was learning in Holland to be a baize maker. And he said it moved him to see you two marrying so bravely, so slight a pair, ground down by work and the world."

There in the forepeak, with their backs to the cutwater, they listened for a few moments to the muffled beating and slapping of the sea, as if the listening itself were some part of their communion, that needed no words. He watched her face, its youth something surely to be pitied. Cruel was the fate that married her a child, that had made of her now a wife of seven years' standing, and sat her now for these brief minutes by his side on the unknown ocean, thousands of miles from England, bound indissolubly to William Bradford. Surely that so quaint and feminine face was the face of the woman who, if the dice had fallen aright, should have been gathered into *his* life, softly, sweetly, in secure and ample living. But they were here, unwashed and a little rank, stiff and forever tired, nibbled by stinking cockroaches and bitten by lice, on a damp-oozing ship beating across a wild, fierce and cold ocean, to what terrors or waste parts of the world no one rightly knew.

"And when Edward wrote that, were you happy, Dorothy Bradford?"

"Not happy; not unhappy," she murmured evasively.

"Were you ever happy?" She shook her head; she did not know. . . . "Not when you were young, a small child like Ellen?"

"I have thought that I was not a child long enough to know."

"Then of a sudden you had to be serious and solemn in a married state."

"I am only a woman; I did what I was told."

"In marrying?" he asked quickly.

"He wanted it." She hesitated. "He loved me so . . ."

"And you, at sixteen—or were you even sixteen?"

"I did what my father told me."

"Ah! And you have been a good wife—how long is it, seven years?"

"Seven years. Cooked and cleaned, mended and worked, and learned to be obedient and loving—and keep silent. Learned to keep myself away from the foreigners, to be spoken to familiarly by no man but my husband." She smiled her meek and apologetic yet sly smile; again as if sharing some little secret joke. "But there, am I not too young to be bitter against the world?"

"Too young not to be," he said.

"What do you think will become of us all, Mr. Winslow?"

"Oh," he shrugged, with a quick sigh, "God alone knows."

She sat silent for a while. They looked around to see the door open quietly and little Ellen Moore steal in with exaggerated furtiveness, followed by two other small girls. Once the door was safely closed again the three children all together broke into shrill babbling with Tandy Fall. Two more little girls came in a moment later, active, pale children with extraordinarily adult, wise faces. They would sit around the oven fire with Tandy and sing, or catch cockroaches for him and put them in a big jar to be thrown overboard.

"Poor William," Dorothy said, smiling with one side of her mouth, her face reshaping and coming together into one of those moments of pure beauty peculiar to her, "I must go and speak tenderly to him."

LOG: NOVEMBER 6TH: I make us to be on the latitude of forty degrees north of the Equator. So we beat due west, with contrary northeast and north winds, at times veering southwest. Expect to see land at any hour, so stand off and on when the night is dark. I calculate to make landfall near Hudson's river, by the grace of God, where our destination in Virginia is.

The stormy weather continued off and on for over a week, before it blew itself out; and then followed day after day of fine, clear near-frosty weather. At night the settlers huddled under every scrap of clothing and covering they had; by day there was much stamping about and blowing in hands. By then they were suffering from stomach pains, sea boils, colds, weakness in the legs, stiff joints and dizzy fits; while many had the early signs of scurvy: depression, sallow complexions, tender gums and foul breaths, with red patches on the skin.

The horizon appeared from day to day to be ever the same imprisoning circle, ever the same in all directions, so that to look at it and think of it for very long brought premonitions of madness; the ship was imprisoned in that naked thin line that extended all round, dividing the sea from the heavens, fixed at some central point of the universe with all sense of direction lost. Day after day, though they could feel the ship moving through the water, the encircling line of horizon remained always there, exactly the same as it had been the day before and the day before that, for apparently as long as one could remember. If it were only possible to jump from the ship and run over the water, surely the horizon could be reached in half a hundred strides, and then it would be possible to look over the edge of the world. Nothing was easier than to believe the Captain and crew to be all crafty madmen, sailing the ship forever around in a circle. And the wind and the sea were so cruel, so purposeless and impersonal; should that sea, so changing, black, or green, or sparkling, get its choppy fingers about your throat, nothing in heaven or earth could save you; the more it was looked upon and thought of the more terrible and terrifying became its immense inhumanity and removedness from the human mind. Should the brightness fall from the air and God forget to make the sun rise again, the ship would sail on and on, but never get a step further, till all had died, utterly lost in that unending chaos, and the ship rotted, fell apart and was sucked down into the infernal depths. For here in this forgotten waste world of God's anything could happen, mountains appear out of the water for them to run upon and be wrecked, monsters swim out of the depths in the night and entangle them with their hundred tentacles or bite the ship to splinters with a crunch of huge and many-toothed jaws, or the sun forget to rise—for the further the ship sailed from Christendom the further it went from God's laws that made the sun come up and go down.

At times they gazed at the sea in a sort of stupefaction until it became too awful to go on gazing, so alien and separate was it from their memories of the friendly land, so bottomless, unending, forgotten. It was easy to say that a man was as near heaven on the sea as on land, but impossible to feel it. The sea was soulless and evil, capable of suddenly rising up, lashing about in a fury and ruthlessly smashing them to pieces; it would play with a man's body like a straw, tear the clothes from it, distend it and blow it up, and take it below for the sport of its monstrous inhabitants.

And how little one could really know about the sea. There were the sailors who pretended to be able to tell the change of weather coming by the look of the sky and the feel of the wind, yet faith could not be put in them because experience proved the sea made fools of them nine times out of ten. But the mind wished to believe the wiseacres, to believe the most unconvincing sailor's prognosticatory boasts, anything to feel, if even only for a deluded moment, that one was not utterly and completely at the mercy of an incalculable element.

They prayed for the circle to break, to come to its edge, to see over it, to glimpse even the smallest island; but each day found them again in the centre of that lost waste of waters, on and on, moving, reaching into nowhere, swinging and creaking onward, but never escaping.

And still it grew colder. They had been on the sea three months since leaving Southampton on August the fifth; and for two months, since Plymouth, sailed west by south. And still it grew colder. A deputation went to Mr. Jones demanding an explanation. Did they, he answered, silly ignorant men that they were, think that in Virginia the sun shone hotly *all the year round*? That there was no wintertime in the New World? And besides, he said, calling on his imagination, they did not know it but the ship was sailing through a great cold stream, thick below the surface with bits of ice, that ran down through the oceans from the north. When they came in against the land and sailed up the wide river—if they found the river before everyone was dead of starvation—then, he said, it would be warm, much warmer than in England.

"That man is so false and evil in his heart," Bradford observed, "I shall not be surprised does he attempt to land us in the snowy wastes of that northern place they call Newfoundland."

Harsh and stormy winds beat upon the ship throughout Monday and Tuesday, the sixth and seventh of November, but Wednesday morning dawned clear and cold, with a steady north wind. Gilbert had a bad night, sleeping very little, and as soon as it was light he went out onto the waist deck to try to exercise some of the cold stiffness from his limbs. He tucked his hands under his armpits and tramped and staggered round and round the longboat.

A small thing like a dead bird caught his eye; it lay within a coil of rope against the upturned boat. He picked it up, a dead bird—not a bird he could name, unless it was a thrush, but it was a land bird. He ran to the side, holding it to his breast, to look all around the horizon, and then to the other side to do the same; there was nothing to be seen but the same dull expanse of restless water stretching away on all sides to the encircling line of horizon. Yet land there must be, somewhere near now, perhaps within a few days' sailing, or a few hours', or just beyond the rim. . . . The bird, he supposed, had been blown out to sea by the storm winds of the days preceding and, exhausted, had taken refuge on the ship, where it had died.

He went below and told the news, shewing the bedraggled little body, the evidence that they were at last coming to land. Then there was constant running up and down to look out over the sea. A kind of suppressed hysteria was shared by men and women alike, as of an isolated community that with joy and dismay were suddenly possessed of an unshakable certainty that the end of the world was at hand. There were women who sat, arms folded, rocking themselves, staring tensely, listening with stretched nerves for they knew not what, like demented prisoners in a deep dungeon, men who looked blankly into each other's faces as if awaiting the hangman's call to execution. Another smiled to himself, uncertain fingers touching reassuringly his buttons, face, hair, like a silly girl going to meet a great personage and overawed and afraid she was not looking her best.

The life of the ship now seemed to be the only life they had ever known, and it was about to come to an end, and they were afraid. In their innocence they saw both ideal and fearsome scenes ahead over the next swell, gardens of Paradise where ripe fruit bloomed effortlessly all the year round, golden valleys of wheat that grew without need of hand to labour; or the black rocks of hell's domain, on which they crashed, bodies washed and flung up to be dragged ashore by tormenting fiends in savage nakedness, their children speared and carried aloft to the gruesome feast, giants, dwarfs, dragons, lions, fish as big as houses that walked the earth on legs like stilts. They had had three eternal months in the airless holds for imagination to breed on ignorance.

After breakfast Gilbert remembered that William Button, Samuel Fuller's boy servant, was so very sick that he had not left his pallet since the breaking of the main beam. He might be cheered to see the bird and perhaps like to have a tail feather for a keepsake. Gilbert also knew that Dorothy had been taking a turn to nurse the boy with other wives who had no children of their own to care for. The Bradfords were in the second hold down, as were Fuller and the boy. At that moment Bradford, Brewster, Carver, Winslow and several others were sitting at the end of the first hold by the hatch steps, talking animatedly. Dorothy had gone down to the second hold a short while before.

Gilbert smiled wryly at his own hesitation and struggle over whether he would go down to her or not. All it could mean was that he should see her face by sickly candlelight for a few moments, and possibly hear her voice addressing a word or two to him, with its suggestion of something shared, a conspiracy. But was it now a necessity? Must he exchange some few words with her every day, or suffer the spasms of that sense of loss and hunger for a presence so much a part of their kind of relationship? A woman desired in the flesh, he thought, feeling a deep pity for himself, was a simple matter. This other state was deadly. Every time he gave in to the temptation of some particular circumstance that allowed them, casually, as it might appear to the rest, to look into each other's faces and hear each other's voices, they wound further about themselves a mesh of pain, built up ever more the store of anguish to come; for marriage here in this time and place meant until death did part. Easier now, he said to himself, caressing the bird's damp feathers with the tips of his fingers, to shut up my heart again and set her back where I found her, an odd-looking little girl that one bid a good morning and a good night and nothing more. There sat her slightly red and rawboned young husband with bright, indomitable eyes, very much recovered and full of life. . . .

But how pathetically she seemed to welcome the smallest moment of his companionship—or was that his own imagination? He got up, excused his way past the engrossed and arguing group by the steps and went down. The second hold below was a low-roofed cavern of darkness in which shewed three feeble pools of illumination, one of which encompassed the pallet of William Button, and, sitting on the deck by his side, Dorothy Bradford.

Gilbert moved down the centre of the hold, pausing for a few moments when half a dozen steps from them. Dorothy sat with her feet tucked under her skirts, her hands resting in her lap, where her fingers played with a strand of coloured wool plucked from the fringe of the heavy knitted shawl she wore around her shoulders. At her side was the boy's bowl of water and a wooden plate holding a slice of bacon, a pickled egg and a biscuit. The youth too was still, and Gilbert thought him to be asleep until he saw that the lad's eyes were open and gazing at Dorothy's moving fingers. She was making some sort of little figure out of bits of wool. The boy's face was a white oval in the bundle of blankets; and in the oval, two deep-sunken, shadowed eyes raising their gaze to her face. And on the ghostly face of the orphan boy Gilbert thought he saw something of adoration in its mute contentment.

She glanced up at Gilbert, and smiled as if she had known all along that he stood there. He advanced to the other side of the bed and sat down on the planks, smiling back at her.

"Our first American bird, Mr. Button!" Gilbert said, and placed it in the boy's thin, damp fingers. "You know what that little bird being blown into our ship means? It means that at any hour some one of us may look out over the sea and there in the distance will be the shores of Virginia."

"I wish it could be me, sir," the boy said. "I said in London . . . I said I'd be the first to see it if I was to keep looking and looking . . ."

"Well there, you hold America in your hand, your little bird is of America," Dorothy said. "And when we come to it the sun will be shining high over Virginia, and there all the birds do sing night and day, and grapes grow on every hedge bush."

"Master Fuller 'as seen savages," the boy said feverishly, "yee, savages wot was brought on a ship."

She patted his hand. "There are no savages where we are going. . . ."

"I see your husband is recovered," Gilbert said to her, "and has his arguing breath back in strength."

"He is a good and—even—a noble man," she answered, with apparent irrelevance, looking him straight in the eye.

Gilbert understood, though he changed his position on the planks uneasily; her unexpectedness could be disconcerting. "You can read thoughts too?"

"Oh, indeed!" she said. "But only with some people. I think it is because your eyes are big like a woman's and I can see into them."

"A happy chance then I was thinking nothing worse," Gilbert laughed, "than of husbands and wives—and of the great mass of matters in their hearts they never tell each other, and suchlike things. . . ."

"But you have never been married?" she asked, pushing her hair back from her forehead.

Round, smooth, serene forehead, he thought. "One lives and learns whether one wills or no, married or not—and thinks oneself clever enough to see the real truth of what others have made. What makes you call *your* husband 'good man,' at so short notice?"

"Your curiosity. You have often wondered what manner of man he is, in truth, that is, not in outward appearance. So I tell you, in case you are afraid to ask! He is a good man, I say, so that there shall be no mistake about that. . . ."

He nodded slowly, and then said, with the slightest touch of bitterness, "Did you think him a good man when he married you, *then?*"

"No. But have you never done a thing your conscience said you should not? Perhaps *he* did. Why should it have been given to him to know what a woman would be like when she grew more fully . . ." Suddenly her mood changed. "He was a man of twenty-three years; he ought to have known that few women live happily with saints. But he wanted to be complete, he wanted to be like others, with a home, an obedient wife——" She stopped, distressed. "Oh, please, let us not talk about me!"

"Very well, we'll talk about politics, money, witches, vagabonds, whether the King is without the law as he claims——"

"No, no," she raised her hands, "tell Will a story. You are so very good at telling children stories, and he is not too old a man not to like a good story about owls or wolves."

So Gilbert thought a moment, and began a rambling story about an owl and a wolf that went on for fully an hour; but he insisted that the owl's name was Dorothy and the wolf's name William.

The next morning William Button stole from his bed and got up into the bows, before the forecastle, while the passengers still slept. Sam Fuller searched for him as soon as he awakened, and found him in the bows, wrapped in a blanket and trembling with the cold; how long he had been there exposed to the elements it was impossible to tell. But that afternoon, following a fit of coughing, he had a hemorrhage, and an hour later, in Sam's presence, died.

He was laid out on his pallet for the last time, and they took turns to pray over him throughout the night. Near morning they sewed him up in a sack, with the dead bird in his hand.

The ship moved slowly and heavily with the swells, as day-light came to the grey sea and the drifting banks of mist; and the eventful day of November the tenth began with no one being able to see further ahead than twenty yards. The *Mayflower* flew a fore-topsail and lateen only, her "nightdress," as they called it; but it would have made little difference if she had had every stitch out; there was not enough wind either to sail with or to dispel the foggy mist.

Mr. Jones continued to lie on his bed, fully dressed in his leathers, long after he knew that the body of William Button awaited his attention out on the deck. He was aware that he approached the most crucial point in the voyage, the landfall, while yet the settlers remained their own masters. When the moment came and they realized where he meant to put down the anchor, they might mutiny. And there was nothing he could do but keep to his course, persuade, bluff, threaten—Weston was quite capable of betraying him on his return, if he did not.

He had again insisted that he must read the burial service, though for this second burial at sea he did not make it a command that the crew be present, nor command that anyone be present, for that matter. Nevertheless he knew that every settler who could get on the deck was there, cursing him in his heart.

They had placed the body lengthwise on the port bulwark; there the side was cut down a foot and topped with a broad plank, for convenience in getting the heavy longboat on and off the waist deck; the remains of William Button rested, therefore, as if on a rough altar between the settlers and the deep sea. The passengers on deck faced the corpse, heads slightly bent, hands clasped, not in the traditional Christian manner, but with straight-hanging arms, praying silently.

Left alone, they would, at the end of their prayers, have pushed the corpse quietly into the sea and gone back about their daily affairs; not because they were indifferent to death, but because they argued it was wrong to have the sorrow and meaning of death obscured and softened by ritual and ceremony.

They were by then used to dawns at sea, to their melancholy and utterly depressing effect and to the ominous suggestions of space and endlessness which came with them, as the grey light first shewed in the east; but the stillness of this dawn added a chilling sense of foreboding to the unanswerable loneliness of the North Atlantic. The senses became so used to the power and noise of the wind that when it ceased they refused to believe it and the quietness was felt like something in an oppressive nightmare.

No rolling of the ship disturbed their attempted meditations; she rode with the steady swells, prow and stern rising and falling with a sort of solemn deliberation. It was the first morning that the weather was not unpleasantly cold.

"Why doesn't he come, and let us send the poor boy to his rest?" Fuller said.

"Little kings must impress their subjects," Bradford commented stonily.

"But alas, he is not clever at it," Edward Winslow said, "or he would know that he should not repeat himself; it weakens the point."

A little cold breeze started up and they saw, with sighs and exclamations of relief, that the mist was moving and thinning out across the water.

"How still it is!" Dorothy said. "Makes you feel frightened." And she broke into a spasm of coughing.

And even with the rising breeze beginning to whisper in the shrouds it was still uncannily quiet.

Gilbert stood behind Dorothy, and cursed himself, as he

realized that he had unconsciously manoeuvred himself near her. The air was as rank with the odours of unwashed clothes and stale sweat as the hold below. Surely, he thought, if someone were to shout at that moment, the masts would fall down! Quiet, murmurs, breathing, a whispering breeze starting up on the misty sea . . .

"Land on the weather!" sang a voice down upon their heads, as if from heaven.

Haggard, shocked faces jerked up to look at the forgotten sailor clinging among the halyards on the mainmast cap.

"Land on the weather!" the mate, Clarke, shouted down the poop hatch to Mr. Jones.

"Lord Jesus—there's land in sight," a woman shouted hysterically down to those in the first hold.

Mr. Jones appeared on the poop deck; and in a moment every sailor on board, it seemed, was clambering up the ratlines. A tumult of shouting and questioning broke out and those below tried to force their way up onto the packed waist deck.

The crowd turned its back on the corpse and pressed towards the weather side; there was nothing to be seen but the mist and the sea. More settlers squeezed up from below, until those on the centre of the deck were forced up onto the cargo hatch cover and pressed flat against the longboat.

The whispering breeze feathered the surface of the water and the last gauze lifted and vanished, and they saw the land. The wind came off the land and the ship's port tack had been carrying her slowly along parallel with a low coast line some two or three miles off the starboard or right side of the ship. In the centre of the coast line there was visible a stretch of highlands. It was the only part of the coast that shewed any appreciable cliff face rising above the sea. Which cliffs Mr. Jones found of considerable importance in his calculations when he went down to work on his charts.

At last the horizon was broken. The eye was stopped by a line of solid land. But belief in its reality did not come immediately. Men stared and blinked their cold lids as if their sight had suddenly dimmed when trying to see some very ordinary object before their faces. Day after day for a seemingly unending part of their lives, regularly and by habit they had searched the distance for such a solid image, and now that it was to be seen the long habit of looking and seeing nothing made them want to shake their heads, afraid to believe, go below and wait for another morning to try again. Then a woman began to beat her breast and at the same time her tears ran down her face; and it was their order of release, as if told that they could then jump up and down, sob in each other's arms, pray, dance ring-a-roses and stare at each other as their tears flowed freely and unashamed.

Coppin and Duff, the bosun, roaring and pushing, cleared the deck to get up a full complement of sail, and in the squeezing, shouting, protesting, someone's back pressed unknowingly upon the corpse and tipped the body of William Button, sewn in his sack and clutching his dead bird, off the bulwark plank and into the sea. When Sam Fuller turned his attention to it again it was gone, but no one could account for its going. Every man stoutly denied any knowledge of either seeing it overset or oversetting it himself.

Book Two

EXPLORATIONS, SAVAGES
AND SETTLEMENT

THE MAYFLOWER

Harbour of the Mayflower

Land Exploration

Fire Signals

CORN HILL

Indian Hut

LONG POINT

CAPE COD HARBOUR

First Two Trips the Shallop

NEW PLYMOUTH HARBOUR

Indian Dugout Canoe

COLD HARBOUR

PLYMOUTH

CAPE COD BAY

Indian Huts and Burial Grounds

Storm

Third Trip of the Shallop

Scale of Miles

0 1 2 3 4 5

Shoals and Tumult Sea

Palacios

14   To get in nearer the coast Mr. Jones had to beat north for an hour and then south again. That the wind blew off the land was most fortunate, allowing him to hug the shore with the minimum of danger.

Coming about and sailing southeast by south again, he found that the coast curved out to meet their course, and he sailed along it slowly, sounding bottom at eight fathoms a mile from shore and opposite the high land that they had first seen. This land he judged to rise about two hundred feet or less above sea level; the coast line north and south appeared to be low and sandy.

An area of broken shoal water ran out here for half a mile from the beach; over this shoal water the mighty green Atlantic rollers broke in a white and seething fury.

About twelve o'clock the previous day the sun had shown its whereabouts for a few minutes and he had been able to get an observation. Now, sitting alone at his table in the Great Cabin, he almost laughed aloud—by good navigation and wildly incredible good luck he had fetched up the very Cape he had set his course for, and that after crossing thousands of miles of ocean!

With the evidence of the sun, the shoal water, the high table of land, flat and straight, the long, low, curving, sandy coast line, and with Smith's *Discoveries* and chart before him, there was little room for doubt. And even if it was not the Cape of many codfish it was certainly northerly enough for his purpose, which was to make a landing somewhere about one hundred and fifty miles north of the long island before the mouth of Hudson's river.

Six years before, the adventurer Captain John Smith had explored, charted and named the coast above the forty-second parallel, and called it New England. Mr. Jones had on the table before him, for his guidance, Smith's *A Description of New England: or The Observations and Discoveries of Captain John Smith in the North of America* . . . with a detailed chart of the New England coast from Cape Cod to Pembrocks Bay, published in Chancery Lane in London four years before. Smith's commentary he knew almost by heart, so that it was no very difficult problem to recognize the landmarks of Cape Cod.

The decisive forty-first parallel, the northern boundary of the Virginia Company's charter, outside whose territory he had made his private agreement with Thomas Weston to land the settlers, was, he knew, roughly only twenty to thirty miles north of the mouth of what was known as Hudson's river. His observation on the sun had suggested that he was well above that danger line and was in fact, as exact as such observations could be made, on the forty-second parallel. Therefore, to reach the Hudson he would have to sail no less than four hundred good English miles by sea south and west. But Mr. Jones had no more intention at that moment of carrying out the original instructions of the London Virginia Company than he had at the start of the voyage—unless the situation broke clean out of hand. . . .

And by the Martyrs the more he thought of Thomas Weston the more his gorge rose. To think that by so simple a piece of buying and selling shares Weston could hold the New World settlement to ransom! For Mr. Jones now had no slightest lingering doubt—Weston had got his fellow merchants in the London Virginia Company to advance money to hire the *Mayflower* and set up a settlement in the Virginia Company's territory at Hudson's river. Virginia Company shares were then of high value, with such an enterprise under way. So he sold them, and bought shares in the Plymouth Company, that held rights from the King to plant in the cold north. And for a hundred-pound bribe was now having the settlers put ashore on his second company's territory. His second company got a settlement for nothing, to tax and squeeze. And even if the settlement failed, he had already surely more than made a fortune on his exchange of shares. A fox! Mr. Jones cursed anew, that he had not seen through the scheme sooner. But he must go through with it; he had taken the money; and what mattered it to him where they made their houses—they'd die in the long run.

He still did not see clearly how it was to be accomplished. The settlers' leaders were unfortunately all honest men, besides being well furnished with descriptions of Hudson's river. Therefore, as they could not be fooled, and he needed a plausible story for his return to England, they must be forced to *agree* to a more northerly landing, to admit publicly and freely that the circumstances of ship and sea somehow forced it upon him as well as upon them; or otherwise they would in time get a true report sent home and he might find himself in gaol.

"Shoal water on our port, Mr. Jones," the mate called down the companionway.

Mr. Jones hurriedly swallowed a mug of gin in preparation for battle, and went above. To get a better view ahead he climbed halfway up the ratlines. Inshore, to the right of the ship's course, a broad expanse of broken shoal water ran along the coast. And now, directly ahead and almost athwart their course lay a fresh area of spume-white tossing water, separated from the inshore shoals by what appeared to be a calm laneway a couple of cable lengths in width. The roaring of the inshore shoals came to him quite clearly. He climbed down again to Coppin and Clarke.

"We stand out, sir?" the mate said expectantly.

"Why, no, sir," Mr. Jones said steadily. "We'll steal on down this road and come out into the clear farther ahead. I keep in close to pick up landmarks and discover what place we are in."

Mr. Clarke did not attempt to hide his surprise and anxiety.

"These shoals are no danger—if a man can read the water," Mr. Jones said loudly and with some condescension. "I've seen the like many a time before. They are but crosscurrents on a sandy bottom. And we have a good wind to carry us out, if needs be."

John Clarke thought that if it were left to him he would not run the risk of getting into such water, to be spun about like a top and ten to one bounced on the sandy ridges of the bottom; but it was not his place to tell the Master his business.

As they crept on and entered between the fields of tumultuously tossing and broken water, which roared expansively and powerfully, Mr. Jones observed with satisfaction that the passengers seemed to have organized their sight-seeing; a dozen or so came up at a time, stayed on deck for a few minutes staring at the land, and returned below, to be replaced by another lot. Good, he said to himself, there was nothing like having the evidence of your own calm eyes when it came to the push.

The channel of calm water continued to be navigable, though Mr. Jones had hoped otherwise, praying for a wind to spring up out of the south in his face, and they left that particular patch of outer shoals behind in less than half an hour. The weather had turned cold and wintry, with heavily overcast skies.

All morning they thrust carefully down the coast, and by eleven o'clock were again threading through a roaring, bubbling and seething sea, but still Mr. Jones held that course, until no one could hear himself speak without shouting with all the force of his lungs for the strange roaring of the water on either side. Now and then the channel they followed diminished to a lane hardly wider than the ship itself and they had to skirt over the edge of one of these areas of boiling sea. The women stayed below, the most with their hands over their ears; even the sailors were frightened and very quiet. It was thought, and not by the women alone, that the ship was running over the homes of the monsters of the deep. And at that moment of mounting bewilderment and anxiety Mr. Jones hurriedly summoned the passengers' representatives to him, and to the Great Cabin, almost falling over each other in their haste and fear, came Brewster, Bradford, Carver, Mullins, Martin, Edward Winslow, Sam Fuller and Stephen Hopkins.

He did not know where he was, he informed them, and would not know until he had seen a great deal more of the coast. Now, it should be plain, even to them, that he could not continue to sail on southwards in this mad and boiling sea much longer; Hudson's river lay to the south, but there it was . . . In a few hours it would be dark and to be caught in the dark in such waters meant only one thing. On the other hand it was impossible now to head out, for if they looked seaward they would perceive that the shoals, a mass of roaring white breakers pounding themselves to foam as if on a beach, stretched for a vast distance between the ship and the open sea. Therefore he was putting about and sailing *northward* again, the only way out of these fearful and dangerous regions.

Earlier that morning, he added, when they had tacked north to come in close, he thought he had seen indications of a good bay; he would head back there and in the morning try to anchor in shelter. Then they might perhaps venture to put a boat out to land, take in much-needed water, have a look round and get their breath. For once they agreed with him wholeheartedly.

All afternoon the ship retraced its way, sailing back past the block of low cliff first seen, continuing north until clear of the shoals, in a gloomy and near-freezing day. Mr. Jones alone knew that they were sailing up the outer side of a vast arm of land that lay out in the sea and which curled in on itself at the tip like a fern. Near dark the *Mayflower* stood out to sea for the night, slowly beating northeast back into the safety of the North Atlantic.

"The young man with the hair sticking up—Bradford is his name—I want you to watch for," Mr. Jones instructed Coppin. "And when he comes on deck slip up to him and speak without any of the rest hearing. Say I want a word with him here in private."

Shortly after, William Bradford appeared at the door, with a suspicious and truculent expression.

"The point is this," Mr. Jones said, when the door was closed. "Take it that we are many hundreds of miles off where we would go, hundreds and hundreds of miles north of this Hudson's river. Very well. Then put against that your poor situation, that you may all starve this winter if not begun to settle within the very month, and my being forced to go speedily——"

"Might I ask is this a trick of your humour?"

"Hear me! Then take it that my ship, and my crew that have been on the sea near four months, are all unfitted to go on searching—that I have in short to stand in to this coast and land you there for your settlement. . . . Suppose that to be our state of affairs, how would your people take it?"

"Ask them," Bradford returned promptly. "Why speak to me in so underhand a manner? I am not their Governor!"

"*You* would not take kindly to it?"

"We are honestly bound in faith to the merchants to go to their territory where Hudson's river is. The smallest child on board can see this coast does not look like any coast of Virginia, that we have heard of."

"It is all Virginia," Mr. Jones said, rubbing the black fringe around his chin, "but this part is called New England." And that for the time being must be all the information allowed them; certainly they must never be told that he had a chart of the whole bay under his hand, to raise up their suspicions further. "True, these parts are above the forty-first parallel—but I have heard it is as good a country as that below, and where you'd be freer of interference——"

"And you have a purpose in singling me out for these confidences?" William remembered that he must be diplomatic even if he could not quite hide his distaste when looking into the black-fringed face.

"The passengers may grow disorderly, when they hear I am forced to drop my anchor at Cape Cod."

"You know the very name of this place?"

"Now, you are a persuasive fellow, and a man seemingly of some influence with them—*you* will be my voice amongst them all, above all amongst the leaders of the fanatics, who now seem to look upon themselves as leaders of the whole ship. However, the others, the loyal Englishmen, they will do as I bid."

Bradford stared at him almost believing his suggestion to be some mad piece of humour. "You're a fool, sir. You cannot dump us where you will like so many cattle and evade your responsibilities and your contract with the Virginia Company. And as for my helping you to do so, I'd see you in hell first."

"No doubt. But you know this ship is lamed and broken dangerously? Yet you do not care to exchange favours?"

"In what way?"

"I have not yet made up my mind whether or no I will return Mr. Brewster to England, there to hand him into the care of the King's Government, who seek him so diligently."

William Bradford's colour, high at any time, flared crimson; and remembrance of the scene at the top of the hatch steps, when in his burst of loud-voiced jubilation he had betrayed the old man's true name to Jones, stabbed back into his mind; and he suddenly felt weak and breathless. Since that day he had often argued with himself that if such a circumstance ever did come to pass the settlers were more in number than the Captain and his crew; to no avail; for the old man would never jeopardize the success of the venture by allowing any act of violence. He knew only too well what Brewster would do—return quietly and without fuss to England, to his death. Jones had no doubt worked this out by now for himself.

"I say," Mr. Jones continued, seeing the success of his thrust and tapping excitedly with his blunt hairy fingers on the table before him, "that I have not made up my mind. Oh, it is my duty! But duty should be tempered with mercy. . . . I could well put it out of mind, forget it; say, if ever questioned, that I had no proper knowledge of his presence on board my ship. Who is to gainsay me? You? Brewster? And yet, I say to myself, why should I act with generosity to men who give me in return but black looks and scant respect? I think you will do what I ask, Mr. Bradford. You will do it or by God I'll take him back to rot in a prison!"

Bradford could not trust himself to speak; he turned to go out, hardly knowing what he did.

"Not such haste there," Mr. Jones said. "Be sure you understand what you have to do."

"Persuade my friends . . . And this is not the territory of the merchants who paid our way, who employed you and instructed you to go to Hudson's river?"

"It may not be, my friend, it may not be. . . . But neither did they instruct us to be near dismasted in a storm. And you would do well to remember something else—your leave-taking from Mr. Weston in Southampton, and how he swore he was cutting you adrift——"

"No sane man would believe that! They'll send out to look for their interest, if we were at the farthest end of the world."

"That we shall see. However, on the business in hand, you

will not of course run to Mr. Brewster's ear, or to any other of the firebrands, with tattle of this, our conversation; or ever afterwards mention it to any man, that's our bargain, and you are an honest man."

William Bradford burst into hard, ironical, hysterical laughter. Jones stood up, frowning, puzzled and taken aback, then angry. These "honest" men were a sore trial.

"My ship is shaken loose in every plank of her," he shouted, jerking up on to his feet, "my mainmast held in the timbers with props of wood and bandages of rope . . ."

After a moment of frozen shame at his lack of self-control, Bradford said in a low voice, "You may rely on me to carry your intentions—though it be not for the ends *you* have in mind. Yes, sir, we will exchange favours! Be at rest. God give you a good night." He left the cabin.

Mr. Jones walked back and forth, thumping his fist in his palm. He had called Bradford to the cabin on an instinctive impulse and a half-realized understanding of the relationship existing between Bradford and old Brewster, having remembered almost with a flash of inspiration Bradford's instantaneous though short-lived change of attitude, his near humility, on that occasion when the old man's identity had been revealed. Blindly thrusting aside his fear of the settlers rising against him, he had tried his hand, to find it work out with complete success, so much so that he had been hard put to it to hide his surprise and delight at his own dark cleverness. The exercise of strategy and absolute command was now surely proven a thing within his powers. Why, he would yet command the King's fleets at sea in the mightiest victories ever known in history, direct men, compel them—or find the secret levers of their being against which they had no defence. . . . Never again would he truck and haul wine, skins and fish. Here was his proving ground, his great preparation as a commander of men.

Bradford went to bed with his mind a tangle of perplexities. There could be no question of telling Brewster of the Captain's threat; the least he could do was to protect him from worry on that score, for the time being. And of course he had given his word to Jones that he would not. But who could tell at this stage just how serious landing outside the merchants' territory might prove in the end? True, the moneylenders could send as well to Cape Cod for the produce of the settlers' labour as to Hudson's river, but would it be legal for them to do so, would they not be compelled, perhaps by the Crown, to write the whole venture off as a loss? On the other hand a landing here would also relieve the settlers of their obligations under the existing and oppressive contract, and would therefore be a dishonest and immoral thing to do . . . unless under compulsion. Suppose the ship to be as badly damaged as Jones said. . . . They had set out for Hudson's river, on another point, because there something was known of the savages and how to handle them; in these northern parts of the unknown New World they might be much more numerous and prove utterly opposed to the strangers from over the sea. Bradford went to sleep at last resolved that Jones must never under any circumstances be allowed to leave them there or anywhere else until it was certain that they had won the savages' friendship and that a settled life was possible, if he had to be kept with them by force even until the following summer. Tomorrow he would talk it out thoroughly with the others, without breaking his word to Jones; and tomorrow they would set their first foot on the soil of the New World. Come, dawn of that long-awaited morrow!

The *Mayflower* started to sail in south by west, with every soul aboard her wide awake, an hour before dawn. But when daylight again came over the sea, on the morning of November the eleventh, the faithful watchers on the waist deck could see no shadow of land anywhere. At nine o'clock Mr. Jones appeared on the poop deck above their heads and made a short speech. He heaved himself up through the hatch and walked rapidly to the railed edge of the deck above the waist as if taking a run at an obstacle, and began in a loud, forced voice to shout down at them.

"We go in here, where we first saw land," he said, "to take a look at the country—and draw wood and water. Let you make no mistake, we are not near Hudson's river, but I cannot risk my ship to go farther in her condition. You saw how, yesterday, I did try for to go down the coast, and how the races and shoals that abound in these seas forced me to turn about—for the safety of your lives. You may thank God you have come to land at all! . . . I have only enough food for my crew to lay with you a month, that is what your delays in starting cost you, and then I must go, for I have to think of their lives now, in all the great and long journey home again. So whilst I stand at anchor in the bay of this Cape, mending the gaping wounds in my ship, pitching her between her planks and strengthening her masts, you may boat it down the coast to spy out the land. As for the weather, you will find the same weather here as at Hudson's river. If you've been told there is no winter in the New World, then you are misled. And if you be in the wrong part of the country for your merchants at home, then they will have to settle it out between them."

"And who knows what savages there are here?" a man called out. "Who knows anything of this place?"

"As much and more as is known of Hudson's river," Mr. Jones retorted. "It is said by Captain Smith that you may have your throat cut on Hudson's river far more easily and quickly than you may here." And now that he had thrown it at them he stopped for breath and dared take closer stock of their expressions. John Carver, Edward Winslow and William Bradford were on the deck below him, with about two dozen other settlers; and neither Carver nor Winslow, whom he looked at particularly, shewed any surprise, but a certain consternation and bewilderment was evident among the rest. "You will find it grow warmer when we come in against the land," he added finally, and turned from the rail quickly and went below before they started asking questions. From then on it was Bradford's and his friends' business to control them and answer their questions.

"If he says he is forced, and in turn forces us, then our conscience is clear," Bradford had said.

"There is the land again," a man shouted. "Look! I see it—there, ahead."

John pushed his way over to the tall, grim figure of Mr. Brewster.

"There, sir, you heard him! This is a cape of land, says he," John said, speaking in the old man's ear. "You remember what it was I heard him say, that day it was I first come aboard, Mr. Weston went to the Great Cabin——"

"I remember, lad, have no fear," the old man answered somberly, without turning his head to look at him. "But there are reasons connected with our merchants at home, that you do not know of . . . And our ship is badly damaged, and we have to deal delicately with Mr. Jones—and our food running short—there is so much mixed up here! So I beg you, young man, not to mention this to anyone else. Be sure that I will talk it out with Mr. Bradford and the others as to whether it is right to put in here. But say nothing of what you overheard, I beg you, say nothing. If we cannot win Mr. Jones to us we may likely all pay for it with our lives. . . ."

Two hours more brought them to within a mile of the low, narrow end of the Cape, sitting in the sea like a lonely desert island, where the wind steadied west-northwest, blowing directly off the land, and all in a matter of moments Mr. Jones found himself in a strong tidal current that set around the Cape's extremity, with the ship in extreme danger of being driven ashore. To clear the waist for the sailors the passengers were sent below, and close-hauled to the last pinch, the *Mayflower* edged out, came around the bulge of foreshore where the breakers smashed in a continual thunder of white foam, and in a choppy sea drove on down inside of the peninsula's head. To the settlers it seemed that they were sailing right around an island.

The Cape was to the port or left side; far away on the other side could be seen the distant line of the mainland of America.

The following wind drove the ship down the inner coast and sailing was child's play from then on. The land by the shore was all low; inland the head of the Cape was a great hill, covered with sea grass and trees, or so it seemed. After half an hour's sailing the land trailed off into a narrow ridge of sand. Standing high on the poop, Mr. Jones could see over the ridge, to the inner harbour lying within the hooked end of the Cape. The narrow bank of sand ran on, curved away to the left, and finally thickened again into a spit of land about a mile long where grew more trees and sand grass. Then it dwindled away to a point and ended. Mr. Jones bore round ever more to port, following the curve of the spit. Now the bowsprit pointed at the inner side of the vast arm of land which composed Cape Cod, and he noted what looked like a river mouth about four miles distant along the coast. The sandy spit dwindled into the sea and the *Mayflower* swung around it, into the wind, came about and sailed in behind the point until the soundsman felt bottom at ten fathoms with his lead; here Mr. Jones bore her around to port again until he had the wind behind him once more, having boxed the compass in coming to anchor. The air was quite suddenly warmer; it was eleven o'clock, forenoon, two hours to high tide, Saturday, November the eleventh.

The settlers below heard the forward anchor drop from the cathead and everyone made a mad scramble at once to get up on deck. Completion of the heavy and laborious task of furling the mainsail had to coincide with dropping the anchor, the ship being steered more by her sails than by her rudder in such a manoeuvre; most of the crew were up above at that task, as the settlers swarmed on deck. The first out on the little deck were pushed forward by those following; they climbed up onto the roof of the crew's forecastle, around into the bows, up the very ratlines and onto the bulwarks. Even Mr. Mullins threw dignity to the winds, pushing, squirming, standing on his toes and almost climbing on his neighbour's back to get his first view of the New World.

John wormed his way across the jammed deck, took Miss Mullins under the arms from behind and hoisted her into the air; and she was too excited for the moment to inquire who it was so kindly enabled her to see over the others' heads. Dorothy was last up but soon got to the side by pulling at men's sleeves and looking up into their faces with a nice simulation of a lost child trembling on the brink of tears.

"There it is . . ." whispered Dorothy to herself, looking upon the lonely spit with a sort of despairing disdain.

They were riding at anchor in calm water, to one side of what then appeared to their eyes to be an enclosed harbour, the waters of which stretched placidly two or three miles in length and a half a mile or more across. The sky was heavily overcast, with a numbing, insistent wind.

"There it is," Mr. Jones said to the mate, with a curl of his lip. "Me it was carried them to it as surely as if I carried 'em on my back—not that they'll ever give me just credit, believing it was rather their own guardian angels."

On the nearer rim of the spit's cold wet beach they could just make out sea birds, trotting in promenade by the disciplined sea's edge.

No human form shewed itself, no smoke or sign of savage life.

Nearest to the ship was the tip end of the spit of land that curled round to form the harbour; between that and the higher land at the back of the harbour was the narrow neck of sand, a connecting ridge, long, narrow, naked. Standish gazed at the tip of Cape Cod, a cable length from the bowsprit, and said to himself that if he could be the first man to set foot there it would be called *Standish Point*. And he thought that there must surely be watching savages concealed there, or he was a Dutchman.

William Bradford looked upon a bleak and sandy New World and saw in his mind's eye, with bitter rage, an image of the dark hair-encircled face of Christopher Jones.

And upon it William Brewster looked and said out loud, as he might have done years ago on an abysmally wet day, "God's will be done. . . ."

It was at the back of the harbour that the Cape shewed in its full character: a waste of sand hills patched with sea grass, and ascending behind them, hills grown over with briars, shrubs, wind-bent and knotted trees, with here and there the livid mark of a swamp. On the scrub-covered hills near the beach the sand blew like smoke. It was a low and desolate prospect, whipped incessantly by a biting wind.

Mr. Mullins' heart sank slowly and surely, as if he had found out some dear friend to be a base and vile liar. He had always been ready to dryly dispel the illusions of other people, but in his strait-laced heart had been many vague hopes and warm yearnings striving for life. This barren prospect could have no possible relation to those engravings of golden, graceful savages walking and fanning themselves with feathers beneath palm trees and amid tropical flowers. . . .

The immediate scene fascinated Gilbert far more than anything he could see across the water: the shoddy, creased clothes; a palliasse straw sticking to a shoulder; haggard, blotchy, tired faces marked by scurvy and rubbed-in dirt, faces framed by greasy head scarfs, with lost and dismal expressions . . .

John Billington turned his scorn upon Edward Thompson, William White's bonded man. "I see no monkeys, Master Thompson, nor grapes to be growing on the seashore. Oh, how the hot sun beats! Here is royal barges all a-made o' gold, with a black-faced king, to welcome Master Thompson."

Captain Jones turned from Clarke and advanced to the edge of the poop deck; the constrained chattering and arguing died away, until again was heard the hum of the wind in the rigging and the soft plash of the sea against the sides.

"This is no happy prospect, I grant," he said hoarsely. "But here is not where you will make your home; it is where I keep safe anchorage till you search out your plantation's ground—which shall be over a-back on the mainland." He pointed westward, across the narrow ridge of naked sand that on the one side separated the harbour from the great bay without. "That is to be searched out in the boat, and if it have a good anchorage—which for your future's sake it must, that ships can come to you—then I will bring the ship there to unload. But my ship's condition will not allow me to sail the open seas farther without I have a delay for mending her; and your food store does not allow of you wasting a day more. Here we have stumbled on a haven, by God's mercy, a calm pond in the wild sea . . ." He indicated the water about, calm, gentle in movement, sheltered from the buffeting wind that beat at the green sea out on the bar. And struggle against it as he might, a touch of some strange emotion was softening his coarse voice, an emotion that had nothing to do with the ship's coming safely into harbour but was in some way connected with the lost expressions of the people looking up at him, and a threatening sense of wrongdoing. And it was a fitting time and place for the Master of the *Mayflower* to experience a qualm of conscience. "A ship might search a year in these parts for another harbour so good as this is," he went on quickly, raising his voice. "And now we are safe you can hear the truth—one other blow needed but to catch us out beyond and this ship would have cracked open and gone to the bottom!" He gave them a few moments to gasp and be properly amazed, as he thought, before he resumed. "For the meanwhile your men may go ashore here and look about them, when your leaders have come to my quarters to be instructed. So you may look forward to having the longboat unshipped and the main hatch uncovered, and with wood gotten on the land have your fire burning. And as soon as you can arrange to start throwing your fishing lines out, do that. And for the moment, keep the deck as clear as formerly so as you do not hinder the sailormen about their business."

He made a dismissive gesture, a commander in the field dispersing his lesser officers to their posts, a gesture which gave a curiously heightened impression of the shortness and awkwardness of his limbs as he stood above them outlined against the sky; then, the determined man of few words, marched aft and descended into the Great Cabin.

An utter silence followed; and those who happened to be looking landward saw how a sudden whipping up of the wind whirled the sand about madly and obscured from sight a section of the bleak desert landscape.

Voices were raised again; some of the settlers began to go down into the holds out of the cold wind and out of the sailors' way; others, men in bond, argued among themselves that if the settlers were relieved of their obligations to the London Virginia Company by landing too far to the north, then they too should also be free of their obligations to those on board who bought their passage and put them in bond, free to do as they liked in the New World right from the start; for it was, they argued, the merchants who had set out every penny. A state of affairs, Winslow and Bradford agreed, that would have to be resolved without delay; the bondmen's debts were to the settlers and to the settlers alone.

Those about old Mr. Brewster turned to him, seeking explanations, assurances that the Captain would somehow be made to take them to a more habitable part of the coast.

"Contentious rascals," he said ruefully. "Here you are, no sooner delivered out of death's very jaws than you set to grumbling and complaining and saying you won't do this and you won't do that—whereas your very first act on seeing your new country should be to fall down and cry out your thanks to God."

He was called upon to step up on the hatch cover and address them, and half a dozen hands helped him up. With the long-boat at his back he steadied himself, stretched his arms out over their heads and said, " 'Our father who art in heaven, hallowed by thy name!' " pausing for them to repeat it after him, and so down to " 'For thine is the kingdom, the power and the glory, for ever and ever. Amen.' And grant us that from this land we may earn our daily bread in all the days to come. I will take you to me for a people, and I will be to you a God; and ye shall know that I am the Lord your God, which bringeth you out from under the burdens of the Egyptians. And I will bring you in unto the land. . . . And I will give it to you for an heritage."

"And on our face," they repeated after him, "we offer thanks for your mercy in bringing us safely over this fearful ocean. Let every man in his secret soul render God his due."

They gazed up with rapt attention at the stern and bearded patriarchal face; until William Brewster smiled, looking down at Bradford and laying his hand on his shoulder, and the graven features of their leader and prophet were instantly transformed; it was the indulgent face of a father regarding his children.

"The old men like Carver and myself," he continued, "must learn to give play to our younger men. It is the young men of fire and zeal who will take up the burdens now, but they must also learn to comfort and inspire if they are to make this country—let their voices be heard!"

He drew Bradford towards him and up beside him on the hatch, stepping down himself.

William Bradford had stood listening, conscious even as he prayed of his greasy underclothes that held no warmth, of his dry, cold lips and face, while he tried to suppress the shivers running up and down his back. But as he found himself looking down and around that clustering of pale mourning faces he knew that there and then he was being tested for the leadership of a New World and his heart beat quickly and his face flushed. He stood stiffly, silent, his mouth unpleasantly dry; not because he had nothing to tell them but because he had so much that his emotion held his tongue imprisoned.

"Well, William?" Carver said gently. "It's not like you to have no tongue."

"Put away your fear, dear brothers." And hearing his own voice, he was freed from all hesitation and doubt and his words rang out loudly and clearly. "You walked without falling through all the dangers and troubles that prepared this, and now you have passed over the vast and furious ocean without mishap. . . . Surely God has chosen you! What cause have you then for fear?"

Dorothy peered shortsightedly towards her husband, and smiled faintly and approvingly, but with a touch of surprise and amusement.

"It is true," Bradford cried, "that we have no friends to welcome us here, no inns to refresh our weather-beaten bodies, no houses or much less towns to repair to for succour. It is true also that now is winter—had we choice we would have landed in the springtime—that this climate may be subject to fierce and cruel weather. Our minds hold fearful pictures of a hideous and desolate wilderness that may lie before us, full of wild beasts and cruel men. But it is good to see ourselves as we are. Throw away self-deception. A man deceiving himself is a man weakened. Whether we hoped for a paradise or no, let us now admit every man to himself to be content with a desert, if God so chooses. For there seems not to be here any Pisgah to ascend and from which to view a more goodly country to feed our hopes. Then, admit who and what we are, cast out false hopes. Summer is done and all things stand beaten upon it—but there is the country."

Withal, a story that hardly needed retelling, Edward Winslow thought.

"These woes let us fairly admit," Bradford went on, "and, once faced, we need not dwell on them. They will not be remedied by making our faces pictures of misery. Think instead of those things we have done. We are poor men yet have moved ourselves from one side of the world to the other. That thought alone, of what you have done, will sustain you; that thought that you might have died in our England, having made no mark either for yourself or for God's freedom and truth than that which your boot made in the earth upon which you laboured. You have done a mighty thing!"

Pausing, he panted in a deep breath, remembering that he must not let his voice run shrill. "For think, oh, think—that we are here at last! We are arrived in a good harbour out of the storms of a vast and black ocean, and thank the God of heaven that He has brought us over that furious sea of enemies and of water and delivered us out of the perils of it and its monsters again to set our feet on the firm and stable earth. Keep it before your mind's eye, that you have done a mighty thing!" He paused again to clear his throat, which felt sore and weak.

Edward Winslow thought a little wearily that William might have said it all with far fewer words.

"For as we read in the Book," Bradford said, "Yea, let them which have been redeemed of the Lord shew how He hath delivered them from the hand of the oppressor. When they wandered in the desert wilderness, out of the way, and found no city to dwell in, both hungry and thirsty, their soul was overwhelmed in them. Let them confess before the Lord His lovingkindness, and His wonderful works, before the sons of men! For though this may prove a desert, we may go in it at will, free men. We shall not want, or die, while we have that faith and hope in Christ our Lord that brought us here. And one day, the children of these fathers will rightly say:

" 'Our fathers were Englishmen which came over this great ocean, and were ready to perish in this wilderness. But they cried unto the Lord and he heard their voice and looked upon their adversity. Let us therefore praise the Lord because He is good and His mercies endure forever!' "

He clasped his hands, closed his eyes, and with his lips moving silently in prayer turned his sharp-jawed, earnest face heavenwards. Every soul on the deck followed his example, raising up their faces to the dark sky.

15   They trooped down in better spirits, though some tears were wiped away among the women. It was time for the midday meal; while they had their food the crew would unship the longboat; in the meantime the longing for fresh food was somehow intensified by knowledge of the near shore. They were delighted to hear each other when speaking in ordinarily low voices even though all the noises of the ship and sea still echoed persistently in their ears, for all the world as if they had shells clapped to their heads that they could not shake off. A babel of excited voices echoed back and forth from the low timbers of the hold, and through it all could be discerned their essentially unworldly and simple though now enfeebled spirit, their lost and homeless state, their eager willingness to be led and guided. William Brewster felt most acutely the responsibility that rested upon him and the other leaders.

Before eating, Carver and Edward Winslow were sent along to Jones to find out what was meant by his command that the leaders come to him "to be instructed." The elder Winslow was chosen to go with the Governor as being the most diplomatic; and this arrangement to stand for the future. They were to appear before Jones not as messengers to carry back his orders but as negotiating ambassadors; they were to avoid antagonizing him further, rather to try to gain more of his sympathy, if such was possible, but on no account to give the impression that the settlers were ready to let themselves be ordered and directed by one who in all justice should be their servant and willing helper, now that they were about to go on dry land again.

"When, sir, do you propose to go on the land?" Mr. Carver asked the Master.

Mr. Jones, to gain a few moments, gave him a long and over-acted stare of surprise, for he was still between the Devil and the deep sea, supposing that he must not shew the slightest sign of leaning towards them for fear the mates and sailors carried back such report to England and he found himself, in the event of any trouble, accused of being a dissenting, treasonable subject himself; while on the other hand, now being come to anchor in Cape Cod Harbour without any great trouble from the settlers as a body, he could afford perhaps to treat them a little less harshly —having to watch nevertheless with an eagle eye that *they* got no actual proof against him that they might in the future send to England on their own account. He shifted on his chair uneasily, and then his long-ingrained habit of opposition and his inner need to dominate pushed him again, instantly, into his old, perverse pattern of conduct. "Man, there is the land. Go walk on it. Or do you expect me to carry you all ashore in your beds and lay you down gently?"

"As long as we know your intentions," Carver said. "The difficulty is in knowing them. It was supposed by us that you would want to lead the way."

"What you mean is that you'd have my sailors go on the shore first, to draw the sting of what savages may lurk in the woods," Mr. Jones sneered. "Well, let me tell you, I need every man for sailing the ship home. I'll lose enough through sickness before we see England again."

"Then you do believe there are savages here?" Winslow asked.

The Master paused warily. At all events they had best be prepared, he said, as they would have to be no matter what part of the New World they first set their foot on. Savages had been seen on every coast of America, but hereabouts many ships had visited from time to time and thus the savages were privileged in having been able perhaps to talk with Christian men. . . . "And though your reception depend on how they treated with the savages, whether they were just with them or slew them and carried them off, you have a fairer chance here than on any other part of the coast of America."

"If they are here they do not shew their faces," Winslow remarked dryly.

"You will come upon them soon enough! And if you mean to be masters you must shew it promptly. These wild men will understand only the semblance of might and force, and God knows

you have poor enough lackeys to pretend courage with . . ."
Mr. Jones smiled in a superior way. "Now that you understand
that the condition of my ship will force me to ride here awhile
I must further caution you: against delay in finding out your
ground. My stores will let me stay with you only a short while;
if the day comes for me to go and you have not found your place
to settle, then I must put your goods ashore and leave you . . ."

" 'What have ye to do that ye beat my people to pieces and
grind the faces of the poor,' " Mr. Carver quoted sadly.

Mr. Jones looked surprised. After all he had only attempted a
fair and timely warning. His future course was as much compelled by physical circumstance as theirs. But they would leave
it at that for the moment. He returned to the subject of making
the first landing, asking why they had been so misguided as to
think that he was going to lead them by the hand like a father,
and so on.

" 'When I was a child,' " Winslow said quietly, almost smiling
at some secret thought, " 'I spoke as a child, I thought as a child:
but when I became a man, I put away childish things.' When
we thought you would want to be first we thought it in charity."

Mr. Jones tried to puzzle out what this might mean. It was
amazing how Winslow had managed to keep himself so dandi-
fied and clean; his long hair was brushed smoothly and today he
wore a well-fitting suit of hard black which suggested more an
ambassador at court than a refugee travelling into the wilderness
to live on roots. He looked away from Winslow's handsome face
with a quick and acute sense of inadequacy, all at once hot under the collar and ready to shout and reassert himself.

"But it was foolish of us to think that you would be affected
by mere sailors' talk," Winslow continued. "So that even if some
do say on your ship's return to London that you feared to go into
the land first—such tongues being always readier to spread an ill
report than a good one—no doubt your repute is large enough to
override it."

"So that's the way you're playing your hand," Mr. Jones
roared. "I was warned you were scheming serpents. But any time
you spend whispering in the ears of my sailors is time wasted.
You may be bent on blackening me as a villain, but they know

who I am. You suppose I called you here to tell you my intentions about landing? I called you here to tell you that no man leaves the ship till I give the order. Now take yourself out."

Winslow shrugged; and they took themselves out without more ado. "He'll be over the side in a couple of shakes," he grinned, "wait and see. I hope they do not put arrows in him, to see what we're made of. . . ."

At the after end of the first hold Mr. Brewster sat on a low stool with a large box before him to act as a table. Here he wrote with great deliberation on a big sheet of rough paper. About him stood the heads of families and others of importance; in the centre of the standing group Stephen Hopkins, William Bradford and William Mullins argued heatedly.

Hopkins was a middle-sized man of thirty-five years, with black wild eyes, a warm, generous and good-humoured face, a simple practical Christian who had no patience with the careful dogmatism of Master Mullins.

"It must begin thus," Mullins pontificated. "*Thus:* Gracious and Dread Sovereign, we Your Majesty's Humble Servants——"

"Pah!" Hopkins cut across him. "You're no sooner escaped the chains of His Majesty's Fleet Prison than you must go about to crawl on your belly and bind yourself with agreements and compacts to that same Lord of Misrule."

Hopkins' voice was nervously edged with malice; they were all cold, padded out and burdened with extra clothes, nervous and short-tempered. Less than half a dozen had managed to continue clean-shaven; most now wore young beards, which completed their appearance of tramps and villains abroad. And common to the majority was a strained, distraught set of the features, as if they had all just collectively awakened from an enervating nightmare. They fidgeted, scraped their boots on the planks and scratched for lice. Coming from above, the sounds of squeaking, pounding and cursing told them that the longboat was being launched.

Bradford threw his hands out, as if to deprive of movement these troublesome stiff figures in their dun-coloured puppets' clothes. Nevertheless, they were Englishmen first and foremost, he repeated with impatience, therefore the customary way of beginning an address or compact was not out of place.

Mr. Brewster went on unperturbed, steadily writing out the agreement that it was proposed to have everyone sign before landing, Carver at one side of him, Edward Winslow coming to lean over his other shoulder.

They never would forget that they were Englishmen, Christopher Martin echoed Bradford, nodding weightily. Mr. Martin was a much changed man, having lost not only his good red colour but such an amount of flesh that his slovenly clothes hung loosely upon him, his face a sickly yellow patched with scurfy areas.

"Use your wits," Bradford addressed Hopkins, "we do not want to give this Captain any excuse to go back and spread reports about that we are disloyal and turbulent people."

"No—but he will!" someone shouted. "They'll send out their spies and governors to rule us, but we'll give them short shrift."

All this whole business meant was that they were putting their hands to a piece of double-dealing, Hopkins persisted, quite useless as an attempt to cow the bondmen. His man Edward Dotey would not sign it, he was sure; he knew his mind, he said, and the minds of his fellows. Did they think these men in bond utter children, to bind themselves further when nothing compelled it? Yet Bradford insisted that they were putting their hands to it in good faith, and whether the bondmen signed it or not, it would be effective by they themselves signing it in their presence. Then they were putting their hand to a piece of double-dealing, Hopkins repeated.

Bradford's temper flared up. Words meant apparently nothing to mad Hopkins. They from Holland were bound together, tested by the years—but what was there then, in that instant of their going forth into the great and distant country before them, to bind Hopkins and *his* kind together?

"It's *unbound* I want to be," Stephen Hopkins said.

Edward Winslow looked up from reading over Mr. Brewster's shoulder, and said, "Stephen, you're acting the fool. This compact is for the benefit of the contentious." Therefore they needed to make it solemn and full of royal authority, he explained, whether they had any or not. If the men they had paid passage for and signed bond for, nearly a dozen in number, were not quickly curbed in thinking that they had escaped all obligation by the ship coming to the land of Cape Cod instead of Hudson's river in the Virginia Company's territory, there would be no holding them when they set foot on the shore. Secondly, the agreement was for the purpose of drawing the new English and the old Holland exiles together firmly that they might rule themselves as a body.

Winslow raised his hands to compel their absolute attention, and said with intense though measured gravity, "What is the deadliest calamity and the nearest that we may easily fall by? Dying of hunger in some cold cave of rocks? Devoured by beasts? Torn in pieces by savages? Lost in the wilderness desert without water to quench our thirst? No! The nearest terror is that we will fall apart, that we will split up, degenerate lower than the beasts, each wandering alone and grubbing in the ground from himself alone, for then we will be truly destroyed, every evil your imaginations can conceive of falling upon us each and every one— hunger, terror, beasts, savages. We must bind ourselves together by every law we can make, even to putting banishment and death on those who break the compact. And this must be done before we set a foot on the shore. So we must have a compact, a constitution, a solemn agreement that we will all obey whatever laws it is found necessary to make. And besides, you blockhead," he turned to Stephen Hopkins, "unless we show ourselves as remaining loyal subjects we will not be left alone by James's butchers."

Hopkins offered no further objections, and set about helping John arrange more boxes, behind which the elder men sat like judges in a court of law, ready to speak to the people.

A few minutes later they heard Mr. Jones's voice above and were told that he was going ashore. The men rushed for the stairs and crowded on deck again as the Captain was climbing down the side. Mr. Brewster continued to write out the compact.

The longboat pulled away for the nearest point of land, the islandlike spit, watched by Mr. Clarke, left in charge on the poop, the remaining sailors in the bows and on the ratlines and the settlers on the middle deck.

Mr. Jones sat in the stern of the longboat dressed in a heavy leather overdoublet and a splendid pair of sea boots reaching almost up to his crutch, armed with an expensive-looking snaphance musket, a pistol, a sword and a dagger. Mr. Coppin was in the bows, holding a musket, while the fifteen sailors who accompanied them were also variously armed with muskets, swords and wood axes. In a matter of minutes the boat was riding in over the gentle inshore waves and they glided to a stop on the white sand.

After a few moments' wait, watching the higher ground, Mr. Jones motioned with his hand and Coppin and two sailors sprang over the side and held the bows. The Captain scrambled forward, balanced on the cutwater and leapt onto the beach. He stared at the dunes warily, then back at the ship and the watching faces on her, before continuing on, ploughing up over the loose sand. Coppin quickly followed with an escort of ten men, leaving the rest with the boat. Mr. Jones led them to the nearest sand hill and there on its summit stood looking about him. It was twelve o'clock noon, a grey and chilly November day, with a calm sea and a steady breeze, the tide one hour from high water.

His plan was to work down through the low-lying tongue of land to where the narrow sandbank connected it with the main Cape; the spit could not be more than a mile in length. If it proved free of savages and other dangers it was an ideal location, being almost an island, on which to build the fishing shallop; no one could approach from the Cape along the sandbank without being seen from the ship.

They started inwards over the sand hills towards the stunted, wind-crippled trees and shrubs that grew in the sand of the interior, Mr. Jones conspicuously leading the way. The first tree, knotted and low-spreading, proved to be no taller than four feet, which from the ship had appeared to be a full-sized tree. Everything that grew here, it seemed, did so in coarse yellow sand. Further in, the ridiculously small trees were so thinly spaced that they could walk through the woody places with ease and without any fear of being watched by hidden eyes. A few dozen paces down the spit they discovered a marshy fresh-water pond.

The going was easier than Mr. Jones had anticipated, although now and then their feet broke through a thin patch of mossy growth and loamy covering to the soft flinty sand beneath. And the only sign of life that moved in that wintry spot was an occasional bird, flying from their approach. So they wound on, noiselessly, in and out amongst the gnarled little trees, skirting out to the left around salt marshes, pushing by the lichen-covered branches, from which many a limb and twig snapped off dryly with a sharp crack. The sailors walked together in a close bunch, holding their muskets before them with both hands, awed by the dead and desolate aspect of that strange place—one imaginative mind nearly persuaded that he plodded thus noiselessly in a dream, for where else but in a dream would it be possible to walk through a wood of ancient trees that only reached to a man's shoulder and which all appeared either to be in the process of dying or to have been fossilized for a thousand years, the whole fixed in desert sand. But for the coarse beach grass it would have been impossible to attach any sense of reality to the place.

At first Mr. Jones marched holding himself very straight, when he wasn't stumbling in a gully or hollow or falling over a clump of grass or trailing briar. Never before in all his journeyings had a more lifeless and godforsaken spot of earth met his sight, and as his spirits slowly sank his head drooped.

When the party on land had disappeared the leaders were again able to assemble the men together in the hold and Mr. Brewster, sitting behind his improvised table, spoke to them.

"At Hudson's river," he was saying, "we should have been in the territory of the London Virginia Company which financed us. But for reasons you already know we are at a place far away to the north of Hudson's river, which place is named Cape Cod. This Cape Cod is the territory of another company, called the Plymouth Company, which has been endeavouring for years to induce people to venture here and live. Therefore this Plymouth Company should accept us readily—as the state of our poor beaten ship will not allow us to go from here—and ought soon to come to an agreement with our Virginia Company when the Captain returns and tells what has happened. Then we can make a new agreement with the Plymouth Company in place of that harsh one forced on us by the Virginia Company and that even harsher one we refused to sign at Southampton. And if we should find a suitable place here to live we shall have a climate like that which we knew in England.

"Therefore, understand that we must here and now, before we set a foot on land, order ourselves for our own governing and that we may hold together with mutual help and purpose. For while we may be in the wrong place, we are still bound under the same scheme, and bound in honour to pay our debts in England to the merchants—we'll be left without a boot to our feet if we don't! As arranged in England, each man shall draw from the common store and have it marked up against him; each man shall work not for himself but for the community, until our debts are paid, and until such time as we shall agree to order our affairs differently and allot land to be owned outright."

After he had quelled the murmuring and arguments he read out the compact: loudly and sternly:

" 'In the name of God, Amen. We, whose names are underwritten, the loyal subjects of our dread Sovereign Lord King James; by the grace of God, of Great Britain, France, and Ireland King: Defender of the Faith.' "

He was interrupted by mocking though halfhearted calls from some of the younger men, with mimicry of King James's Scots accent: "Gude die and gude gang wi' yee!" And, "The dirty Scot that we made a gentleman." "By cheatin' an' lyin' he plays his game; let him go to the Devil from whence he came!"

Mr. Brewster stared them into silence, and continued. " 'Having undertaken for the glory of God, and advancement of the Christian faith, the honour of our King and country——' "

Even the well-behaved women at the back made sad, clucking noises at that point.

" '—A Voyage,' " the old man went on resolutely, though now, when it came to reading the agreement he had written out, he began to feel a little ashamed, " 'to plant the first Colony in the northern parts of Virginia; do, by these presents, solemnly and

209

mutually, in the presence of God and of one another, covenant and combine ourselves together into a Civil Body Politic, for our better ordering and preservation; and furtherance of the ends aforesaid: and, by virtue hereof, to enact, constitute, and frame such just and equal laws, ordinances, acts, constitutions, offices, from time to time, as shall be thought most meet and convenient for the general good of the Colony; unto which, we promise all due submission and obedience.' " Here, he looked up very pointedly. " 'In witness whereof, we have hereunder subscribed our names. Cape Cod, eleventh of November, in the year of the reign of our Sovereign Lord King James, of England, France, and Ireland eighteen; and of Scotland fifty-four. Anno Domini sixteen hundred and twenty.' "

The first to sign were Carver, Bradford, the elder Winslow, Brewster, Isaac Allerton and Miles Standish. John had been listening to the proceedings with a massive, earnest attention, feeling his orphanhood, that he was apart from them, allowed to look on at a large family's business if he kept his peace. But as Standish put down the pen, Brewster, looking about, caught John's eye and beckoned. He went forward supposing that the old man wanted him to fetch him ink something from his cabin. Brewster dipped the pen in the ink and held it out to him.

"Yes, lad—you. Not if you don't wish it, but we are agreed it is the least mark of respect we can offer you for your willingness and good faith."

He took the pen and tremblingly signed his name; and went back smiling sheepishly and without being able to utter a word. That he should have been asked to sign it at all, not being a settler, was compliment enough; but that he was called to sign immediately after the leaders and before such men as Sam Fuller and William Mullins was so unexpected a mark of favour that he felt like expanding his lungs and making some huge and gleeful noise. He sought out Mr. Mullins with his eyes and looked boldly in that gentleman's sick and doleful face. Priscilla was at the back of the hold; he turned and stared at her until he caught her eye, and winked. She looked down at her fingers as if she had not seen it.

The Compact was then signed, or marked, by all who were

asked. Nine of the men in bond did not sign after all; but of these four were sick and it was thought best not to bother them with it just then; the others, being unwilling, were not pressed. Contrary to Hopkins' opinion, when it came to the turn of his own bondman, Dotey, the man signed his obedience without objection.

An hour later Jones and his company were back at the water's edge opposite the ship, without having discovered any sign of human life on the spit. He set the sailors to cutting firewood and digging a fresh-water well in the sand.

Mr. Jones returned to the ship pondering on his future course of action. He had made the grand gesture and led the way ashore; he alone was aware of how safe a spot he had picked for his setting foot on the earth of the New World. Yet dare anyone ever say he did not lead the way!

The spit's beach would serve most excellently for rebuilding the settlers' boat. He knew very well from Smith's chart just where lay the best location for a settlement; and that was right around the bay in a harbour marked by Smith "Plymouth," in honour of that Plymouth in England from where so many ships set out to explore the wide oceans. But he could not tell them that, no more than he could, that morning, sail to it directly. That would have been to shew his hand too openly, Mr. Jones thought. They must believe it to be their own discovery when, by his manipulation, they came upon it.

He had reckoned out on his chart that by land the distance from where they lay anchored to the new Plymouth was roughly something over thirty leagues, or a hundred miles; to sail around the coast, twenty leagues; and to sail directly across the open sea, as the crow flies, a bare eight leagues. A small boat coasting down the arm of Cape Cod and up the far mainland must inevitably hit on it. He would then sail the *Mayflower* over to unload.

His log would read: "Strove to go south, where we fell into a vast boiling sea of shoals, which turned me back. On the morning following put into Cape Cod safely, from where I durst not move until the ship was remedied of her grievous damage taken in the mighty storms. In the meanwhile, their food running so short, an awful threat staring us all in the face, the settlers sought out a place to plant themselves, and found the very favourable spot where they now are, which is called New Plymouth."

It all fitted together, Mr. Jones thought, as the longboat slid in under the line of anxious faces looking down at him from the bulwark of the *Mayflower*, and he could not be found at fault on his return to England.

The first business then was to bend all effort towards speedily getting the timbers of the shallop out of the hold and onto the beach. The settlers no doubt would discover the savages soon enough. . . . "You can cease your praying," he said as he came up over the side, "there are no elephants."

"Are there people?" old John Carver asked quietly. "We are not so concerned about elephants. If men live here, then we also can find the ways of sustaining our lives."

"We searched far and wide for them," Mr. Jones declared grandly, "but saw we none. Do you expect them to live on a sandy spit in the ocean? They'll be over across the harbour. But you can be sure they will hide until they know we mean them no harm." Moving across the deck to the poop door, so that they would be forced to follow at his heels for further information, he noticed in the crowd men armed with matchlock guns, with powder horns and bags of shot tied at their waists, belted and buckled and equipped as if for war. Between a dozen and twenty of the ablest settlers were thus accoutred. He swung round to the group of leaders. "You suppose to go ashore now? Your first work is to unship the shallop, get it to the beach and have the carpenters to work!"

Mr. Carver pointed out that there were more men on board, crew included, than could in the very restricted space profitably work together unpacking the boat. So while a dozen or so assisted the crew in this another party would go ashore to another part, stretch their legs and spy out the land for themselves. For after all there might not be savages in any of these parts and therefore they would not be able to obtain corn seed of the kind that grew in the New World and which they must have; or, if there were savages on the main Cape they might be so completely hostile that any attempt to make a settlement would be sheer waste of time and life. And until they found these things out it was no good building the fishing boat.

"And how do you think to find these things out *without* your boat?" Mr. Jones snapped. "This isn't England where you can walk abroad in the land. This is a vast country, all overgrown. If you do not find your corn country on Cape Cod you'll find it twenty miles down the coast, or fifty. But it must, for speed's sake, be done in your shallop, with which you can cover distance. There are no roads here to walk on, no single path even. A man would not go more than a few miles in a week, pushing over brambles and swamps. You can go in the longboat to the spit, if you wish—but my longboat must leave you there and come back to the ship."

"Very well, sir," Mr. Carver said quickly, before any arguments could break out. "Our hired sailors shall take us, and then we'll send back with the boat."

The fifteen able men who had been selected to compose the first scouting party included Miles Standish, as military leader, William Bradford, Edward Winslow, Gilbert Winslow, John Alden, Stephen Hopkins, William White, John Billington, Christopher Martin (who had insisted, though they told him he did not look well enough), Isaac Allerton, Sam Fuller, and the settlers' own three hired sailors, English, Trevore and Ellis.

Mr. Jones gave his orders about the unshipping of the shallop, and ascended to the poop deck. He was extremely hungry, but paused, intending to wait a moment and see the boat put off.

Mr. Coppin affected much amusement at the settlers' appearance. Leaning over the side, he called down as if to a party of schoolboys, "Let you little lads take great care for the boat, or it will go hardly with you."

The others in the boat looked towards the landing with anxiety and suppressed excitement; but John's exhilaration knew no such self-imposed restraint, and his natural antagonism to the second mate burst forth happily in a prompt retort. "Get forward, you filthy cockroach. I handled an oar before you was in your mother. Back to your hole! Your smell sets all a-puking. Sailor filth!"

Coppin was then engaged shouting down at Standish, who, the last to climb down the side, wore a breastplate over his jerkin and held a smoking slow match in one hand.

"Look to it you don't blow the boat up there," Coppin shouted. "And don't fall in the water, your lordship, or you'll go straight to the bottom. You, boy, keep a civil tongue," addressing John, "or you are like to get your head broke. The oars, gentlemen, go in them locks on the gunwale. They're not for floating in the water, or pitching at fish."

"Sailor filth!" John roared happily at the top of his voice. "You it is we should have pitched over the side before now, like any scabby louse. Come a day, Master, I'll smear your filth in the decking with my boot. Back to your galley slops, whore's gut!"

Had there been anything handy to pitch at him Coppin would have pitched it; his anger at the unexpected retort was quick and violent. But he was fortunately held in by the press of settlers at his back. He spat down copiously; the boat was already moving and his spit fell short.

Her four oars dipped rhythmically in the ruffled surface of the grey sea as the longboat drew away from the ship and swung around in a wide arc, heading towards the farther, main beach, and not the nearby spit.

"Nay, nay—ahoy!" Mr. Jones bellowed, waving his short arms and pointing back at the spit. "In the Devil's name, are you all mad, or blind? You go in the wrong direction."

The four rowers rested their oars at a word from Edward Winslow. Bradford stood up precariously, cupped his hands about his mouth and shouted back, "We go to set foot on our country. We have no time to waste on spits of sand in the ocean. Over thither is where the land begins, and there we go." He sat down abruptly and the rowers resumed their strong sweeps.

Instant realization that if he proceeded further in that particular situation he would be made to look a fool came to Mr. Jones. He choked back his words as he was on the point of ordering the rowers to return forthwith. The settlers' three sailors might obey him; but on the other hand they might not; and he dared not put it to the test with the whole ship looking on. "Wherever you go, here or there, the longboat must return to the ship when you are set ashore. If you be caught by murdering wild men, and have no boat to escape, that's your own lookout."

Bradford pointed at the nearer horn of the main beach, which curved around the back of the great harbour and ran on down the arm of the Cape. "We go there, and will send the boat back. Keep a watch for our return."

"I'll keep watch to teach you one day to address me as a cabin boy," Mr. Jones said to himself, and swung down into the Great Cabin to his meal.

The distance from the *Mayflower* to the main beach appeared to be something under a mile: a matter of thirty minutes' good pulling. The men in the open boat settled down more comfortably, tucking their hands in their sleeves or otherwise out of the keen, cold wind, their eyes constantly scanning the long rim of beach ahead. Their elation at having foxed the Captain, even in such a small thing, was quickly forgotten. William Bradford knelt in the prow of the boat, thrust forward like a figurehead, his lean face blue with the cold.

Nearer came the shore, until they could see the boles of the pitch pines behind the sand dunes. How good it would be to walk again on the firm and stable earth, to feel the blood warming through working muscles!

Back on the ship, voraciously spooning steaming lentil soup down his throat, Mr. Jones vowed that he would not be tempted into going above to see how the landing party fared. Huddled in mufflers and capes, the watchers in the rigging and on the waist deck followed the longboat's course, tensed and silent as the boat suddenly stopped moving while yet some way from the rim of white beach and the toy figures of men, so minute and lonely against the wide sweep of land at the back of the harbour, appeared to go mad and jump into the sea.

It was then three o'clock in the afternoon and the tide had run back sufficiently to reveal to those in the longboat that extensive flats stretched out from the shore under shallow water. The keel of the laden boat grounded firmly and there was nothing else to do but step into the water and splash the remaining hundred yards to the beach.

Thomas English, the leading sailor, came on shore with them, while Trevore and Ellis floated off the longboat and turned it back towards the ship.

The settlers stood on the wide and empty beach gazing about them silently. Nothing further needed saying then: Brewster and Carver had talked to them carefully about the rules of conduct to be observed—not to go too far from the beaches, not to separate, not to go in thickly wooded places; if meeting savages to shew the most friendly attitude; on no account to use their weapons except in the direst emergency. But they stood, close together, as if waiting for someone to speak, or for something to happen, breathing the air of the New World and feeling its strange and sickening movement beneath their feet; for the ground under them swayed with the old movement of the sea!

"It's a time before you get your land legs back," the sailor, English, said, and began stamping his feet. They all laughed and moved slowly and cautiously up the beach, swaying a little drunkenly because of the apparently gentle seesawing earth, the surface of the sand ahead appearing also to swirl in half circles.

The party trudged up over the first sand hills at the back of the strand and there halted, scanning the nearer brushwood and the vast curve of the beach. On the flat, naked sand of the beach objects stood out with astounding clearness, circled with vague haloes of light; that which from a little distance appeared to be a large boulder or quiescent animal proved on closer inspection to be nothing more than a big crab shell or a starfish. Cast high up on the beach were the shells of crabs and huge lobsters, the greater number bleached white. A stone's throw away a gull and a crow hopped about a dead crab; a passing party of mackerel gulls turned aside to circle above the explorers' heads, either in playful curiosity or expecting to find food near them. The lobster shells were a good sign. They talked of how they would make traps to sink in the bay. What a wonder of God it was, they said, that such homely and common things of the Old World should have been so kindly planted here in the Other World to meet their eye. For suppose the lobsters here had been twenty foot high, and the inhabitants two-headed (of which there was no sensible reason that they should not be)?

On the wrack line they could see several trunks of trees that had been washed up at one time or another, some half buried in the loose sand, some nearer the water, fresh from the recent tide, damp, wormy, waterlogged and bestuck with barnacles.

Despite the sounds created by the wind and the plashing of the sea behind, the silence was frightening. For months they had lived, awake and asleep, in the company of the singing rigging, the slapping of fierce water and the creaking of the ship; now the silence was oppressive and stupefying. They shivered, feeling helpless and a little sick, keeping tightly together, blindly willing to be directed in the smallest matter.

"Lord God," Gilbert said to his brother, "what a great beach! How vast space is when you can set out to walk over it at will."

"Distances appear doubly great when your feet are wet," Edward Winslow answered wryly.

Standish set out in the lead, walking along the beach. It struck him that he'd feel a good deal safer were he walking *behind* his clumsy warriors, but that would hardly do. . . . The threat of lurking wild men worried him far less than the thought that at any moment a gun might explode accidentally behind him and fill his back with bird shot. Weavers and suchlike indoor workers, after being cramped in a cold hold for two months, stiff and awkward, made not the best material for skirmishing adventurers! Above all he knew that for the first few months they would have little chance of hitting anything they fired at; matchlocks even in the best of trained hands were instruments more useful for frightening than wounding; for which reasons he had dealt out bird shot. A sting from a stray pellet was better than no hit at all, if trouble did come, and should any one of them actually succeed in getting his gun to fire. . . .

The men walked so close together that they continually stumbled against each other; when this had happened several times and Christopher Martin, his hands stiff with the cold, let his gun fall, Standish began to whip them up with grim curses, in his harshest military voice.

"Jesus help us! Were I a savage and saw such a miserable

huddle of frightened rabbits I'd think a dozen of you too small for my dinner. Heads up! Walk apart, four abreast, muskets on right shoulder!"

Bradford had a small pudding-shaped bundle, wrapped in a piece of cloth, tied to his belt. Asked by Edward Winslow what he carried there, he replied, "Trinkets—beads and glass mirrors. We cannot talk with the savages in their tongue but even a savage will understand that a present means friendship." Laughter followed his declaration; any form of noise served to lessen their sense of isolation and loneliness, intruders in a strange, spacious, sandy world, human specks on a great ribbon of beach that faded into the distance.

How many of them felt the wonder of what they were doing? Gilbert thought. Hard-working, patient souls, simple men cast in a drama far beyond their comprehension, beginning the most extraordinary venture the world had ever or would ever see, like sleepwalkers in a sick, cold dream.

Trudging along the wide-open beach became unbearable, as well as obviously pointless, and Edward Winslow suggested cutting in through the trees to see what kind of land lay further in. "It is known that there are savages here," he argued. "Good. But —we see no sight of them. Therefore some pair of eyes, perhaps many pairs of eyes, are watching us, hiding in that they are afraid or mean to attack us. If they are afraid only, they will fly from us whether we walk on the beach or inland; if they mean to attack us they will do so sooner or later, and better it is sooner, when they are the less prepared and gathered together. Let us make a bold stroke and get it over then—or do we rather wait till the women and children are ashore with us? . . ."

Standish and Bradford agreed, and the party turned inland, found a gully where the growth was sparse and proceeded up through the trees, few of which grew higher here than twenty feet, the loose sandy loam in which they stood affording no grip for anything weighty; trees grew as large as the earth would allow, and were then blown down, as was plain to see.

"Look you!" one of the men exclaimed. "There's winds here, by God." He pointed at the topmost branches of an exceptionally tall pine, where, twenty-five feet above the ground, sand clung to the windward side of the branches like snow. In other trees they noticed the same thing.

There were evergreens here and there, but otherwise the dead hand of winter had already stripped the trees. Nevertheless, between them they managed to identify over a dozen different kinds of tree and shrub: boxberry, shrub oaks, oaks, aspen, beech, wild plum and cherry, holly and juniper.

They trudged up a shallow gully in single file and came out on a low-lying level expanse, a few dozen acres in extent. Here in yellower sandy soil grew a mossy sort of poverty grass, beach grass that rustled dryly, sandwort and a few other hardy weeds. They walked on amongst the stunted oaks, giants in a dwarf world, glancing askance at the witches' trees; knotty, gnarled trees, hugging the ground, the elders dignified with a sinister yellow lichenlike rust and hung with long grey beards of moss that swayed in the breeze.

The air was softly alive with the sighing of the wind, cut with the dreary peep of the piping plover; but these sounds, though there, were hardly heard; the landscape impressed a feeling of stillness and utter abandonment.

Beyond this small, dead plain was a stretch of marshy, pond-ridden ground; from the dark brackish water a huge crane rose into the air and winged away in slow motion, followed by the quicker flight of a cloud of waterfowl. The mossy beards hanging from the branches waved at them as they stole on.

Digging a hole in search of earth, they found, a few inches below the surface of loamy crust, only the ubiquitous white flinty sand. Nowhere had anyone seen a rock, or even stones; sand, sand everywhere . . . It seemed therefore that they would have to go farther down the Cape before they discovered the real earth capable of growing good crops.

Every other minute someone fearfully said, "Listen! Whist . . ." and they stood for a few moments peering about and listening.

Now the early winter dusk was already darkening the air; and they had seen no single sign, no least indication of human life in that place. Of animal life, tracings at the edge of a marshy pond suggested the presence of rabbits and either foxes or small wolves. In fear of being lost in the dark the party retraced its footsteps back to the beach, their hands numbed with cold and the effort of holding their heavy guns, their stomachs empty and their every muscle ready to creak aloud in protest against the un-accustomed exercise.

And what in the Lord's name would they say to the poor people when they got back, Bradford wondered, as they ploughed and stumbled through the loose sand of the dunes and staggered down onto the beach? By all the signs nothing lived in this sandy mockery of a country but the wild fowls of the air.

"What can we tell but of what we saw?" Edward Winslow said. "Or do you not remember your brave words of this morning—that we be content with a desert if it is cast for our lot?"

"Words are easy deeds," Bradford muttered. "Scoffing at ghosts, that is one thing, but meet the risen dead face to face, that is another."

Where they had splashed ashore from the longboat Standish fired off his gun as a signal to the ship and they set themselves to wait, hunched in the lee of a sand hill.

It was almost dark when the boat came for them; the hired sailors had tumbled into it on hearing the signal shot and put off without asking leave of the Captain or crew. The party on the beach shouted for its guidance, paddling out over the flats to meet it. They rowed back in the dark towards the beacon lights of Mr. Jones's stern windows.

16   The first hold was momentarily brightened by an orange glow, as the wood fire in the brazier resettled and red embers fell down upon the thick hearth of sand spread beneath it on the planks. A settler near by rose from his cold bed to pile on more of the fresh, odorous wood of the New World; his face looked up at the open hatch, through which the smoke escaped. Dawn was showing; time to wake everyone up. Hello—a star; a

patch of clear sky was visible through the misty air. And as he gazed, warming himself by the fire, the star faded.

He turned an ear towards the square of light; out in the harbour all seemed silent, the water lapping gently against the hull. A sailor should be on watch above—but he was probably asleep in the shelter of the bulwark, wrapped in his dirty blanket.

In the Great Cabin Mr. Jones sat up in bed, gazing with watery eyes at his candle's flame and holding his hand to his jaw, where his left upper canine throbbed fiendishly. He had reached a point where he wanted to jump up and punch his toothache hard.

And at that moment Priscilla Mullins took her young brother Joseph by the hand, and walked with him out on deck to see what kind of day was dawning; and to allow her father and mother to get up and dress in a private, seemly fashion.

The settler standing by the brazier and watching the sky lighten was about to shout out that it was dawn and time to get up and welcome their second day in the New World, when the planks in contact with the soles of his feet trembled perceptibly. He opened his mouth in surprise, while a further series of more violent tremors shivered through the ship, as if it stood on ground agitated by an earthquake. There was a curious grating—like . . . an elephant rubbing itself against them. An animal—a sea monster! Then to his reeling senses it seemed that the whole ship was being rocked from side to side. His breath came back in a rush and with it he was able to utter an incoherent cry, as he ran towards the after-end stairs to get up on deck; in the course of which he tripped and sprawled over the end of a pallet.

Others had been awake in the first hold when the tremors and the grating noise began, and four dark figures collided, trying to get up the stairs together. The scratching reverberations ceased as the four men cautiously ventured out on the deck and, two of them holding hands in frightened silence, tiptoed to the side and looked over at the sea.

Priscilla was standing near the mainmast, holding the child tightly against her skirts, not daring to move. Through the open cargo hatch with the fire's smoke came women's voices, awakening sleepily, and the whimper of a child; then the sound of Miles Standish's boots coming up the stairs.

It was a calm morning, with a mist lying low on the surface of the sea; and when the men at the side first looked down into the water they could see nothing unusual. They strained to hear, putting their hands behind their ears. Standish, who had been up and dressed an hour before, preparing for the coming day, appeared on deck from the poop hatchway, and Stephen Hopkins, one of the four there listening, called him hush. They all listened. The movements of the harbour water were oily and quiet, long low swells appearing to glide under the surface.

A moment later they all heard a deep and hoarse sound of breathing coming from the sea; then hissings and blowings from near and far, the breathings of strong and mighty creatures surrounding the ship and hidden by the fog. "Hear them now? Monsters, *big* monsters," one of the men whispered. Standish's gaze rose above the poop and his eyes met those of Mr. Jones; then the others looked up and saw him. The Master stood motionless, one hand resting on the scuttle of his hatchway, the other holding a red handkerchief to his jaw. In the pale bodiless light of the morning, framed by the shrouds and rigging and outlined against the sky, he appeared like a timeless idol, set up and forgotten. He heard the breathed words of sea monsters, and nodded slowly and silently; the half of his mouth that was visible folded into a boy's mocking grin. But he said nothing.

Priscilla gasped, holding little Joseph to her closer still.

The ship shivered under a heavy dull blow, as the sperm whale that had lazily rubbed the barnacles on its great square head against the keel flipped its tail and glided, a creature of over a hundred tons and longer than the ship itself, from beneath her. They had at last encountered the physeter. The harbour was occupied by shoals of resting grampuses and whales, lolling, asleep on the surface of the foggy sea.

The girl stood rigidly, staring up at the high deck and the Captain, as if praying to the heavens.

Inspiration leapt to life in Mr. Jones, making him forget even his throbbing tooth. He stuffed his handkerchief away, moving across the deck, bending forward with outstretched hand and whispering loudly, "Keep silent. I'll deal here!" He suddenly straightened and strode to the side, clapping his hands hard and bellowing, "Whoa! Whoa! Whoa!"

A huge black forked tail rose out of the oily water, near enough to be clearly seen, and came down with a mighty smack; a whale slid beneath the surface, leaving the water heaving and tossing. Smacks, bellowings and gurglings sounded all around, quickly moving away into the distance, while the surface of the water about the ship became broken by small tumbling points that washed against the hull.

Standish, knowing the worth of a whale in meat and oil, though he had no near idea of how hard it was to kill one, shouted at Hopkins and they both ran to get their guns—which were stowed conveniently at the end of the first hold. Cold and sleepy people got in their way, but they feverishly thrust them and their questions aside and took up their muskets.

The frightened young settler who had been first on deck stood halfway down the stairs, shouting, "It's monsters, monsters!" until half the children were howling and many of the women screaming. Standish and Hopkins had to pause to quiet them.

John, who had been sleeping with the locker door open since the ship had come to anchor, ran out in his shirt and breeches, his pistol in his hand, and was up on the waist deck ready to repel wild men a few moments after Hopkins and Standish regained the side with their muskets. But the fog was still thick enough to obscure everything from sight beyond twenty yards.

Mr. Jones remained a while longer, uneasily observing the crowd, seeing the story of his dispersal of the monsters pass from lip to lip, until every face was turned to gaze up at him. He tried to look stern and forbidding and unaware of them, yet could not turn away, for at that moment he was the centre of the world. A woman, clutching a young child in a blanket to her breast, pointed out to it the Master on his deck, smiled up at him and timidly waved her fingers.

His round tortoise head came forward, peering palely at one and then another, and he saw that the smiles of the women were smiles of friendly gratitude, and the fact that they were *women*, feminine creatures, caused him such strangely violent embarrassment and upsurging of crass bad temper that could they have seen his face as he turned about sharply and climbed down into his cabin they would have seen that he was blushing even through his leather-coloured cheeks.

John stood before Priscilla, curling his bare toes away from the cold deck, grimacing at his feet and then at her.

"Can anyone see them?" she whispered, looking anywhere but at him.

"Them? What's them?" he grinned, rubbing at the rising goose flesh on his arm.

"The monsters the man in Southampton told of," she said, as if speaking down to the child.

"Them's no monsters," John laughed, quickly sorry for her; her face was white and frightened. "Only fish, girl, big, black fish that needs come up to breathe and blow and give their young suck."

As the morning light increased the fog became less dense. John Billington saw, about thirty yards from the ship on the outer side, a black hump appear gently at the surface of the water, accompanied by what looked like a jet of steam. The people on the deck were silent, listening. "There's one," he said in a hoarse undertone, and pointed. "Save your poor flock, Captain Standish," in part terror and part mockery.

The settlers crowded back as Standish and Hopkins aimed their muskets, each with its slow match clipped over the flash-pan.

John raised his pistol, running to the side, and took a pot shot at the whale; his wheel lock whirred, sparks shot from the flint, the pistol bucked in his hand, going off like a small cannon; Standish's gun misfired, making a red flash in the pan, casting soot in his eyes; Hopkins' gun exploded with a dull and violent roar, and fell to pieces in his hands, the stock coming away from the barrel and the barrel splitting in two along its entire length.

As the two reports echoed across the harbour the shoals of big fish sounded and raced for the open sea.

No one on deck was hurt by Hopkins' bursting gun, though he himself was deafened and half blinded for several minutes, burned on the hands and rendered pitch-black in the face.

Captain Standish flew into one of his quick tempers, exclaiming that Hopkins' gun had exploded simply because there must have been several previously unexploded charges in the barrel. Only by virtue of the grace extended to fools and children had he escaped having his head blown off, not to mention the danger to innocent bystanders. The little military leader stamped his foot, wagged his bright red beard, and shouted hoarsely and furiously; Hopkins, half stunned by the explosion, blinked at him out of his coal-black face, dazed and astonished.

John was the only one present who seemed to see anything funny in the scene. The deck had now become packed and no more could come up. They listened to Standish's tirade with absorbed attention and solemn faces, like people in a theatre.

"Did you shoot the monster?" Priscilla asked John, at last looking him straight in the face.

"Dead as a doornail. Didn't you see him sink?" And he tried to sound careless and as if she were but a casual bystander he had never spoken to before; unfortunately, in nothing but his shirt and breeches, his teeth were by then chattering with the cold. "My pistol here is no penny firecracker, but the finest made."

She went back to her parents' cabin with a pleasurable sense of pride, repeating in the back of her mind: He wanted for to kiss me—he killed the whale—he wanted for to kiss me—dead as a doornail!

There was no question of observing their first Sabbath in the New World as a strict day of rest; time was too precious; God would understand.

The day set in blowing coldly; later, between rainy periods, the sun shone at rare intervals. But when the sun did shine even the dullest were aware of the crystal quality of the atmosphere.

John, with Francis Eaton and a dozen helpers, all with some little if not very useful experience of carpentry, were sent ashore to the spit to begin assembling the shallop. The timbers had been unloaded the afternoon before, lashed together and towed to the beach, while Standish and his party had made the first exploration. Behind them they had a guard stationed with primed muskets; five men were also sent to watch on the sandbank connecting the spit—or as they had already christened it, Long Point —with the main beach.

The leaders through Governor Carver began from that day to institute a rough form of local government. Parties were organized to draw water from the pond and freshly dug sand wells, cut wood, check and list goods and the remains of the food store, set up a sick bay where those who were ill, six in number, could be cared for all together at the end of the main hold, overhaul hooks and lines for fishing, and arrange personal goods and chattels for unloading. They expected to find a site for settlement within a fortnight, allowing five or six days to rebuild the fishing shallop.

Of the hooks and lines it was pointed out by Mr. Clarke, kindly enough, that all their hooks, besides being eaten by rust, were far too large to catch anything but porpoise or shark; for which Mr. Martin was wholly to blame, though he protested, shivering from a chill, that Mr. Cushman had bought them, and Mr. Cushman, having turned back at Plymouth, was not there to answer the charge. So the smith must set to and try to fashion smaller ones from iron wire as best he could.

The ship, sitting so calmly within the encircling hook of land, was a busy house in which there was little or no privacy now that the sea noises were no longer present to drown everything but the loudest shout. Mr. Jones had his Great Cabin, but ears quickly became so accustomed to interpreting sounds through the bulkhead partitions that he might as well have performed most of his private actions in full view on the poop deck. He was not a person of gentle movement. They knew when he was eating within his cabin, sleeping, reading, talking to himself—and now, especially, when he was distressed and in pain. The second day in Cape Cod Bay began with sounds of his walking back and forth, calling for hot water to stupe his face, and moaning as loudly as if he desired the sympathy of every soul on board.

When the boat builders had been put ashore on the near spit the settlers asked to have the longboat to go over to the main beach across the harbour. This the Master refused point-blank.

His temper was against his tooth, that it dared to hurt him so agonizingly and fill him full of fear that he was going to die, and this he displaced upon the luckless settlers as if their asking for the use of the longboat was the very cause itself of his tooth flaming in his jaw.

First, he would have them know that he had not forgotten their conduct on the previous day when, trusted with the long-boat to carry them a musket shot to the spit, they had made off to the other side of the harbour, defying him in his face. There-fore, and secondly, let them bend all their energies to seeing that the shallop was builded as speedily as could be. The rest of their energy they could devote to getting themselves and their goods in shipshape order for that near day when they'd go ashore lock, stock and barrel. He remembered having heard, he said, that the entire end of the Cape was nothing but sand all the way up for five or six miles. He had to shelter in the harbour with his damaged ship, he repeated, until the fishing shallop was finished and with it a safe harbour across the bay on the main-land discovered, but in the meanwhile he meant to allow no waste of time through the fine gentlemen taking Sunday walks. When the shallop was ready they might rest assured that he would set out exploring parties in proper style, covering more parts of the coast in one afternoon with the sailing boat than could be seen on foot in a month.

His attitude seemed completely incomprehensible to the set-tlers. Here was the land, and yet he did not appear to want them to go on it. For what harm could follow if those unable to work on the shallop spent their time walking down the Cape? If trouble lay in store for them there, better they found it sooner than later. There could well be good fat growing land a half a day's walk away for all anyone knew. And if they discovered in-habitants these same, could they but somehow communicate with them in signs, might indicate where lay the best untenanted land, whether on that far mainland that could be seen from the rigging, or on the Cape itself.

The settlers' ambassadors were interrupted by the entry of Giles Heale; he was the purser and sailmaker, and was supposed handy enough to act as ship's physician in dire emergencies. He appeared at the door very timidly and apparently unwillingly, and, moaning with pain, Mr. Jones waved the settlers out.

What took place in the Great Cabin then was known from one end of the ship to the other, in exact detail, even as it was happening.

Mr. Jones had concluded that, rather than die in agony, he would have Heale draw the tooth; for certainly the pain of pulling it could hardly be worse than that which he already suffered in every particle of his face and skull.

He sat squarely, gripped the edge of the table with both hands, threw back his head, closed his eyes tightly and opened his mouth wide. At the first trembling touch of the cold iron pincers against his sensitive canine, he bellowed and pushed the sailor away with a sweep of his arm. Then they took the cold out of the pincers by holding it near the charcoal brazier, and Heale tried again, this time with Mr. Jones standing up.

The purser managed to grip the brown tooth with the corners of his pincers' jaws; an excellent tool for drawing six-inch nails out of planks. Mr. Jones panted with the frenzied terror of a drowning man, holding Heale by the shoulders. Trembling nervously, the purser gave a gentle tug, while the Captain's fingers dug into his shoulders until he squirmed, and tugged harder. "Let go! Let go!" Mr. Jones howled. But the purser was then too frightened to do anything but hold on. They swayed around the table like drunken dancers, till the smooth jaws of the pincers slipped from the tooth, and Mr. Jones was free to fling the purser to the other end of the cabin. He pulled him to his feet by his neckcloth, opened the door and pitched him forth, picking up the rusty pincers and flinging them after him. Then he fell upon his bed, moaning and wiping away his tears of pain.

There was no order against being rowed to the near spit where the boatbuilding was proceeding, so Bradford and Standish gathered a party together there on the beach, with the intention of walking down the spit, continuing along the sandbank and getting onto the main Cape that way. At that time, eight o'clock in the morning, the tide was fully out; they removed their shoes and stockings and paddled ashore from the longboat, over the mud and grasslike seaweed, from which, when trod on, clams squirted muddy streams.

John was working on the boat with Eaton and their helpers, laying the keel and sorting out the pieces; Gilbert was one of those standing musket guard near by; and Sam Fuller had remarked mysteriously that he had "some business of God's" to transact with the Captain; otherwise the party was constituted the same as the day before: Standish, Bradford, Edward Winslow, Hopkins, White, Billington, Martin, Allerton, eight men.

Half a mile along the spit's beach a large expanse of sand and mud flat opened out on their right, a square mile patched with seaweed that stretched between them and the real head of the Cape, and now exposed by the ebbing tide. Thinking of the already abused leather of their shoes, they did not venture to cross it but continued on and crossed over by the dry sand of the connecting bank. Here, for the space of a mile, they were exposed to the open Atlantic winds, and plodded on as fast as they could, till they had come around the full half circle and onto the main beach that faced the ship like a white crescent, the little hills on the head of the Cape rising up on their left to a sandy ridge something above eighty feet above sea level.

"Each of us," Bradford said, "will keep a strict watch for any movement of men amongst the trees, for signs of men living here, and note where we may take wild fowl or other food." All watched the sand anxiously for any sign of a footprint. To know even that savages lay in wait to murder them would have been a relief; where savages lived they were sure they could also live. Bradford prayed for a sign of human life, any sign, in that primordial and fearful landscape that surely was the same as existed before God created man to till the ground and banish the terror of utter loneliness.

At the sea's edge they examined a wine-coloured jellyfish, over a foot in diameter; then turned up the beach, crunching over razor-clam shells, and crossed the dunes. Their plan was to ascend to the top of the head and get a comprehensive view of the whole end of the Cape.

Very soon their hopes of keeping their feet dry vanished, as they had to pass over swampy ground, skirting desolate ponds where tall flags grew, before getting onto the higher ground. Then the land was all small hills and fissures, covered sparsely with bushes, briars and small trees. Some of the bushes carried grey berries clustered on short twigs; they were creased, waxy berries, with a beautifully odorous, spicy smell. "These we will call the *bayberry*," Stephen Hopkins said. He found them so waxy that the tallow easily rubbed off on his salt-hard shoes.

Not twenty minutes after Mr. Jones had flung the purser out and his pincers after him he was disturbed by an authoritative knock on his cabin door. Samuel Fuller entered, bid him good morning and closed the door behind him; he advanced to the table as briskly as his ambling gait allowed and there, uninvited, deposited his linen roll containing surgeons' instruments, and a small green bottle.

Outside, some of the women edged down the passage, to listen.

Seated by his glowing charcoal brazier, set under an open poop window, Mr. Jones was warming his aching face and beginning to drink a mug of brandy to dull the pain. He twisted his bullethead around and stared at the intruder.

"This is fine comfort you have," Fuller commented expansively, rubbing the side of his long nose. "And room for a man's head without banging it off the beams!" However, he thought, the Master might keep his floor a little cleaner, and not walk grease and lumps of biscuit into it. He glanced about with a pleased expression at the chairs, chests, books, and the low, roomy bed screwed to the decking.

Some minutes before, Mr. Jones had burst out into the passage and shouted at some children running up and down making a noise; at which a woman settler had appeared from the waist deck and called him a "black-faced villain." If this wart-ridden skeleton was come to complain, then by the living God, Mr. Jones swore, he'd take to violence.

"What leave have you to walk into my quarters?"

"I thought you'd care for to have your pain gone," Fuller said, almost gaily. "Indeed, you know, sir, the whole ship is anxious for your condition."

"Anxious for my decease," Mr. Jones snarled, with as cowing

a snarl as he could effect with his stiff face. He would have told him to get out there and then, but there was a certain comfort in having a human presence to snarl at.

Sam nodded benignly, clasped his long fingers together and scratched under his stubbled chin with his horny knuckles. "Foul humours of the body, like those of the soul," he began, casually, as it were, "are usual to be accompanied at their cleansing by much pain of the body or soul, as all experience teaches us. But I am not one of those who preach that suffering is necessary for man's good *in every circumstance.* God's good for man works differently. There are many who believe that travail and pain is the only path to the beauty of Godly knowing, as if we were created for no other purpose than to burn in hell. But suppose a man escaped a great pain by having his festering tooth drawn, let us say, with no hurt to him at all, would he not be just as likely to see God's goodness in sheer thankfulness? Of course you will understand," he added a little sharply, "that it was therefore needful for me to argue with myself, to wrastle a long while before I came to the belief that sometimes it is a good thing to, let us say, draw a tooth without pain—*and then go forth and learn how this delicate thing might be done!*"

"It cannot be done," Mr. Jones asserted, trying to hide his intense interest in Sam's discourse. "I've had enough truck with your class of physicker today to last me a lifetime. If your kind's power was as great as your wind and spit we'd none of us have a moment's ill."

The women outside listened, tensed and still as statues.

"Certainly, a man cannot be relieved of his pain if he will not have it," Sam said, "nor even resolve to give it trial. So he must be left to beat the air, and there's an end to it." He began to gather up his little green bottle and linen roll of tools, as if to depart; but this he had no intention of doing until he had dealt with Mr. Jones as he intended, tooth and soul.

Mr. Jones finished the brandy and threw the mug down on the floor. "A man that says he can take a tooth from another man's head without pain should be flogged for his lying presumption."

"No man can know the joys of being a good man, until he has

231

been a good man," Sam continued, in his pleasant, ambling way. "And many a man will not go towards the joyful state of being a good man because he fears it is something terrible and hard of accomplishment; no more than he will take courage to have a tooth drawn, though it makes his life hell's misery itself."

"If you, sir, would leave preaching and tooth drawing separate, you might have yourself understood clearer. For how dare you come to stand in my cabin and preach at me as if I were as without knowledge of religion as a savage!"

"And so you are," Sam would have liked to have said, but smiled instead, brushing away a drop from the end of his large, beaked nose. "It is a weakness in us all, to preach the way," he said. "So you must bear with us for what we are—if only for the sake of being mended. I wish myself to attain to being a good man, a good and a tender man, holding all men as my brothers, which," he added, looking down pointedly at Mr. Jones with an openly ironical expression, "which would be well-nigh impossible if I did not constantly remember what poor fallen creatures we all are. But there are rewards, we fondly hope—rewards like having a pit of flaming pain in your face, and then having it gone . . . we all search for courage, to do in the end what it is easier to do than not to do!"

Mr. Jones had not eaten that morning, nor slept the night before, and the brandy had gone quickly to his head. His cheeks glowed like two red shining apples in their frame of black hair. "Courage!" he exclaimed, beating his breast and letting his head sink down. "Courage—we are all cowards."

"Alas, that is true." Sam laid down his bottle and roll again quietly. "To be cruel to others is easy—but to ourselves, ah, there's the rub." He moved around the table and stood by the Captain's bent back. "Yet *you* are a brave man . . ."

"Hush," a woman in the passage whispered, "listen to that!"

"I am a cowardly man," Mr. Jones moaned hoarsely, dribbling on his hands.

"So we all are," Sam consoled him, patting his shoulder. The Devil's curse of strong drink . . . well! How men abused the gifts of God. "Until we know that it is easier to do a white act than a black one. Come, I'll give you a potion to remove the pain." He took up the mug from the floor, half filled it with brandy from the bottle on the table; then shook his own green bottle vigorously. Mr. Jones raised his face and watched him anxiously as he measured drops from the green bottle into the brandy, nodding to Sam's counting of the slow, oily drops. ". . . seventeen, eighteen, nineteen, twenty, there!" Mr. Jones's pale eyes were unusually moist-looking.

And that, Sam said to himslf, should lay a horse on its back. Indeed no, he amended, a horse was a delicate creature compared to men. Well, he added, it'll lay the Master on his back, I pray God. "This potion," he said aloud, "is of that called opium, which is got from the poppy that grows in the East. I learnt of it in the university at Leyden, when in Holland doing penance for the King's sins."

At which mention of Holland Mr. Jones stiffened slightly, and then forgot it, as he was handed the mug.

"Swallow it down," Sam said kindly, "to the last drop." He stood by while Mr. Jones swallowed and gasped and gulped in the mug, and coughed violently. The Master stood up, swaying, and slapped his chest. "Now it is best to lay down flat," Sam advised, taking him by the arm to the bed. Mr. Jones suffered himself to be helped down onto the bed, and have his head raised and a pillow put beneath it. "Close your eyes," Sam said, "and be as if you are going to sleep."

"He has put him lying on the bed," it was reported out to the deck.

"You are a man of conscience," Mr. Jones mumbled, feeling deadly sleepy and dazed. "And you swear you can draw a tooth without pain . . . I will not be hurt; I will die first. If the pain ceases I can keep the tooth . . ."

His mumbling grew deeper and more drawn out. Sam turned his back to him and unrolled his implements; it never did to let the patient see the tool, if that could be avoided. He took from his roll a large Italian forceps with rounded jaws, adjustable with a thumbscrew—which he had also picked up in Holland—and slipped it up his sleeve. Then he drew up a chair to the side of the bed and asked the Master to open his mouth. "So as I may look at it and give you a true report. Come, there—wide open!"

233

Mr. Jones's breathing had become long and restful. When he closed his eyes he swam dizzily in a warm dark sea of forgetfulness; again it was as if he were forever tipping back in a rocking chair, always just on the point of sinking backwards into blissful oblivion; all his pain was gone.

"Just here it is?" Sam asked, gently touching the swollen side of his face. "Put your finger to it."

Mr. Jones, after several efforts, managed to raise his arm and touch the offending tooth; he gurgled words of nonsense like a child talking in its sleep. Sam said a silent and fervent prayer for the safety of his fingers, and inserted them in the Master's mouth, talking soothingly. Very gently, with forefinger and thumb, he started to press the gums behind and before the tooth, to deaden it, gradually increasing the pressure. Mr. Jones began to move his head a little from side to side and grunt, opening his sleep-heavy eyes. For safety's sake Sam deftly propped a wooden gag in the other side of his mouth, and further increased the pressure of his fingers.

After three or four minutes he took his forceps from his sleeve, slipped the jaws behind and before the tooth, and tightened the thumbscrew. Now he felt that having to treat a grown man as a baby was disgusting. Here Mr. Jones showed weak but definite signs of life and tried to push him away, grunting and moaning unintelligibly.

"Jesus, my Lord, protect me," Sam said aloud, with some emotion. He placed his left palm firmly on Mr. Jones's forehead, gripped the forceps with his right hand, and pressed his knee and shin decidedly down on Mr. Jones's lower middle. Yet it was no such uneven battle as the purser had engaged in. Sam had drawn many a tooth, though not with the help of opium, and knew precisely how to loosen a tooth while retaining a sure grip of it.

Mr. Jones still had enough senses left to utter a feeble, half-choked scream of rage and terror, but could never quite get sufficiently back from the edge of oblivion to marshal his strength and throw off the fiend that clung to his tortured face. On the other hand he could not be quite sure that it was *his* face that was out there so far beyond him and dimly suffering the tortures of the damned.

The women outside moved away from the door at the low sounds of the Master's half-choked cries; now surely Sam was choking him to death on the bed. But their fearful curiosity brought them back, closer than ever, a few seconds later.

Sam's breath came fast and he grew quite warm with the exertion. Mr. Jones's teeth were strong, though not large, and rooted most firmly, for he was still a comparatively young man. God forgive me, Sam thought, for this which I do. It was a horrible great swelling Mr. Jones had, but if left to itself it should have gone down in a week, and as the tooth had only a small hole at the side, ten to one the trouble would have cleared itself up completely if left alone. But drawn the tooth must be, for the sake of Mr. Jones's soul and for the sake of his relations with the settlers. Though Sam might later feel guilty over the morals of his action, he was then convinced that Mr. Jones would one day be thankful from the bottom of his heart for the loss of his tooth. But surely a tooth for a soul was a good exchange any day?

Bending on his forceps back and forth, he felt the tooth loosen in its socket. Mr. Jones's hands clutched at him weakly and his watering eyes bulged. Sam gave the tooth a final loosening twist and pulled it out cleanly. Mr. Jones almost swallowed his tongue, coughed it free, and lay limply, breathing hard.

Sam turned him on his side, placed his handkerchief between his cheek and the pillow, and covered him up warmly. "Now, sir," he said close into his ear, "you needs rest yourself and try and sleep. You have had *no* pain, and you will have no more pain. Let the matter drain and spit it out."

The Captain half turned his face into the pillow. From his blubbering Sam caught the words ". . . stay . . . stay . . ." So he drew up the chair again and sat by the bed.

A little later he gave the patient a drink of warmed brandy and water, with a few drops of opium, and a half an hour after the extraction Mr. Jones was asleep, breathing deeply through his open mouth and occasionally uttering a little sobbing sigh.

Before Sam left the cabin he placed the tooth conspicuously on the centre of the table.

Outside, he shooed the women away, nodding and smiling. "Fear nothing, good wives, the battle with the Devil is well begun and half over—soon we may expect in his place a shining angel with a black beard."

Half an hour of slow and erratic ascending brought the exploring party at last to the highest part of the Cape's head, which was no more than seventy or eighty feet above the sea's level. Looking north, away from the ship and the bay, they saw a gently sloping desert of wind-blown sand stretching down to the open Atlantic. At moments the air about them was thick with dust and stinging sand, forcing them to all but close their eyes. Far away on their left, across the sea, was the mysterious line of coast, the mainland of America.

From where they stood, amidst the last of the sea grass and shrub oak, it was possible to see over the entire head of Cape Cod. In a boisterous and bitter wind, closing their eyes to slits against flying sand, they saw that they were upon a huge curled hand roughly triangular and about three miles across at its widest. The arm of the Cape curved away from them towards the mainland, sinking almost to sea level at the wrist, rising again, apparently thickly wooded on the broadening forearm, ten or fifteen miles away.

A green and wild Atlantic broke on the bar around the outer side of the Cape. For half a mile out it was a mass of white breakers roaring over shoal ground and tumbling in broken foam to the strand. Out beyond the mile of sloping desert sand that composed the northern half of the Cape's head, coots and other seafowl rose and fell over the white-topped breakers. The sun burst out for a brief spell, turning the grey-green ocean a sparkling blue and touching the tops of the rollers with rainbow tints.

"Praise God," Martin said hoarsely into the roaring wind, "this is a wild, a terrible country!"

The Master had spoken the truth when he had said that the inner harbour was a haven, a calm pond in a wild ocean.

At midday Mr. Jones was still snoring heavily. Sam, looking out across the harbour, thought he could discern the exploring party on the top of the Cape, and offered a prayer for their safety.

For the fact of being denied an hour's use of the longboat their trip entailed walking all the weary way around the harbour by the sandbank and back again, three miles there and three miles back that could have been covered with little or no effort in the boat. And on the spit the building of the fishing shallop was not going forward as speedily as had been supposed possible; he had been across to John and the boatbuilders in the small jollyboat, to learn that the portions of the shallop had become so decaulked and damaged by people lying in them throughout the voyage that the job would take not less than a week and possibly more. . . . A week, when their very lives depended upon having a coasting boat immediately. Sam's thought ranged anxiously back to Mr. Jones. Having done the deed, he had fallen to doubting. The tooth drawing might have some effect, but he did not now feel inclined to rely on it making any difference whatever; the Captain might be too far gone to the Devil for a single operation to bring him back as much as a step. For Sam was keen-witted enough to realize, or at least feel, that if the Captain's intractability was a hate and fear partly based on a sense of wrongdoing—because of his harsh and stupid treatment of them —he was likely to sink deeper in vileness as time went on, in sheer self-defence. Therefore the long-awaited advantage of the tooth drawing must be followed up, the treatment extended without respite until he was well and truly wrung from the Devil's grasp. Samuel Fuller would rather have died than admit that any man lived in the world and had not a spark of grace in him somewhere. But every man that had come against Mr. Jones so far had failed. Every man? The corners of his wide mouth lifted, and as the idea developed his eyes lightened and he gave the sea a knowing wink.

Thus it came about that Mr. Jones returned to the world from his deep sleep to find Dorothy and Priscilla tiptoeing about the Great Cabin, tidying, wiping and sweeping. He lay on pretending sleep for several minutes, alternately fuming and relenting, in his thoughts scattering the presumptuous busybodies forth with a shout, only to feel grateful for their presence the next moment; until necessity became so pressing that he had at last

237

to move. He moved, making an embarrassed noise, "Har!" clearing his throat. "Har!"

"Oh, Lord save us," Dorothy exclaimed mildly, "the man's awake."

This one was a charming little thing, Mr. Jones had admitted to himself when he had lain looking at them through his eyelashes; a pity he liked the other one better. They were neat, the fanatics' women, their woollen and serge dresses homely without being dull, their hair always combed and tied back in a ribbon. The Mullins girl did not look at him; with her back turned she was hastily rubbing at his big chair with a rag. As he sat up he suddenly became aware of his left jaw and touched it with his finger. It was sore but the tooth was gone.

Dorothy laid down the shirt she had been folding and came over to him, looking at his face both inquisitively and sadly. "Mr. Fuller asked us to tidy up," she explained, "and to be here to look after you when you wakened." She handed him a cup of water as if he had asked for it.

Mr. Jones felt suddenly relieved; she spoke simply, like a child; there was no mocking laughter waiting to burst out, no viciousness, no slightest sign even of resentment. He wanted to stand before her and examine her face closely. Instead of which he set down the cup of water, sprang up and walked straight to the door. His head instantly began to throb and feel heavy on his neck. He turned for a moment, snorted in his bull fashion, waved his short arm at them and said with a touch of mockery, "Do not let me disturb you ladies!"

The door closed behind him and Priscilla threw down her cleaning rag. "Now do you believe the man a very toad? He's a bad, wicked, ungodly man. Do you see the way he looks at *me*? I shouldn't have let myself be so lowered as to be persuaded by your Mr. Fuller. We'd best not be here when he comes back."

"Are you going to leave me?" Dorothy asked. "That wouldn't be at all proper. Sam said we must treat him with womanly tenderness."

"We are both going," Priscilla said firmly. "We have finished our work, whyever should we remain longer?"

"I think," Dorothy said patiently, "that we should speak with the man, vile man though he be. Surely that was part of Sam's purpose?"

"You are free to do as you wish, I have more respect for myself. . . . The smell of this quarter," she added lamely, "makes me sick."

"We all smell nowadays." Dorothy shrugged and turned to the charcoal brazier, bending over it and blowing.

Priscilla frowned perplexedly at her back, her long pale face becoming stubborn and therefore very young-looking. She poked her head out to see that the passage was clear of Mr. Jones, and hurried to her father's cabin.

When the Master returned several minutes later he found Dorothy standing by the brazier, which was glowing brightly. "The cook has your dinner ready," she said. "And if you want it now I'll tell him." The Master did not appear to know what to say. "That is your tooth on the chest." She pointed.

He picked up his tooth and examined it with immense interest, while watching her out of the corner of his eye. She came and stood by his elbow and pointed at the tooth with her little finger. "There's a hole there, and there's the badness on the top that caused your pain." But still he said nothing. "I'll tell Tandy you are ready for your dinner."

"Wait," Mr. Jones said, as she was going. He lifted the lid of the chest and took out a couple of shrivelled lemons. "Good for all manner of sickness," he said curtly. "Give one to the other wench. And be pleased not to make a practice of coming in my quarters but when I request it. Here, take your medicines with you."

Dorothy took the lemons and proceeded out, too hurt to speak. Priscilla was peeping from her cabin door, her mother standing behind her. "Mr. Jones sends you some medicine." She thrust the lemons into Priscilla's hands and went on.

Well, Mr. Jones said to himself, banging the table with his fist, the Captain's quarters are the Captain's quarters, not a kitchen for women to come and go in as they please. But he was glad he had given her the lemons. He got out a mirror and looked at the gap in his teeth, feeling his jaw and nodding wisely. All a matter of courage, he said, nothing more. A man can have an arm cut off if he has the courage to let it be done. But at the same time he was struggling at the back of his mind to cast out from his imagination the memory of Sam's face, benign and earnest, humorous, likable, and the echo of the lanky fanatic's voice: "Many a man will not go towards the joyful state of being a good man because he fears it is something terrible and hard of accomplishment; no more than he will take courage to have a tooth drawn though it make his life hell's misery itself." He banished the echo by stamping up and down and cursing furiously.

Gilbert came aboard from guard duty to take his midday meal and, seeing Dorothy standing on deck looking across the harbour at the head, stopped awhile to speak to her and reassure her that in the event of any danger overtaking the exploring party their gunshots would be heard on the ship.

"That should prove most consoling, Mr. Winslow!"

"If they would bide themselves in patience a few days, till our boat is ready, they would seek out the land with little or no danger."

"It is the danger they are in now, a handful of silly, simple men, wandering abroad . . . the savages laughing at them and waiting . . ."

He tried to take her attention from the Cape across the harbour. "Some of our men dug up clams this morning and eat them in their hunger for fresh meat. But they're feeling very sorry for themselves now!"

"Oh, Gilbert, what heroes they all are!"

"To eat clams out of the mud?"

"To be venturing by themselves over there." While she, she would not accept the pains of a heroic life, pretend to be cheerful, and full of hope.

"And how is the Captain behaving himself?" he interrupted her again.

"Don't speak to me of that vile, ill-mannered man. If the ground opened under him and swallowed him I'd look the other way." She reverted to her general woes. Half the ship would go back now, if they'd but admit it. But they had a certain roughness to protect them, an ability to go on blindly in this mad and

240

disastrous adventure, able to live like rabbits on top of each other. To Gilbert she poured out her detestation and scorn, her horror at that grey and windy and sandy New World. A New World! Why had they not simply banished themselves to the salt marshes of England's Wash?—it would have been so much nearer. They might think themselves all fine adventurers but for her part she'd rather be in England with a fire and a kitchen of her own. And when she thought of William Bradford in the innocence of youth throwing up farm and land to fly about the world for "principles"! . . . No, no, she was not one of the chosen people who set their faces to the desert. "I hate it, I hate it!"

Before he could gather his wits together, after so unexpected an eruption in her mild-seeming nature, she had turned away, to run to the hatch, and gone below. He followed, determined to console her, so pitying and tender that he cared nothing about what might be said by the good-living settlers' wives.

Blue with the cold, the exploring party descended the head, back the way they had come. At least they had proved that the whole head of the Cape was useless as land on which to build a self-supporting settlement.

"Halt!" Hopkins called out, and pointed with the barrel of his gun towards the distant high ground on the arm of the Cape. "I see smoke."

"Smoke it is or I'm a Dutchman," Captain Standish shouted, dramatically extending his arm as if to halt an army, although the little party behind him was already standing stock-still. He instantly smelled his slow match. It was out, as was everyone else's, blown out by the Atlantic winds on the head of the Cape. However, the smoke, if smoke it was, appeared to be well beyond ten or fifteen miles away.

The haze of smoke suggested a very large fire; which meant that there were human beings on Cape Cod other than those from the *Mayflower*. And the savages could hardly be unaware of so large a thing as a ship, sitting there in the harbour.

A whole day at least would be necessary to get to where that trace of smoke appeared out of the woods, and another day to get back. On the morrow, they decided they would try Mr. Jones for the longboat, and outfit their expedition more practically, with food and camping implements—a few hours out on the Cape made a man uncomfortably aware of his empty stomach. The little party proceeded back more slowly, cautiously stopping, peering, listening, looking on all sides for the peeping brown face they expected to find behind every bush, expecting the horrible thud of a barb in the back or a club stick on the neck; or they might come at them in a screeching mob, three-legged, hopping on hands, with single eyes in their foreheads blazing fire, giants with an extra pair of hands where their feet should be and hairy and matted from head to toe. No one spoke of his private terrors for fear of being laughed at; yet each man's fancy was very like his neighbour's. The broken and hilly country they descended through again, with its gullies of sliding sand, sorely tried their soft muscles; and several noses were already red and running, with Mr. Martin beginning to have a painful cough. It was an immense relief to get down amongst the trees again and try to rub some life into their hands.

On the way down Bradford found a small tortoise, which Allerton put in his jerkin to bring back to his children.

17   The next morning, Monday, November the thirteenth, which began the third day in Cape Cod Harbour, those who had not yet been ashore got lifts back and forth in the longboat, ferrying between the *Mayflower* and the boatbuilders on the near beach. While windy, it was a singularly mild day for a northern November, and after breakfast the men on board began to notice a certain concerted activity on the part of the womenfolk, which took the form of getting out dirty clothes and tying them in bundles, binding their hair up in kerchiefs and pinning on themselves warm shawls. The women saw no reason why they should not also go ashore. Near where the boatbuilders worked there was a fresh-water pond, and there they could wash their

clothes and lay them out on the bushes to dry. Every man had something to do, fishing, digging clams for bait, cutting wood, building the boat, et cetera, which gave them an immediate chance to move about and get over what they called their "weakness in the knees." The women rose determined not to be denied the same opportunities.

Bradford thought he knew what the Master would say on getting wind of this, but Sam suggested that they leave Mr. Jones to him for the next few days and even undertook to get the jollyboat freed for their use. The jollyboat only held four but it would be most convenient for the women to go back and forth in it to do their washing. Also the men could use it for fishing. Some smaller hooks had been made and the settlers looked forward to eating fat codfish for supper—a hope in fact that was not to be realized once during all the time they lay in Cape Cod Harbour, named for its abundance of fish.

"I come to inquire if your face be well?" Sam greeted the Master, when he paid his call to the Great Cabin.

Mr. Jones replied that he was as well as could be expected; that all he felt was a sensation suggesting he had been kicked in the face sometime recently by a horse. Sam assured him solemnly that it would pass, holding his clasped hands under his chin, his head on one side; the poisoning tooth was gone and the rent would soon heal up.

There was a tendency in Mr. Jones during the early part of their conversation to turn his back and appear otherwise engaged; and Sam was not unaware that this was due to a certain shamefacedness of the Master's because of his deplorable conduct during the operation. But while Mr. Jones felt that his conduct on the morning before had been a trifle odd, the details were mercifully blurred and lost. There then followed perhaps the first neutral conversation held by the Captain of the *Mayflower* with one of his passengers since the start of the voyage. He asked about the potion used to dull his pain and Sam returned a short and learned disquisition on drugs and alchemy, not one half of which Mr. Jones understood but to which he listened as it were under a sort of self-imposed duress. Nimbly Sam led the conversation around to the jollyboat.

Mr. Jones had no objection to their using the little boat; but to hear him grant this tremendous favour a listener would have supposed that it was to Sam alone it was given. Questions about the use of the longboat, however, brought a different response, given with all the Master's usual egocentric, declamatory self-importance. Contact with what he thought to be learned men, though he would not have admitted them to be so, brought out, as before, every last ounce of pompous phrasing of which he was capable.

"Can you not see that I have every sailor, all and every sailor, working might and main to restore the ship while this fair weather holds, and must watch to appear that I treat them with all care, lest they turn troublesome? The longboat is the crew's safeguard. How should I fare with the crew were you to lose the longboat in some misadventure with winds or wild men? It is their right to always have the longboat with the ship. In a sudden gale this harbour's currents might be our doom, had we not our boat to hand to pull us about and get to sea. When I use it, it is a different matter! But the sailormen like you so little they are forever ready to cry out against you."

But this Sam knew to be untrue, although he could not say so.

"Your own boat will be ready in a day or two," Mr. Jones said. "What is a day? Go hurry it."

There Sam thought it prudent to leave the matter, for the time being.

Sitting on a sandhill above the boatbuilders, his musket by his side, Gilbert was jotting in his notebook. The morning air was so mild that it was not only possible to write but a pleasant occupation, and a very necessary distraction for his thoughts.

NOVEMBER THE 13TH. Before me on the beach John Alden works with a giant's happy energy. I would wish to understand why some have kept their health through the voyage (mine is good, thank the Lord), while others are sick and weak and will certainly fall prey to the scurvy before many more weeks have passed over our heads.

Writing in his notebook helped him to push thoughts of Dorothy back into the darker recesses of his mind, the recurring visual memories of her thin pale face, now grown beautiful to him beyond all power of reason, her gestures, her back as she walked across the deck, the soft throatiness of her voice with its instinctively artful catches and dying falls, the natural grace and delicate femininity that her presence seemed to effuse like a subtle odour. He wanted to write about her alone, everything he could think of, preserving and recording, memories, even futile imaginings of what might have been; anything wherewith to seize something permanent of her. Because at times he was filled with sad and wild forebodings, that their ways would part or she fall sick and die; she was too unchangeably a child, too incapable of dealing satisfactorily with time; it was as if he had some pre-knowledge which told him that her kind did not grow old, or older, their petals fell early or they lived on unchanged for their short spell until a sudden withering and embittering transformed them into something other, so different as not to be recognizable as the former person they were. And when he thought like that he felt a melancholy anguish, that he had found her only to find her lost to him.

But he did not then or ever at any time write the intimate loving remarks he desired to record; it would not be fair to her to have such things in his notebook, to be read by whoever found it if he lost it or himself met an unwarned death. So he wrote carefully and deliberately of everything but her, seeking to forget her for the while and his searchings and anguish for her.

This morning the women began to ship themselves ashore with their two and three months' dirty linen, and now not only their washing but their children. The first over was Mrs. Ellen Billington, a heavy, strong woman, larger and stronger by far than her husband. She is one of those collected up in London by the merchants to give us a full complement. I have no doubt but she is thought of privately (or publicly for all I know) by the more godly kind of wife and wench as a coarse, common and degenerate person. Myself suspects she is the right kind of freedom-loving woman, big and ripe, that many a day has

paid her penny for a place in the playhouse to view the
great deeds and doings of the world. Her voice may jangle
the ear but she is as brave as a lion. This morning she
came to the side and pitched down into the longboat—
already full—a great bundle of washing, not only not asking leave but daring anyone to lay hand on it. Then she
follows it down the side and squeezes herself into the boat
with great jolly jollity, ignoring protests and pushing out
of the way anyone she thought fit. But that not being
enough, she brings after her her two young sons, one of
eight years, Francis, and one of six years, John.

And so she comes on to the shore with them first, and
the two little boys run wild on the sand, while she stands
and shouts back to the women on board not to be denied
and to follow over.

Knowledge of this gets to the other children (in number
about thirty) and hell's hullabaloo breaks out there, so
that in the end nothing will do for the women but to
bring their children with them too. Some of these small
ones stand about on the sands with solemn well-behaved
faces, others run mad like dogs on grass, chased by their
mothers with bundles of washing and fistfuls of soap, till
all sorts itself out and they trip and swarm over to the
pond, leaving the virgin beach a picture of trampled disaster.

And here for history's ear be it noted (and what one of
us is not daily aware that he takes part here in history's
making with every breath), that this virgin beach, the
first we had set foot on in the New World, was trampled
up by a generation that will change the world's face, or
so the hope is—and their parents know so, guarding them
as the absolute prizes of their lives, giving them the very
food out of their own mouths. And there they go running
into the New World: seven boys and three girls between
the ages of ten and fifteen, eleven boys and four girls between the ages of five and ten, three little boys of not more
than three or four years, and two infants in arms; such a
party as you might see any summer Sunday in England

going to the sea's side to play with the sea and eat their bread.

The jollyboat is now brought into play, manned by a capable young fellow who plies to and fro with the washerwomen as fast as he can.

From where I sit on guard I can see the ship, harbour, Long Neck, boatbuilders and the women washing, and have paid no penny for my seat at this great play.

Later I see John Alden take up a little bundle he has brought ashore and laid by and snatch a minute to go over to the pond with it. It unrolls in his hand and it is a shirt. At this time the Master is ashore and moving about the pond like a little king inspecting his subjects, attended by Mr. Coppin with a firearm. John stands by where William Mullins' daughter is kneeling over the water and would appear to offer her this his shirt. She seems to be bothered by his request, looking around to see if there is not some other woman he could go to, but at a word from her mother near by she smiles up at him (to show she has a good heart), takes his dirty shirt and throws it on her pile, turning back to her washing without more ado. He returns to his work.

Jones and Coppin see this, and I swear Coppin says to the Master, "Why do not we also have our dirty linen washed by these foolish women?" They pass by close to my sand hill and Coppin leaves the Captain to go back to the ship, the Captain calling out after the mate to bring some of his the Captain's linen and where to find it.

Those who went exploring yesterday are nursing their sore feet and stiff muscles on board. Some of them appeared this morning, like cripples that had lost their crutches; you might hear their poor joints creaking like old chairs if near to them. They mean to rest today and tomorrow busy themselves about the ordering of the many different kinds of stores on board, sorting out and packing nails and hoes and hatchets and spades, etc., drawing up lists of persons and ordering thereon to what families the single persons will be put to live with to save building extra houses. If on tomorrow evening the shallop is still far from finished they will have themselves outfitted and ready to go exploring again, this time with blankets for sleeping out and food to last several days. Thereafter they will not hang on the Master's pleasure they say, but go around onto the Cape again by foot and proceed down it twenty or thirty miles, to search out the savages. They will light fires at agreed times, to shew the ship whereabouts they are come.

To follow out the comedy of shirts: Coppin comes back ashore, after a while, and he has a bundle of shirts under his arm. The Captain is standing a little ways off from our New World shipyard, watching how the men work fitting together the planks of the boat. The mate shews him two of his, the Captain's shirts, that he has fetched ashore for him. But Mr. Jones looks to have changed his mind about having his shirts washed by womenly hands; it is the presence of Coppin with his own bundle of shirts and smirking face that irks him.

Mr. Jones now says that he does not favourably consider interfering with the settlers' women at all: the ship's crew has remained successfully apart from them and so it must continue. There is a certain slight but unsavoury insolence about this Coppin, who is a big greasy-looking fellow, young in years; he is as big as our friend John Alden. Coppin says they have risked their lives for these fanatics and a shirt washed is small return.

The Master asks him who it is he proposes to have wash his shirts, drawing him out. Coppin gives his own sort of dirty laugh, and says he has a certain nice young woman in mind. "That is as I supposed," Mr. Jones says, changing in an instant and giving him an ugly look. "Well, my man, I will order this for you—but not to your liking! Go to that big forward-looking woman." He points out Ellen Billington. "Offer *her* your linen. If she does not accept it readily, come away. That is then the end of it." I see Robert Coppin's face turn sour and black, while the Captain his own eyes half shut and his face tighten like a small boy daring a big dog and secretly afraid of it. I see now to be true what I had but before suspected to be true: our Master is a little in fear of his savage crew. He flies into contrary moods, ill humours and quick passions to help him deal with them as a Commander should. And his treatment of all men must spring from the same. "Then," says the Master, "as a lesson to you, you will give *my* shirts to this comely young woman you have in mind, telling her they are mine and it is my request. And in the future keep your distance from whatever of these young women you have a fancy for." And so he turns his back on him and walks away like an erect little beetle. If he had any humour he would be smiling, but he has none.

The mate goes too, not before he has given foul looks at the Master's back, and does as bid. Mrs. Billington takes his shirts with no apparent ill humour, and the mate looks about for his next. Our Miss Mullins is some way off laying washing out on bushes to dry and gather the sand in the air. It is to her he goes. And now her mother is not near to make her keep up her nice show of good temper. Whatever he says to her, with winks and grins, it angers her. I do not hear but I understand: he is turning the tables on the Captain by speaking to her in such a lewd manner that she must fly to indignation and reject the Captain's washing as if its acceptance would cast doubts on her chastity. So Mr. Coppin returns to the beach with the shirts to find the Captain, and with insolently solemn face tells him he has been rejected. The Captain says little; sends him back to the ship with the offending shirts. I have enjoyed this comedy of the shirts.

These people insist on being the same as if they were at home in England; but this adventure is going to make many of them very changed men, if I live to see it.

Written on Cape Cod and on the ship *Mayflower* during the week beginning November the thirteenth.

After dark the men worked on by the light of a ring of fires on the beach; the daylight was awaited impatiently in the morning, its going in the evening lamented, the contracting of the days as the season of winter advanced viewed with dismay. By the fourth day coughs and colds were spreading alarmingly; except at high water, going to and from the spit meant wet feet and sometimes wet breeches and shirts.

By Tuesday night they knew that there was no hope of the shallop being finished for another four or five days. The sky remained cloudy but the weather kept dry and tolerable. Day and night a watch was kept for the savages, but still no sign, signal or glimpse of them was seen, though many swore they saw the fleeting movement of a form here or there, which of course could well have been a bush moving in the wind, a scuttling fowl in the tall sand grass. How long, it was wondered, did Mr. Jones intend to stay with them? His answer was, as long as his food stores would allow, which they took to be another way of saying as long as he pleased, or as short.

On Wednesday John and Francis Eaton, the smith and every hand that could be of use to them, were off to the spit and ready to work on the shallop with the first streak of dawn, having been exhorted on the deck by both Mr. Brewster and Governor Carver to work with the utmost speed. A flaming torch carried with them to the shore kindled their fires and the cold dawn resounded with sleepy voices, the clinking of iron and smacking of mallets.

From the off side the fishing lines were hauled in—and the hooks came up as they had been put down.

Near eight o'clock Standish's exploring party began to gather on the deck. As the shallop was not ready they would go again on foot, this time with cheese and biscuit sufficient to last them several days, each man bringing his cape and blanket slung from shoulder and belt with which to cover himself in camp at night. Captain Standish proudly let it be known that his own equipment included a compass of a half a pound in weight housed in a square wooden box that would have held a man's head. They agreed to stay away not more than three days, travelling twenty to thirty miles down the Cape towards the mainland and in that direction in which the smoke had been seen when they had climbed the head. At twelve o'clock every day as near as they

250

should be able to judge the time they would come to the inner beach, visible from the rigging and the spit, and by the water's edge light two fires with an interval of five minutes between, to shew the ship where they were.

Sixteen men, whose health was judged adequate to the journey, were ready to set out: Gilbert Winslow, Edward Tilley, Isaac Allerton, John Billington, William White, Stephen Hopkins, Sam Fuller, Edward Winslow, William Bradford, Captain Standish, John Tilley, Thomas Tinker, Degory Priest, two bondmen, and Master William Mullins—who had proved himself singularly contentious and useless in every task that had been allotted him so far.

Mr. Carver repeated the rules of conduct to be observed and Mr. Brewster refreshed them concerning the rules they had agreed upon to observe in all dealings with the savages: "Our actions towards what people are here shall be different to that of other ships calling at strange parts. Every evil done to savages, no more by Spaniards than by Englishmen, has been excused by a plea of fearing treachery and attack. Do not hurt unless it is to save your life *when you are already attacked,* and even then fire off your arms rather to frighten than to kill. That is the order and rule of our coming. Ships touching have trampled the faces of many a poor savage, but we are come to live in peace and friendship and win their souls. Thus neither must we ever steal from them by the smallest token. The savages will not understand that we are not come to steal without we teach them the truth of it from the very first; so it is as teachers we come amongst them also. We will remember that they are men and that all men have souls. Certainly if they've before known any sea captains or roving sailormen they'll be hard put to it to believe us honest and understand it! . . . But it must be. We will give them something useful and of equal value for everything we get. You will also keep it in mind that these wild men are never to have any understanding of firearms and gunpowder. We are few: that secret is our strength."

It was then discovered that the longboat was waiting to take Mr. Jones and a bodyguard across the harbour, where he intended having a morning out in the swamps on the head, shooting fowl for his table.

The Master on the other hand knew of the party gathered without on the deck, and was hesitating about passing through them to the boat, having refused them the immediate use of it for a much more serious purpose than he intended himself. The soreness had practically gone from his face and he had risen in a good humour; which inclined him to reason that as they did not have their own boat ready yet with which to go around the coast and "discover" Plymouth Harbour it could make no odds if for a day or two they walked abroad on the Cape. He resolved the difficulty by sending Mr. Clarke to them with the information that when he had been put ashore himself he would instruct the longboat's sailors to do likewise for the settlers' party—as they seemed bent on wearing out their shoe leather tramping about the Cape.

He was in fact in such a good humour over his cure that he nodded to the settlers right and left on his way to the boat, going even as far as to call a good morning to Sam in such a way that it took in the rest of the deck. And Mr. Fuller winked at Mr. Brewster.

The Captain and his bodyguard were set ashore on the far side of the harbour, and the boat returned for the settlers' party. Every woman was like a mother running to the door to look after her son. As the longboat lingered by the ship's weather-beaten side while a laggard fetched forgotten bullets and a wife called halt to go and get a leather jacket and make her husband take it because without it he was like to cough his insides up sleeping in the wilds, Dorothy peered down at William, in one end of the boat, and wanted to smile at Gilbert, in the other end. Yet she knew that could she see into Gilbert's eyes clearly she would be frightened. For she had seen something in his face that told her that at any hour, given the right kind of opportunity, he would speak of what had come now to be between them; he might believe that he never would, but she knew better, yearned for it and at the same time dreaded it with a sick fear. She had avoided Gilbert's glance; she must avoid it forever. There sat Gilbert, expressionless, yet self-confident, like an experienced gambler who had thrown down his stake and awaited his fate with a certain amount of world-weary acceptance and curiosity. And there sat William, determined to appear unflinching, forthright, fixed in his aims as the North Star, God's selected vessel; in his heart a boy hurt by the world and oppressed by a strange sense of ignorance and unworthiness. She loved as it was forbidden to love, and did not love he whom she was under a commandment to love. Mayhap after all she had died and come to a cold bleak sort of hell. She coughed and the pain of it racked her breast.

The wives looked down at a boatload of homely little men with pinched faces, who held their heavy firearms as if they expected them to explode in their hands at any moment, fitter figures to gossip under the eaves of a sheltered street than go as warriors to the mountains and the far places; and Dorothy's was not the only woman's breast to contract painfully, if not for the same reason, nor the only female mind to wonder what they were doing under God's heaven in a ship, at that place, and at that moment.

Farewell, they called from the boat, all in muted tones, farewell, Dorothy, Rose, Eliza, Sally, Beth, Ellen, Mary and all.

Keep warm, they called from the ship, keep warm by night, don't be led astray from your being a sensible man. Don't be too proud to run and live to fight another day; and quiet tears wiped away in the corners of scarves. God protect them from lions and bears and falling into holes in the ground, from giants and wild men with hairy brows, and "things."

So the boat moved off across the calm water till the faces in her were indistinguishable. High water had been at four o'clock in the morning; they would have to splash ashore again from the longboat through shallow water.

The party sat on the sand to put on shoes and stockings; from the swamps above the beach a shot resounded, where Mr. Jones fired, missed, and frightened off every fowl for a quarter of a mile around him.

They rose, hitched up their bundles, belts and breeches,

waved to the ship and set off down the beach in single file; which order of march, Captain Standish said, made them look purposeful and not to be trifled with, and also prevented stragglers from straying about; what eye watched them from what bush should carry off a good impression.

From a hill by the side of a pond their setting out was watched by the Master with mixed feelings of struggling resentment and disquiet; their jogging backs, a line of awkward townsmen proceeding in a stumbling heavy-footed march down the centre of a broad flat expanse that curved away before them as if into eternity. Standish saw him, and waved an arm in recognition. Several sailors in the Master's party waved back and one cupped his hands about his mouth and sent after them an ironic cheer.

For the first few minutes when not looking at the white sand flying in the wind from about their feet, sticking in their stockings and filling their shoes, they each and every one felt it a duty to watch the sand dunes to the left; which accounts for the fact that Mr. Jones, four hundred yards behind them, saw the black dots of human figures three quarters of a mile away along the beach before they did. Five or six men were coming along the shore towards them. They saw them without shock, thinking they were some of the Captain's sailors who had gone down the Cape on higher ground and were coming back by the beach.

Gilbert and Edward both had keen sight; shortly they discerned, almost simultaneously, that the five or six figures ahead, now halted in a still group, had a dog bounding about them. "A dog? It is a dog!" They halted while Standish passed about his smouldering slow wick and each set a glowing tip to the end of his own salt-petred cord and clipped it in his gun in readiness.

"Quicken pace," Standish threw back over his shoulder. "Can anyone distinguish their colour or what clothes they wear?" No one could as yet. The figures ahead appeared to be moving towards the sand hills. Standish and Bradford forged on at a jog trot and the ragged line trailed after them with pounding hearts and panting breaths, until Standish himself had to slow down with a stitch in his side. As they progressed, stiff bodies in stiff clothes, holding their guns before them with already aching muscles, a thin stream of smoke from each wick issued into the

254

air, like creatures engaged in some ritual on an open plain, their variously garbed and bound heads thrust forward with straining eyes.

The figures in the distance moved towards the sand hills at a quicker pace, and disappeared. The settlers re-formed their ordered line and marched on steadily, tramping by the water's edge to have the greatest distance between them and the dunes in the event of being surprised. Each dune and clump of scrub and sand grass appeared very much the same and it was impossible to fix a landmark to point where the savages had disappeared; but the sand must tell them all they wanted to know.

In a little more than five minutes they came up to the footprints, where Standish ordered them back until he had made a closer inspection; in the firm sand below high-water mark were the imprints of naked feet and of feet so thinly covered that the foot had made its own imprint through its skin covering; and all about, the imprints of a dog. The track came towards them by the water's edge, stopped short in a huddle of marks, out of which the track of footprints emerged again at right angles to the sea, ran up the beach and vanished in the sand dunes. Here were the savages and if they wanted their friendship and their corn seed they must chase them; while the realization sunk deep that at any moment, around this hillock or the next, they might come face to face with their first savage.

Standish allowed no hesitation; his comments and answers were all of what to do in this situation or that. Some slow matches had fizzled out; they were relit, and the line turned up the beach, following the trail of footprints.

At the back of the beach the sand was soft and sliding, except where held together by sand grass. The Indians' trail ran in and out across the low dunes, which stretched inland here four or five hundred yards to higher, hilly ground where grew undergrowth and trees.

By their splurged and sliding imprints it was obvious that the savages were running at a speed the settlers could not hope to equal. But if the trail continued plain it must lead either to the feet which made it, or, as they hoped, to an Indian village.

With their eyes closed to slits against stray particles of flying sand, the sixteen ploughed over the dunes. The undergrowth and trees were cut into islands by twisting gullies and rivers of sand, ideal for springing an ambush. The trail wound on, the savages apparently making no attempt to hide their footprints either by separating or going through the grass.

Standish slowed his line of men and they proceeded cautiously up through the trees by gullies and small open spaces, some men detailed to watch to the right, some to the left, some behind, and the leaders to the fore, as the column crossed near the Cape's wrist towards the Atlantic side of the peninsula. It was not unthought of that these half dozen they followed were decoys to lead them to waiting hundreds, but it was not given a voice. They were in the hands of God.

They came into a small valley that funnelled the wind, whistling and rustling, through the wizened branches of starved pines, where, above to the left, ran a thinly spaced line of the same trees like leaning sentinels. "Whoo!" mocked the wind, in so startlingly animal a voice that they all looked around and back and halted as one man.

Behind the thin trunks of the line of trees above on their left, a white shape ten foot high reared up and glided after them, nearer and nearer and with a long-drawn whooping and dying cry. Their feet froze in the sand, breaths stopped and cold skin prickled. "Oh, Lord, Lord . . ." someone whispered.

The howling ghost gliding down on them behind the trees vanished in a cloud of sand, no more than a whirling eddy of sand sucked up by the wind into a gyrating column.

"By God, I thought my starry crown was near at hand," Hopkins gasped, and the rest laughed with him in relief, and they went on.

Somewhere about eleven o'clock, the sixteen men were led to the base of the highest hill they had yet seen, and around it, and up the back, seeing how the savages had ascended there out of sight and from the top—here were the marks of their stomachs—viewed the surrounding wilderness and spied on their clumsy pursuers. Then down the hill again ran the footprints, and across another small valley of naked sand, and up its gentle side to a bare ridge.

They paused, and their eyes followed the swooping trail down, and up to the sky line; it was suddenly a more ominous thing there than it had appeared to be anywhere else. For how straight and true it travelled, as if with a purpose; straight to the ridge on the sky line. . . . Did the savages intend to ambush them, then that was the place. From behind the ridge they could leap up and send their arrows down amongst the unsheltered men toiling up through the loose sand.

The ascent to the ridge was not difficult, though the cursed sand slid back from under their feet; two or three minutes would bring them to the top. Aching and numbed in mind and body by the unaccustomed labour of walking and by the cold, windy, rich air, the terror of what could well lie waiting behind the ridge above, outlined against the high grey sky, held the half of them back in the rear, while those in the lead climbed steadily: Standish, Bradford, Fuller, Hopkins, Allerton, and Edward Winslow, shoulder to shoulder, behind their smoking slow matches. Gilbert and the bondmen followed next, then the rest; with William Mullins last, an angular, flapping scarecrow panting in winded distress.

Their feet plunged in the sliding sand; no voice broke the empty silence of insistent wind and space; until the leaders' heads rose to the ridge, guns held forward, tailors, hatters and wool carders, topped it and looked over.

No one. Nothing. Not an ambuscade. The trail of disturbed sand ran away down again into weeds and bushes and brambles; and as they raised their eyes from it they saw the outer Atlantic not a half a mile away, driving its white horses in over the bar in mad fury, and farther out, white fields of shoal water. Their pursuit had brought them from the inner side of the Cape's arm to the outer side. Here, with a clear view all around, they sat down to break their fast.

By that time Mr. Jones had returned to the ship and his sailors spread the news that the exploring party had sighted savages and followed them into the woods. Mr. Carver enjoined the women to trust in God and pray for their men; to which they replied that the husbands, fathers and heads of families should never have been allowed to go while the young men of no responsibilities like John Alden and the hired sailors played at boatbuilding on the spit, and a demand was put forward for a party to go after the explorers and rescue them from being flayed alive by the savages. To which the Governor was tempted to reply that if that was the way they felt they ought never to have come to America; instead, he said that women must keep to women's affairs, and firmly closed the argument.

Mr. Jones spent the afternoon overseeing work in the first hold, where he was having an extra prop lashed under the broken main beam and the whole strengthened and rebound. Unexpectedly he found himself being addressed by a determined Ellen Billington, with other matrons at her back.

"It's this 'ow, sir, that we beseech your honour, sir, to go after them poor fools, our poor husbands—you have your pack of sailors would make short work of any murdering wild men——"

He watched her broad, hairy, masculine face for some moments, its distress thrown into sharp relief by the shadowy half-darkness of the hold, before raising his hand to silence her. "Your people scorn my sailormen no less than myself, spurn my advice —but think to call me as a nurse to wipe your noses! Did I not order them to wait another day for their boat, and with it keep on the waters of the coast? To damnation with them. Go, leave me to my business." But they stared at him like unjustly scolded children, and did not go from before him. And feeling in danger of giving in to speaking kinder words, he scowled and left them there standing.

Washing down their cheese and biscuit-bread with water from a marshy lodgement, the explorers shouldered their guns and travelled on towards the broad Atlantic, until they stood on a crumbling bank above the wild beach. There the footprints ran down through the freshly churned sand of the bank, on to the wide, sloping shore, marking a line on its surface that stretched away into the immense distance where lay the unknown America. There they rubbed their eyes and squinted and saw again the barely perceptible dots, the savages; saw them run until they were out of sight once more.

"They keep a nice distance between us," Gilbert said.

"They knew from the start that we were after them," Edward answered. "I wish to God we could fathom their game—or why they did not go back on the inner beach, the way they had come."

"It could be that we frightened them," Bradford said, voicing the hope that they all held to, without much conviction.

Miles Standish grunted, and led them plunging down the bank and out onto the wind-swept beach. It was between one and two o'clock in the afternoon, they thought, and their twisting course had already covered something between eight and ten miles; men who for two months before setting foot on Cape Cod had not walked more than twenty feet in a straight line.

Travelling down the beach, all sense of time became lost; the air was heavily damp and salty with spray, and they knew not how soon the darkness would fall and force them to crouch down for the night, to sleep on that immense and forsaken landscape. On by the thundering waves led the footsteps of the unknown, and the solitude was of the ocean and desert combined; an army of thousands could not have seriously disturbed those empty spaces of beach, sea and eternal sand.

The afternoon wore on. Their feet dragged over long strands of kelp weed thrown up by the waves, disturbed at every step a host of skipping sand fleas, and the lonely sea birds continued to hover and skim over the spume as if men had not only not come, but never existed. The dunes on their right grew higher, until in their place came cliff-like banks of sand. Three miles along the beach they climbed wearily up the sliding, shelving cliff of sand, to look at the interior. They were passing around the head of a large tidewater creek which began almost on the outer edge of the Cape and ate across it diagonally towards the head of the peninsula, opening out into broad salt marshes near the inner harbour where the ship lay anchored.

On, and on . . . and on . . . and on, the bemusing footprints ran away, forever away before them on an endless beach, until the track attained a hallucinatory fascination for its own sake, and they must plod on drunkenly for weeks, months, because it would not let them stop. And it seemed that they had been weeks already on their feet, lift and fall, up and down, the dead thud of sand under the sole, each foot shod with a leaden boot.

At last the very palpable darkening in the air reached through their numbed senses and they knew that night was coming about them. By then they were travelling past broad gullies that ran inland from the beach, where the coast looked as if it had been beaten and flattened by some tremendous storm.

A straggling, stumbling group of men turned from the savage green and yellow ocean to find a hollow in the coarse grass wherein to lay their weary bodies down; and they agreed that come what might in consequence of it a fire was absolutely necessary; to keep them from shivering to death in the night. Thus, while the camping ground would need to be in the open, for safety, it must be near wood. Their dragging steps were painfully slow. The dusk appeared to fall with startling rapidity.

Spread out in a disorderly procession, they moved inland; and in the half-dark Bradford tripped, clutched at Mullins to save himself, and both slid sprawling down into a hollow. Their fall made no sound, and they were momentarily separated from the main body. Both men rose to their feet to find themselves in a soaring cage of ivory. Mullins stumbled blindly about in terror, fell against the gleaming, arching struts of their trap and the whole structure rocked with the rocking world and collapsed upon them in a heap of monstrous, bleached bones. The elder man's broken voice cried into the night, "God forgive my sins, God forgive my sins, it's death, I die!"

And even after he had been pulled free and it was explained to him that the bones were those of a whale thrown up by a storm, he continued to moan, "Lord have mercy on us, we shall die, we shall die," though they spoke to him harshly to give over his mewing like an old woman.

A place was chosen for the night and the men set about gathering a pile of twigs and dead branches from a wooded valley near by, three standing guard with freshly primed muskets, slow matches glowing in the dusk.

Priscilla sat in the dark on the edge of her bunk, tensed and quivering. Her small brother Joseph slept in his mother's bed a few feet away. The door on to the poop passage stood open. Mrs. Mullins had gone down into the first hold to sit with the other women in the glow from the brazier. Outside the night had almost enveloped Cape Cod and the ship.

Her mother had gone out and left her lying down; the moment of her going she felt to be an age away, as far away as London, Southampton, Plymouth, John the carpenter's kiss in the sail locker. "That was his answer," her mother had said, speaking of the Master, "that we have always and ever scorned him and spurned him. As if any of us ever said one crooked word to him. It is his own wickedness. Not stir hand or foot would he if they were roasting our men there on the beach. Scorned him and spurned him indeed!"

Scorned him. She had turned and twisted on her hard plank bunk, seeing her father's ungainly figure climb down into the longboat, his solemn and disgruntled face, as it pulled away. The men had gone forth into the wilderness with hearts heavy with disquiet. And the savages had played them on and led them down into their country, led them on to where they waited in their screaming thousands. And Mr. Jones would not send after them or give the boat for others to catch them up and warn them of their folly, because she had scorned him by not washing his shirt.

It was simple plain. Nor would the Master go out in the morning with his careless, cursing sailormen, to find Gilbert Winslow and Masters Mullins and Bradford and all, because the Captain had singled her out ever since Plymouth, sent her presents of lemons, and she had scorned him. That was the real meaning of his answer! Her guilt and fear choked her and she began to cry. She would be the cause of her father's death and of a great and general disaster, punished because she was wilful through life, wanton, sinful in her secret heart. She stood up at last, trembling all over hysterically, biting her knuckles and swaying her head from side to side as women did in other times and places when whipped to religious frenzy by the rasping or hotly passionate voices of men preaching the nearness of doom and descent to the flaming pit.

Mr. Jones, with a candle on either side of the table, bent over his chart of New England, and inked in a cartographic correction of the shape and length of Long Point, otherwise the spit at which the prow of the *Mayflower* then pointed. Correcting the self-vaunting Smith's "fair discoveries" ought to provide him with many hours of pleasure in the weeks to come.

The latch lifted and the door opened, but he heard no one enter, so did not look up, until the door closed and the latch fell into place. Priscilla walked in stocking feet across the greasy boards, with short noiseless steps, and stood by his chair. She had not thought to put on her shoes, nor would she, in the state she was in, have remembered or stopped to put on a dress had she been in her shift.

He glanced down at her stocking feet; blue woollen stockings wrinkled on her ankles. The inch off her heels made her surprisingly smaller. And, looking up, he experienced a shock of pleasure: her face was the face of the martyred Christ he had once seen painted in a church in the Low-countries and before which he had stood long in awe with his young cropped head bared and his sailors' jelly-bag cap screwed to a ball in his fist, dumbly struggling to comprehend a first dawning recognition of beauty beyond the flesh. So thus, that face, it was the girl; the skin pure, cleansed, of a radiant paleness, the eyes heavy-lidded and drugged, the lower lip trembling with the merest movement; her unbound hair black in the candlelight, hanging straight down from the smooth crown of her head, touching each cheek, revealing a white cave at her throat and rippling out in soft disordered ends over her breast. She stood with the stiff posture of a wooden image, her hands tremulously clenched and twisting on her thighs. She whispered; perhaps she had been whispering to herself as she entered the Great Cabin.

"Speak up, girl, I cannot hear you," he said at last, his own voice lowered and softened by surprise and acute discomfort now that the shock of her face had passed. But her being a woman, and her beauty to him, was from that moment on somehow connected with God, religion, churches, prayer, and he began to be

262

eased as if from a burden. He heard her whisper and it sounded as if she was saying:

"I am the lamb of God . . ."

After a few moments her voice became normal under his repeated suggestion that she speak clearly; and though pitched on a high, quavering note, yet was slow in articulation. ". . . Love is that. Love is love for all. I love you as I love my father. Christ loved all men, the saved and the sinner."

It went on, over and over again. He shook her arm, perhaps to awaken her, and she took his hand and held it. He saw the whiteness of her forearm in the candlelight, and also a sort of shining dew on her forehead close by the line of her hair, while she lifted his hand and held it against her breast so that he felt her live heart beating. What would she have of him? Why did she come so? Slowly he rose, pushing back his chair with one leg. Why did she come to him?

"You did want me to come. You will not leave them to die in the strange country? I am at your will, stand before you, am all submission."

She seemed to be coming back to a more waking state; it was no longer possible to believe that she might be asleep. How very large were her eyes, he thought, moist and bright with compassion.

"But what is this you expect?" he said, feeling the warmth of her bosom entering his hand through the soft folds of hair.

"You are not spurned—what do *you* want of me? Men would kiss me. Do you want that? Nothing is denied you—oh, believe me!"

Their eyes were on a level; she was no longer taller by an inch than he; and with shivering, warm emotion he stood close against her, looking into her face, his mouth open.

Stretched for the night in a hollow, the long sand grass gathered under them, the explorers prepared to try to snatch some sleep. "Thou must ere long go to the bottomless pit," William Mullins' voice muttered deliriously, as with bloodshot eyes protruding from their sockets he stared about at the dark night outside the rim of illumination cast by the fire. On higher ground at one end of the camp stood Bradford, at the other end Edward Winslow, taking the first turn of an hour to stand guard, the great curved stocks of their matchlocks in the crooks of their arms, smoking cords in their left hands, by which marked lengths they could measure time.

To some sleep came immediately, to others, like Mullins, the aching fatigue of body made resting itself an added torture.

"Sleep, man," Hopkins growled, "sleep!" and fell asleep himself as he spoke.

"The damned increase in sin in hell. There is found no eating, drinking—consider, God Himself shall be the principal agent in thy misery—consider how we must come to a place prepared by God on purpose to exalt His justice. Hell is that place! Our stolen waters shall burn us woundily and our dancing be on fire, fire kindled with the bitter sins, the sins of the damned!"

Mr. Jones continued to look into Priscilla's face, letting the slow tender tide overwhelm him and, as became his absurd and primitive side, felt a sunrise in his breast and in the humming of the wind in the shrouds heard a heavenly choir sing his glory with piercing and confused sweetness. And in his soaring and intoxicated mind her child's voice asked its question, declared its intention. He suffered his revelation to invade him wholly. Time passed. His thought floated together again, the golden rain thinned and faded and he returned to his body in the Great Cabin.

She thought, the child, that the world began and ended with nothing more than a kiss! She was as unaware of the true nature of what she offered as an infant in arms. What more wonderful thing could happen to a man? There was an absolute goodness and innocence in the world past all understanding. He knew it, he knew it at last, and he let the earthquake rock him, and he held on and breathed deeply until he felt secure enough to speak. A fear for her sprang up, an anxious desire to protect her.

"You must go back to your quarters," he murmured. "To be seen here, child—it will not be understood."

"You will not leave them to die?"

"No, no—be assured!" He disengaged his hand clumsily and drew back. "We'll see the smoke of their fires tomorrow. And if we do not, why then I'll set out and bring them back."

Steps sounded out in the passage: the settlers were going to bed.

Priscilla began to feel exhausted, chilled, numb and ashamed. She realized that she had no shoes on, stood in the Captain's cabin with the neck of her dress unbuttoned and her hair loose as for bed. She walked backwards from Mr. Jones, buttoning the neck of her dress, and only then knew what he had said: that if he saw not the smoke of the settlers' signal fires next morning he would go to seek them. And now he was looking at her with a doting smile—not having exacted the penalty of one kiss. . . . Had she loved *him* and all the world with an unbounded love but a little while ago? True, he was not so goatish and frightening when you knew him. Oh, what a problem men were! And her head buzzed and throbbed so.

She gave him a wan smile; and he hurried to open the door—sure sign of his utter overthrow.

"God bless you, sir," she said as sweetly as she could, gazed in bewilderment at his pale swimming eyes, shivered, and glided out.

The Master stood motionless for a little while, before returning to his chair at the head of the table. That he had suffered a conversion he accepted unconditionally. He sat very still, like a man afraid of discovering broken bones after a fall. His whole being felt warmed, enlarged, eased of constraint. These people were no dangerous fanatics! They were but simple children, *all of them*. And somehow it seemed that he had known that for a long time, but had never till that moment been able to admit it. Who but simple children would have brought their wives and young to the uttermost ends of the earth where nothing was but the wild beast and the savage? But they were children of knowledge and wisdom also, however it was.

There was the strange Mr. Fuller, who, as often as you reviled him, was ever ready to turn the other cheek. Mr. Jones absently fingered the gap in his teeth as if it were a keepsake that recalled a fond memory. What a wonder-working lesson! "Many a man will not go towards the joyful state of being a good man because he fears it is something terrible and hard of accomplishment." And Dorothy and Priscilla, when he had awakened! And yes, the whales, and how the women had looked up at him! And the settlers' child that had approached him with a child's soft rambling words of friendliness—from which he had turned as if in shame! There was another world that he had not known, a world in which a girl could be reared in a state of sweet innocence. One of the candles, reduced to a liquid pool in its iron cup, went out. Mr. Jones felt that at last he had come home, after long wandering and tossing on many a dangerous sea; but he must feel his way carefully, making an exploration of his own soul.

"Realize the truth, I beseech you," William Mullins raved, stiff upon his cold bed of sand and grass, "God can be merciful . . ." He muttered and twisted, until he fell into a half sleep, roving in nightmare on a desolate plain of rippled sand that was peopled everywhere in the distance by running, hopping, naked things, half sea flea and half savage. Over in the trees a screech owl defied the wind with his rasping squawk, the blown sand hissed in the grass and the Atlantic beat out its confused and never ceasing roar. The sentinels wore their blankets around their shoulders, listened and peered and at every suspicion threw a handful of dry grass and twigs on the fire—to shew the eyes of the night that they were awake, unafraid, and not to be taken by surprise. Then the stars came out; and Degory Priest, standing his hour's turn, looked up into the universe and remembered his distant, improbable and highly extraordinary life as a sober hatmaker in a hushed little back lane in the snug town of Leyden. Could that have been him? It seemed hardly possible.

So the night passed.

18   In the clear morning light the pounding lines of white-topped breakers stretched along the coast behind them and before them, in a straight line in either direction as far as the eye could see. On that shore, Gilbert said to his brother, a man did well if he managed to conceive of himself as being of more importance than a speck of spray or skipping sea flea.

The footsteps led on, now fainter but still clearly discernible. Not five hundred yards past where they had camped the trail turned up off the beach and plunged inland. Here the country was more wooded and grown over than anything they had so far experienced; but the sand persisted, yellow in the interior, like coarse salt, as it was to persist wherever they travelled on the Cape. It was hard at times to believe that it was all sand. Bradford repeatedly dropped on one knee and shovelled at it with cupped hand; and always beneath it was sand and more sand.

Very quickly it became apparent that the savages meant to lose them here; where they might have gone over easy ground they had deliberately gone through the worst patches of thorn and scrub and dead weed. A dozen times the trail was lost and they went back and retraced it, only to find it came to an end by the swamps at the head of the great creek they had discovered the afternoon before. The leaders' disappointment was a little lessened by the sight of numbers of all kinds of waterfowl about the creek, from water hens to fish hawks and majestic cranes. Standish and Winslow crept away to try a shot for breakfast but hit nothing. On their return the party sat down in shelter for thirty minutes to rest and discuss the situation. From then on it was more than possible that they would be the ones followed, and by the same savages they had been before pursuing; all the more reason then to appear bold and undeterred. The important thing was that they now had proof that savages were on the Cape, and if they continued on down the arm must discover their village or habitations, where they would try to trade for the

267

vitally necessary American corn seed; sowing English wheat would be a useful experiment, but to have to rely on it might mean disaster.

Standish consulted his compass. Stiff, cold and thirsty, the sixteen men in breeches and woollen stockings trooped in single file by rounded hills and hollows, due south, till the Atlantic's roar grew faint in their ears. But despite their desire to present a brave front there was many a halt, stock-still, in a huddle, while they listened and looked on every side.

A yellow fox's tail whisked out of sight in the long grass. No men ever told each other, "There goes a fox!" with greater relief and joy. America was not wholly a desert if it harboured foxes! And so on, pushing through the trees and kicking the dead leaves, with constant glancing behind.

In less than an hour the inner bay was visible from a hill; three or four miles to the west, behind the spit, lay the anchored *Mayflower*. Midday had been the hour agreed on for the lighting of signal fires; it was then early in the morning, but they decided that when they reached the beach they would "have one for nothing" and give the "all well" nevertheless.

The way led down through scrubby trees and thistles and into another curving valley, and there, miraculously appearing to float on desert sand, was a chain of clear pools. The water proved real enough; when they threw themselves down and cupped it up it ran delightfully through their fingers, tingled on their faces and tongues.

The landscape of stunted trees and tangled bush growth continued with unrelieved monotony. Here and there an aspen or beech struggled for life with the birch, pine and holly. Gilbert lagged behind, tasting various berries, examining spider and scorpion. Beneath an odd-looking little tree with pendulous branches and grey shaggy bark peeling from its trunk in strips, he found a thick-husked nut the size of a walnut, the kernel of which was white and delicious.

"Hasten!" Standish ordered. "Only thus will your stiff legs loosen."

Through twisting gullies and lanes, feet shuffled over leaves and sand; there was sand in their shoes, stockings, breeches, hair.

More water, a green swamp, roundabouts where the grasses seemed greener, tenderer, and evergreens grew in profusion. Surely soon they would see the last of the sand.

In a clump of bushes the leaders thought they saw movement again, and halted the column.

"Come forth," Standish shouted, "come forth," and waved his arm to indicate what he meant. Out of the bushes bounded a little hornless deer and disappeared into the thicker undergrowth in the blink of an eye. They saw him again for a second as he sped swiftly into the bright and living green of a thicket of pitch pine and holly. Here was the best sight they had yet seen in the New World; and with luck they might enjoy a dinner of fresh meat that day.

On the inner beach were lit the smoky signal fires, one first, then the other; lit and put out, lit and put out for twenty or thirty minutes, until answering blobs of haze and winking pin-points of flame were seen on the tip of Long Point.

Then, turning their backs on ship and harbour, they continued on down the Cape, plodding on the harder sand of the beach, deeper into America.

Before the midday meal Mr. Jones came ashore and stumped up to the litter of planks and trestle benches where the unfinished shallop sat on the sand, rubbed his hands together, twitched his shoulders and bid John and the others a very agreeable good day. He circled about, tapped the keel with the toe of his boot, bent to examine, peered within critically and grunted with satisfaction. Behaviour so unusual and alarming that the men watched him warily from the corners of their eyes and were inclined to step aside silently out of his way. But when he spoke it was evident that he was not drunk.

"We progress, sir," John said, with unmistakable unfriendliness. Ellis had seen Priscilla coming from the Great Cabin the night before, and told him so. "We go forward as best we can. And quicker we'd go if more on them knew a chisel from a tree-nail. Or if we had help from some . . ."

At moments there was a certain amount of apologetic embarrassment in the little Captain's manner. Then, a few minutes later, he startled them all by saying outright, "I'll send ship's carpenter! It's of no purpose getting my ship in trim, if your boat is not ready and trespassing the wide bay for a place to seat yourself. Come to it, give me your chisel, till I pare the transom into a better fit!"

He pottered and banged with them on the boat until it was time for them to go aboard for their hot midday meal.

John wandered down the first hold with his steaming dinner bowl in his hand; he could have sat down near the smoking and cheerfully blazing brazier, but moved on and came to a stop before Mr. Brewster, who was sitting with his family, his back against a beam, already engaged with his own dinner. As the young carpenter continued to stand before him he patted his son Love around to his other side and gestured to John to sit down. John seated himself by the old man and during the next few minutes, munching solidly, looked around at him several times.

"What's the trouble, lad?"

"A girl, sir," John grinned, "so I'm come looking for your advice. This is the way of it—she give me back my shirt what she washed, she give it me back this early morning with not nice words——"

The old man, wiping his beard down with his handkerchief, raised his hand. "Pause! I'd be blind if I didn't suppose this is William Mullins' daughter?"

"The same, sir."

"Was your shirt not washed clean then?"

"White as a daisy! But it's as she wants me for to court her father when it's her I would court——"

"Hothead. This is hardly the time or place to start letting your fancy cast about at young women."

"Ah," John said impatiently, "you cannot stop the young grass growing. You cannot see your nice young girl, day in day out for a month and double, and stop your fancy turning on her. All a man asks is to know where he stands. Then Ellis says to me last night he seen her come out from the Master's cabin in her stocking feet—mark you, in her stocking feet!"

Mr. Brewster smiled, shaking his head. "You can be sure her

mother was close by. Put no seem on tales of that kind, my boy. Besides, inquiring for Mr. Jones's health is part of Mr. Fuller's campaign, or so it would seem. No doubt she was returning Mr. Jones his clean shirt too—you'd be sure of that if you knew the stern William Mullins as I do!"

"In her stocking feet?"

"Now, now! I will have nothing more of that. What did the girl say?"

"She sent the shirt by little Ellen. So when I seen her this morning, she is going ashore in the longboat with us, I whisper in her ear. She says to me, 'Don't you be presuming to tell me where I'm not to go in my stocking feet.' But I see a blush come on her, and press the matter—true enough I picks her up against her will like and carried her off the boat to the beach, where she near tears me in pieces with looks like daggers. 'Master Jones,' says she, 'is a right proper gentleman, for all his swearing.' Oh ho, think I, is that the way the wind blows now—but not meaning it at all! 'You was nicer to me a time back, my pretty,' I says. 'You make your peace with my father,' she says, 'if you wants me for to speak to you nice. You very pagan atheist,' says she, and more words of that like. 'Who am I courting,' I says, 'you or your father?' 'You make your peace with my father,' she says, as she has ever. More words pass and she flounces off in a huff. I gets high and shouts somewhat after her, that we'd see who'd be gentlefolk come another day, and that two can play a game of catch me who can and scream to be culled——"

"Do you not stop to remember where we are, and what we are at, and what kind of strange people are Mr. Mullins and his generation?"

"Waste my chances, and many another likely young man on board the like of Mr. Gilbert to pluck them from me? There's this I've learned, it'll be many a day before there's high-nosed shopkeepers here to play the game of selling their women for the highest bid."

"You are a hotheaded fellow," Mr. Brewster sighed. "Is there no way of staying you? Why do you not make your peace with William Mullins if you are out with him? We do these things in the open; if you will pay attention to a daughter do it with her father's consent. Because we will have no baiting rings for men to whip the blinded bear for their cruel sport, nor priests with the power to hang, and so forth, it does not mean we are going to throw over all the best of our English ways of living. You understand that, my boy, and understand it well. First, be on good terms with the girl's father."

"And there's the rub—he would the sooner wipe his feet on me. So will you advise me?" John put down his bowl and rubbed his mouth with the back of his hand. "He calls me pagan, ungodly, that I am not of his. She follows suit. But she never will say in what way I am not—not of them, unless it's their pride, that I'm a hired man. Always and ever it is, I am not one of them, not one of them, not one of you. But how does a man become one of you? You advise me, sir."

Mr. Brewster played with the ends of his beard for a moment, almost smiling. "Here Mr. Mullins is as yet but a man standing by himself, like many another. Only very few of us agree exactly in what we're about. And so we must remain, men thrown against each other, for good or ill, until we have houses to live in and a church to meet in. Then perhaps will come a day when all on this ship will combine in belief and principle and government, and may rightly be called a true body combined, and you will know where you stand. Your being a hired man is nothing against you. My advice to you is that you go back to the boat you build—if you're finished your dinner—and build and build for your dear life's sake, for all our lives' sake, and in the course of time you'll see God's true ways and understand with us and be one of us."

"And for the meanwhile," John expostulated warmly, "I am the dog that needs be kept outside the back door!"

"No, no, lad," the knobbly-faced old man protested. "You know right well how we value you."

"But will not spell out the mystery! Value me to hammer and haul for you. What makes me dirty dog and Mr. Mullins what's run in face of the lockup be full of grace?"

"Mullins is as he is after long years; you are a very young man. Am I to begin telling you the difference now when we are engaged for our lives with this savage country? Do you suppose that what has set this great enterprise afoot can be explained in a word? Can I explain to you in five minutes what it has taken men years to discover in their hearts?"

"If you cannot, sir, there is little truth in you," John said, turning away, and without knowing the pertinence, even profundity, of his thoughtless comment.

Here the old man looked at him keenly, nodded wisely, looked into the distance for a while, twisting a horn in his beard, and nodded wisely again. "Lad! That's as true a word as ever was spoken. And you are right, what time is there ever like the present? You shall not come for advice and go unanswered, were we both drowning in the wild sea and yet had a moment of free speech. I tell you what I will do. Come to me every day, or when you will, be it only for a few minutes, and I'll do my best, I will, humbly and gratefully. But this you must remember, that while I may explain us as men seeking to get back the primitive love and truths that were when men first began to be Christian in the world, both now and in time to come there will be other voices proclaiming how we must come to our desire. I may say for us all now: We will be true Christians and brothers and do no hurt to any man whatsoever; but you may live to hear others of us say: We will be true Christians if we have to beat and slaughter every other man in the world to come to it. But I anticipate. When men were early Christians there was a true love and goodness amongst them, but it became lost in the courts of kings and in the big cities, until the world came to the state of unhappy vileness it is now in. That shall be the text of my sermon to you for these daring days.

"But first you must be warned, in all fairness, of the penalties that attach to being what you call 'one of us.' You will have seen men shivering in the iron cages of the market place for not attending at the King's church but if you become one of us and go back to England you will preach the way and you will be like to lose your life on the common gallows by the side of thieves and murderers. Will you remember that? Will you think about it now when building the boat? By tomorrow you may have changed your mind and no longer wish me to instruct you."

"I wish your instruction, sir," John said, and realized that he could stay away from his boatbuilding not a moment longer. "You shall see me again."

What will a man not do for a pretty woman? Mr. Brewster thought, when John had run up the hold and bounded up the steps, and he shook his head and combed his beard with his fingers. Still, what did it matter how the spark of grace came to be fanned in a man? And who was he, Will Brewster, to suppose that the God responsible for William Mullins and for worms with forty-eight legs apiece had no sense of humour in regard to young men and their ways with girls?

Gulls, flying high, spaced out in isolation, winged their way down the Cape as if in slow deliberation bent on some undeflectable purpose; yet, close to, their glass eyes would have shown no purpose, only a reflection of an immemorial scene: in the green sea two nearly parallel ribbons of beach stretching north and south, between them land marked by brown patches, glinting water, ragged splashes of living green and erosions of sea and bright sand; the outer beach with a white lace frill of breakers, the inner forming an even line, the whole an immense shape with the proportions of a human arm that narrowed northward to a thin wrist and, where the hand should be, a great parrot head with a cruel hooked beak—within which nestled the foreign shape of a ship.

And five miles from the ship in a straight line across the water to the inner side of the Cape, some gull's sharp but uninterested eye must have recorded a movement of men trooping inland up a shallow fissure, and how the dots stopped moving, drew together and remained stationary.

"By the living God you're all blind," Hopkins swore. "It is a man's footfall printed plain. Here is the big toe. They must use this way for coming and going to the beach. If the sand were but less wind-blown . . ."

The leaders resumed march, forging up the inclined gully, which resembled a river of sand between high sloping banks. Another hour had passed since lighting the signal fires. In all they had now wandered a good thirty miles since the morning of the day before, although the distance back by the inner beach to where they had been put ashore by the longboat was not as much as twelve miles.

Distributed between the sixteen men, half a dozen slow matches burned, both in readiness to shoot bird and beast and because it was felt that they must stumble on a savage encampment at any moment, or be attacked. The gully they travelled up from the sea was long and tedious, and the country about tangled and broken.

Standish, Fuller, Hopkins, Bradford and the elder Winslow paused at the gully's end, their eyes level with a small plain, uttered grunts and exclamations, got their breath again, and quickly ascended the last few feet. The others hurrying after crowded up and they all found themselves standing on the edge of an irregular field of stubble. It was a large-stalked, thinly spaced stubble, from what unmistakably had been a planting of something that gave a larger stalk than English wheat. Bradford bent and examined the cut and broken ends protruding from the heavy yellow sand, while Standish and Winslow spread the others out in a line and watched the surrounding trees. This was it; men had sown here in the sandy mould, and reaped. Around the edges of the extensive field Gilbert noted many nut trees like the one from which he had tasted nuts earlier in the morning; but these trees were larger and the ground about them appeared to have been kept clear of other growth.

At the far side of the field was an opening which seemed to lead to another patch of cleared ground; through this the explorers proceeded cautiously.

"There is our second discovery," Winslow whispered, "*there has been a house!*" They filed across the clearing, crunching on more stubble, watching the trees, here tangled in places with creepers and vines. They came to a standstill and gazed down at what had been a human habitation. Half buried in the sand were four weather-beaten balks of wood of uneven lengths and thickness, ship's planks, which marked out a square of about ten feet by eight feet. That was all. The sand around was rippled into waves by the action of the wind. Four planks to one side of a field where plants had been sown and reaped during the summer past; had they been carried to that spot from a lost ship by savages or sailors?

They ranged all over the smaller clearing, but the woods remained as silent and mysterious as ever; nothing, nothing but the four ship's planks and the stubble left in the sand—the curious sand that supported ponds of water and in which grew tree, weed, vine and rose.

Mr. Mullins had sat down in exhaustion on one of the planks; after a few minutes he revived sufficiently to lift his drooping head and observe the others, who were gathered in the centre of the field, Bradford kneeling and with his knife digging up a root for examination. His feet still plodding wearily though they rested in the sand, Mullins reached down in somnambulistic torpor for a rusty-looking stick by his side. But when his fingers closed around it in the sand he did not seem to even have the strength to lift it. He pushed the loose sand away from it on either side; it was a hoop of iron, firmly held in the ground, reminiscent of something he knew well, but his mind, as his fingers, was incapable of coming to grips with it.

Nothing was to be learned from the root of stubble Bradford had dug up and Sam Fuller came over to see how Mullins fared, intending to give him a mouthful from the small bottle of gin he carried as medicine; he sat holding the partly revealed hoop of iron and staring at it. Sam threw down his gun and began digging in the loose sand; by the time the others came over he had the handle and top of a five-gallon kettle exposed. A half-dozen hands dragged it forth and emptied it. Rusty but otherwise in sound condition, it was brother to the kettle Tandy Fall used in the ship's galley. There was no sign of the lid.

Captain Smith's men could have given it in truck to the savages when he explored parts of the Cape but six years past, Mullins said, or even Gosnold left it, or . . . or . . .

"Or the wild men killed some ship's crew," Hopkins added, glancing about with his wild dark eyes, "and took their ship to pieces." A ship's kettle would be the last thing to be given away.

They brought the kettle along, agreeing to carry it two at a time; kettles would not be so easily come by in the New World that they could afford to leave one buried in the sand. If an owner turned up, then it could be returned or paid for. But the greater number of them left the deserted clearing with something of the shyness of men getting out of a church or a house in which they had no right to be. A path led forward between thornbushes—it could have been a path, or just another naturally formed alley.

A halt was made in silence, listening; no sound, only the rustle and sigh of wind. The way led upwards once more, and out upon another plain of hacked-off stubble thirty or forty acres in extent, circled again by patches of tall waving sand grasses, thorn trees, pitch pines glowing green, laurels and briars. The sky had lightened in texture and the day had a sharp-cut brilliancy that never was to be seen in England at any time of the year. The bumpy surface of the field lay in hard relief.

At first glance it seemed no different from the other fields, offered no further evidence of human life than the broken withered stalks thicker than men's fingers. The party's tendency to gather in a group at every halt, making an easy target, worried Standish; he harried them out into a long line and they started across the field like beaters at an English shoot.

"Halt," he called in the middle of the field, and they obediently halted and made a close scrutiny of the trees on every side. Winslow detected what looked like the oblong mound of a grave against a background of singularly sturdy pines, and there they directed their course until near enough to see that the mound was covered on top at one end by a woven mat, yellow and weathered. Round about was a clear space of free, loose sand, and near by, half in the trees, a pile of stalks and large withered leaves the size of a man's hand. But the mound was newly made, the sand and mould still a little damp and retaining the imprints of the hands that had patted it into shape. In size it could well have been a large grave.

"I firmly say we should dig into the end of it," Winslow argued, principally against Bradford, who shewed hesitation over disturbing what was to him obviously just a grave. Even savages would be angry to discover their grave disturbed. "If there is nothing to be learned we can again put the sand back as we found it," Winslow added.

Standish fingered the mat, frowning; he was not the man to experience any moment of wonder on coming upon a woven mat in the wilderness; and with an expression of angry impatience cupped his hand about his mouth and shouted across the clearing, "Hallo-o! . . . Donner und Blitzen . . . Where are you?" A bird like a magpie squawked in a laurel and flew off low between the trees.

"Dig 'er up and to 'ell with it," John Billington said. "Who knows what's hid?"

The faction that favoured digging up the mound prevailed; at the least it would give a short respite from the weary labour of walking. And there was a certain attraction to digging that stirred the imagination and turned it away for a few moments from cold anxiety and the heavy-headedness of fatigue. Dig, they clamoured, dig, dig. Who knows? . . . An Indian king with jewels in his ears, baskets of gold nuggets, or a fresh store of food, roots and game . . .

Swearing an oath at the bondmen, who were sitting down with their guns lying on the ground, Standish prodded the pair to their feet and set all the rest out in a circle, facing outwards from the mound. Let watching eyes observe that they were no mere hungry rabble.

Allerton, Winslow and White laid down their guns and with their knives and hands began to scoop a hole in the end of the mound not covered by the mat. At a foot's depth their fingers came against a hard woven surface. Feverishly they clawed the dry sand away and still on their knees pulled out a little old sack-like, loosely woven basket, its opening drawn to and knotted tight with a leather thong. None of their stiff cold fingers were capable of picking the knot and without further ado Allerton cut the drawstring and pulled open the neck. Winslow put in his hand and drew out a spilling fistful of large yellow shining seeds.

All eyes were on the basket. The men standing out in a circle closed in nearer; Billington broke out of the line and stood over the three kneeling, the word "gold" forming on his lips.

"The golden seed of our bread . . ." Bradford answered him, with a suggestion of superstitious awe and disbelief. "I have seen it pictured; it grows on plants, in the shape of fat rods. And that we should have been led to this spot in all this waste of country . . . 'And when the children of Israel saw it, they said one to another, *It is manna.* . . .' "

"It is the New World's wheat," Winslow confirmed. "And here is our bag of seed! Now we ought for policy's sake place it back, cover it up as we formerly found it, and search out our savages to truck with them for it."

"We'll not put it back!" Billington shouted. "Did we not come to get it?"

"This will not be the only corn seed on the Cape," Winslow began.

"Take it we should, while we have it in our hands," Standish said, "else like these wild men it'll have vanished away when we come again."

Then ensued a heated discussion, during which no one thought to watch the trees except Gilbert, who idly wandered about the field with his musket on his shoulder; having once seen the contents of the basket, not interested in arguing the toss. He observed that a cold yellow tinge was coming into the high dome of cloud overhead. He went on, looking for a couple of stones to crack open an assortment of nuts bulging his pocket. But now that he came to think of it he could not remember having once seen a single good-sized stone since setting foot on the Cape, either inland or on the beaches.

When he looked back from the farther side of the field, having wandered right around its edge, the discussion had turned on whether or not to dig out the rest of the mound, and Edward was pointing out in his practical way that if they took the seed they would then be forced to find the owners, or have the savages automatically take them for enemies, having to all appearances stolen their food.

Gilbert strolled on. The cleared ground sloped upwards gently from the mound end of the field and at the top suddenly fell away again. Looking down, he saw through sparsely growing trees another of the Cape's innumerable small valleys filled with scraggy pitch pine and holly, and between the trees, in a hollow, the outline of what he would have described as a little barn covered entirely with matting.

Over the ridge and down, he descended a few steps, halted and reminded himself that he was a cowardly fellow if the truth were but known. Yet the savages could hardly be sitting calmly at home in their little barn with all that clamour of voices going on not a hundred yards away. His slow match was smoking faintly; he blew on it, tightened the screw that held it in the lock of his gun and edged down the slope. The dry weather was kind to gunpowder; a shot would bring the others running up the field in a matter of moments. He pushed through the tree branches and slowly descended to the edge of the hollow, not knowing why he did, but knowing he ought not to, while he began to whistle softly the air of Dorothy's favourite song, "So I'll go down to some lonely waters," to keep away panic. Forcing oneself to overcome one's cowardly nature was a good exercise, he felt, without any great conviction; in any case some of the party at the mound could not but have observed the course of his wanderings.

The hut or barn below came clearly into view; all in all it was no more than forty paces below the end of the field. It had a perfectly curved roof running down into the sides, its flat end, facing him, semicircular, the whole wonderfully neat and symmetrical. He surmised that long thin sapling had been bound into lengths, and both ends driven into the ground, to form a series of arches, over which the rush matting was neatly spread and bound on. Its height would just afford a tall man standing up room, with a floor space of perhaps fifteen feet by ten feet. In the roof there was a square opening, smoke-blackened, with a hinged flap lying open. Looking at it, he thought that the men who possessed the New World, whoever they were, could not be as savage as they had been painted.

He circled the house slowly, his lips pursed in a soundless whistle; and circled it again, nearer, listening for any sound from within, coming to a standstill before the end that had faced him as he came down into the hollow. Here there was a division in the matting for entry and egress. He stood still, perhaps for minutes, before urging out his painfully inadequate voice, "Within?

Hallo? . . ." Nothing stirred inside. He looked quickly behind him; the wind again, cracking off a dry twig; and slowly drew the matting to one side with the barrel of his gun. It was dark inside at the first glance, but in a moment he could see. No one. Holding the mat back with one hand, he poked his head in and looked around.

On the centre of the sandy floor were black and dead cinders, white ash and half-burned sticks, across them a pot stand or spit made of forked sticks supporting horizontals.

The house was double-matted, the mats attached to the frame inside clean and fresh, crudely coloured in broad stripes of yellow, green and brick red. On the sand at the far end were clay pots and bowls, some enamelled black from the fire, a bright red hand basket that seemed to be fashioned of crab shells fastened on a wicker frame, a large coarse wicker basket filled with yellow corn, and smaller black and white baskets holding knobby roots. Lying in a corner was the head of a hind, the eyes glazed, the sand beneath it blackened with blood. Hanging in bunches on the walls were eagle claws and the pointed ends of horns or antlers. There was also many other small baskets of seeds and acorns, and a folded pile of soft-looking skins.

On the pile of skins there was an earthen platter containing what was unmistakably a fat grilled herring.

A faint call came down on the air to him: Standish bellowing his name. Gilbert shouted back that he was coming, though it was doubtful if they would hear him, and took a quick look backwards around the clearing and immediate trees; still no sign of life. Did they have burrows in the sand into which to retreat? Already he felt an affection for the simple, wonderfully clever matted house, with its peaceful, domestic air. He had only to go up and call, and the others would come, crowding and pushing in with their heavily clothed, uncouth, stiff bodies, poking and prying, Billington stuffing his pockets with whatever he could lay his hands on.

Gilbert propped his gun outside, ducked in, tore the fish in two pieces, replaced one half, and came out taking a bite at the other. He dropped the mat, picked up his musket, and walked up out of the hollow as quietly as he had come.

Gaining the end of the field, he looked down and saw that the others were busily digging up the rest of the mound, half a dozen of them at it now, and had all but demolished it, sand flying out backwards from their hands as if from the paws of burrowing dogs. He waved to the sentinels reassuringly; they were just too far away to see either the piece of fish or that he was eating. Chewing slowly, spitting out bones, he savoured its full, rich, fresh flavour. Surely no man could know the true joy of taste till he had half starved on bits of salt pork and smoked beef for a couple of months? And when he had finished and wiped his lips he walked down the field and stood with the other guards, scolded by both his brother and Standish for going away, but said no word about the pleasant domestic scene he had so curiously discovered.

By then a second and much larger basket had been unearthed, of a newer appearance and stuffed tight with corncobs five and six inches in length, which passed from hand to hand to be examined, smelt, tasted. It had also been decided that they should take as much as could comfortably be carried in kettle, pockets and handkerchiefs, put the baskets and the rest back, and go on in search of the savages. But many of the men, all dog-tired and weak from lack of a solid meal, desired to return to the ship there and then. Winslow and Bradford, however, were determined to find the savages and somehow explain that their taking of the corn was done under dire necessity, because they must have seed, and was no unfriendly act.

The rest of the day passed very much as the morning and the day before—with not a sight or sound of savage. Half a mile further on they came on the remains of an enclosure, such as might have been set up to pen animals, made of stakes driven into the ground to stand shoulder-high, as if men had dropped from heaven into the wilderness, made it, and disappeared back whence they had come without leaving any other evidence of themselves. Then near midday their course was barred by a broad double-armed tidal inlet which, from high ground, could be seen to extend inwards across the Cape. This, it was conjectured, was the river mouth seen from the *Mayflower* when coming in around the head. It was full of seaweed and as desolate and blood-chilling as only salt marshes can be. But the leaders trooped doggedly on, roaming inland by its course, and back again; and on a sandy bank by the water's dark edge found a dugout canoe. At first sight they mistook it for a very large log, too large to have grown on the Cape, and went to look at it closer.

It consisted simply of a tree trunk shaped cunningly by fire into a long narrow boat. They saw how patiently it must have been worked upon, burned out with small successive fires, chipped and smoothed until the sides were an even two inches in thickness all around. Eight paddles, made of interlaced sallies bound to a handle, lay in the bottom. It also might have been dropped from heaven simply to perplex and frighten them by its lonely solitary appearance. A single set of footprints ran from the boat and disappeared in the slush of the marsh.

Billington, lightheaded from undernourishment and fatigue, pitched one of the paddles out into the water like a child in wanton play; which was retrieved by Edward with a willow switch and replaced in the boat. Hopkins and White wanted to take the dugout and paddle about in it, being only dissuaded not to by threats. Then it was suggested that four of them take the boat and paddle home to the ship with the cumbersome iron kettle, the sea of the bay being reasonably calm. There was a feeling perhaps that they ought to *do* something with the canoe as a gesture, set it adrift, take it away; remove it somehow, so that the landscape was freed of such a sign of prior human proprietorship, that they could feel this world their own, free of interference; and also as a token of revenge against the savages for hiding and keeping them so long in suspense.

But in the end the sane council of Winslow, Fuller and Bradford led them away towards the harbour and the ship, leaving the canoe as they had found it; and they came without further event—other than losing themselves twice, completely, and having to retrace their own footprints—to a large fresh-water lake near the inner beach, halfway home, where nightfall overtook them and forced them to make camp.

And their bulging pockets, filled with corn, had a certain connection with the immense fire built as if in defiance and the brave barricade of thorn branches and rotten sticks stuck in the sand that they set up around them. The barricade, however, would not have kept out a calf. Each man stood his hour of sentry go with another for company. Early in the night an ice-cold, penetrating rain began to fall, continuing on and off until daylight, soaking their capes and blankets. In the morning every gun had to be reloaded with fresh powder.

Throughout the previous afternoon everyone had taken his turn carrying the heavy kettle and most of them were sick to death of it. On leaving camp another argument broke out, between Bradford and Standish, and Hopkins and White. The latter pair, whose turn it was to carry the kettle, wished to put the corn in a blanket and hide the kettle until they could come for it another day. Their irritated, desperate shouting and wrangling terminated in Hopkins pitching the corn out in a spasm of temper, swinging the kettle at arm's length and with incredible strength sending it sailing out to fall with a splash in the pond.

Then shamefacedly he packed the corn in his damp blanket, slung it on his shoulder, and the sixteen wet and hungry, cold and irritable men wended their way onwards.

By going too far along the inner beach, before remembering that they must recross the Cape to the outer side to get around the inlet that cut into the wrist of the peninsula, they had to make their way back, losing an hour, with considerable bad temper.

On the head a shot was fired, to tell the ship of their coming, and at twelve o'clock they at length stumbled down onto the harbour beach and saw in the near distance the longboat, waiting, with Jones, Carver and Brewster on the shore. The explorers wanted nothing so much in the world as to sink down and fall asleep and sleep and sleep, and sleep.

It was the afternoon of Friday, the seventeenth of November, and they had been away two whole days and a half and the ship had not sunk, disappeared, or been invaded by wild men.

19   Awakening late the next morning, the returned explorers, heroes and mighty hunters, were relieved to hear that in fact things had gone on aboard as they had from the beginning of time, or whenever it was in that long ago that the voyage had started. Tandy Fall was still entertaining the children with scraps filched from the crew's meagre rations and looking more than ever like a spider that had fallen into a vat of grease. Mr. Jones had shot a fat duck—and eaten it. Isaac Allerton found his wife, who was going to have a child, very well considering all; and William White found his wife near her time and also well. Three people now had the bleeding gums, purple patches and swollen muscles of scurvy much advanced into consumption— James Chilton, Ellen Moore's elder brother Jasper, and William White's bondman Edward Thompson. And Bradford returned to a Dorothy as pale and quiet as ever. John had the fishing boat within a week of being ready for the water; while stories of Mr. Jones going on the beach and forwarding the work with his own hands made them curious to see this strange conduct with their own eyes and renewed their apprehension about how soon he meant to sail away and leave them to their fate.

There was some dissatisfaction reported, more on the part of the crew than the settlers, that, being now anchored against the land for a week, no fowls, fish or fresh meat had yet been enjoyed by anyone except the Master with his one duck. For the scurvy was also showing amongst the crew, though in a milder form, and they believed that the only sure way to check it was to eat fresh meat.

Many more people had coughs and colds, but otherwise from the general quietness a stranger would have thought there to be no more than a dozen persons on board instead of a hundred and thirty. And this was because they suffered a growing awareness that though the ship could be full of life and small voices float over the water, they were terrifyingly alone, a minute effort of

life confronting a trackless immensity of stillness, alone before
the outcrop of a forest that perhaps stretched to the other side of
the world, alone, to enter and by their own small effort penetrate
the mystery, and live with it. From the land came only silence
and a small whining wind, and England lay at the other end of
the world. A man might lie shivering at night convinced that
they were all dangerously mad to have brought themselves to
that pass, but the day had to be faced, and the next, and all the
days to come, many or few. . . . The ship must soon go. They
felt their loneliness and isolation like a pain.

In the afternoon the leaders of the expedition were sufficiently
recovered of their ordeal to comply with the Master's request to
talk with him in the Great Cabin at a sort of general council,
and there they betook themselves from much-needed rest, creaking in their scurvy-tainted joints but with a new fresh colour in
their faces, to endeavour to fathom in what this hinted change
in the Master consisted.

"Be welcome," Mr. Jones began, in a very ordinary voice,
though in himself he was sure he felt as extraordinary as a singing horse in a Christmas play; but as modest to hide his warmed
heart as a girl with a forbidden love, out of inexperience of what
to do with it and in mortal dread of being discovered in some
fashion and laughed at.

Standish was accounted important enough a person in their
affairs at that juncture to be brought in; as was Stephen Hopkins, representing with Martin and Mullins the Londoners and
"merchants' men." Brewster, Carver, Fuller, Martin, Winslow
and Standish were accommodated at the table; Bradford and
Hopkins stood, Bradford because he felt at more advantage
standing up like a felon in the dock.

Fuller, pleased to the bone in his own unassuming way, gave
the Master an account of their adventures; and Mr. Jones listened, leaning forward in his chair with his fingers interlaced,
his tense expression heightened by the fact that his eyes appeared to bulge more than they had ever been noticed to do before.

"The corn comes as a good omen," Mr. Jones agreed, as if he
was having a little trouble with his breathing, "but our better

news is that we have the shallop near ready for the water by two or three days' work."

It is "we" now, Bradford thought, not ceasing to watch the Captain. Before it had always been "you" must go do this, "you people" must go do that. Today he sat with them like a gambler who had been caught out cheating but who was nevertheless determined that though he had suffered a reverse he was not going to let his discomfort shew. The Master had set himself on some new tack, Bradford was convinced, wherewith he hoped to quickly wash his hands of his cargo of souls, and get away. And this new tactic involved a greater seeming co-operation. The more he saw of Mr. Jones the more he approached a belief that their coming to Cape Cod was all part of some evil plan of the Government in England to abandon them on the barrenest spot to be found across the ocean, where they must all perish of cold and starvation. He was surely a very devil and needed watching like a hawk. And Bradford bitterly regretted in his narrow and honest heart the promise he had given Jones never to speak of what had passed between them concerning Mr. Brewster. But it was on that same night, he never forgot from one day to the next, that he had also sworn his oath not under any circumstances to allow Jones to sail away until they were sure they could live and grow; he swore it anew then. Moreover, remembering the Master's threat to return Brewster to England in the event of trouble it suddenly revolted him to see them sit at the same table together, the Captain's small, round, smooth, dark face turned to Mr. Brewster as he spoke of going with them, to help in person find the best place to make a settlement.

Bradford's wind-scorched face flushed a deeper colour, and he looked away, at the smoke-blackened beams stretching low across the roof of the Great Cabin.

"We should take twenty—thirty men," Mr. Jones was saying, "sailing the shallop down the coast's shore for a week of days if needs be, and find some safe harbour, where the earth is fit to grow your seed, where fish are, and deer——"

"It must be free ground!" Bradford cut in harshly, without looking at the Master. "We have not the numbers or the strength in our people to clear forest trees in winter weather."

287

There was the matter of the corn, Mr. Carver began to explain, it was all very well talking about it as manna from God, as the rank and file of the settlers were doing, in their simplicity, but the fact was that they *must* find the savages whose corn it was and prove they were not enemies, before the word spread from one end of the coast to the other. It must be discovered why the savages kept hidden, whether the reason was innocent or if they were preparing to attack.

"All the which we can do very speedily for ourselves," Bradford said stubbornly, "if not hindered further."

The rebuff did not pass unnoticed by Mr. Jones, but he tried to believe that such things no longer had any power to raise his temper; the primary sensation of standing on a threshold, of soon partaking of some inner peace and secret well-being enjoyed by certain of these people like Fuller, Brewster and Carver, was acting as a sort of buffer between himself and the stings of the world. At that moment Mr. Jones thought himself to be a very good man, or rather that he had always been a very good man but had not before seen himself in his own true light. His sensations were emotional, simple, but he was sincerely struggling to *be* a better man, richer by his revelation though not yet strong enough to be unashamed of a good action or resolve his guilty conscience.

"We should look to Mr. Jones to lead us in our expedition," Sam said, smoothing over Bradford's retort, "ask him in fact to captain our shallop and generously give us the benefit of his wide experience of coasts and seas—could he spare himself from the ship . . ."

Standish glared at Fuller, and Bradford looked at the long-nosed physician with an expression suggesting that Mr. Fuller had suddenly gone mad. But Martin, Mullins, Hopkins and the rest agreed with Fuller without question, as did Carver, Winslow and Brewster.

"Will you thus join hands?" Fuller said. "Will you captain our boat, sir, help us the which are but babes in the wood?"

"If you all think it fit," Mr. Jones replied, with an expression they should have taken as one of humble dignity but were not prepared to, while his gaze remained turned upon his clasped hands resting before him on the table.

There was something very near a shocked silence for a few moments, as they realized fully that indeed some particular and peculiar change had overcome the Master in their absence. But the effects of long hostility were not to be wiped out in a moment. If he meant to be a true man with them let his acts prove it. Yet the leaders later said that they thought things were at last taking a hopeful turn as far as Mr. Jones was concerned; all except Bradford and Standish, the one deeply suspicious of devilment, the other without sufficient experience of the Master before that moment to know that anything odd was or might be happening at all.

So it was decided that the first moment the shallop was ready for sailing the waters of the bay a party should return to the place they had named Corn Hill, make another attempt to find the savages and pay them, and try to get more corn; then undertake a major exploration right around the shore of the coast.

With so much settled soundly and briefly, Governor Carver broke up the meeting there and then, before anything could go amiss with it, and they left the Great Cabin still on the same surprisingly good terms with the Master—to hurry below and discuss him exhaustively.

While the meeting went forward in the Great Cabin aft, talk of a very different nature was flying about in the crew's mess, below the galley. On such a ship no hierarchy ascended from cabin boy to ship's Master. The Captain was still in theory a feudal lord, master of life and death. Except in emergencies he ruled through his chief lieutenant, the first mate—the only man, other than the Captain himself, allowed quarters in the poop. Every other member of the crew slept and messed forward on an equal level, second mate and quartermaster alike. Nevertheless distinctions between members of the common crew were finely drawn, but related both to individual strength and each man's function in sailing the ship and not to any rank or privilege.

A Master maintained his absolute will through his power to punish or hang any sailorman, provided he had evidence against him and could force the rest to carry out his bidding, and through the general knowledge that ready gallows waited in every home port and that port authorities would string up troublesome sailormen with a ready and ferocious alacrity any time of the day or night, feast day or fast.

In the mess at dinnertime that day, Coppin, Bosun Duff and the quartermasters, the lesser lords forward, were prompted to speculate as to how soon the ship would return home by the small quantity of spiced beef and boiled barley sent down from the galley for the midday meal.

"I wallops up what I'm give per man," Tandy Fall said, raising the trap and descending half a dozen steps from his galley. "An' where does I git it from? From Mr. Clarke, what 'as 'is orders from the Master. Go pull the Master's beard." And would give them no more, returning above and banging down the trap.

"And the longer we do stay, the less we'll have to put in our bellies crossing back," one of the quartermasters said, faithfully echoing Coppin.

"There comes bad weather against us," Coppin said. "We starve, die of hunger. Not the Master, with every key in his pocket, 'e won't starve, it's the poor sailormen will." The oldest argument on the sea, and the most effective.

Few mutinies have not had unsatisfied stomachs behind them; the half of the crew there gathered to their meal about the greasy table listened to Coppin with ready attention. He was also the tallest and strongest man amongst the crew. "There is no cause to sit 'ere longer than needs to put the ship in good shape, and she is near that now," Coppin told them. "The Master 'as done 'is job. We 'ave these psalm singers where they would go. So they're here. So we go home. So we go home before the snow falls and freezes the sails to the spars. Bless me from dying of the hunger for men that haven't no God, who will not use the sign of the cross to save their life—but who to look at them, the sons of witches—would have you believe they kept God in their pockets. Do us a Mullins, Tom."

And the bosun dragged down his cheeks with finger and thumb, piously turning his eyes up. "Brothers, we are with God, the Lord is our help. Brothers, we will walk the straight path";

and mouthed nonsense in a melancholy voice, amidst howls of laughter.

Throughout Sunday, Monday and Tuesday, John worked desperately to get the shallop ready and rigged for the sea. The weather grew colder, and one morning the ship was powdered with frost. Gloves appeared on the hands of those lucky enough to have them; others wore socks on their hands or made mittens by binding on bits of rag; while orderlies kept the fires blazing on the beach, hewed and sawed firewood.

Not once but many times John regretted his coming to the New World—where the sun did not shine from morning till night "like a brass plate, and every bird and animal in the world was, with grapes growing in the woods. . . ." Lord save him. He cursed the cold sky; and changed his mind again, on seeing Priscilla Mullins, thinking that but for her and old Brewster he'd risk breaking his contract to stay a year and smuggle home to warm England on the *Mayflower* when she sailed. But with the boat afloat there was surely going to be a lot to see and do! And the tall old man said he had taught Bradford to read Latin, a foreign tongue in which men wrote secret books of knowledge, and when they came to be settled he might give him such learning also and set him on the high road to becoming a man of weight and means. While the men were working on the boat the older children were allowed on the beach and with mufflers around their heads and socks on their hands ran about and played, so that the scene was not altogether without its hopeful and homely aspects.

On Tuesday afternoon flecks of snow fell out of a grey sky. The women on board flocked up on deck and stood there awhile feeling the cold feathery touch on their cheeks like the fingers of death. The sailors on Mr. Jones's orders rigged a tarpaulin on four spars over the open cargo hatch which allowed the smoke of the brazier beneath free egress but would keep the snow from falling into the hold.

The shallop's little forepeak half deck had yet to be put in her, but as soon as the flakes of snow fell the leaders decided to launch her that evening, as she was. Sailors and settlers went ashore with ropes and tackle and pulled and hauled and pushed the tubby fishing boat down below high-water mark where the full tide at nine in the evening would float her and from where she could be rowed to the ship and tied-to. In this strenuous work the Master directed his unwilling sailors like a mule driver. But the threatening snow, as if in part answer to prayers, cleared off, and in the night gave place to gusts of driving rain and sleet.

By midday of Wednesday the mast was rigged, leeboards and rudder lashed temporarily and she was ready for try-out runs. A clumsy, open, wide-beamed boat, she could carry thirty men at the utmost, with safety, and was sailed with a sort of lateen used in a primitive fore-and-aft manner. The hired sailors, English, Trevore and Ellis, with John sailed her back and forth on the wind across the harbour mouth until they felt they could manage her in more open weather, discovering that her awkward sail made her not at all seaworthy in high winds—but for that matter they could always down sail and take to the oars. She was no very proud vessel to carry the lives of so many people.

But all day Thursday the men of the exploring party kicked their heels in impatience, every bite of food bringing them nearer the day when there would be no bite for man or child, while violent gusts of wind swept the bay outside and set the usually calm sea on the inner side of the Cape dancing in white clothes; and so continued all day Friday and Saturday and Sunday morning. Then on the evening of Sunday all was clear again and the sky full of light, the driving rain and sleet vanishing; hopes were set on being at last able to make the necessary journey over to Corn Hill the following day, Monday, the twenty-seventh of November, which they did, though in the night it snowed heavily.

Of this second major exploration Edward Winslow later wrote an account:

> . . . Master Jones was desirous to go with us; and took such of his sailors as he thought useful for us: so as we were in all about thirty-four men.
> We made Master Jones our leader: for we thought it best herein to gratify his kindness and forwardness. . . .
> The wind being good, we sailed to the river we formerly

discovered, which we named Cold Harbour, to which when we came we found it not navigable for ships; yet we thought it might be a good harbour for boats, for it flows there twelve feet at high water.

We landed our men between the two creeks, and marched some four or five miles by the greater of them; and the shallop followed us.

At length night grew on, and our men were tired with marching up and down the steep hills and deep valleys, which lay half a foot thick with snow. Master Jones, wearied with marching, was desirous we should take up our lodging, though some of us would have marched further. So we made there our camp for the night, under a few pine trees; and, as it fell out, we got three fat geese and six ducks for our supper, which we ate with soldiers' stomachs, for we had eaten little all that day. . . .

When we came to the creek [next morning] we saw the canoe on dry ground, and a flock of geese in the river, at which one made a shot and killed a couple of them. And we launched the canoe and fetched them; and when we had done that she carried us over by seven or eight at once.

This done, we marched to the place where we had the corn formerly, which place we call Corn Hill, and digged, and found the rest; of which we were very glad. . . .

Whilst some of us were digging up this, some others found another heap with corn, which we digged up also.

So as we had in all about ten bushels; which will serve us sufficiently for seed.

And sure it was God's good providence that we found this corn; for else we know not how we should have done. For we knew not how we should find, or meet with, any of the savages; except it be to do us a mischief. Also we had never in all likelihood seen a grain of it if we had not made our first journey, for the ground was now covered with snow and so hard frozen that we were fain to hew and carve the ground a foot deep and then wrest it up with levers.

Whilst we were in this employment, foul weather coming up, Master Jones was earnest to go aboard [the *Mayflower*], but others of us desired to make further discovery and to find out the savages' habitations. So we sent home, with him, our weakest people and some that were sick, and all the corn; and eighteen of us stayed and lodged there that night; and desired that the shallop might return to us next day and bring some mattocks and spades.

The next morning we followed certain beaten paths of the Indians into the woods, supposing they would lead us to some town or houses; we lit upon a very broad beaten path, well-nigh two feet broad. Then we lighted all our slow matches, and prepared ourselves, concluding we were near their dwellings; but, in the end, we found it to be only a path made to drive deer in, when the Indians hunt, as we supposed. . . .

Whilst we were thus ranging and searching, two of the sailors, which were newly come on the shore [from the returned shallop], by chance espied two houses which had been lately dwelt in, but the people that owned them were gone away. They, having their arms, and hearing nobody, entered the houses; and took out some things, but dared not stay, and came and told us. So some seven or eight of us went with them; and found how we had passed within a bowshot of the houses before. . . . Some of the best things we took away with us, and left the houses standing as they were.

So, it growing towards night, and the tide almost spent, we hasted with our things down to the shallop, and got back aboard the ship that night, intending to have brought some beads and other things to have left in the houses, in sign of peace and that we meant to truck with them. But it was not done, by means of our hasty coming away from Cape Cod: but, as soon as we can meet conveniently with them, we will give them full satisfaction. So much of our Second Discovery.

The very children on board now knew that the Cape was peopled with wild men, savages, Indians. Their houses had been entered, the food of meals seen fresh in bowls, their corn, wickerwork and clayware brought back for all to see. But of the people that there lived—they might have been bodiless ghosts or men possessing the magic power to render themselves invisible, a thing not to be ruled out of court, seeing that they were reputed pagans and devil worshippers anyhow. But though their eyes looked over the surrounding water with mounting dread and anxiety, the advancing figures were never to be seen; silence and mystery. The land was patched with bright snow, on which surely the smallest movement could not but be seen.

To know that the savages, whatever manner of men they were, lay gathered, hidden, to burst upon them, would have been somehow better than knowing nothing. Mr. Mullins was pestered to consult his book. But his book, he said, was of Virginia, and this was not Virginia. . . . Would to God they had gone to Virginia. Would to God, Mr. Mullins thought, he had heeded the old mapmaker in Southampton.

Then, as if playing some diabolical game with them, no sooner had the shallop returned than the weather broke again and kept all to the ship for another four days, while the ship heaved and strained at her anchor cables and the wind and rain howled over the water. It was during those days that the cry first began to be heard openly from some of the settlers that the ship should try to return to England, that the whole impossible venture be abandoned, come what may, or that they attempt to go south to Virginia, as was originally intended.

But who could swear that there was not snow also in Virginia? Mr. Jones said the weather was no different there. Mr. Clarke said the same. And in the north, if once they got a footing, they had a better chance of continuing free of interference by the Crown. Also the shallop was now built. And further, there was not enough food to venture going south.

By immediately finding a spot on which to settle, there and then beginning to eke out the food store with fowls, fish, deer and anything else to be got such as corn and roots from the savages, the remaining provisions might somehow or another be stretched out to last over to the spring. The simple truth was that they were trapped there, and there they had to stay, live or die. The food store would not even carry them back to England. Patience and prayer, patience and prayer . . .

Patience and prayer, the women cried, and everyone turning into frozen sooty sweeps on a smoke-fouled, snowbound ship! That was what the unbending muddleheadedness of men had led them to. And the whales were about again and would one night stave in the ship's sides, Lord have mercy on them!

And on one of those dark whining nights the second child to live was born and added its wailing to the crying of the wind. The first born had been named Oceanus, coming into the world on the wide ocean; the second was named Peregrine, a wanderer.

Log: December 5th: Rest still at anchor in the harbour of Cape Cod. A child born, of William White, which lives. It is to be named Peregrine, and is a male child. Died: one Edward Thompson, a man brought under bond by the same William White, who thus, though he gains a son, loses the passage money he expended on this man. Will be buried on the near shore of Long Point. Harsh and foully blowing weather keeps all to the ship.

20   Edward Winslow opened his account of the third major exploration, which he later wrote, by saying:

Wednesday, the 6th of December, we set out again, it being very cold and hard weather.

At length we got clear of the sandy point and got up our sails; and within an hour or two we got under the weather shore [i.e., the inner shore of the Cape, from which the northeast wind then blew], and then had smoother water and better sailing; but it was very cold, for the spray froze on our clothes and made them like coats of iron.

We sailed six or seven leagues by the shore . . . and found a fair road of a bay, a league over at the narrowest and some two or three in length. But we made right over to the land before us, and left the exploring of this income till the next day.

As we drew near to the shore we espied some ten or twelve savages very busy about a black thing; what it was we could not tell. They saw us and ran to and fro as if carrying something away.

We landed a league or two from them, and had much ado to put ashore anywhere, it lay so full of flat sands.

When we came to the shore we made us a barricade, got firewood and set out our sentinels; and betook us to our lodging, such as it was. We saw the smoke of the fire which the savages made that night, about four or five miles from us.

In the morning we went to explore this place (and look for the savages), but we found it to be only a bay, without either river or creek coming into it. Yet we deemed it to be as good a harbour as Cape Cod. . . . We found also a great fish, called a grampus, dead on the sands.

We then directed our course along the sea sands, to the place where we last saw the Indians, and there saw it was also a grampus which they had been cutting up.

We followed the tracks of the Indians' bare feet a good way on the sands and at length saw where they had gone into the woods, by the side of a pond [Great Pond, Eastham]. One said he thought he saw an Indian house among the trees, so we went up to see; and here we and the shallop (and the men left in her) lost sight of one another till night.

Se we lighted on a path but saw no houses, and followed it a great way into the woods. We found where corn had been set, though not that year (as at Corn Hill). Later we discovered a great burial place, one part of which was encompassed with a large palazado (a fence made of stakes). Within it was full of graves, some big, some small, some also paled about; and others had like an Indian house made over them, but not matted. Yet we digged none of them up, but only viewed them and went our way.

Also, a little further on, we found two baskets full of parched acorns hid in the ground, which when we began to dig we supposed to be corn; we cast earth on them again and went our way.

All this while we saw no people. We went ranging up and down till the sun began to draw low; and then we hastened out of the woods, that we might come to our shallop; which, when we came out of the woods, we espied a great way off.

They were exceedingly glad to see us, for they feared, because they had not seen us for so long, thinking we would have kept by the shore side. So, being both weary and faint, for we had eaten nothing all that day, we fell to make our camp and to get firewood, which always cost us a great deal of labour. By the time we had done, it was night; and we fed upon such victuals as we had, and betook us to our rest, after we had set our watch.

With a doubled blanket shawlwise around her head and shoulders, Dorothy rested her elbows on the bulwark and stared out unmovingly across the dull waters of the harbour. Rain had washed the snow from Cape Cod that Thursday afternoon and the evening was fresh and cold. Long Point masked the outer bay from sight; looking past its tip, the eye saw only the distant inner shore of the Cape. But somewhere out on the wide bay, coasting by unknown shores, ran the little shallop bending from the wind, carrying a handful of questing, desperate men. Gone with them was old John Carver, his bald head hatted and muffled with a woollen scarf; and young John Alden; and with them were the mates Clarke and Coppin, experienced men of the sea, strong in wind and limb, ordered forth by Mr. Jones from his sickbed, to speed the settlers.

She had come but a few minutes before from looking in on Mr. Jones on Sam Fuller's instructions, to see how he was. Several had taken chest complaints from their former adventuring about the shores and sleeping on the ground in the wet, of which Mr. Jones was one, and Gilbert another. The Captain was making a quick recovery, his fever passed, but Gilbert was likely to take longer in getting better. Sam had remained aboard to care for the sick.

Dorothy had stood so for two or three minutes when the Winslows' adopted waif, the child Ellen Moore, came very quietly behind her and gave a gentle tug at her skirt.

"Mr. Gilbert wants for to talk with you, mam. 'E arst me to say that, as 'ow 'e'd like your company 'fore you went to your bed."

Dorothy took her by the hand and they went in to descend the poop hatch. "Talking of bed—it's time little girls were all in bed and covered up to keep warm. How is your brother Jasper?"

"Doin' badly, mam," the child said, with grown-up self-possession. "Mrs. Carver says for me to pray to God for 'im, which I suppose I must."

Ellen's calm acceptance of illness and misery, the fruit no doubt of a close acquaintance with both since infancy, suddenly hurt Dorothy as if she had noticed for the first time some horrible physical deformity in the child.

In the wide, low hold, peopled by moving shadows and the pale blobs of faces, the brazier flickered and glowed beneath the open centre cargo hatch. Down at the far end, on a shelf projecting from the galley bulkhead partition, near the bunks of the sick, stood a hand lamp shaped like a shoe, from the toe of which spouted a small clear flame; only one candle was lighting elsewhere. Candles had come to be deemed too precious to be burned except during dire necessity.

The air, as usual, was sharp with wood smoke. All the settlers were there in the first hold, in their family encampments or sitting around the fire. To the right at the forward end, beneath the lamp, the dozen rough box bunks fixed to the decking and partially partitioned by dividing screens had been given over to the seriously sick. Quiet voices echoed about the hold; a copper bowl dropped on the deck gave out a clang; what noise there was came mostly from the children.

Ellen's clinging hand led Dorothy firmly down the centre of

the hold and then across to Gilbert's pallet. It was difficult at first to see where he lay, but as her eyes became accustomed again to the gloom she saw his outline, his face, and lastly, his eyes. The child walked away soberly, her mission accomplished.

"Come closer, Dorothy May," he said, his voice noticeably wheezy and hoarse. "I have waited, through a very long afternoon, but you never would come over to me." She continued to stand a couple of paces from his bed, looking down at him, silent, her white hands fidgeting on her bosom, so slight and girlish a figure. "Come, sit on my bundle, Dorothy," he whispered.

At last she moved around the end of his pallet, felt for his clothes bundle with her hand, and sat, thrust her toes under the edge of the mattress, cupped her face in her hands.

"Surely it is a very honourable occupation for young women, to sit with the sick? None watch you, dear Dorothy," he whispered reassuringly, "they are all too busy with their own affairs —their own fears."

"Stop talking nonsense. Do you feel better? You've kept warm?" She could now see his face clearly, the soft brown, uncombed hair bunched about his ears, his smooth round forehead, and his dark bright eyes. . . .

And just there, in that part of the hold, odorous with the smoke of fresh wood burning and the smell, not so pleasant, of a hundred stale human bodies, her senses were conscious with a quickening pang of recognition of Gilbert's own individual odour, a pleasing tang of must and leathery sweat.

He coughed, and lay still for several moments, breathing deeply. "I'll live," he said; "not that my doubting presence will have any great effect on the affairs of the New World. . . . You have been on deck again, looking for the boat's return—not yet. . . . Two days will not do to discover a seat for a new world to build on. Your William must be away from you a week or more, this time. So you will have to make do with my poor consolation." His voice lost its bantering tone. "They are twenty good men and strong; fear nothing. Have you no word to say to *me*?"

She shook her head.

"No. Then if you will not tell me a story I must tell you one. I will tell you of a bower in the wilderness; a lonely bower of peace and rude comfort, which I saw with my own eyes—and where I was entertained to dinner on a roasted fish!" And he told her of the Indian house, describing it in detail.

"You should have brought them to it," she said, not meaning it. "Which is the kind of conduct that—that makes you not well thought of. . . ."

"It is your good thoughts of me I want—yes, yes, don't say it, I speak in a fever, near sick unto my death, or else how could I speak so! Ah . . . if you were but a savage maid," he said in a soft humorous murmur, that gradually grew in strength and seriousness, "and I a strong hunter, how we might fly to the wilderness! Far into the wilderness of great trees and bunchy grapes, and build us a house with a hooped roof of woven mats——"

"So did William Button think he would be a king—but he died of coughing," Dorothy said uneasily, wishing that she could think of something innocent to talk about and lead him away from these their unfulfillable intimate hungers. But . . . finding words had always been difficult when the warmness rose choking in the throat.

"I am not talking of any William Button," Gilbert said urgently, "you know that well. Oh, Dorothy, admit our state! That, alone, may give a mite of satisfaction."

Admit our state, William's favourite words, a mockery in Gilbert's mouth. "No," she whispered, "no, we must not, ever. Think of *them*, out in the loneliness, William, always alone——"

"We are all alone, man is born alone. Deny yourself you, if you will, but I will not. I am no frightened girl, nor ashamed to say how my thoughts reach about for you through the long day. Do not speak to me of sinning! That pious language has no meaning in my ears if it's of you and me. To know, to admit, that is at least something; I've learnt that in my ten years longer on the earth than you, Dorothy May."

"Gilbert—quiet your voice. You are sick, in a fever. Why must I live only to make others unhappy?"

"But you do not deny it," he whispered, staring up fixedly at her and raising his head from the pillow. "Mumble of your Wil-

301

liam how you like, your William that stole you from me as a child, it is you and me, you and me, you do not deny it—the sin is out and about between us——"

"Stop," she said, laying her hand quickly on his mouth, and as quickly withdrawing it again before he could catch it up in his own. "Please do not talk so now, not now, not now, oh, please?"

"Very well," he said, sighing, "as you will."

He turned his head away; but his gaze came back to her white face after a moment, and he faintly smiled with an expression of tender affection and unconditional surrender such as she had never had from any man before in her short life. Her whole being seemed to expand and for minutes on end float with a kind of soft delight. They continued to look at each other in silence. Until she remembered the shallop again, out seeking on the cold waters, and her guilt returned, and she glanced away from him, confused and afraid.

"I—I did dream of Ted Thompson," she said jerkily, anything to get back to playing the role of good Christian speaking to ill Christian. "A strange dream it was . . ."

"Thompson?" he frowned. "Thompson, what Thompson?"

"Mr. White's man, that they have buried on the shore amidst the little savin trees. He that used to talk so of—of being warm, of monkeys and coloured birds. God have mercy on him, he looked never to have been warm in all his life. And then he bled and swelled up and turned purple, and coughed—the very first to die in the New World. . . ."

Her continued preoccupation with illness and death now worried him again. "And you dreamed?" he prompted gently.

"I dreamed I saw him in a garden, all full of flowers; and next he was taken there, by men, and dragged away. They tore the clothes from his back, and branded vagabond on him. He was tied to the tailboard of a cart, by his wrists, the way they do tie them, and whipped through a town. I woke up all wet on my face, crying tears out aloud. That was the night before last night. William was not pleased to be wakened, going out as he was in the boat in the early morning. But he talked to me most kindly."

She went on, with more of herself and her husband, and Gilbert smiled to himself; she was reminding both herself and him in her simple way of her fixed and immovable married state. "So your William treats you lovingly?" he said coldly. "You are a very pair of doves. What trash. I am not deceived with a word, like a child. I'd stake my life he went forth, not knowing if he'd ever return, with no more than a pat on the head and a 'Be diligent, my good woman, and say your prayers!' "

"You think wrongly," she began defensively, "there is no fault in him but what——" She broke off, as if what she had meant to say had unexpectedly become lost in her mind.

"How *did* he go forth from you?" Gilbert asked, suddenly knowing that something had happened that she wished to hide from him.

"Thinking not well of me," she whispered. "I am not a good woman, to tell lies! He said that I had slipped away from God; but he meant that I had slipped away from him—as so I said, so rashly, rashly, and we parted the morning, he with an offended heart towards me, because I was unrepentant. And so it is: there has been a greater coldness in me for him, since the days we first sat together in the galley, you and me . . . in deceit. My thoughts were elsewhere." She spoke quickly and breathlessly. "When I bursted to sing, swelled with love to live, I had no words to share it with him, and make it of God, as he would. Not ever, not then. My eyes looked no more at him with undeceiving affection. . . ."

"Did you ever look at him with true affection?" Gilbert asked, jealously and bitterly.

"Always I did, until then."

"Dorothy, you never knew what love is. How could you know your heart with a cold stranger?"

She coughed, and when it had passed, covered her eyes with her fingers, trembling.

"We could go back with the ship, to London," he whispered. "They have nothing against me at home. You could be hid on the ship, until she was on her way."

"Don't," she said, "don't!"

"You want to live a good life, a life of warm love, of love of

303

blood and heart, not of mouthy prayers on stiff lips—to live, to live, do you not want to live?"

"I do want to live, oh, I want so to live, Gilbert, as you say," she wept. "I want to live a-times so much, so large, so great, like I was hungry and hurt, burning a fever in me—but it passes, then I know I will not ever, but will die. Death has his hand on me and catches my breath."

"Don't think of these deaths! It works in your brain. Think, oh, think, that we may be together, and live—I can hide you on the ship before she sails back."

"What should I tell William?"

"Tell him? Tell him nothing. You are gone, that's all. He will soon make his own life afresh."

"Lie to him? I would not do that. How could he marry himself another wife if I was not dead?"

"Not lie to him, just say nothing on it, or he'll prevent it— he'll prevent it, in as he owns you with his bed and his prayer book."

"You would have me a liar and a husband deceiver?"

"Yes, dear love. To have you I'd bargain with the Devil. You will come, you will?"

She stood up, breathless, her heart pounding, her hands fumbling in agitation to draw her blanket around her, although she felt to be burning in a fever. "No, no, no, don't look at me so! Wait, wait for time to tell——"

"But say it, say you will, Dorothy!"

"If I stay with you longer you will make me say everything you want . . . and I want . . ." She hurried from his bedside, to the centre of the hold, where she stood, breathless, leaning against the base of the mainmast.

"Come back and talk with me, Mrs. Bradford," he called, loudly. "I am most lonely this evening."

His suddenly loud, hoarse voice booming in the hold caught the attention of the others there, particularly a group by the brazier sitting with their knees drawn up and staring at the fire, of which group William Mullins was the centre. A moment of panic overcame Dorothy, seeing them all look around at her. She took a few steps towards the fire, her hand to her forehead.

"I am so tired," she said. "I will go to bed. . . . Mr. Winslow would be glad of company." Then she turned away and went below, feeling her way in the dark till she found her own pallet down in the second hold and crept beneath the blankets.

Mrs. Mullins touched her husband's arm; but he frowned and said under his breath, "The sick cannot console the sick. I am in meditation." His wife leaned towards their daughter and whispered in her ear, "Go and talk with the young man—more worthy of your attention than some I could name. . . . You have our leave. We are all here."

Gilbert did not see the girl come to his side; but when his eyes focused again she was there, sitting where Dorothy had been sitting. And he thought, What a silly vacant face she has, the vacancy of innocence and inexperience, and though he appeared to continue staring at her, forgot her; until Priscilla, frightened by what she took to be a frenzied and mocking expression directed at her in cold silence, picked up her skirts and left him without a word spoken.

Far into the night Gilbert lay awake, gazing up at the shadowed beams; and down below, by William's vacant bed, Dorothy lay awake, with her face turned into the pillow.

And at four o'clock in the morning, in the end bunk beneath the shoe-shaped lamp, Master James Chilton, a consumptive tailor, of Canterbury, with his wife watching by his side, gave a long-drawn sigh, closed his eyes for the last time and without the least fuss slipped away into death.

Well before daylight the camp was awake and breakfasting around two large blazing fires; the men warmed their feet and dried some of the night's dew out of their capes, as they munched biscuit and saveloy meat. That Friday morning found them only ten miles further along the coast past the inlet they had named Cold Harbour, on their journey around the sixty-mile perimeter of bay formed by the northward-bending arm of Cape Cod and the mainland, in search of a safe harbour to take deep-sea vessels and having clear ground and good soil.

The two great fires threw warm light and dancing shadows

out across the expanse of flat sand surrounding the camp, and upwards inland over the desert sand for two hundred feet, to where the edge of the woods lay.

Boughs had been thrown the night before into a loose horse-shoe-shaped barricade, the open end facing the beach; which at the most would have served to trip any intruder running upon the sleeping explorers.

In the half-dark the men began to take their guns and stuff down to the shallop, which lay anchored in a shallow cove, some distance from the camp. The cove was watered at low tide by a seaweed-lined inlet that wound through the wet sand to the waters of the bay, and would thus enable the shallop to put to sea again while the tide was yet out.

The night had been clear, without frost, and it looked like being a raw windy day, good for sailing.

Clarke, Coppin and the sailors went down to attend to the shallop, with the bulk of the men, leaving Captain Standish, Bradford, Edward Winslow and Alden at the camp. Standish and Alden, sitting on the sand with the powder keg between them, reloaded the muskets which Standish thought had got damp during the night. Bradford and Winslow were taking the last turn at sentry go, standing with their backs to the fires and looking out over the low barricade of branches.

"With Coppin out of earshot," Standish said to John, "you mark this: one or other of you should have been left behind. That fellow's fur rises up like an angry cur's on your near presence. You will today keep the length of the boat between you."

"If he do I won't be so tempted to tip 'im in the sea," John said.

"You will do in as I order. As he is, he is of use; you go to set him at loggerheads and he won't be. Don't ram your rod so hard down the barrel."

William White trudged in out of the darkness and, kneeling by the fire, rolled up his blanket.

"Where is your gun, Mr. White?" Standish asked.

"With the boat, Captain!"

"The order is, Mr. White, to keep your firearm with you, till we know more what we're at."

"I see no good reason to wrench my arms further, lugging that piece of iron up and down the sand with me. I only wish I had brought me a good old English longbow across the sea, and you might keep the rest. I put no faith in a damp firecracker to save my life if all comes to all."

"By God," Standish began, "had I you gentlemen one month——" and stopped with his red mouth open in his red-bearded, flame-lit face, a bullet in his fingers poised over the muzzle of a musket.

From the edge of the wood that lay, hidden still in the morning twilight, two hundred feet away, a bedlam broke forth as of half a hundred demons shrieking, whistling, mooing, owling; wolf howls intermingled with the banging of sticks; barks, shivering screams and shouts in guttural tones:

"Hoo-ah-h! Hoo-ah-h! Hoo-ah-h! Woat! Hoo-ah-h! Woat! Woat! Woat! Ha-hee-ha, ha-hee-ha, ha-hee-ha, ha-hee-ha, ha-hee-ha! Woach! Ha! Ha! Woach!——"

Standish dropped gun and bullet and bounced up onto his feet, jerking at the pistol in his belt. John scuttled across the sand on his hands and knees and pulled out his pistol from his rolled blanket. From the beach the calls of the men there came up faintly through the clamour.

"Arm, arm!" Standish roared back.

Bradford and Winslow had dropped to their knees behind the screen of boughs and were straining to see out into the half-dark, while at the same time blowing up the sparks in their slow matches. On Standish's cry Winslow stood up, and shouted in the direction of the boat, "Stay as you are—look to the boat."

A figure came running wildly and heavy-footed over the sand, tripped and sprawled with a splash of flying sand; Standish, straddle-legged, pointed his pistol, steadied on his left wrist; the figure rose up, proving to be Stephen Hopkins, saw the firelit Captain pointing a muzzle at him, and threw out his hands. "Jesus—hold." He stumbled into camp and sank onto his knees, panting. "They are *men*," he said, "they are men. Get from the firelight and you will see them."

"We have no light to our guns," the powerful voice of Coppin boomed up from the beach. "Shall we put off?"

"Shall we come to you?" Mr. Carver's voice cried, shrill and trembling, from the water's edge.

"Scatter the fire as we can't be seen," Bradford shouted.

"Stephen, run with a brand to the boat," Winslow said. "Tell them to light every match but to fire not."

The clamour of yelling and screaming rose in waves of intensity until it seemed to be shrilling and barking and echoing on every side.

"Let us retire to the boat," Bradford cried.

"And lose our food and powder to them?" Winslow shouted. "They keep off—this is all to affright us—there is not one to be seen. We gather ourselves up in good order and shew we do not fear their magic."

Hopkins had pulled a branch as tall as himself from the nearest fire, and with it on his shoulder, flaming and smoking at one end, ran out and down the beach. Bradford with another bough proceeded to scatter the fires.

"Fright us! I'll fright them, the devils," Standish answered Winslow and, standing back from the barricade, levelled his pistol arm at the edge of the trees.

"Let them yell," Winslow shouted, stretching out his hand to stay the Captain. "If we fire or run they will come at us. They are like children mooing in the dark."

"I am the commander here!" He shook off his hand.

"In Christ's name leave the fires," Winslow screamed in anger at Bradford, and turned again with the intention still of preventing Standish from firing. But as he did the little Captain's pistol bucked, flaming, his ball whistling high over the trees. As its thundering echo died, the howling and barking in the wood lessened, sank, and ceased as if a heavy door had closed.

"There!" Standish said half under his breath. "The ordering of these matters is mine. Damnation with the fire——"

The remains of the scattered fires were glowing like a hundred little suns and, smoking tenfold, filled their eyes with tears.

"Listen," John said.

A whispering sound had sped over the camp and terminated with a dull thud out on the sand. Another followed. And then through the branches of the barricades something ripped, passed over the smoking embers and hit a cloak hanging to air on a stick. It fell to the ground; John darted to pick it up—a feathered shaft tipped with a black claw sharpened like a double-edged knife point.

"Down to earth," Standish bellowed. "Present your arms to them."

Five men ran in from the direction of the shallop and the pale waters of the bay: Hopkins, the mate Clarke, Isaac Allerton, John Howland, Carver's bondman, and Degory Priest. They threw themselves down with the others between the remains of the fires and the barricade, facing the woods, muskets propped on the branches before them, throwing out question and comment. Arrows came in humming flights of half a dozen, and then a dozen or more together.

"There is not more than twenty of them," Winslow said, "for see how thinly their arrows come when they might come in droves and flocks. And that noise was all done by the same small number of men——"

"Each fire when I order," Standish commanded. "Degory, fire off at them. Go to!"

Degory Priest pulled his trigger, and in surprise felt the gunstock jump back beneath his armpit, saw the gush of sooty flame, and the crashing boom struck every ear like the cuff of a heavy hand.

"Reload," Standish said curtly, peering through the branches like a bellicose goat.

"I see them," Winslow said. "Keep your eyes to the clear spaces of sky between the trees."

"Alden, fire off."

John aimed up the incline, low along the sand, and cursed blasphemously when his musket misfired with a damp hiss.

"A man stands out," Clarke said. "I see him by the larger tree, the one like a mushroom."

"Hold," Winslow said, "I see him. Let us hold fire."

"Fire, Howland," Standish ordered.

Howland's musket lashed out its tongue of crimson.

"No hit. The fellow eggs his cowards on," Standish said scornfully. "But they stay hid, for all his yelling."

A tall figure was silhouetted against a tree-framed silk screen of sky, waving his arms at the camp defiantly. They could see that he was a man, but nothing more; a black jigging shadow.

Standish took up his own superior silver-chased flintlock musket and aimed carefully. But when the smoke of his shot had whisked away on the breeze the savage was still jumping up and down against the sky, yelling incitement to his companions.

The Captain reached another musket from one of the others, and aimed again. The serpentine clicked down; nothing happened. He threw the gun back angrily and called for a second, biting his lips and breathing deeply.

"Standish, I forbid this," Winslow said. "Let us lie and wait to see."

"Let us hold," Bradford backed him up, "wait awhile and see——"

The Captain aimed deliberately, while an arrow swished past his head. As if to help him, the silhouette stood still for a moment, turning aside, speaking excitedly. The gun in Standish's hands belched red fire; but the figure remained, jumping up and down again.

John had quickly run a handful of bird shot into his barrel and reprimed the flashpan. Saying nothing further, he aimed into the tree above the savage's head, and fired. A shower of twigs descended on the figure's head, followed by a dead branch which struck him on the shoulder and broke in pieces.

The silhouette gave a startled whoop, jumped like a jack-in-the-box, turned and crashed off among the trees. Heads bobbed in the woods, and in a few moments howls and cries were fading into the distance.

The woods returned to their old, mildewed silence; daylight flooded the eastern sky. The settlers' first encounter with the inhabitants of the New World had come and gone almost before anyone knew what was happening, to pass into history as "the huggery at Nauset," leaving them unscathed but for the sand in Stephen Hopkins' eyes and the handful of savages as confused as the handful of settlers.

310

The same morning they sailed on down the coast with a strong wind; and about nine or ten o'clock it began to veer to the north and east, bringing showers of sleet.

The squat, thick boat, with its large loose sail, at home on the waterways of Holland and the lower Thames, was there, where quick gusts and gales blew out of nowhere, a dangerous craft to sail, lurching and creaking and bending over at alarming angles.

Noon came; a watery ghost of the sun peeped out at a gap in the clouds, shewed its face and slipped away; the sleet was in at their necks, soaking chillily against flesh, blankets and capes sodden, the inside of the boat gleaming wet and slopping with water. Opening up a wide break in the sandy coast line, they sidled in as the tide began to ebb. Following the coast on their left hand, a neck of sand came to meet them on the right and the shallop entered a broad shallow inlet a half mile or more wide at its mouth, where wind-rippled water stretched away into the desolate flatness of a great salt marsh.

Old John Carver was huddled in the bows in a near coma from cold, wet and exposure; so the shallop was run into a cove —rising flocks of fowls—near where scrubby wood grew, and there the afternoon was spent in drying themselves out by fires, getting their circulation moving and rigging the sail as a shelter from the fits and starts of rain mixed with snow.

It took perhaps an hour to strike a light and start a fire with some of the precious supply of dry sticks and grass carried in a waxed cloth; but at length before the shelter on the wet sand grass a fire was got going and extended patiently into a tremendous crackling, smoking bonfire, and they felt their lives to be saved only in the nick of time. And when they had some heat in their bodies and damp clothes steaming, the early winter dusk was ready to come down.

The night passed with no more disturbance than from the quacking of ducks; they felt themselves to be quite safe in such a godforsaken morass of swamp, sea and sand.

Morning came, and revealed a desolation of mud flats abandoned by the tide; and there they stayed on until nine or ten o'clock, in gusty weather, drying themselves and their stuff out thoroughly. That day it was resolved not to attempt so much, but to start out late and put in to land again early. Their course from then on would be along the coast of the mainland proper— the Cape roughly joining the mainland somewhere about where they then were, so Clarke said. And he further said that Mr. Jones had instructed him about a harbour the Master thought to be on the mainland somewhere opposite the head of the Cape. Mr. Jones had spoken of remembering having once seen a chart whereon this perfect harbour was marked.

William Bradford scowled and Edward Winslow shrugged. Mr. Carver said that they were in God's hands, looked absently from one of Mr. Jones's mates to the other, and that he had a dreadful cold coming in his head. William Bradford thought privately that, whatever could be said for Clarke, the hulking foul-mouthed Coppin could never be mistaken for God's agent under any circumstances. At the back of his mind, as with the other leaders, was the persistent worry about how long the *May-flower* would remain with them in the New World. Jones had spoken originally of how he must keep a sufficiency of stores to see himself and crew back over the ocean, that when his stores approached a certain level he must dump the settlers on the shore with their own stores and go; but how near the ship's stores were to that danger point only the Captain knew; and William Bradford trusted Mr. Jones as much as he would have trusted a ferret in a nest of young rabbits.

Sailing west, the head of Cape Cod began to drop out of sight and the sand hills of the peninsula changed to solider-looking, well-wooded country, broken down flat every few miles by inlets and marshes.

The water fretted and struck at the bows of the shallop, cuffed her and gurgled by her sides, as on she lurched and splashed in a mounting northeast wind, racing at the beach, tacking off and plunging in again.

"We are come thirty leagues around the bay," Clarke kept saying encouragingly. "We must find a harbour any hour if only we keep forward."

But the afternoon wore on, darkening, blustering, and no harbour fit to shelter the *Mayflower* came into view.

"Darkness comes on apace," Mr. Carver shouted from the bows, back against the tearing wind. "If you will not go in let us put the sails down and row with our oars—or this gale will take them down for us. With rowing we may at least keep ourselves warm!"

Those at the other end of the boat did not hear him, both for the noise of wind and water and creaking rigging and because Hopkins, Standish, Bradford and Winslow were arguing about whether to continue on or try to run the boat on the beach—a dangerous proceeding since by then they were far enough up the west side of the bay to be exposed to open North Atlantic weather. No longer did the waves hit gently on the beaches as in Cape Cod Harbour and on the inner side of the arm; at one spot where the coast bulged out the waves smashed on rocks, shooting spray fifty feet into the air.

And from a quarter of a mile out it was not possible to tell just how strongly the inshore waves were hitting the beaches; the shallop might ride in to the sands without being swamped, and she might not. Their leading sailor, English, was against taking such a risk with the onshore wind so high, as were Trevore and Ellis. Coppin said that if he was given the tiller he could do it. While Clarke thought it better to risk freezing on the sea for the night, or part of it, than founder on the shore. But he agreed with Winslow and Bradford that if by the time dusk, then beginning to fall over the land, was halfway advanced and no opening had shown up, they would head onto the nearest beach and trust to luck.

The wind whipped shortly into a small gale and the desert of water ran with sudden ridges of flaring white, the laden boat's wake smothered in its inception. With the changes of wind the boat creaked, canvas flapped madly, and the spray hissed over the bows in drenching showers—to complete the work of an earlier shower of sleet; the chuckle of water by the boat's sides all too quickly changed to a frantic slapping and beating and the sea surged by on the lee side half a foot from the top of the gunwale.

In the crashing and running of waters Clarke heard a snap, felt the tiller lurch in his hands, and knew the top hinge had broken. He held on, his shoulder wrenched, but in a matter of seconds the lower rudder hinge went also and he was half dragged over the stern, holding a free rudder trailing behind the boat.

Freed of her rudder, the shallop slewed around and before the sails could be loosened took a small hurricane of wind broadside on. From the weather side stays ripped out and cleats flew from the timbers with splintering cracks. While each man held on for his life the mast split off short and sails, rigging and mast went overboard.

Without wasting time or breath in words the twenty men fell each to what task lay nearest to hand. Clarke, John, Coppin and English, with a couple of coils of rope, lashed two oars, one on either side of the stern, by which to steer; others freed the rigging with their knives, lifted aboard the mast and clawed the dripping sails over the side after it, banged in the row locks and set out the oars. The wind pushed them insistently shoreward, the sky blackened over and sailing, swirling curtains of icy rain beat with a hissing noise the sea about the gleaming shallop and the streaming, struggling men.

When the mast went overboard the swells were rolling shorewards unbroken; by the time the steering oars were lashed and the mast and sails got in, the swells lifting the boat had curly white caps, and by that sign showed how horribly near was the shore.

Through the rain and darkness their tired, cold eyes strained for a sight of the land, sometimes seeing a hundred feet, sometimes not more than ten.

With six men rowing as hard as they could against breaking swells and the wind that beat shorewards, no man could yet tell whether they moved backwards or forwards. After a minute Trevore called out that he saw the shore. None heard him in the howling wind but his rowing companion, John, who looked and thought he saw it also. He in turn yelled out to the men steering, Coppin and English.

The shore, seen now in glimpses through the darkness and

driving rain, appeared to be but a few hundred feet behind and nothing more than a sandy beach all but smothered by white foam.

Numb and wet to the skin, the settlers left the boat's management and direction entirely to the sailors, while those of them that had minds still capable of it said their prayers. The steersmen began to bring the boat around, to point her at the supposed beach; and the shoreward-racing swells quickly helped to swing her broadside on to them, lifting her up and swinging her down, each moment the men expecting the next roller to turn her over.

"The beach ends in a point!" John shouted. "There is the last of it. The tide races on the point—keep her off . . ." But the tillermen shook their heads, seeing nothing. At the same time John began to notice a hopeful sign: the swells were surely smaller and no longer so broken on their tops. He shouted advice again to keep the boat on her course parallel with the coast, as she was, for apparently they were riding in behind some protecting outcrop of land; but once out of the breaking swells, the steersmen seemed to lose all sense of direction, and he felt that the boat was actually heading back into the rougher water. Giving his oar to Standish, whom he unceremoniously dragged onto the seat with one arm, he scrambled into the stern and before Coppin knew what was happening had shouldered him from the port steering oar and sent him sprawling forward. Fortunately Coppin was held back forcibly by Hopkins, White and Allerton, while John and English steered in the direction the young carpenter thought they should.

The rain thinned and fell away, the wind lost its smothering force, and the water grew calmer; the six panting men on the oars pulled on, their feet resting in half a foot of water. They were in a harbour, there could be no slightest doubt. It was almost dark, yet there was light enough to see what looked like the wooded end of a small island sitting in calm water, right ahead.

And they bore on to it, having come at last into their New Plymouth Harbour, frozen and drenched to the skin, twenty shivering, exhausted men in a small boat.

21   LOG: SUNDAY: DECEMBER 10TH: Cape Cod. A high tide in at noon, a very flood tide. Today a clearer day, the bad weather past. Shallop still away discovering. Saw the smoke of fires distant on the Cape, know not if savage or of ours. No wild man yet shows his face, which causes great general fear, for that they hide to prepare mischief against us. Many are in ill-health. Some of the crew also complain of sickness and more particularly of the cold. Dies Jasper Moore, an orphan lad brought by John Carver. In the morning will be buried the boy, on the Long Point.

Only on the surface was the water alive; below, surely, Dorothy thought, it was always asleep, still and asleep, drifting here and drifting there, cushioned on the yellow sand. Another Monday morning, and the longboat over on the empty beach where the shallop had been built, and tiny figures to be seen among the trees, digging a grave. She was alone in the prow of the ship, looking over the side and down at the green water. The morning was the best time to be out and about in the New World, when the day was good, for the air could be crisp, dry, light. But what of the pink smear? She shivered to remember that after a fit of coughing she had seen for the first time a pink smear on her palm. So William Button had died, with blood in his mouth, and Edward Thompson.

She tightened her shawl around her and looked over the side again, straining to peer into the depths, down through the glinting water, praying to God to let her forget her eating fear of death. The ship was peculiarly still, the decks deserted: fear for the men absent in the shallop, prayers for the boy being buried ashore. There in the prow she was cut off from the rest of the ship by the forecastle house, with its iron spout smoking in the clear air. Unexpectedly the sun shone and she was sur-

316

prised at its warmth; a thick dust of frost on the ship was beginning to melt. Death. Please, O God, let me think not of death,
which is a sin. I want to live and not be sad—the sun shines!

There were half a dozen empty casks in the prow, all
powdered with frost and bejewelled with daggers of melting ice
where the sleet and rain had gathered on the tops and frozen in
the night. The sun striking down on the calm water attracted
her so much that she put a small cask by a larger one and
climbed on the taller, to be able to lean right over the rounded,
wide-topped bulwark and look straight down into the sea. What
was it that Gilbert had once said? "Then you will begin to believe it and put your face down to the sea." She saw her palm
again, the pink smear of fresh blood, her life's blood.

What waved there below in the sleeping depths? Seaweed,
eelgrass, green hair. Hair combed by the ebbing tide flowing
swiftly and silently out of the harbour. In the green depths, no
pain, no unhappiness, no hunger to hear the voice of one, no
shame before the face of another; only the sunshine coming
down on summer days to warm the yellow sand. Voices sounded
deep in the ship, as if in the sea itself, soft women's voices,
sailors' hollow, entombed voices.

Pushing, tiptoe, she balanced over the broad rail and spread
her arms down over the bellying side of the ship, with her finger
tips making wriggly patterns in the melting frost; deep below the
green hair rippled and waved in silence, silence . . . Look
down, look down deep, she thought, into peace.

Her feet slipped on the frosty barrel's top, shot backwards and
up and the weight of her upper body drew her down the other
side; her palms slid down the wet iced side of the ship as she
frantically tried to push herself back. Then she knew there was
no saving herself: she had overbalanced and was falling into the
water. And as if time stopped for a spell, she was able to feel
surprise and indignation—because she was going to die after all
in a silly, accidental way, with not a soul to see the manner of
her going, and not having given Gilbert his answer.

Face first she struck the upward-rushing water, then was beneath in darkness going down, head over heels, felt the searing,
shattering shock of icy coldness in every shrinking particle of her

317

being; her mouth opened, gasping to scream, the freezing water sucked down her throat into her lungs and there turned to fire. An orange glow blazed into her mind's eye, flashing and dazzling, sank, died, faded out, and she slid into the utter darkness, and peace.

The swift sure currents of water being sucked out of the harbour by the ebbing tide took her gently and rolled her away towards the deep sea, her skirts billowing slowly, a sea anemone, her hands white fingers of coral, her hair fine streaming sea grass.

The sun flooded the ship brightly for a full ten minutes; some women and children came up onto the waist deck to see the marvel; and the white frost on the grey wood turned to bright tears and trickled away.

Across the bay the men in the boat thought the high and distant sky augured well for them that Monday morning; for once again, having spent all the previous day upon the little island inside the new harbour's mouth, resting, drying out their clothes, mending the mast and praying God thanks in their minds for their deliverance, they were on their way, crossing inside the harbour mouth that was formed by two sandy spits; and, at last, approaching the shore, following a channel of deep water.

Just then the sun shone out. Their eager eyes saw weedy and grassy banks ascending from the water of a river to cleared, rising ground, the banks neither too steep nor too high to clamber up in half a minute. Their deep channel led to the little river's mouth.

The boat stood off for ten minutes: but no arrows flew, no savage shewed, and it was safe open country.

They entered the river mouth, gliding through still, clear water and over to the right bank, slow matches on guns smoking in the brilliant winter sunshine. The crisp, buoyant air, the warmth of sunshine on face and hands, infected Bradford with a moment of glorious recklessness. Leaving his gun aside, he put his foot on the gunwale and, near to a willow, leaped to the bank, landing not on sand but on solid grass-covered earth and rock. Using both hands and feet, he clambered up the bank, ignoring the warning voices behind.

318

He came up onto the broad back of a hill that ascended inland, level, clear but for a few pines here and there, and marked by fields of stubble.

There he stood, breathing deeply, while the others came up to join him. Across the river there was more cleared ground, hills, and trees that in high summer would be feathery, majestic, beautiful—and here was country surely rich in wild life, *food*.

He loosened earth with his heel and collected a handful of soil. It was rich, black soil, and he held it out to shew to the others, as they came up the bank. And the sun shone on for ten minutes, while they looked about and ascended the hill before them, talking and shouting and walking like lords in a park.

Wednesday afternoon came, and Gilbert roamed the ship still, the blankets of his sickbed trailing about him, with weak aimless steps. The longboat had scoured the harbour for Dorothy's body, and although no one hoped to find anything there, the spit had been searched as well. Mr. Jones dismissed any probability of her having got on the land either through the agency of savages or in the longboat or jollyboat. There had been found no tracks on the spit, Monday evening, except those of a party that had gone to cut wood and draw water and the tracks of the group that had gone to bury Jasper Moore. Moreover, both boats could be accounted for from the hour she was last seen on the ship on Monday morning until noon on the same day, when Mrs. Brewster first discovered her to be missing. Stories were revived of creatures that reached up from the sea and plucked unwary sailors from their ships. But however it was, there could be no doubt that the sea had taken her in some way or another.

The weather was clear, and Gilbert had spent many hours that day, and the day before, gazing into the water, possessed of one insane hope after another, never quite believing that her disappearance was final, that there was no awakening as from a bad dream. Perhaps the shallop on its way back would find her—but then she would be dead in that case. . . . Nevertheless he watched for the shallop as desperately as others watched for the return of their husbands. And because so many fathers of

319

families were out on the unknown and the fear was general that the boat might not come back at all out of that distant fabulous land of mystery and invisible men, concern for Dorothy's disappearance was lost in the greater anxiety; until many a time Gilbert wanted to shout in this face or that: "She is gone! You should weep that she is gone and the clods remain. There is not enough beauty in the world or spirit in our dull hearts that we can let her go without crying out aloud!" And much more; yet he spoke to no one, only in his own distracted thoughts.

So he looked down into the sea, as she had done, but with his hair tangled, eyes sunken, unshaven face grey and haggard as a drunkard's from a month's debauch, and whispered Nashe's song. "'Brightness falls from the air; Queens have died young and fair. . . . Dust hath closed Helen's eye. Worms feed on Hector brave; Swords may not fight with fate. . . . Heaven is our heritage, Earth but a player's stage. Come, come! the bells do cry. I am sick, I must die—Lord have mercy on us!'" A prayer for a time of pestilence. The beauty of it moved him cruelly, and he wiped away an itching tear from the side of his nose; and wondered had she gone to escape *him*, as well as the cold, harsh uncertainty of life that William had brought her to. And what if he, Gilbert, had never discovered that sad, half-hidden starry crown about her head, would she still be alive?

A sailor's shout rang out, "There's our bird winging home!" followed by excited voices, and a moment later the pounding of feet coming up the hatches. Gilbert crossed the deck and stood in the press of women watching the shallop round Long Point and sail in, bending on the wind. The figures in her waved and shouted and the ship answered with an outcry of hallooings, women's glad high voices and children's excited shrieks.

Nearer, and those on the ship could count the returning explorers. Twenty. They were all come home: old John Carver, hat bound into a bonnet with his scarf; the big, brash, grinning young carpenter, hero of the broken beam; Edward Winslow; the ship's mates; Hopkins, Billington, White. Quickly the women picked them all out. "Isaac Allerton's there, man, be easy." "I see your man, Edward!" They were all there.

Soon boat and ship saw each other's faces. Sailors ran up the ratlines. Mr. Jones ascended to the poop from his cabin.

"There is William Bradford—wearing the orange shirt his Dorothy dyed sticking out at his neck." A guilty silence seemed to spread in quick, shocked waves out around the woman who had so thoughtlessly spoken. Mr. Brewster's tall form pushed forward to the rail, mute pain on his large, lined face, to be the first to greet his difficult protégé, his namesake William, and somehow, with God's help, ease the blow.

"Arrows!" Hopkins yelled, himself like some savage of dark face and wild eye and black lank locks. "The savage men tried their hand with us—and we frightened them to the middle of yesterday. Arrows!" He waved the bundle of arrows aloft. The shallop came alongside, full of red, wind-whipped faces, every man an experienced, confident traveller and conqueror.

Now we will come heart to heart, William thought, thinking of Dorothy, as he had thought all across the harbour. A woman's lot was hard. They would give each other more. He would make it up to her in little ways.

"We have found our harbour," they shouted. "The land the good Lord left over for us since the beginning of the world!"

Bradford forced himself to sit on in the stern and appear calm, strong, while the others jostled good-humouredly to get up on board, so that he was the last to ascend the boarding ladder and throw his muddy-breeched leg over the side. White, Billington, Allerton, they were all with their women and children; shouting, hugging, tears—indulgence not quite to his taste or approval. Mr. Brewster faced him; and was here taking him with an arm around his shoulder and drawing him aside beneath the projecting weather-beaten deck of the poop.

"It is true—we have found our harbour, sir, we have found our home. A harbour to take this ship in comfort. And there is cleared ground." He could not keep the note of triumph from his voice. "And good soil, where corn is grown."

The older man was strangely silent, wetting his upper lip beneath his brown and white moustache with the tip of his tongue. William remembered Dorothy and looked about quickly. "Dorothy? She is well? I have not seen her." The old man gripped his arm so tightly that it hurt. In his eyes he saw a fullness, as of tears.

"Our Dorothy has gone, Will. How, we don't know, but gone she is to eternity," the old man said, speaking faintly, close into his face, searching his eyes with helpless pity. For though he had thought of many words to say at that moment to prepare the way, he knew then that it was better that way, to say it simply and directly. "She is drownded since Monday gone, as if the earth had opened and swallowed her."

Mr. Jones, coming down off the poop deck to the waist, paused near by, and seeing close up the frozen staring face, rawboned, harsh-featured as if with all the suffering of common man moulded in the likeness of a driven animal, that was the younger man, and the openmouthed, helpless face of the old bearded one, hurried uneasily among the gabbling throng.

"No, no—leave me to be alone," Bradford said at last, thickly, through his squeezing, choking throat. He turned to go below into the darkness, so that no one should see, not even the older man he so loved, what must by all tokens happen to him very soon—the frozen immobility inside melting, the welling up of what was underneath, his collapse into womanly weeping. He went down the stairs slowly.

The bulwarks were breast-high; through months of storm and tossing no one had fallen overboard; how then could one fall overboard in a calm harbour? She had taken her own life, the most heinous crime possible to a human creature in all the calendar of sins then known to Christian man. He passed in a cloud across the hold, descended again into complete darkness. And down again, until he was in the cargo hold. There he stumbled about with little half-formed cries, seeking a corner in which to hide; finally, falling on his knees, covering his face with his hands and bending forward half doubled up, he slowly banged his head against a barrel of meal, calling her name aloud.

On deck, the prevailing genius for organizing took a hand in the telling of what had been seen and done, Governor Carver being deputed to tell the tale as a single voice and straighten out the tangled threads being so wildly flung about the deck by everyone all at once.

Gilbert stood by his brother and Mr. Jones and listened to the surprisingly gentlemanly voice soothe the rough throng, listened and did not hear, like some savage intruder, passive, tight-mouthed, arms folded in his blankets, staring across the dark water at the lonely Cape whereon was his fancied lovers' bower in the hollow by Corn Hill.

"By their noise," Mr. Carver was saying, speaking of the savages' attack, "we guessed them to be forty or fifty; though some thought that they were many more. Edward Winslow thinks they were at first trying their kind of magic, to send us back over the seas from whence we came. But how no single one of us was hit when the arrows came so thick we know not, unless it was of God—for these savages must know how to hit the fleet-running deer, as their very lives depend on it. So how it was that no one of us came to be struck, while our capes hanging by were hit many times through and through, we know not—unless it was, as Edward swears, nothing of their design at all to wound us, but to fright us from their places of habitation. But however it is, we mean to give them a wide berth for a long time, to let them cool, before we go near them again to render accounts for their corn. But of the harbour! . . . Well, the harbour is a most hopeful place, full of byways, sideways, banks, islands, with the greatest flocks of wild fowl we saw anywhere, and cannot but be a natural ground for all the fish, in their seasons. There is there an abundance of mussels, the biggest and best we've yet seen—we'll not fall down while we can make a mussel stew! And signs of lobsters and crabs there are many. And there the ship may go straight without delay, to a better shelter than this. Mr. Jones may have no fear on that score."

"The land is excellent black mould," Edward Winslow continued the story. "We roamed it all about, seven or eight miles, without seeing a single sign of savage or of their houses—only where corn had in years past been planted. The river is not navigable, it is true. But there are plenty of small running brooks to the sea, of very sweet, fresh water. Some great oaks, pines, walnut, beech, ash, birch, hazel and the sassafras tree, for medicine oil to ship to England."

"With vines everywhere," Mr. Carver resumed. "Cherry trees,

plum trees, and many others which we knew not. Oh, and herbs we found! Yes, in winter. Strawberry leaves, sorrel, watercresses and—what do you think? Beds and beds of wild leek and onions. And there is excellent clay for pots, that we washed with like it were soap. But above all there is the cleared land, and the brook to come up in our boats to it. There is a hill on which we think to set up the big guns, our own big magic, which will command all round about and from where you can look far over the ocean and see even this place of Cape Cod. So there, with God's help, we must go, without delay."

Gardens to make, houses, fishing, furs; but go across the bay and the new life in harbour and forest could begin tomorrow! And Mr. Clarke was there to testify, as had surely been the very purpose behind sending him out, that the new harbour was fit to shelter the ship. Mr. Jones withdrew from the waist deck; the women were raising their voices and calling for him to up anchor and sail there and then. . . . He went into the poop without mentioning that entry into New Plymouth Harbour must wait on a following wind, in fear that the excited women would somehow set upon him and tear him in pieces if he announced any such thing. And a nice state of affairs, he thought, when Christopher Jones ran from his own decks in face of mere women; and stranger still by the same token that he found himself more concerned for them than put out. How times changed, indeed! May God send me my east wind, he prayed, and felt a greater depth of satisfaction in the prayer than he had ever had before; as if it was the very first prayer of his life; which indeed it was, in a sense.

Midmorning, Saturday, December sixteenth, the wind blowing at last from out the quarter necessary to get the *Mayflower* into the new harbour twenty-five miles across the bay, the ship's already green and slimed cables were wound in and the anchor lifted. With the shallop sailing ahead and the longboat tugging at a tow-rope behind, she moved out from the shelter of the Cape, awakened from her sleep, and became again the old live ship, creaking her timbers, singing in her shrouds and butting doggedly at the waves.

The die was cast, the spot of earth chosen; and Fate perhaps had already drawn lots for who should live and who go to the wall, for scarce one half were to reach victory in the unequal struggle of will and idea against physical circumstance, the greater number destined to defeat by death taking off their weakened, half-starved bodies. Four months and eleven days had come and gone since the ship had sailed out down Southampton Water in August sunshine, with thirty-four men settlers, sixteen bondmen and hired hands, twenty women and thirty-two children, to try to make the first English settlement in North America.

Being on a dead course for the harbour's mouth with a following wind, the mainsails prevented Mr. Jones from seeing his objective while standing on the poop, so he came down and went forward into the bows. In the forepeak crouched a cold sailor with leaded line ready in his purple fingers. And standing in the shelter of the forecastle house were William Brewster, John Carver and Samuel Fuller.

"An hour will see us in," the Master said, in answer to a question put to him by Sam. "If the wind holds; it's but a freak wind." He stood with his back to them, small round body tightly filling out his leather jacket, his hands, blackly ingrained with charcoal, clasped behind him, legs apart, peering through red-rimmed, half-shuttered eyes at the looming coast ahead.

They had apparently come to accept his making landfall so far to the north, he felt, as a thing forced upon him—as he was believing more and more every day himself by a not unusual process of dismissing certain hard facts out of hand—and appeared to be prepared to make the best of a bad job. And in point of fact it might yet be proved that he and he alone had saved all their lives by that very act of putting in straight to land. To go south, looking for Hudson's river, would have meant a further and fatal delay and expense of supplies. But the margin of food he had thus saved them might be the very means by which they were enabled to tide over into the summer. Moreover, *he* could not be blamed for the *Speedwell's* defection, consequent loss of food and space, and addition of more mouths to feed.

He had done them wrong, he did not deny that to himself, and had tried to believe that they were many times damned and dangerous men. But that was all behind. He was growing, so mad was the world, to crave their respect and friendship; certainly of Brewster, Carver, Sam Fuller—and, perhaps, Winslow. . . . Bradford alone appeared bent on keeping him an enemy, but the death of his wife seemed to be working a change in him. So that all in all the coming days looked hopeful.

"We were just now discussing our harbour, Mr. Jones," Sam said. "We all think it must be the place named by Captain Smith 'New Plymouth.' Your Mr. Clarke is of that opinion too. We have all been great readers in years past of the discoveries made in America—you can well imagine why! And Mr. Brewster in point of fact had his well-thumbed copy of Smith's *Discoveries* packed up in England at a friend's house, to ship with us, but . . . well"—Mr. Fuller nudged Mr. Brewster slyly—"he had to leave in something of a hurry."

"I remember to have had some of Smith's charts myself," the Master admitted, "and do recall that he named the place New Plymouth. But names are made by use, and I see nothing against your giving it a new name."

"New Plymouth . . ." Mr. Brewster said. "It is a good name. And I remember, as if it had been a sign, that we were handled very kindly in the old Plymouth."

"It is Captain Smith's name," the Master said distastefully.

"Nevertheless," Mr. Carver said, "we do not suppose names will be worrying us a week or a month from now. Patience works all."

On the waist deck John leaned over the side and looked forward at the shallop dipping ahead; and, as many another, the end of the sea voyage in sight, his thought turned back to some of the things that had led him to it and that had happened during it. It was a strange thing, he felt, how just some certain scenes and faces stuck in the memory, were always to hand for an odd moment, as it were, when much else that at the time had struck home as being of great import seemed to want to be forgotten. There was the dead face of the old geographer, laid out on his four-poster to be washed for burial. A sight he was sure he would not forget as long as he lived. Perhaps it was the way you came on them out of the blue. The way he had come on poor Mrs. Dorothy on the quay with tears in her eyes, as if she knew even at that early day that she was going to the fishes. How came it that he remembered, as clear as if it was yesterday, William Bradford's stiff walk towards them across the cobbles—and that he wore an orange shirt? Or old Brewster's apple cheeks as he chucked the sheet from him in the sail locker? He'd far sooner remember Priscilla's face during the times she was being nice to him. . . . Plainly, there was no sense to what you remembered and what you didn't when it came of its own.

The cold had got into him; he clapped his arms, and went to go below for a while; but saw Priscilla standing in the poop passage, with a long black cape on and a shawl about her head. "If you come and look dead forward you'll see where the harbour is," he said to her.

She nodded out at the sailors on the deck. "They will not let us go out when the sails are to be swung, you know as well as I do; especially a woman."

"They will not let? Who are they to let? What if I let you? Come out, Miss Muffet. The sails are set." He took her by the arm and drew her across the deck. "There is a fine open hill there, that we walked up and saw all the country roundabouts; and the which you may walk up before the day is out, if you're lucky and have me take you ashore."

"Are there rocks and trees?"

"Big trees, real trees, not the like of them we've left behind. Mostly the shore is sandy inside the harbour, but that's only the shore. There's a lot of mud and thrash right up to the land when the tide be out."

"They say there are black clouds of birds."

"Oh, birds aplenty, birds you've never seen. And wolves to be howling behind the hill."

Robert Coppin was above on the poop, his large hands in leather mittens gripping the lateen halyards, with the helmsman below holding the ship before the wind. He glanced down at their backs with a curl of his thick lip.

Out from beneath the poop stepped William Bradford, and went to the side. He glanced forward, but for the rest of the short while he stayed above looked back fixedly at the fading outline of the head of Cape Cod. When it had dropped out of sight he returned below, and sat down beneath the shoe-shaped lamp near the galley door. The ache and heavy-headed bewilderment that had lain on him over the past two days was passing. What eased her death for him most was the belief that she had taken her own life, a deed which he held unforgivable by either God or man. There he remembered that he should make some notes in his pocket book. Someday he would set down a history of it all, and shew the world what was done and what was suffered—what was fit to be shewn. Under "Deaths," he wrote, "December 11th. Dorothy, Wife to Mr. William Bradford"; and hoped in his simplicity that by dismissing her thus and speaking of her no more she was out of his life and thoughts from thenceforward. There was work and enough for hand and mind amongst the people; he got up and went over to a settler, who lay sick, and forced himself to talk to him.

Now over a third of all the settlers had signs of scurvy, and it was already foreseen that the healthy would spend as much of their time nursing as in building houses. Each man had only to look in his wife's, child's, or neighbour's face, to see the result of being cramped for four months in a dark, damp, smoky hold on a daily bowl of porridge and a scrap of dried meat. They reminded each other of nothing so much as poor half-killed gypsies after a spell in prison, with their lanky greasy hair and yellow smoked faces.

Further down the hold Gilbert lay propped on his elbow, with his brother Edward sitting on the side of his pallet. While the people waited in nervous impatience for the end of the last lap of the voyage, while the ship's cook in the galley listened to the wise talk of little Ellen Moore, John succeeded again with Miss Mullins, and the Captain and Sam Fuller talked in shouts in the bows, while William Bradford forced himself to what he conceived to be his stern duty, Gilbert told his brother of Dorothy and himself, in a rambling, hoarse whisper. And Edward said that while he understood how such things happened he must banish it from mind. It had been difficult enough getting him into the company at the start, Gilbert not being a person with either a shilling in his pocket or a conviction in his head; and so far his lazy conduct had done everything except prove him a man of worth. But if it leaked out that Mrs. Bradford's death had been occasioned by him in any way at all he might as well stay on the boat and go back to England. Not that he believed him to be responsible for her death; but others might not think so.

"Banish the thought? Tell me to fly like a bird and I'll do that too!" But he could say no more. Telling Edward had been a mistake; this was an absolute thing that had happened to him; words had no power to relieve or comfort; he could only go on twisting about in the dark of his mind, or give it up, as she had done. Well, he thought bitterly, men were never so badly off that they couldn't find means to hurt themselves further. But how could he have foreseen, even though he had gone on in it against his reason, that it would end in the cutting off of the sweetest being he had ever known? "Dust hath closed Helen's eye."

Opening up the harbour mouth, the mainsails were reefed to the usual accompaniment of shouts from the sailors, hauling, pulling, and squeaking of blocks. The ship, following the shallop closely, made straight in through a channel of deep water, between stretches of tide-exposed sandbank and the harbour's two low, protecting sandy arms.

Inside, her drift carried her around in a wide arc to the left, topsails flapping loose, the sailors on the spars leaning over to gather them up. The shallop rowed on, behind the harbour's left-hand spit, and waited, marking where the *Mayflower* must come to anchor. An incoming tide let the ship's weight carry her on. Very slowly she drifted around the long arm of sand, sea grass and a few twisted bushes—another bit of Cape Cod—and her anchors were let go, dropping through twenty feet of water into mud and sand.

It was eleven o'clock forenoon, Saturday, December sixteenth, the tide one hour past low water.

Cold and quiet, the men and women came up on deck, and with drawn faces looked about their new haven, their journey's end.

Between the ship and the open sea was a long, low arm of sand; they were in a calm channel of water, perhaps a hundred feet wide, that ran along on the inside of the spit. In the opposite direction and exposed by the tide there stretched from inner water to shore proper a mile of uneven mud flats, intersected by innumerable runnels and pools. It looked immense, abandoned by God and man since the waters of the Flood receded and exposed a drowned world. Patched with salt grass and drying seaweed; here and there the bones of large fishes lay on the sand and mud, festooned with decaying green and brown ribbons. Mud, eelgrass, pools, runnels, seaweed stretched flatly across the harbour to the right almost as far as the eye could see; through it a shallow stream wound from the river mouth to where the ship had come to anchor. But over beyond, the solid land rolled down to the shore, a virgin land of forest, hill and swamp that after Cape Cod looked, even in the distance, a very paradise. And God sent the snow away.

In the air, above the spit behind, gulls stood in the cold northern wind and cried; from far off came the quacking of duck. Otherwise there was no sign of life, no smoke of savage fire to be seen anywhere through the bright winter air; here, if anywhere, they should have the world to themselves, if God would but keep the wild men away also.

No sooner were the anchors down than the Master came back to the leaders. When he spoke to John Carver his hoarse voice was uncertain and his weak light-coloured eyes searched their faces anxiously.

"The wind changes," Mr. Jones said. "Another hour and we should not have got in! I hope in God you inspected this place well, Mr. Carver, I hope in God it will do for you. . . ."

The Master of the ship stood foursquarely before them and addressed them, anxious for their welfare. There could no longer be any doubt about his attitude then, whatever it had been before. Surprise and gratification stayed their answering him immediately. William Brewster glanced at John Carver, and Samuel Fuller twitched a drop from the end of his long nose and gazed upon the Master as pleased as if he saw a lost child return. Mr. Jones thought he felt the eyes of others on him from behind, their crowding about, curious of what was passing between him and the leaders; but he gripped his courage tight, determined there and then to begin establishing himself with William Brewster and his companions, if it cost him his life.

"*It is land,*" John Carver said cautiously, his silver beard ruffled in the breeze. "And it is for land we come, to make our homes. Let all examine it, and answer for themselves."

Sharp and clear, above the low voices of the settlers packed on the waist deck on the other side of the forecastle house and the sailors' louder shouts and calls, the Captain and the leaders, standing in the bows, heard a loud, ribald voice ring out:

"Reef 'em fer easy flyin', lads, this is their graveyard we're comed to. We'll be out for home in a week an' they can set in buryin' each t'other!"

It was Coppin, standing halfway up the ratlines, shouting to the sailors tying up the main topsail. Such callous joking was common among the sailormen, and none had ever given it much heed, least of all the Captain. But there they saw him stiffen and his face suffuse with blood.

"Very true," Sam Fuller said dryly, to the Master. "Land is of two particular uses to men—to live by and to bury each other in."

22   Cold, misery, uncertainty, toil, darkness, lack of time; all worked against Gilbert's habit of recording events in his pocket book, so that by the middle of February but half a dozen pages had been added since his last entry at Cape Cod on November the thirteenth; these, though written over a period of five or six weeks, he headed February sixteenth.

Two months have passed since we sailed in here to New Plymouth Harbour and the sick set themselves to tame the wilderness wastes. And our plain tale is of cold, weariness, hunger, death.

And strange it is that for myself I still feel that I do stand outside this adventure and but watch it. For it is not of me or my nature, a passion of body and soul to succeed, as it is of Bradford and the others. I do but behold it; and must one day go back whence I came. Since she has died I know I shall not stay where her troubled spirit is. There is no golden land; it is a land to put iron in the soul. It is winter. True, I have seen with my own eyes that it is a new world, not the backside of the old; but of quaint coloured peoples, none; of palm trees and hot sands, none —but of the snake that crawls in every Eden, he waited not even for me to get to the shore, but bit me on the way.

It rains and blows, and then again the frost is thick all day, but of the latter not much. Our feet are ever in wet stockings. Mr. Clarke says that it freezes all through the winter in these parts; yet it looks as if it will continue to be an open winter this year. Some say it is God's grace marking out a chosen people. Every man to his own belief. The mate says also that the summers are warm and good. Live, horse, and you'll get grass.

Mr. Jones has made no move to go, as our fear was and is; yet he must go any day now or surely his sailors will have his life.

On the right side of our river ascends a very level rise of ground, which stretches inland a pace to where it overlooks the country around. Here behind on top of the hill a party of us under Standish build a platform on which to mount cannon, to frighten the neighbourhood in case of need. Felling wood, which is a little way off, dragging it up, sawing it and fitting it, is heavy, slow work for hungry, creaking men. But they say this work must go on, to impress the savages, when we might be building houses. They swear there are savages in the woods about; but we see nothing of them except the smoke of their fires at a great distance.

Despite my cast-down spirits it was a great and moving thing to walk up here on the first day, and look out and about. I had thought my heart to be so shrunk up and dead that nothing would ever move in me again, and it did. (Had I the way of putting it down then it would not now be so halt and lame; work, weather, cold, have afforded little chance to clerk it with pen and ink.)

The first sight of the trees away over the river is alone enough to lift a man up; see them there, as they have grown pure in nature since the beginning of the world, feathery, unlooped kings.

Then, as I came out on the top end of the hill and with man's first eyes looked across into the distance of the vast overgrown land, that certain passion of my own rose up to grip me in the throat. Oh, Lord God, I said, what a country here is! Surely it is God's especial gift for the hungry and the landless men of the old world? the denied and the depressed, who are born to slavery, without rights over the rags on their back, may come from every corner of the world, and herein vanish into a mighty bosom of land, finding a plot whereon to stamp their feet, and say, "This is my own!" From where they cannot be whipped and hounded out, branded or hanged from the gibbet to ease the press of vagabonds. But when I had stood long and looked at it, the coldness crept back into my bones. Men are but fallen creatures; they may make it as easily their hell as their paradise. Look back here out over the harbour; there is something here like unto a man. When the tide is run in it is all grandeur, full, sparkling; but the tide goes out, and shews what is beneath, vile mud.

It is the getting wet of cold poorly fed bodies and the going back and forth to the ship to sleep, in all weathers, that kills us. Twenty-one are dead in the two months gone, of a sort of coughing, galloping consumption that when once it gets a grip tears through the scurvy-tainted, half-starved body and carries it off in a matter of a week or less; which is that we call "The Sickness." It is no unusual thing to awaken in the morning to a lamentation for a poor soul slipped away in the cold night. So we have a little more room in the holds. The most of them went in that fashion; Degory Priest at the beginning of the month past, January; and Rose Standish at the end of it.

Poor Rose's going somehow surprised no one but the

military Captain, though one day she seemed to be up and about and the next cold clay. I do not ever recall her speaking above a murmur at any time; being the wife of Miles Standish would necessarily quiet any woman, let alone a timid one, prime chattel of this age. So she went, fearful even to tell him she was going, for fear no doubt of disturbing her lord and master. For his part he appeared to be angry that she had done something without his express permission, but quickly lost himself again, once she lay buried, in the general press of matters that takes our short day, and soon was as spry as ever he was. Yet he is as ordinary kind a man as any, when he is not being stupid.

It is this fever to get a roof over our heads and a spade in the ground that leaves no room for sorrowing over the dead. The truth is that when the first one died we were all brought up halt; but the next and the next is like an old man telling the same story over and over again. Hurry, hurry, says the cold rain patter, you may be next. And we hurry by, to the task we hope will save us from the same fate. Christopher Martin, that we saw at Southampton a very bellowing bull or lumbering boar that seemed sure to stand when all else fell, is worn down to a crying wreck and whisked away into his grave. He did go with a lot of noise and crying out, but go he had to in the end. Farewell, earth's bliss. Here I should tie on my rag of Latin, but am in no humour to it. Learning will be scant in this hard land for many a day, if its demanding toil let any in ever.

Here follows, Brother Edward, the order of deaths, as near as I can recall them, not being at the time able to set them down: Edward Thompson, the first to die in the New World, where he found no monkeys; Jasper Moore; James Chilton; *She who went to heaven on Monday December 11th;* Richard Britteridge, 21st December, the first to die in New Plymouth Harbour; Solomon Prower, 24th December; Degory Priest, 1st January; John Langemore, also at that time; Christopher Martin, 8th January, his wife some time after; Rose Standish, 29th January;

and four of the bondmen that were sick since Cape Cod. Then, this month beginning, the sickness at a great height, five die: Thomas Rogers, John Rigdale, John Turner, Richard Clarke, Tom Moore; and others lie at death's door. Twenty dead up to this middle of February.

Which has reduced us by fourteen grown men: so that with our sick we have scarce twenty men and boys able to stand guard, build housing, seek out the savages for our informing and trade, hunt food, &c., &c.

So much about death and dying! I had thought in the beginning that the ship was let go quietly from England because it were easier and cheaper so to let it go than to keep the most of them that went in her in prison. But it appears that there may be more to it, that someone instructed: "Put them to the North, that they may die the quicker." Come, come, the bells do cry. There are no bells to cry for us. But is there not the man still amongst us who should be made answer for these deaths?

And many more will each give up his ghost before this tale is wound out to the full. Scarce half the men working are able for it; while much time is taken again in caring for the sick ones. Thus, while lots were cast for the sites of houses at the beginning of January, only the large Common House is finished (cowhouse were a better name for it), a little house for the sick, and a storehouse; the other houses are still very unfinished. But there is no greed or pushing of one by another here; everyone knows he must lean on his neighbour, like brothers of one family; and indeed I never thought I would see men work together for each other's good as these do. All is order, agreement; the sites for houses are laid out to make a neat street running up the hill, with the river on the near side, so that in the future a man may land from his boat in his back garden. The size of each family's house is to be according to need and not to what money they have put into the venture. It is hoped to have the others still living aboard ship housed ashore in some fashion by the middle of next month, which is about the time we should begin to prepare the ground to put in seed—if the sailors have not thrown them in the sea by then and sailed away. If that happen we will lose half our stores and all the cannon, which are still aboard, since there has not been time or strength yet to get them up and bring them the mile to the shore.

Of notable things that have happened:

On Christmas day Mr. Jones gave us a barrel of his own beer to cheer us up. But this the sailors did not take well and made some sort of outcry to him, rumours of which we heard. It had been very wet and stormy that week.

And at that time also we had been getting little game and less fish. So the Master went out in the longboat with some of his men, to have sport, as he said. A storm came on when he had gone out and up the coast but, lo and behold! he returns with three very fat and heavy sea creatures, monstrous fishes with the faces of cats, which are called seals. I have heard of them in English waters, but many here had never seen their like before. He divided them up between the crew and our people, and they were very good to eat. Our spirits raised and we felt well.

Mrs. Allerton bore a son, the first to be born in New Plymouth, but it was stillborn. It is remarkable how men will not take an ill thing as a mark from heaven as readily as they will take a favourable sign.

Two men went out hunting and were lost for the space of several days, during which there was some snow and frost. But they found their way back alive, though with frostbitten feet &c., and swore they heard lions roaring.

The roof of the Common House, where Governor Carver, Bradford, some others and some of the sick, were sleeping through the night with a big fire, took alight and half burned off. The fact that it had been raining so much saved the thatch from altogether going up like a dry sheet. A week of fine weather followed, and a-times the sun shone out.

A man met some wolves, and threw a stick at them. We

said why did he not coax one back for the stewpots, instead of throwing sticks.

We got many of the hogsheads of meal ashore and into the store hut, during the fair weather; and threw the last of our bad dry-salted meat, smelling to high heaven, into the sea. In the least we may have a handful of meal each till the summer.

Ten days ago or so it began to be rightly cold and frosty, and to sleet; so that we lost many a day's work.

Today, February sixteenth, was an exceedingly cold hard day again; and if the rain holds off we may get something done tomorrow.

I think of that butter going off on the cart in Southampton; but I cannot be the only one that remembers it with hurt in his stomach. We may go down for want of that butter. Smaller things have changed the face of the world.

By Friday, February the sixteenth, John and Gilbert could look down the hill, from where they worked on the gun platform, at a scene of varied human activity set against the wide sweep of harbour, anchored ship and the Atlantic outside. It was a day of frost and biting northerly winds.

The tide was half out. On the mud flats, within calling distance of the Common House, Ellen Billington and some of the elder children were searching for clams. To the north, in the harbour, the jollyboat shewed as a small black point on the grey water. Every day it went out to fish, manned by two heavily muffled men; now and then they hooked a cod or a lonely bass.

On the right side of the rise by the river's mouth, the chimney of the squat, earth-coloured Common House smoked in the clear air. A large shed, twenty feet square, with a pine frame, heavily thatched roof and mud and wattle walls, it had one low door, and four very small windows of oiled paper. Next it stood a smaller storehouse, and another completed house, half the size of the Common House. Then, continuing the line were the frames of two other houses, half completed.

Down there Brewster, Bradford, old Carver and the rest

worked mixing mortar and mud, making doors and windows and sorting marsh grass for thatching; a couple of men worked clearing ground for the spring sowing, the women were cooking, and washing was spread on the ground, held down with stones.

To the right the river came inland to a swamp; to the left were the woods in which Standish and the rest of the platform-building party were felling oak, and into which part of the country Mr. Jones and a party from the ship had also earlier disappeared, on a deer hunt.

At midday Edward Dotey came up to stand sentry by the platform and John and Gilbert went down to eat. They left the top of the hill, where they had set their mark on the earth with spades, boots, picks, beams of oak, chips of fresh wood and sawdust, and wended their way down over the path trod out of the grass and brambles. The few trees had been cut down early; the stumps were already weathering.

Their eyes by habit constantly probed the country on either side, scanning the river, swamps, boglands, hills and forest for signs of movement or smoke. During the first few weeks on Plymouth Hill Standish had gone out with parties in search of the savages; but each time it had been the old story of Cape Cod—figures in the distance, an abandoned hut, an old deer trap, two skeletons in a forest glade, silence. But from the hill smoke had been seen in the woods many a time.

When the two men were some way down the hill they observed a small, solitary figure coming up to meet them, the orphan child Ellen Moore.

"Here comes your young woman again," John said, amused. "I wish mine was off the ship and here housed, that I'd get a look at her in the long day." He looked out at the ship, riding within the long arm of sand, on board where something less than half the settlers still lived and slept.

Gilbert did not answer. These days he kept his silence for hours on end. Their lack of conversation, working alone that morning on the platform while the others of their party felled in the woods, reflected the prevailing sense of foreboding that lay heavily upon all. But his gloomy expression lightened as the little figure came nearer, head and shoulders wrapped in a piece

338

of blanket, painfully thin black-clad legs picking their way sedately along the rough path. Without a word she turned with them, taking Gilbert's hand. He felt the rags that were bound around her palm and fingers against the cold.

"I thought Mrs. Winslow forbade you to climb the hill alone?" Gilbert said. "Suppose a wild man was to run up out of the river and take you home with him, what would I do?"

She frowned.

"There's someone digging a fresh grave," John said. "Take you on it's John Tilley's woman 'as died."

"It is Tom Tinker and Mrs. Tilley are died this morning," the child said matter-of-factly. "Mrs. Tilley's wits came unhinged, they did. She cried out at the last—about the bad men what's brought 'er here to die, she said. They put us away, not to hear. Her eyes went stark staring mad. I saw. Then she died. Are they all bad men what brought us here? Is Mr. Brewster a bad man?"

John Tilley stood in the shallow grave that was to hold the body of his wife, on the other side of the hill from the Common House, slowly throwing out fistfuls of earth with the tip of his spade, a wiry, red-faced man, dour, dogged.

We are grown red-faced, Gilbert thought; if it were but good health, instead of the north winds; and wondered what his own face looked like with a two months' beard. Cold and squeezed stomachs: the hair on one's face grew just the same. Every man had a hairy chin now.

They came to the huts. The smaller completed hut housed four sick people (curious it was that the children did not much get it), each on his pallet and heavily covered. At the fireplace end Mrs. Carver and some women were cooking, boys chopping firewood; dozens of eating bowls stood in lines on the earth floor, ready to receive the contents of the cauldrons that bubbled over the flames. But they were not allowed in to stand by the fire; there was little enough room; if they wanted a fire they must go into the Common House.

Ellen surrendered to Mrs. Brewster, and John and Gilbert passed on, Gilbert reluctantly; for there were sick and dying in the Common House in greater number; almost every day for the past week there had always been someone in the last throes. Gilbert, admitting freely to himself that he had not the Christian fortitude of the Brownists in particular, would not now enter there unless of necessity, or unless he was in such a state of fatigue that he could fall upon his pallet by the door and sleep though the heavens fell and the odours of hell thickened the air.

Ironically, the Common House had been built so that its width was very nearly the same as that of the first hold, though but half as long, and admitted as little daylight, day or night; so that but for the absence of a rocking movement and the sound of slapping water one might still be on shipboard with the rest.

And it stank. Above all it stank of death, sickness, excrement. A blazing fire always burned on the five-foot-wide hearth, yet with the tang of fresh pine there hung in the air the suggestion of putrescent wounds; for the breath of the man infected with "the sickness" was very foul. The gums bled, the teeth dropped out, red patches appeared on the skin, later becoming purple, and the muscles and joints swelled as if monstrously bruised; bleeding took place from the mouth, ulcers appeared on the body; death followed at any stage of the illness on catching a cold. Or the patient took a violent cold and fever before the scorbutic symptoms appeared at all and virulent tuberculous consumption killed him. In the latter stages he had to be handled like a child and soup spooned down his reeking throat. Yet the leaders, especially, attended the sick as though they were their own children. A shiver ran up Gilbert's back. They were incomprehensible men.

Since the beginning of the month death had visited the infant colony very nearly every day. Two more today, the sixteenth of February. Therefore, he reckoned, they had already lost a third of all their number. Truly, as old Brewster had said, saying prayers there the night before, they were at the pit's brim and in danger to be swallowed up without trace. Thus then the ship would return to England, saying how they had found the land, and died on it. A very strange tale to set down: Death leaping into the story at the end, bestriding the stage and sweeping the boards clean of every poor hope and fear, till only Himself remained, and the silence fell down on the trees again and the grass grew on the rotting beams of their endeavours.

John pushed the heavy door of the Common House open and strode in; Gilbert stood a moment, watching his thick leather-clad body become an outline in the gloom within as he ambled up between the two rows of beds towards the glow on the hearth, until a weak and peevish voice from a pallet told him to close the door. He closed it, behind him, and went up to the fire, and held his hard, dirty, chapped hands out.

Standish and the wood-felling party were not in yet. They were the only two about the fire and waiting, idle, for their dinner.

It was dim. The oiled paper of the windows were no more than pale blobs in the gloom, until the eye accustomed itself. John squatted, sighing, on a pile of firing, and gave all his attention to the heat. Gilbert, after a moment, turned his back to the fire and looked about, with perhaps the same compulsive curiosity that had a moment before driven him into the Common House.

His eyes ran up and down the line of blanketed pallets on either side of the big hut: six to the right, six to the left; at night four more were set out in the centre of the floor. Five beds were occupied that midday. Thank God they were quiet, poor devils. What a way to end, on a far, hostile shore, after accomplishing the impossible! Suddenly he saw William Bradford to his right, crouching by the very end bed. At first he watched him out of the corner of his eye, and then openly, in numb fascination. Here was how one spent his dinner hour. . . . Bradford had drawn the clothes back from the figure lying on the pallet before him, a lividly patched, emaciated corpse surely, but for the little weak breathless coughs that broke from the man and the fever-ishly moving eyes; his joints were swelled grotesquely. William had taken the cloth from under him, fouled by the sick man in his helplessness, and was manoeuvring a clean piece of coarse stuff under him to take its place. Even from where he stood in front of the hearth Gilbert could smell the individual and to him revolting sick smell of the settler, Thomas Williams, whom Bradford attended. And after a morning in the fresh air his senses tended to reel. So then must Bradford's. The sick man was one of the "strangers" gathered up in England by the merchants; and the man was assuredly on the point of death. Anyone who had seen the others could tell that at a glance. Yet William bent upon him closely, sponging him with warm water and soap, just as Sam Fuller was probably doing on board ship for the one or two sick there, giving that last comfort of clean skin and a clean bed. But it was Bradford's face that brought Gilbert's shock of realization somehow to a head: it was itself the face of a sick man but lately up from his own sickbed, and it was softened by an absorbed tenderness and patience. Now and then he whispered to the man, as he moved him gently, though Williams could surely not have been able to hear him, let alone understand him.

Then William, dipping his rag in the bucket by his side and squeezing it out, noticed that he was being observed, and some of the old gaunt hardness came back to his face.

William had changed most decidedly since Dorothy's death. The extent of that change Gilbert only then, at that moment, fully realized. He had quickly come to be less shrill. He now rarely lost his temper, as he often did formerly, was silent, concise, reasonable, yes, and tolerant—in a word, he was reaching or had reached his full state of manhood, and with it the knowledge that to love one's brother was the easy and natural thing and not something to be desperately striven after; every man, caught as he was in the trap of life, was deserving of pity and love one from another. He was become a leader of men, Gilbert thought, because he had become master of himself. Through *her* death? No, through this venture of life and death that had wrought a marvellous change even in the very least of them—all except perhaps he himself, Gilbert Winslow.

What mysterious urge worked in such simple plain men, he wondered, that throughout their lives they were dedicated to the preservation and furthering of life? "We are but instruments"; a favourite phrase; and telling. They were all mad, in their different ways, with the same blind sense of *mission*—to push the human race on a step further, though they sacrificed their own lives.

342

With his back warmed by the fire, a cold wave of shame suddenly grew in Gilbert, his throat constricted and his eyes became moist. He hurried down the aisle between the beds, dragged the door open, and stepped out into the keen air, breathing deeply.

The primordial, withdrawn stillness of the forest was at intervals rippled by bird song and the occasional *craak!* and quacking of waterfowl. Stephen Hopkins squatted on the frozen mud, screened about by reeds and branches, his gun on its rest, pointing out over the water of the boggy creek. Above, the sky drifted clouded but bright. Some small animal cried out shortly. The sound of a hammer hitting an iron spike came to him faintly from the settlement hill where the cannon platform was being set up. Standish and one or two others should be felling timber somewhere in the woods about half a mile away, but of them he could hear nothing; for he had walked perhaps nearly a mile before judging that the wild fowl would not there be disturbed by saw sounds and hammer blows.

But he was alone, he thought, as no man ever was alone in the world before. True, it was madness in the first place to have come out alone; but then it had been he himself who stood out stoutly to so go alone, and not out of sheer bravado surely, but by circumstance of the sick and the amount of things to do otherwise. . . . Nevertheless, he had been a fool, he thought, not to have had at least one of the elder boys come with him and to hell with the women's moans on the danger of it. The silence was hard to bear, the silence accentuated and made oppressive by the birds.

He was afraid, he admitted to himself. It was not the cold alone that was making him shiver in his shoes, but that he was cut off, alone a mile from his kind, a mile of tangled forest and swamp between him and help, a very long mile further into the unknown New World than the others, further perhaps than any other civilized man had been in that part of the country. But it was not wild men or animals that he feared. It was the silence, suggesting immense distances, that was so frightening; silence, emptiness, a forsaken world. It was the listening and staring that undone one.

Stephen Hopkins was well hidden; he was not afraid of sav-

343

ages, but, simply, of giants, Things, presences of such a vast, unknown and apparently uninhabited land that God had forgotten. He prayed for a duck to shoot at, for a heron to sail by, for anything to which he could give attention.

There were pine needles under his feet. He picked up a weathered cone a full half foot in length, and fingered it curiously; looked from it to the white pine near by, rearing its plated blue-black trunk two hundred feet above the earth and there spreading out its pagodalike top. Up there in the branches flitted small birds with sharp tinkling voices. To a dead branch half a dozen paces from him a bird as blue as any summer sky fluttered, settled and began warbling with short rich notes. A thing like a ball of leaves hung close to hand; he took it, pulled it to pieces, found a cocoon, and inside a grub, stirring. Spring.

Elm, alder, birch, hawthorn, hazel, he could recognize, but wherever the eye turned it could find a strange unnamed weed, shrub or tree. Someday men of learning would come and give names to everything that grew, and then the people would feel at home. He began to forget his fear and loneliness. Spring was near at hand, he said, spring was stirring about. The bush or little tree at his back, already opening soft buds, would be in full flower in a matter of days.

He sniffed, thinking that he could smell the coming spring in the air. And he felt that he had come alone to that spot for a very private purpose. It was to stand thus, and feel it, the opening, stirring world, the edge of mystery, behold the great pine in solitude, the essence of the secret and majestic country, feel it all, alone, undisturbed, like God's first man. It was cruel that he could not sing, raise his voice, shout that the spring was in the air, was underfoot, in the pines, buds, blue birds.

Two drakes flew towards him, scraped the water with stiff heels and came to rest. With stealthy movements he adjusted his slow match in his gunlock, blew on the spark gently, keeping his head down. Two ducks were better than none, if they would but come nearer and keep close together. . . . He held his breath.

And because he was holding his breath he heard all the more clearly a human voice speak in the woods, in the forest where anything might have its life; a voice answer, and after it other words, scattered, near, far, living tongues, how many he could not tell. The words were nothing intelligible; low, monosyllabic utterances. The ducks rose out of the water, beat their way into the air and flew away in a wide-curving flight low over the bog. Again there was silence, twittering, rustling.

Stephen crouched down on the frosty mud, his gun by his side, and peered through his screen of branches and reeds. There was an open space between the edge of the bog, where he lay hidden, and the nearest tree, the great pine. Immediately to the right of the tree and from a gap in briar and holly, the figure of a savage emerged, paused and passed on across the clearing and out of sight. Another tall savage followed the first, and another, spaced out, two . . . three . . . four . . . seven, each savage a dozen paces from the heels of the one preceding him.

With quick presence of mind Stephen nipped out the spark of his slow match in case the smell of the burning cord blew over to them and gave him away. Eleven . . . twelve—a dozen of them exactly passed a stone's throw away. They appeared to be all and every one tall straight men, nearer over six feet than under. Each carried a great bow as tall as himself; some had only a few arrows in their hands, others bundles of them slung on their backs. One or two, as far as he could remember afterwards, also had long thin spears or pointed shafts.

As quick, they were gone, with long, loose, tired steps, disappearing into the forest in the direction of the settlement hill. If they continued on the way they were going they must come upon Standish and his party felling trees. . . .

Nevertheless he allowed a minute to pass before he stood up and set out for home. At first he had thought of following the savages and trying to warn the woodcutters; but after a moment he knew that his greater duty was to try to work around to the settlement by another way and bring word there. The wild men would surely be come in numbers of scattered parties, and if he went crashing through the woods looking for Standish, ten to one he would cook his own goose and the settlement would get no warning. Standish would not be so foolish as to work without a sentry.

With every step he was conscious of his clumsy, noisy progress; and soon he cast caution to the winds and ran. When his breath gave out he paused to rest in a thick clump of holly. No gunfire, no unusual sounds came from the direction of the settlement hill; nothing could have happened yet. He shouldered his musket and wound on with more caution.

He tried to hold every detail of the Indians' appearance in mind; for here he had been the first to see them face to face, as it were, and would be called upon to give an account of them. But his excitement was also in part that of a man who had been granted an unexpected and magnificent privilege, and in part because the natives were so like himself in more than having eyes, hands, toes. . . .

Though he gasped for breath he thought of what he would say: "Why, man, they look like me—toes on their feet and noses on their faces—I could pass for one of them any day, so they must be gentlemen."

Their appearance and disappearance had all been so quick, quiet, unspectacular; but by the time he reached the hill, saw the cannon platform above and a single sentry walking back and forth by it, he had a comprehensive description ready. No shots still; all was well. How he would astonish them! "They are men like Jews," he would say, "but with lean sad faces of a dirty yellow or smoked colour. Their hair is long behind and many have it twisted or bound into a fox or cat's tail, which bobs on their back and gives them a great grace of walking. They have leather to their feet and legs, muddied as with journeying, and soft skins on their shoulders in the shape of capes, but otherwise very naked and hardy men. Their language is babel. Thus are they, a tall, yellow-to-brown, beardless and brave-appearing people. Did I not see them with my own eyes?" and so on.

"Savages are in the woods coming upon us, keep a lookout!" he shouted at the sentry, and ran on, stumbling and panting, down the long gentle slope towards the squat Common House, shouting at intervals. Figures stopped moving, turned to look at him, Standish appeared to spring out of the door of the small house, an eating bowl in his hand spilling soup down his

346

breeches; the wood fellers were home for dinner, thank the Lord he had not wasted time looking for them.

"Wild men in the woods," he shouted, "stealing up on us."

23   Several hours later, the same afternoon, Mr. Jones ascended the side of the hill near the burial ground, followed by the mate, Clarke, the two quartermasters, Williamson and Parker, and three sailors, whose names were James Hinge, Bart O'Neil and Jeff Daggot. The quartermasters carried the latter two sailors' muskets, while O'Neil and Daggot struggled with a pole on which there hung a fine, heavy young stag. The Master, Clarke and the other sailor, Hinge, were each burdened with two fat geese.

Mr. Jones was much thinner. During the month past he had developed a troublesome and persistent cough. His face seemed to have shrunk in size; but there had come on it a greater depth of character. Today the icy winds had reddened his nose and at times so caused his weak eyes to water that he appeared to cry; but at the heel of the hunt he was returning in triumph, laden with fresh meat such as the settlers had not seen before, and thereby sure of a very warm welcome.

They toiled up from the lower ground along a rough path of sandy earth and grass, around shrubs and through thickets, and, coming within sight of the level plateau, the Master was surprised to discover that all work had ceased. Higher on the hill two lots of four settlers each marched up and down, with shouldered muskets, in full view of the surrounding countryside. Up by the unfinished cannon platform were two or three more, marching back and forth. Other lookouts were posted between the Common House and storehouse, watching the far side of the river, while more stood on the opposite edge of the hill looking north.

A big fire burned in the open before the Common House, and

round about it were the rest of the fit men, perhaps some fifteen in all. Alden was there, Bradford, the Winslow brothers, Brewster, Fuller, Standish, Hopkins, each man armed, some armoured in quilted waistcoats, belts, powder horns, bags of bullets, knives and swords; a few were cleaning and reloading guns. There were no women or children to be seen.

The Master trotted forward, his two geese, tied together by the feet, jerking on his back and breast. He threw them down by the fire, turning to the old men, Carver and Brewster.

"Savages, sir," Brewster told him, a weary tremble in his voice, "coming in the woods. They passed Stephen Hopkins two hour since, but have shewn no sign. Your return is very welcome, safe and sound. You saw nothing of them?"

Mr. Jones shook his head. "Only their sign here." He indicated the deer on the pole, which the sailors were setting down.

"We have just gotten the last of the women and children off to the ship," Carver said, in some excitement. "If they are coming to attack us we think to wall ourselves up in the Common House—if they are many. We sent to Mr. Coppin to come ashore to us with what fit sailors he had, but he declined——"

"He refused point-blank, the cur," Standish said angrily.

"He said he dared not ask the sailormen," Brewster explained, "in that they'd make a great outcry. And he said he would not come ashore for our defence without your warrant, to leave the ship unmanned."

"We fear that if the savages are gathering they wait for darkness to come," Edward Winslow said. "We were debating to send two or three of us to search them out, and make plain we were come in peace—but they would not understand a flag of truce, we think, and so perhaps murder our messengers."

"What is this sign of savages you spoke of?" Mr. Carver asked the Master, touching the dead deer with his toe.

The men had gathered hungrily around the spoils of the hunt, fingering the plump geese, smoothing the stag's fur, the imagined smell of roasting meat in more than one nose.

"To speak truth we found the beast dead," Mr. Jones admitted. "So fresh killed he lay warm. The fellows in the woods that keep hidden did it, and vanished away." The Master, with an air of caution, recounted how, returning with the six geese they had by the greatest of good luck shot on a creek, they had heard a sound of scuffle or movement in the forest, which they took to be a deer bounding away in panic from their approach. But a few moments later they came upon the young stag lying dead, with a wolf dog beginning to tear at its throat.

The deer had not been killed by the wolf, but by a shaft, shot through the side of the breast. Whoever had killed it had just finished cutting off its horns, and carried them away with them. He concluded that the sounds of his party's approach had sent the savage or savages concerned into hiding. The wolf dog ran off. As no answer came to their repeated shouting all about the spot, they brought the beast home. Now the savages had at least one reason to come to them. If they felt that it was stealing, he said, attempting a joke about their stern ideas of honesty, they could mark it down with the Cape Cod corn: Owed; to wild men; one deer.

Mr. Jones paused, looked around the faces gathered about him attentively, and pointed at the six fat geese and deer. "A good supper will bring up a man's spirits. It is not meet to fight, either men or storms at sea, on a tight stomach. Here is fresh meat, after scarcity and want. You do take half, and the other half to go aboard for the crew."

"God will requite you, sir!" Mr. Carver exclaimed.

"By St. John, you are a man. God will bless your works," Moses Fletcher said loudly and fervently. The others joined him in praising the Master, and one settler clasped him by the hand with tears in his eyes.

Mr. Jones pushed out from amongst them, silent and embarrassed. Fletcher the smith set upon the deer to skin it and cut it up. The geese were seized to be plucked there and then, the feathers being tossed in the air. Mr. Clarke, the first mate, with one of the quartermasters, walked over to the guard post behind the Common House, to scan upriver through his spyglass, where smoke was to be seen rising out of the woods.

The remaining four sailors stood in a group to themselves at one side of the fire. Whirled about by the wind like snow, the small breast feathers from the geese blew into the men's faces

349

and stuck in their beards. Standish received a fistful in the face and spat feathers and oaths, and left them in disgust, going up the hill with Bradford to observe the distant smoke from the gun platform. All the six geese were taken up; every man tried to pluck a handful of feathers and toss them into the wind. In a few moments it was a game that everyone wanted to play, a relief from tension, inactivity and cold. Mr. Jones, telling more of his adventures, moved off with Carver and Brewster.

A muttered consultation took place among the four sailors; then one, James Hinge, strode around the fire boldly, dragged the goose from off the wizened Francis Eaton's lap and tossed it back at the feet of his companions, saying, "Be we damned body and soul if we cannot pluck our own fat birds—and eat them!" He gripped the next goose nearest him by a leg, but John and Gilbert were plucking at it and John refused to let go, staring back with a wooden, mocking expression that dared him to go further. A hubbub arose around the fire, all in a matter of seconds, in which there were cries of, "Shame, sailormen, shame— or would you shame your Master, the good Captain?" Each of the four sailors, fully as starved for fresh meat as any settler, raised his voice in defence. "They are our own, masters, our birds." "We'll not be robbed of our long and cold day's profit." "We brave it into the forest for our meat. You sit in your houses waiting for the showers to pass." "The sailorman dies for food as quick as the man on land—when, but for you, we should be home to England a month past!" O'Neil, Daggot and Williamson, shouting and arguing, tired, hungry and angry, followed Hinge's example and tried to take the other geese; while a tug-of-war went on between John and Hinge, John holding the head, the sailor the feet.

Mr. Jones saw what was happening back at the fire out of the corner of his eye, but hesitated, looking the other way and hoping it would blow over. The temper of his crew, kept day after day, week after week, in the desolate harbour of New Plymouth, when they should have been on their way home long ago, he was well aware had reached a dangerous point. But when Brewster and Carver turned, startled at the sudden uproar, and hurried towards the fire, he was forced to follow.

"Your fine friends are a-stealing our meat, Master," Hinge shouted. "Is it just, Master, is it just?"

Fletcher the smith stood up from the deer with bloody knife in blood-soaked hands. The sailor Daggot patted his own right shoulder. "Here, Master, are we blistered carrying our deer. But had we been acquaint 'twas all for other men's suppers we'd have left it lay! God's truth!"

"You are to have the half of all we got today by God's grace," Mr. Jones answered. He spoke with the reasonableness that they still found bewildering, always suspecting him of trying to lead them into some trap; had he frothed and bellowed they would have felt happier. Tensed for a storm, the wind fell out of their sails. But no doubt he would soon give way and return to shouting, blustering and issuing dire threats of punishment to be meted out on their return to authority and England; then they would again know him to be a fearing little man and hold him in silent contempt.

"Meat you have this day, but there will be no guzzling aboard while any woman or child here goes hungry," Mr. Jones continued quietly. "Take you three of the birds, and get to the river; await me in the shallop; our share of the deer will follow."

"We shot the birds, Master," Hinge said, taking courage at Mr. Jones's quiet tones and hesitant voice for all his apparent intention of being firm, "so should we not have them to portion out as we think?"

John leant towards Hinge and said quietly, "Go quick, go to, Mr. Hinge, or by the martyrs we'll all here take you be the slack o' the breeches and walk you into the water, to swim for it. Get off!"

Mr. Jones looked hastily backwards, to see where Clarke the mate was. Mr. Carver made motions with his hands to say that the settlers must let the sailors have all the geese if they insisted, while both he and Brewster felt anxious about the Master's increasing docility. But Hinge, cooling, gave up, swung the disputed goose angrily from him, took up the one lying on the ground and marched off towards the river mouth. The other three sailors were about to follow him when a shout came from the direction of the Common House and a young settler, a lad with an old and rusty sword stuck in his belt, ran towards the fire.

"There is a noise of men," he cried, "from over at the back of the Strawberry Hill across the river. Over beyond we can hear them when we keep still."

All ran back with the youth and crowded out behind the Common House. Standish and Bradford were to be seen running back down the hill. Mr. Clarke called for silence.

At first they heard nothing but the humming and whispering of the wind in their ears; then out of the far distance came a wave of sound that was no more than faintly audible, as of a number of people shouting and singing, not in unison, but like men shouting and singing and cheering one against another as the inclination moved each individual.

It was judged not to be the noise of a vast concourse, but of some few dozens at the most.

A movement was seen on top of the round hill across the river, as Standish and Bradford, panting from their run back down the hill, joined the general body.

"Men," Hopkins whispered. "There! . . . They shew themselves. . . ."

Dusk was beginning to fall. Two small moving figures were suddenly to be seen coming up from behind the hill across the river and standing plainly in view. They were over a quarter of a mile away from where the settlers were grouped behind the Common House, but the savages' gestures were broad and easily discernible. Each figure carried what appeared to be a bow; they waved their bows at the settlement and stamped their feet, uttering unintelligible howls at the darkening sky.

The demonstration lasted a few minutes, after which the savages vanished again, apparently returning down the far side of Strawberry Hill from whence they had come. Some of the settlers thought it an attempt on the savages' part to rouse their own courage, as a man will whistle in the dark, others that it was done in an endeavour to draw the settlers into the woods; or, again, that it was done experimentally, in great daring, to see what reaction came from the settlement and the strangers that were come from over the ocean.

Standish proposed to take a dozen men, go there and then with a bold front, and endeavour to find the Indians. However, darkness was falling, and the leaders thought it best left till the morrow. If the coming of the savages meant war it were better to be attacked behind the shelter of the Common House than in the trackless woods.

Had they but one cannon mounted on Plymouth Hill to let off with a boom and a belch, they would have felt far safer; for the red-mouthed roar of a cannon exploding two whole pounds of gunpowder at one burst would be surely the most fearful thing on God's earth to ignorant heathens.

The matter was being discussed again and plans made, when the Master of the *Mayflower,* by then as concerned for the safety of the settlement as any settler that must stay out the night on land, announced that, come what might, work on unloading the cannons should begin the very next day. Pressed to promise outright that he would have his sailors give some help, he hesitated, remembering the temper of his crew.

But at that moment there was seen a great column of smoke rising out of and dissipating itself over the forest, a mile distant, which could only be caused by a very large campfire or fires started up with grass and fresh wood.

"Tomorrow," Mr. Jones said, "I do promise, we will get your cannons out of the hold by some manner of means."

He went back to his ship in an uneasy frame of mind, both because of the lonely group of men left behind on the dark land, and for what lay ahead on the morrow. It was not only that he looked forward with misgivings to the task of driving the reluctant, bad-tempered sailors into manhandling the awkward and heavy cannon out of the bowels of the ship, getting them to land and dragging them all the way up the hill, but that he seemed no longer capable of working up false courage with shouting and cursing, that he had no stomach any more for bellowing and horse driving.

Time went by so quickly in the New World; tomorrow he would do this, or tomorrow he would do that, and suddenly, in hunting, walking, exploring the harbour, having a river named after himself, a few expeditions, a week was past, a month gone.

Few slept in Common House or on shipboard throughout the night. Women's voices sounded on the deck all night as one or another came up to look anxiously across the black, silent water at the faint yellow gleam of light in the Common House windows. True it was that they would hear shots if anything happened—but it took so long to get from the ship to the land that all there could be murdered a dozen times over before help arrived. If Mr. Jones went at all . . . If the fit sailors did not refuse point-blank to risk their lives for the settlers . . .

All night sentries stood at each corner of the Common House with smoking slow matches burning on their gunlocks. Inside, half the men at a time lay down in their clothes, while the others remained awake by the fire, nursing their weapons. A great fire was kept blazing in the crude stone chimney and the lamp alight; the savages knew exactly where to find them; there was no sense in cowering in the dark. The country around was black and silent.

Sometime near dawn, when it was Gilbert's turn, amongst others, to stay up ready dressed and armed, he found himself standing apart, before the wall near the door where several large sheets of coarse paper were tacked up, and reading the spidery, crabbed writing thereon, which set forth the working rules and regulations for the infant colony; though he had read them many times before.

A Draft of Rules Hereby Agreed Amongst Us . . . That the land shall be in common right held . . . until such time as our great debts are paid. . . . That we do continue in all honest endeavour to hold to our agreements originally made with Thomas Weston and the Merchants aforesaid of London. . . . All that is above our Company's needs that is grown of the land, found, bartered, made or got in whatsoever way shall go to the repaying of Our Debt in London and shall be rendered up to Thomas Weston his Merchants . . . for a period of seven years. . . . Everyone to have their needs out of the common stock. . . . Kept to hand at New Plymouth where all may read . . . should any man not understand clearly how and why we thus work together as one loving family. . . .

What fools! he thought. What honest, Godly fools! He was reading on mechanically, sleepy, yet gripped in nervous tension, when a premonition of the coming of some longed-for little pleasure overcame him and he halted short. Then he almost moaned aloud and beat his forehead with his fist. Dorothy . . . It was the knowledge of her presence for so long on the ship carried in the back of his mind; a habit of thought springing out to catch him unawares. Forgetful, unthinking in quiet sadness, the little intimation of love and wonder, hope to see her, hear her voice, would stir in him, making him look up, the expression of his eyes brightening—and with the cold blow of realization, remember. . . . Where is she? What doing? I'll search about to catch a glimpse of her. Nowhere. She was gone. Dead. Emptiness.

Time, please God, must wash the recurring sense of her imminent presence away; and then he would not start up in forgetfulness any more with that warm stirring. Remember, he thought, with tight-clenched teeth, that is not her humming her song. Nothing but the wind. She was dead. Gone. Do not start up, looking around to see her like a fool out of his memory. She is no more.

And perhaps that was why he did not care very much whether the savages came that night or not.

The day was dawning again; and the woods remained silent, still a mystery. In the night another had died in the Common House. Two went to dig a grave with the first morning light. Twelve went to seek the savages once more, and again found no slightest trace of them. Either they had gone back whence they had come, or they were concealed in the very air, in the reeds and trunks of trees, waiting.

Log: February 21st: The great scare of savages is past for the time being. In the week past hauled one of the settlers' cannon up out of the hold, and ashore with it. This is a minion, some eight feet long and a full thousand pound in weight or more. It took every fit man on ship and shore to drag it up the long hill to the platform. By what means it did not go through the bottom of the shallop I know not.

I thought it good to engage the healthy of the crew to this work, both to keep them fit and to give their hands work. Holding command of them becomes a task that keeps my attention day and night. Yet if I am hanged for it I cannot and will not go, and leave these sick women and children without a roof over their heads. Though their fathers be very felons—and I know not the truth of that—are they not, these children, innocent in Christ's eyes and in our own, though the puritan swear they are all born stained in deepest sin?

Since last I writ here on the 17th, there have died, Thomas Williams, John Turner, Mrs. Thomas Tinker, Mrs. Edward Fuller. William White and William Mullins lie aboard at death's door.

John had come with the shallop and the hired sailors for a load of goods, and from the deck he spied Miss Mullins coming along the poop passage, a jug in one hand, and wiping her eye in the corner of her head scarf.

"How is your father today?"

She shook her head, blinked red eyes. "Mr. Fuller and Carver are with him. They have made him his will for him."

"It is said he is mortal bad."

"He is making his peace with all," Priscilla said, with an air, oddly enough, of pride.

"Would he make his peace with me," he asked on the spur of the moment, "if I spoke with him?"

"Is it not for you to make your peace with him, not he with you?"

He shrugged. "I see it no different. Since Mr. Brewster has been learning me in what this man and the other holds to, I hope he has his rights—but I see him no less the harsh man! But I'd speak a word to him kindly, if you would give me your help. . . ."

"I cannot say," she said, downcast and with a quivering lip, and passed on, to go below.

A little later she came to John in the cargo hold and told him that her father would see him, if he so wished. "But you must not speak loudly," meaning that he must do nothing to anger him, "and can stay only a very short while."

She brought him to the door of the cabin and nodded to him to go in; she herself remained outside. After the bright, gusty deck it was dim inside, the air heavy; and he was embarrassed to discover that Mrs. Mullins was in her bunk also, wrapped in blankets, with Priscilla's young brother Joseph by her side. He pulled off his cap and bid them good day. The woman nodded dully; the child was asleep. Mr. Mullins lay under thick covers, breathing heavily. There was hardly room to turn around between the bunks.

The sick man opened yellow eyes, in a stubbled, parchment face of death and stared up at the young carpenter; his voice came rustling weakly from some hollow place. "God is just," he said warningly, "but God is terrible in His justice. Do not therefore let us vaunt our young strength; the tallest grass falls first."

"I am come to ask you have you all your wants met, sir—not to vaunt over you," John said respectfully, but firmly.

"Are you turned to God?"

John shifted on one foot under the stare of the yellow, dying eyes. His intention in coming had been to humour the father and thereby gain favour with the daughter. He nodded seriously.

Mr. Mullins sighed, as if in relief. "From whom do you take teachings?"

Not knowing exactly what he meant, John answered, "Mr. Brewster, sir."

"Very extreme, but a good man; very lax, but a good man——" He began to cough with his mouth roundly shaped and tongue protruding. John's own mouth felt thick and dry in the heavy, sick air. Mr. Mullins' head raised on the pillow, his dirty yellow eyes bulged and his death's face turned scarlet under its bumps and sores.

A hand pulled John out backwards. Priscilla said, "No, no, go away," and stepped in quickly. He returned to his work with

357

a feeling of escape. And from then on he knew that she would be no longer uppermost in his mind as a desirable young woman only; he thought of the pale, proud, cold-faced girl with warm, resentful tenderness, and cursed the Captain, the ship, crew, New Plymouth Harbour and the rainy, gusty weather. Her father was as good as dead; and her mother was on the way. The Sickness had a habit of carrying off whole families once it got a fatal grip on one member. He worked that day with fierce, desperate strength.

On shore that night John learned that Master Mullins died at six o'clock; and that Master William White had followed him an hour later. The next day, at noon, he was told to go out to the ship and bring the bodies ashore for burial, and collect a sack of nails and a load of iron bits and pieces.

The day was again squally, with quick showers blowing up and passing off all morning. On the waist deck about a dozen sailors, under Mr. Clarke, were attempting to haul up one of the smaller cannon on the derrick rigged to the mainmast. As John came aboard with Ellis and Trevore they were complaining that they could not lift the cannon.

"We are iller men, sir, and by your leave, than them whose work we do," one said. They looked extraordinarily hairy, demoralized and dirty.

Mr. Clarke asked where the quartermasters were. The sailor Hinge replied that they were sick and would not come to the work, as the rest of the crew were sick and would not come to it.

"Bring up the other men," Clarke told Coppin, "or we will still be lifting this gun next week."

The second mate, leaning against the bulwark, made no attempt to do as he was told. "They are sick," he said, "sick like to go home! Whilst any of us are left alive." The sailors let go of the ropes and stood idly in a group, with their hands tucked in their breeches and jerkins out of the cold. John, waiting in the poop doorway, thought Coppin's insolence but a show put on for his benefit.

"I have a notion as to what this sickness amounts," Mr. Clarke

358

said. "The sooner the work is done the sooner the ship is freed. Back to work!"

But the sailors had drawn around Coppin, urging him to speak for them.

"They say these goods are the madmen's business," Coppin said, coming forward, hitching up his greasy leather breeches. "That it is three months since the day we come to land. Let not the passengers waste time bringing their dead to the shore, then they would have time enough and to spare. The sea is good burial enough for sailors!"

Four more sailors came out from the forecastle in a leisurely fashion, and joined the others. They argued amongst themselves in a knot to one side, ignoring the first mate's repeated order to go back to work, pretending not to hear him for the sound of their own voices. Mr. Clarke left the waist deck and went towards the Great Cabin.

Meanwhile, the body of William White had been brought up from below and John was helping to lower it over the side, into the shallop. The wife, Mrs. Susanna White, a young woman, followed, to go ashore for the burial of her husband. Trevore and Ellis then carried the shrouded body of Master Mullins out on a plank, and it also was lowered down to the boat. The half-dozen women still living on board gathered on the deck to see the boat put off.

Three more sailors emerged from the forecastle as soon as Mr. Clarke left the deck. Shouts came from the sailors, "Why do you not all get from the ship?" "Get off the ship, and leave us for to go home!" Coppin, speaking loudly, said to them, "Once I was favoured of the Captain. But nowadays he thinks not of his sailormen—only o' them gaolbirds he has brought out o' England. Now they are all his concern, and we can rot. Now it is that the Master 'as turned against us all, and will see us here die."

Priscilla crossed the deck swiftly, her face half hidden in the hood of her black cloak. She was going ashore for the burial of her father. John handed her down the ladder to the boat. The shallop was then ready to put off, but he lingered, sitting on the bulwark, watching the morose, arguing sailors. Nor did he bother to disguise his contempt for them; were he Captain he would tie each man up and beat him soundly—if only for not having enough sense to cover their cold and dirty bodies with warmer clothing. They had not the good sense of dogs, which in the least would lick their own sores clean.

Mr. Clarke returned from the Great Cabin to the middle deck; a moment later Mr. Jones appeared above on the poop deck.

At the sight of the Master the noise the sailors were making increased. "Come down off your poop, little man," a voice shouted.

"Put the boat off," Mr. Jones called down to John. "Put off. Go. This is none of your business."

John went down the side slowly, but halted when his eyes were level with the top of the bulwark. The women on the deck, taking Mr. Jones's order to apply to them also, hurriedly cleared off the deck and went below. A voice yelled hoarsely out of the forecastle, "You be afeared to come down off your roost, to see how it is with us—that you'd get hurt for your pains!—that you hold us here to our death. Our bosun lies dead below!"

"Put off," Mr. Jones repeated, unsteadily, "put off the boat, I say, and get about your business."

John reluctantly descended the rest of the way, and the shallop pushed off. The wind caught the sail as she left the shelter of the ship's side and she slid away, leaving Mr. Jones standing silently on the high poop, facing the muttering, desperate crew.

24   But while he stood, expressionless, Christopher Jones's world was for the second time turning upside down within him. For years, surely, his nightmares had been concerned solely with facing just such a day and hour. The crew feared nothing any more, were moved not a whit by the threat of an awful punishment at the end of the voyage. Death passed to and fro daily; their companions died next them in the forecastle; the foul

breath of the Sickness arose from their beds; better to hang from a gibbet at home in England than rot their way to death and be tipped in the Northern Seas a thousand leagues from home. So it were come, the Master thought, and suffered a second revelation. But as his first had been through sentiment and released pity, his second was the real and true revelation, coming not as raw experience, but as if it was the result of a great experience, fully grown and planted firm: he no longer feared being thought a fool, no more felt the inadequacy of his short body; therefore, he feared nothing. And as he realized it he smiled to himself a little and looked down at his boots.

He climbed down the ladder to the waist deck with what he thought in all simplicity to be Sam Fuller's easy, confident movements and strong benign expression. Robert Coppin watched him with a brutal, pained look, whispering, "Burn me, by God, if 'e's not mad. . . . The Master's as wicked with madness as an old witch!" And they drew apart, warily watching the dangerous madman, until he stood amongst them, glancing about into their faces inquiringly, looking, as it were, with fondness into their desperate countenances, sick, dirty and as scabbed as men escaped from dark dungeons.

"Well, lads?" he said. "Who shouts? I am come down. Let me see how it is with you." No one answered. They stood around him in a circle, staring at him, puzzled; though had one struck him from behind all would have fallen upon him. "Would we be men, or rather be like the beasts out of hell?" the Master continued; while Robert Coppin and the sailormen heard with horror an echo in his voice of the preaching gentlemen who had led the fanatics across the Sea of Darkness to their death—and here kept the ship while their great Sickness crept from themselves to the crew. . . .

"For only beasts," Mr. Jones said unctuously, with never an oath nor a hot breath, "would sail out to leave their brethren— would you leave your brothers and sisters so weak and struck down, with yet but one foot on a savage coast?"

"Brothers and sisters!" Coppin muttered, and swore obscenely under his breath.

"No matter that when we are home to London I may never

get another ship to sail," the Master said, with a nice touch of the martyr. "Be that as it may!"

"Where's our right for to truck for gold and skins?" Hinge asked truculently.

"All men shall have their rights," Mr. Jones said philosophically, "when every man admits to his fellow also having rights." A bland goodness of heart almost shone out of his face, which sickened and frightened them. Small chance for a ship to get back a thousand leagues of perilous ocean with a mad Captain. "Moreover," he reminded them, "we have yet to find the savages."

Daggot took up their complaints. "We signed, Master, to go where the savage was—and had our right laid down to truck for gold and skins, that what we got we kept. Here are no savages—but sickness and dying, while our stomachs go short!"

"Let us back to our work," Mr. Jones said, "and I will make no mention of this mutiny. We will go from here when God's mercy sees fit."

"How shall we go," Coppin burst out, "if we lose any more in the sickness? Who will sail her? Bosun lies dead!"

"I will go see him," Mr. Jones announced, with the tones of William Brewster.

He went firmly from them, descended forward through the forecastle, an unheard-of condescension, and saw with his own eyes that the bosun had died that very hour.

He observed the condition of several other members of the crew who were lying sick, and promised them to institute a system—as the settlers had—whereby the fit would take it in turn to tend the ill. More, they would have clean grass brought from the shore for their bedding; while each man must have clean water carried to him daily and be washed. And he would shoot deer and fowls himself, that they always had a supply of fresh meat for their weak bodies. And he would visit them daily!

"And he will wipe us after," Coppin said later. "Christ crucified! He is contaged with the same madness as drives these fanatics to their deaths. We are lost men all if we do not put him down in irons."

Ashore, in the burial ground facing the Common House on

362

the other side of the hill, the newest graves were smoothed over, trampled flat and sown with sods; a measure they thought fit of late, to prevent the savages observing by how many their numbers were being decreased.

Later, the same evening, the second mate descended into the bottom of the ship, with a lantern in one hand and the key of the spirit room in the other. Robert Coppin was a young and lusty man with a large and hungry body, a small head, and the sentiments of a boar; and he had a certain regard for the preservation of his own life. "Rot," he said to himself, "rot we will, rot, rot, rot!" How to get home? . . . It was no longer impatience that devoured the crew, but an obsession that if they remained sitting in the slime of New Plymouth Harbour very much longer none of them would live to see the Old World again. And there was not apparently as much as a savage woman in New England. Here was but a waste of life; no drink, no food, no women.

It was the Master's intention to give John Parker, the sick quartermaster, half a mug of spirit as medicine. Mr. Coppin would go below and get a bottle of brandy. But Mr. Coppin knew that if Mr. Clarke had not been on the shore working for the fanatics like the fool he was, he, Robert Coppin, would not have been trusted with the key of the spirit room—or had the Master not lost his wits to the new religion of the fanatics and begun to talk of "brother" and "sister"! . . . How let Mr. Jones know, *by action*, that the crew had no intention of rotting in that muddy waste? By the entry to the cask room his foot kicked against a crowbar from the settlers' goods.

He paused. He was entirely alone in the lower part of the ship. . . . The men had shouted out against the Master. They would be blamed. The Master was not to be feared any longer; he was become an old woman.

He had to do it quickly or not at all; he could not stay down there alone all night. He put the padlock key of the spirit store in his breeches pocket, jammed the chisel-edged end of the crowbar in the crack of the door, and with a couple of powerful heaves burst the door open. Then quickly he took half a dozen bottles of brandy and a half-gallon jar of Holland gin, and buried them in the ballast bags of sand forward in the cargo hold.

With the required bottle of brandy he made his way above and to the Great Cabin, and reported to Mr. Jones, "There is rogues on the ship, your honour, have broke their way into the spirit store! The doors is agape and the shelves is half empty." He observed the ensuing actions of the Master with satisfaction, and contempt. Mr. Jones sent an order to the crew that the spirit, valuable medicine, must be returned, and supervised the rehasping of the broken lock by the carpenter.

The spirit was not returned; but no order of general punishment was issued. In point of fact had Mr. Jones desired to punish the crew as a whole there was no way he could do it there and then. His only weapon to hand, once he abandoned physical force, was the food, and that could not be curtailed further without outright starvation. But matters would be well again shortly, he prayed, when once, the spring breaking out, they started getting about further afield and securing fresh meat regularly. The deaths had reduced his crew by five men, while another four lay sick, and the general health was bad. So they would sit a while longer, to gain strength. And no one could gainsay him when he returned to London, and say that that was not the chief reason for his delaying in the New World. . . .

From February the sixteenth to March the sixteenth Gilbert's pocket book recorded another eleven deaths.

Edward Tilley, Mrs. Mary Allerton, Thomas Tinker the younger, on the 25th of March; the young Mullins child, Joseph, the 28th; John Turner the younger and William Holbeck, the 7th of March; John Crackston, the 9th; Sarah Eaton, the 10th; John Rigdale and Mrs. Anne Tilley, the 12th. Forty are gone since William Button. We shrink to a handful. Some whole families remain untouched, such as the Brewsters, Hopkins, Billingtons, while others entire are gone to the clay. Today, the 15th of March, dies Mrs. Alice Mullins. How wise the savage men are to hold off. Shortly they may possess their land again here but for the trouble of kicking our bones out of their way.

On the day they buried Priscilla's mother, next her father and brother, the shadbush was flowering everywhere, reminding them of the apple trees and the hawthorn of England—they had named it the shadbush because it bloomed at the same time that shoals of a small bony fish began to swim up the river to relieve their hunger, and which they called shads. The open winter was running on into a mild spring, and growth was early. The sods were laid over the remains of Priscilla's mother in bright sunshine. The Sickness was abating. From that day on the girl would live with the Brewsters in one of the row of thatched and mud-plastered cabins that stretched up the hill from the Common House. In the afternoon Mr. Clarke rowed her back to the ship to fetch ashore the remainder of her goods and chattels.

Seven days later, on Thursday afternoon, which was a very fair and warm day, Mr. Jones came to her by the riverside below the Common House, where she was alone, washing pots, and appeared to want to speak to her. He took off his worn and greasy knitted cap, and stood by for almost a minute in silence. Then he sat down, a little above her, and plucked blades of grass.

"We are all alone on the ship," he said at last. "This morning went the others, the women and the children, to their finished houses. None remain."

"We had thought you would have sailed away long, long ago," Priscilla said, with gravity and melancholy.

"My sailormen were sick," he said instantly, as if in fear it should be thought that he had remained for any other reason. "But now comes the time when we can make do, at a pinch, to sail her home. The day is near. Time grows short for what we have to say and do. . . ."

He gazed at her in appeal, or so she thought, with his pale, weak eyes. She suddenly noticed that his face was unusually clean, and that he was carefully shaved above his jaw-liner, while he also had his best boots on, waxed and polished. But she felt no unease with him.

Mr. Jones stood up awkwardly. "So I must go," he repeated, avoiding her inquiring eyes. "Yet—I am asking if there are some that would return. One or two would not burden the ship's stores. . . . I am asking to take you back to England," he said outright, and with a most visible effort. "Your family are gone. Here, you are bereft—no life for you but hard toil. . . ." He gazed past her, across the river, towards the edge of the forest running out to the point on the coast. "When the next ship comes they may find no man left here, as happened in another part. . . ."

"I must stay," she said. "It is all there is—you have done much for us, sir, much, much!"

"I would marry you," Mr. Jones said, his clean face smooth in the bright light, but set and tightened with the effort he made. "I am a man no more than in my prime! I would leave the sea, get a farm of land at home . . ."

She shook her head. "Dear sir, be not offended with me. I'd do you no hurt in the world—you saved us. But . . ." She shook her head sadly.

"But you would not marry with me?" He looked into her hooded face, his gaze very slowly dropping from eyes to mouth, chin, and arms folded into her shawl.

She thought suddenly to ease him with a lie. "I would, sir—but there is another." But when she had said it she knew as quickly that the latter half of her statement was no lie; there was another.

Mr. Jones sighed and nodded. She smiled at him in relief, the first smile of her young mouth for a fortnight. He was not going to prove difficult. "You will have my prayers forever, sir."

"I will be in need of them—come the day I again drop anchor in the Thames. . . ."

Then the Master carried her pots for her up the path, and she went into the Brewsters' cabin where she lived, her sharp good looks softened, her expression abstracted; while Mr. Jones wandered up the hill with his hands behind his back and his eyes turned downwards upon his so carefully polished boots.

It was the day on which the settlers began to sow their first garden seeds.

25   On the Thursday following, March the twenty-ninth, the day the savages came, the weather was again cold and changeable. After an early start, clearing and digging over the fields that were marked out before the mud cabins and up the hill, the settlers ate of dumpling pudding, peas, lobsters from the harbour and some morsels of wild duck.

The meal over, the men stayed on in the Common House, now no longer used as a hospital, with the intention of drawing up what Standish called "Military Orders." For a long time he had wanted to have set out and ready a definite organization for defence. Forty, all told, had died of the Sickness: twenty-two men, eleven women and seven children. So that they were then twenty-eight men, of whom twenty-four were fit in some measure for service and work. Standish wished to have a permanent organization of four companies of six men; each company would have specific duties, and take it in turn to stand guard at night; and in the event of an attack, he said, they would not be falling over and getting in each other's way.

They sat on boxes and barrels around the fire, resting after their meal, while Standish outlined his "Military Plan." They would draw lots, he said, for who should be in each company and which company take the first watch. But in the middle of their business a shot sounded from the top of the hill; it was faint, coming from above where the sentry stood, but unmistakably a gunshot. They were thrown into confusion, and all ran together to get out of the Common House.

Up on the gun platform the lookout was waving and pointing towards the river ford. They saw, from the side of the hill half-way up, a man come striding, who was none of theirs. He came on with long, easy steps, a tall savage in leather leggings and short mantle. The women rushed to bring the children indoors. Fast he came and easy, with serene, expressionless face; before anyone had time to gather their wits, the savage was before them. He stood and looked from face to face, at their clothes, their weapons, the solid mud and thatched cabins, his dusky naked breast rising and falling heavily as he got his breath back.

He was a tall, handsome but very thin man, neither young nor old at the first glance; of a glowing brown colour, his eyes very black, no hair on his face. His head was shaved or chopped close over his forehead and ears, the lank black hair from the top of his head drawn back and bound at his neck into a long, soft animal's tail. He had no knives or weapons but a bow and some loose arrows.

The savage raised his hand in greeting. "Welcome!" he said in English, suddenly smiling, nodding all around. "Kekutto kâunta. Welcome mens do come London." He laid his hand on his breast. "Neèn Squanto! You ale have? Squanto, me. I like ale." Then rapidly, "Me come London. There, over far sea, Squanto live, in London. London. Neèn Pinese; great man; nétop. Cowaun cham amish." Pointing over the river at Strawberry Hill, the way he had come, he continued, "Neèn womasu Sagimus, comes!" He gestured at Winslow, Bradford, Carver, who stood to the fore, speechless. "Sachem? Sachem you?" and pointed back again across the river. "Sachem. Massasoit—King. There, Cantaugcanteest."

"Father of all wonders," Gilbert whispered, "a Cockney savage! . . ."

No one had attempted to speak to the man, so fascinated were they in listening to the English words on his lips. But at last Edward Winslow, seeing the savage begin to looked puzzled and hurt, nudged Standish and whispered, "Put your pistol away for the love of heaven." Winslow advanced a step, bowed, cleared his throat and said, "Greetings, brother. We are happy to receive you."

Behind, Mr. Brewster told a settler to fetch a mug of beer for the visitor; and agreed with Fuller that Trevore and Ellis be dispatched to acquaint Mr. Jones of the savage's coming. Then, while Winslow was questioning him further, Standish sent parties up each side of the hill to keep an extra close watch on the surrounding countryside.

"Your name is Squanto?" Winslow asked.

"Squanto," the savage agreed, slapping his breast proudly. His voice was of a middle, level tone; he paused on every other word for special emphasis. "Pinese, that is, great man of his people—who are they here dead, Patuxet." Now he walked towards the Common House, jerking his shoulders, saying, "Wekíck nittóme. Yo ntéatchin! Let all go in. Petiteaûta. Brrr-brrr, cold. Very good have fire. Cold."

"Squanto does not go in," Standish barked, blocking his way. "He is come to spy us out, what is our strength, dispositions, numbers. Why have they hid till this day, only coming beyond the hill to howl defiance? We have not been here days, but months. None have shown a face, never mind a sign of friendship. I forbid him going in the houses. Bring our seats and firing here. Question him in the open."

Standish's attitude seemed very unreasonable to most; but Governor Carver would not risk raising the military Captain's quick temper, already testy at being called "Captain Shrimp" by Billington after dinner. Wood for a fire was piled in the open space before the Common House and seats brought out.

The savage had immediately become less talkative. "Cold," he said, frowning, and would answer no more questions. He stood stiffly, with a look that suggested he had been deeply insulted.

"Perhaps a present would bring back his good humour," Bradford suggested. "Let us give him a mirror."

The beer was brought. Squanto drank it off with slow swallows, dark eyes ecstatic, the long brown fingers of both hands clasped around the mug. He had fingernails; one looked at his own and compared them. He had hairs in his nose. Fears began to sink away. There was nothing about him fundamentally different.

"I say give him a coat to keep him warm," Sam said. "We have the old red one in the trade goods."

Mr. Carver sent for the coat. They seated themselves around the fire. An old coat like a long red hunting jacket was fetched out of the storehouse and Sam offered it to the savage, holding it out for him to put his arms in the sleeves. In the meanwhile Squanto persisted in his silence, only shrugging now and then and saying, "Ahhe, ahhe," to everything, like a sulky child. But the coat, slowly at first, began to bring him back to a better humour. He held out his bow and arrows in a lordly manner for one of the settler boys to hold, while he put on the red coat.

Clasping it around him, he looked down at it sternly and critically. "Man. Maunek nquit tìas híagat!" He raised the skirt, felt the stuff, looked at the lining like an old-clothes dealer with something hardly worth considering. "Eatawûs. Old thing. Quttaûnch!" He sat down by the fire, grunting and scratching himself inside his leggings. "Fleas?" he said. "Fleas? In coat?"

They protested that no one had worn the coat for a very long time.

"How do you speak English?" Winslow asked him again, and everyone gathered closer, craning their heads in at the man straight out of a nightmare.

"Beer," Squanto said sulkily, looking through them all into an immeasurable distance with his strange black, animal eyes and caressing his smooth chin. "Great hunger." He belched hollowly and apparently at will to show how empty he was. Fortunately Mrs. Carver came to his side at the same moment, bringing a platter with peas, dumpling pudding and broth.

"Tush, the man shivers, the poor man," she said. "He has taken cold."

The savage seized her hand and kissed it; dropped it and set to eating. But immediately he looked up, as if struck with a thought, brighter, eager, put the platter down hurriedly between his feet, clasped his stomach with both hands and rolled his eyes sickly. "Wuttáttash. Brandy," he said weakly, shuddering and making his shoulders shake as hard as he could. "Nummâuchenèm. I sick. Naw watuck nôte shem. I come far—brandy, lords!"

"This is a very civilized fellow in truth!" Mr. Brewster said, aside. "We'll give him some spirit. He would seem to be well acquainted with it. It will help him find words. And poor man, he has a cold in the head."

He should have some spirit for his stomach's sake, Brewster

told the savage, brandy. Squanto resumed eating, gulping the food hungrily. A mug of brandy and water was brought to him. He tasted it and instantly his face was happy again. A couple of children escaped from one of the cabins and were dragged back indoors with screams and protests; they could be heard crying inside. The Indian stood up, looking inquiringly across at the cabin. "No beat, no beat child," shaking his head. He looked worried and indignant and lapsed from his little English into his own language, saying something heatedly which it was plain enough meant that the Indians did not beat their children and that to do so was shameful. He nodded, sat down and finished his brandy, handing back the cup in the bland expectation of having it immediately refilled.

"You speak English," Sam Fuller tried again, speaking slowly and distinctly, touching his own lips, then pointing at Squanto's mouth. It was as good as a miracle to be sitting talking to the man. The wild man even had a cold in the head to prove that he was like any other poor human being.

"Ahhe, ahhe, I do, great speak," Squanto replied, smiling; and pointed out over the harbour, repeating the word as if he liked the sound of it, "speak, speak, speak. In London, Squanto learn speak. Tell. Ahhe." He looked towards the empty cup, rubbed his stomach, "Maskiet . . ." He raised his hand, shouting out, overjoyed to remember and say a long and difficult word, "Medicine! Medicine!"

They nodded, in good time; let him tell who he was and where he came from first. "You tell us," Winslow persisted.

Squanto took a deep breath, sighed, stood up, and waved his arm for the circle to widen out and give him plenty of room.

There then followed a curious demonstration resembling that of a corn-cure quack at a fair and a good mummer miming the story of his own exploits. When he could not remember a word he acted it in pantomime, with considerable talent and naturalness, so much so that they concluded this manner of conveying knowledge to be of common practice among the Indians, which indeed did later prove to be the case. They understood his story clearly enough, though the chronological sequence seemed to be muddled in his mind, not that that greatly mattered.

First he made them understand, the smoke of the fire and the Atlantic Ocean his backdrop, that captains from over the sea had often in years past come to parts of the coast to fish for cod and salt it and trade for skins, particularly to the north. He blew great winds with his mouth and rocked his body as if in a boat. Some captains were good, some were bad, some stole and killed. In the beginning the people of Patuxet, the hill on which they then stood, the Nausites of Cape Cod, Massasoit's people behind, inland, the Narragansetts of apparently further away, et cetera, would come to a ship like children. Sometimes all was well. But again there came men in a ship who robbed them of the very skins from their women's backs and went off laughing. A ship came to Plymouth. A captain's name was Pring. A ship came and men from it died there of spots and sores on their faces and were there buried. Soon the spirit of death escaped out of the graves the strangers had made and went into the mouths of the people.

"We sauas haum itch. Great plague come. Ka kit onck quêban. Dead. Gone away. All dead mens." Squanto acted a great plague sweeping the country all about New Plymouth Harbour, rolling his eyes, clasping his stomach, staggering, falling down. The bones of the dead lay everywhere in the woods, the houses rotted and fell quickly upon them, the fields lay untilled. The land thereabouts was swept clean.

Miracle upon miracle, Sam Fuller exclaimed, with clasped hands and open mouth.

Only he, Squanto, escaped, the last of his tribes—because he had been carried off on the bad Captain's ship. The Nausites of Cape Cod were very angry against the men of that ship and against all men who came in ships, because they took their people away, and that was why they had attacked the settlers and tried to drive them off. The Captain of the bad ship had been named Hunt. He had come about the coast trucking for skins, looking for gold and fishing in the cod season. Pretending it necessary for the purpose of trade, this Captain Hunt got twenty of the men of Patuxet, New Plymouth, on board his ship, having already secured seven of the Cape Cod Indians, and carried them off across the ocean. There, in a far strange country (which the settlers guessed was Spain), he sold them as slaves for twenty pounds a head! He, Squanto, was one of those thus carried off and sold.

There was much shaking of heads and indignant murmuring, and it was made clear that it was none of their purpose to do the like, but to live there in peace and treat all men honestly.

"King," Squanto said sadly, patting his breast. "Squanto, King, Patuxet, have no peoples. But he shews how corn grows, no fear, no fear," which meant that he would shew the settlers how to grow corn.

"But you are brought to Spain," Standish reminded him suspiciously. "How you come from Spain back here, eh?"

"Place from—from Málago to London, a good man's help," the tall savage answered. It appeared that in Spain Squanto was rescued from the slave market by some kindly priests, who gave him his freedom and put him on a ship going to England. Whether word was sent by the same priests to certain people in England was not clear, but a Master John Slany of London, a merchant and Governor of the Newfoundland Company, took Squanto from the ship at London and into his home. There he stayed, in London, for over a year, serving Master Slany. Until Slany, sending a boat out to the Newfoundland Banks to fish, dispatched Squanto back to the New World, with instructions to his Master, Captain Dermer, to get him ashore as near his native hunting lands as was possible.

Now the Indians feared all men who came in large ships, feared terribly their weapons that went HUMPHF! with red fire. When those present first came to Patuxet and started digging and building on the hill and burying their people one after another and trampling on their graves after their fashion, there was no one to see them. And when word did come of them, the Indians watched and waited, and remained away.

The powahs, the men of magic, gathered in a swamp and for three days and three nights together made a great magic to drive the strangers and their big ship away. But the strangers and their ship did not go, and the sachems, pineses and powahs knew not what to do. Until, hearing that Squanto was come back and in the north, the King Massasoit sent for him, and he agreed to go forward first and speak with the hairy men from the ship, for he was brave, and though he had been carried away he had known kindness by them.

Squanto was sad, he said, sad but proud to be the last of the Patuxets, a clan of the great peoples known as the Massachusetts, who were before the plague many, many thousand and a brave and strong people. Now, in the interior, their bones rotted in the glades and grass grew in their houses.

At that point Trevore and Ellis returned with Mr. Jones and one of the quartermasters, Andrew Williamson.

"Give him another portion of brandy," Mr. Brewster whispered, "the poor lad is overcast with memories and despair."

Standish frowned, but the brandy was brought; and very soon Squanto was smiling and nodding again. Though the brandy was well watered it had a potent effect on him. He sat down and looked around as if expecting acclamation.

The settlers were silent, trying to digest so much new and strange information; or talking to each other in low voices and with sidelong glances. The women had edged up and stood around the outside of the circle, children at their skirts.

Squanto sighed. "Wùskont peyâuog. Now comes the King; Squanto must be in his shadow." He gestured tiredly in the direction of the hill across the river.

Who and how many were coming? they wanted to know instantly.

The great Sagamore Massasoit was coming, Squanto said, as he had told them already once before. He was the Sachem of the nearest tribes to New Plymouth, who lived many days' journey away. Squanto had been sent first, and if the men from the ship were not bad men and meant to there stay in Patuxet, he would give the signal so that Massasoit might come over the river and make peace with them.

Standish jumped to his feet. "How many? Many—you understand? Numbers, how many. Fingers, see, understand?"

Squanto shrugged. He wiped his nose, that was long and straight and flat at the tip, with the back of his hand, and stared at nothing, motionless. Then his jaw was very square and firm, the lower part of his face European, but his eyes and forehead and hair were of the rocks and the rain, cold and remote, the eyes set close together, the forehead small and narrow to sit on such a big face, which gave him a deformed, mad, dangerous look. So it was they suddenly saw him afresh in all his strangeness.

He waved his hands vaguely, all the life gone from him, saying, "Nquit pausuck owash. Many come, many as birds, like leaves in tree."

Standish, with the leaders and Mr. Jones, withdrew a little way, leaving instructions that Squanto was not to be allowed to give any signals for the meanwhile.

"First," Bradford said, "the King is on his way. How shall we entertain him?"

"Caution first," Standish affirmed, "until we get the truth. Are wild men in the woods, waiting but their signal from this tricky man to fall upon us? What do we know of their ways? Or do they see it easier to fall upon us when once in our midst? Here we can lose our precious lives in a trice—with one false step. All must be treated as we were at war, parleying to be done at a distance from our camp, hostages given into our keeping who are persons of rank amongst them, for their good conduct. This business falls under my command, and if you are not led by me——"

"Tush, man, give over," Brewster said. "If there be these thousands of them and they want to kill us, why they'll do it and the Lord have mercy on us and that's all. The best we can do is try to impress them with some little ceremony, while we keep the most out that we can. This is a friendship full of risks, but have their friendship we must."

"If they are allowed to come amongst us," Standish persisted heatedly, "they will soon learn how weak we are."

"Their envoy there already knows that," Winslow observed, "and he is not dumb by any manner of means. If their King is coming we must receive him. Then we can get their measure; they have ours already, if we let this man go back to them. . . ."

"Mr. Jones thinks he's all but ready to sail," Bradford said, glancing at the Master with a hard look. "Comes therefore these advances from the savages only in the nick of time; for the ship cannot sail until we know if we have the friendship of the wild

men. With their friendship we have a slender chance to live until relief comes; without it we might as well all walk into the sea."

"I am for trusting Master Squanto from London," Sam Fuller said. "Here is a very miracle from heaven and you all ignore it. And the reason is that miracles have been freely worked for us—if you will pardon the Popish word!—from deliverance at sea to finding our corn seed all ready for us on that Cape beyond. Captain Standish winces at words like I was at him again with the knife."

"Fuller will have his joke on the gallows," Standish retorted. "I am for a proper conduct of this affair, or will have no responsibility for it."

"I think the savage may be trusted," Bradford said, "as well as many another we have had to trust in. . . ."

They argued back and forth, and finally hammered out certain guiding principles, in the forming of which Captain Standish had much of his own way. First, no signal to be given by Squanto to bring the savages into the settlement. Second, Squanto to go and meet the King and lay certain conditions before him. Third, a parley to be arranged at a distance. Fourth, hostages to be exchanged. Fifth, the King to come into the settlement with only certain of his followers. They returned and with great difficulty made each point clear to the Indian toasting his feet by the fire.

Fed and warmed with brandy, he was unwilling to move. "Wuskont peyâuog!" The King was coming! "Aquie iack qussaûme." They were soon to learn that when displeased or merely lazy he would use more and more of his own language. Why should he go and get his legs wet again crossing the river just to meet the King? The King was coming; he would shew himself any moment and send more messengers. It had to be explained over and over again to him that a state visit from a King could not be handled with such casualness.

Until at length he consented to go; after being presented with an old hat, shoes, stockings and shirt. He was outraged, with a stiff, impassive countenance, at the suggestion that he should leave his new clothes behind and don them dry on his return.

He set off with the black felt hat jammed tightly on his head and his long red coat buttoned up to the neck; from under the coat emerged his own leather, fringed leggings, while on his feet he wore the shoes and stockings in place of his own rawhide slippers. Upriver he walked through the shallow water, erect and solemn, and crossed the cleared ground on the other side, leaving trails of water from his coattails. They concluded that his foolish conduct must have made him feel very cold about the lower parts, and that the solution was that he would at all costs appear back before his companions in his new clothes, that though he forbore to shew any enthusiasm over them he was secretly very proud and pleased.

It was decided not to send the women and children on board. There would not be time, the Indians being close by, and it would make it appear that they were in fear of them. But should Mr. Jones bring the greater part of the crew ashore, or would it look better to make a show of having many men on the ship? Mr. Jones was agreeable to either course, but foresaw some difficulties with the crew whatever was done. It would be well-nigh impossible to keep the crew aboard once they knew that friendly savages were crowding the shore, bringing furs and food and God knows what. But on the other hand anything might result from letting them loose among the savages. . . .

Bradford argued that they should stay on the ship. They would be better without them. Winslow and Carver thought also that it would be safer to keep the majority of the crew on the ship until they on land had some experience of the savages at close hand. It was agreed that Mr. Jones stay on land with one or two of his more trusted men while Clarke kept command of the more unruly on board.

As Squanto disappeared across the river frantic preparations were set afoot to receive the savage King with as much impressive ceremony as possible. Here, Bradford, who had voyaged to the New World a young man unsure and gnawed by self-doubt, was a fully-fledged organizer, quiet, efficient, determined, persuasive. The last of the hoarded butter and pickled eggs were got out, muskets primed all around, the drum and trumpet found, presents selected, rusty swords cleaned and buckled on,

377

the cannon on the hilltop loaded, lobsters boiled, "the street" swept, while the children ran about in great excitement. Then on top of all it began to rain. So they prepared, and waited, and watched, and said their prayers in case they did not have a chance to do that last again in the world before nightfall.

An hour had passed, when one dot was seen to appear on Strawberry Hill across the river. Then another, and very soon the bulge of hilltop seemed to support a multitude. But now there was no howling or shouting or banging of rattles. All was silent.

The Indians remained on the hill and Squanto appeared again at the other side of the river. The King was come with his brother, Quadequina, he said, and would have the Sachem of the men from the ship come to him that he might see his face and look into his eyes and discover if he was to be trusted, that the powahs might touch him and divine if he was evil or not.

Old Mr. Carver, as Governor, was willing to go; but here Standish insisted on keeping to the rules. Let Massasoit send his hostages forward to a point on the other side of the river, to which spot they would also send their hostages. And let all be done without any delay, Standish shouted, shaking the rain from the brim of his hat; for if it was not arranged soon there'd be precious little time to have talks before nightfall; they would not have strangers in the settlement after dark, kings or beggars. Squanto went back.

In the meanwhile lots had been cast to determine who should go as hostage to the savages, and it had fallen to Edward Winslow. Winslow's wife being then ill, they wished to relieve him of it; but he said he would rather go, as it had fallen to his lot. Some thought more than one should go; but Edward only remarked that if any lives were to be lost better one than two or more; then they were glad he was going, knowing him to be the best amongst them to parley with the King.

Very soon six savages appeared with Squanto at the appointed spot and laid down their bows on the ground. Winslow, unarmed, holding a large platter before him, crossed the river at the ford to them. In turn the six Indians that were to be held as hostages in his place came over, and were taken to one of the cabins and placed under guard.

Winslow ascended the hill, following Squanto in his red coat and black hat with foxtail bobbing on his back; and as he came close enough to distinguish the faces of the gathered Indians a hush fell upon them all; he saw with relief that their total was not more than between sixty and a hundred, feathered, furred, painted, with small bright dark eyes, standing as still as rocks. Some one of them made a sign with his hand and all sat down, excepting a group that stood to the fore. He had time to notice that behind there were many women squatting about, many with their children with them, which seemed to be the very best of signs.

Squanto led him forward towards the standing savages, to a tall, portly, grave man, where Edward laid down his tray of presents and bowed.

In silence they looked at each other. Massasoit was dressed very much as Squanto had been, in slippers, leggings, loincloth, a kind of shirt, a short cape or cloak. About his neck, however, he wore a chain of large white bone beads and teeth and, hanging on a string, a little leather bag. His face and head were greased so that the rain, then ceasing, ran off him; beneath the grease his large, solemn, melancholy face was stained or painted a uniform and not unpleasant mulberry colour. The clothes he wore were made of fine deerskin, patterned with tracings of colour and fringed with silken fringe. Over his arm he carried a coverlet made of soft black and white skins. He was perhaps forty years of age, a big, stout, soft-eyed man.

Close by the King's side stood a younger savage, the Sagamore's brother, Quadequina, who looked like a tall, handsome, well-proportioned young Jewish gypsy. But Winslow had no time to marvel at their Jewish features. Squanto seized the white man by the shoulders and kissed him on both cheeks, apparently to demonstrate on what good terms he was with the bearded man from the ship. He grasped Edward's hand and kissed it, took Massasoit's hand and placed one in the other. The King bent over and gravely kissed the back of Winslow's hand, dropped it, and held his own hand out. With equal solemnity Edward kissed it in turn; it was dirty, wet from the rain and a little acrid to the nose.

"Speak, Winsnow," Squanto said, with deliberation pushing his chest out, gesturing, shewing how a speech must be made.

Winslow made a speech. King James saluted the King of the Massachusetts with words of love and peace, accepting him as his friend and ally; and the Governor of New Plymouth desired to look into the face of Massasoit, to trade with him and his people and make a treaty forever as good neighbours, et cetera, et cetera.

Every savage listened intently; but before Winslow was half finished Squanto burst out, interpreting him to the King. And Winslow wished indeed that he knew what Squanto was saying. . . .

At the end the King nodded; at which the savage in the old red coat indicated that the presents should then be given. "Wiaseck—knife—give presents."

To Massasoit Winslow presented a pair of steel dinner knives, and to Quadequina one knife. The knives were polished brightly, and though the King and his brother managed to keep their reserved expressions they were obviously pleased. For the King he also had a copper chain with glass pendant; for his brother, a smaller piece of coloured glass to hang on the ear.

Next, he presented to the King a dish with a piece of butter in it and a bag of biscuit-bread, feeling that settlers and Indians were at least equal in their poverty. He spread pieces of the biscuit with butter and offered it to them. The King smelt the butter carefully, and shook his head. But when Squanto took some and ate it, apparently to demonstrate that it was free of poison, both the King and his brother took of it, licked at the butter, munched and, later, belched appreciatively. Winslow presented his last gift, a bottle of brandy and water. The King sipped, his brother sipped, and the bottle was passed around behind them.

The ceremonial eating and drinking gave Edward a chance to look more closely at the whole body of Indians. Their eyes were inquisitive, but when one found himself being looked at his expression became haughty and solemn, as if determined that his face should give nothing away. Neither from their clothes nor from their weapons could he gather any information about their real intentions. All the men had bows and arrows, clubs, spears. Some wore leggings and leathern shirts, and some did not, but all had warm skin capes. The women and children were much more heavily dressed and protected against the weather.

Squanto spoke at length with the King, pointing over at the settlement hill. They prepared to cross over.

Massasoit kissed Winslow's hand, and set out, led by Squanto and followed by twenty of his men; while Quadequina very respectfully brought Winslow to the centre of the hilltop, where a skin was laid out for the hostage to sit upon. Skins were placed about his shoulders to keep him warm, meat and pounded Indian corn placed before him. Surrounded by silent, painted faces, he prepared to wait, praying both for his wife and for patience.

At which time, as Edward Winslow sat, cold and patient, the object of a hundred dark and unfathomable eyes, his wife died in the hut reserved for the sick across the river.

Above the ford on the settlement hill Captain Standish and Captain Jones, matching each other in both small size and warlike appearance, with swords and daggers and their best pistols in their belts, met the King. They were attended by a guard of six settlers with shouldered muskets.

Jones and Standish, marching abreast, led the way up from the water's edge. The savages followed in a bunch, and after them came the six musketmen, two by two. Massasoit and his twenty warriors kept as close behind the Captains as they could, without treading on their heels, giving many backward and uneasy glances at the heavy weapons of their guard of honour. Up and down the near and far sides, and back and forth across the summit of the hill, pairs of settlers with shouldered muskets marched smartly.

The procession turned down the hill, until it reached the seventh dwelling house in the line, which was still in the process of being built. Here, against the front of the cabin, a sort of flooring or verandah of loose boarding had hurriedly been laid down, spread with blankets, coloured rugs and shawls, while in the centre, to receive the King, was a large green tasselled cushion of Mrs. Brewster's. Before the platform a fire blazed.

The King was seated, his warriors dispersed about him. Up the street an uncertain trumpet sounded, followed by the banging of a small kettledrum, and from the Common House emerged old John Carver, Governor of New Plymouth, who was preceded by a youth with the ancient drum and flanked by two settlers holding rusty swords before their noses. Governor Carver had a green feather in his hat, a sword buckled on his belt, a red sash, and marched as well like a king himself as he could for the rheumatism in his hips and knees.

Before Massasoit he saluted by raising his hand, and the King of the Pokanokets returned the salute likewise. Squanto indicated that a speech was required and Mr. Carver repeated more or less the same speech that Winslow had made and which was again interpreted by Squanto.

Before the Common House the trumpet sounded again. Stephen Hopkins advanced down the street with a cushion for the Governor. He had meant to walk before him holding it at arm's length, but had not been able to find it in time.

The portly Indian Sagamore looked closely into Carver's face and said in a deep, pleasant voice, "Cowaûn kamuck."

"Massasoit greets you," Squanto interjected.

"Asco wequas sun nûmmis," Massasoit said, with a frown at Squanto. "Ntússawese Massasoit."

The Sagamore took Mr. Carver's hand, apparently on instructions from Squanto, and kissed it; and the Governor returned the compliment. The ceremony of kissing hands, they could only conclude, was something invented by Squanto out of his European experiences.

Mr. Carver seated himself upon his cushion of state. Then followed the other settler leaders down the street, with trumpet and drum, and grouped themselves about the Governor. Mugs of gin were presented to be handed around among the visitors, both as a friendly gesture and as a demonstration of the potent powers of combined fire and water which the Englishmen held captive in bottles. Mr. Carver could only hope that the women had scraped together enough food to make some kind of meal for the savages—and that the visitors had not too large appetites. It turned out that they had very large appetites and good strong teeth; they cleared everything set before them, and skimmed their platters clean with their fingers.

Though the savages all kept stiff public faces, some with unrelaxing self-important frowns, or so it seemed, their eyes were bashful, dark and sad in the way that certain dogs' eyes are; but the English, in their turn, stared boldly at them, nudging, whispering, gazing with awe and fascination. In what shape and form had they expected them to appear? No one rightly knew. But certainly not so like to themselves in every physical proportion. That somehow was in the nature of an affront. Mayhap they would in some way or another have been more monstrous and beastlike. Many there were who were prepared to see tails growing from them behind and little horns sprouting from their foreheads. But they were nothing if not human, despite their skins and feathers and paint, quiet, dignified, bashful and downcast of eye before the strangers, absurd and childish with their paint-smudged faces as children dressed up in great solemnity to fright other children.

Most of the warriors had painted their faces for the occasion with varying stripes and patterns of red, yellow, black and white, which sweat and rain and brushing leaves had daubed and mixed with the most fantastic effects.

The warriors would have liked more gin, but Squanto was asked to explain to the King that spirits were only used on certain great occasions, wherewith men pledged each other good health and long friendship.

Then the King called for a long special pipe from one of his followers. "Squuttame!" And filled it from the tobacco bag at his neck. A light was brought to him and he exhaled smoke through his nostrils. And this, Squanto told them, was a ceremony of *his* people. The long pipe was passed around politely, in deep silence, while Brewster, Carver, Fuller, Bradford and the rest each drew some smoke from it and blew it out.

Very soon the few men and boys not otherwise engaged had edged up to stand around and stare at Massasoit and his twenty seated warriors; and though the women had also been told to keep to the cabins, before long they were craning their necks with the rest.

"We would make a treaty for peace, to live in love with all neighbours," Mr. Carver said.

Which desire Squanto communicated to Massasoit. The King spoke to his followers in low tones, and the warriors, the pinese men and the powah men, agreed with gestures of their hands and heads, grunting "Ahhe, ahhe," all sitting stiffly upright, crosslegged. Before they had only moved to scratch, the hair of their heads much adorned with the nits of lice. These also, as the savages Hopkins had seen in the forest, had no growth of hair on their faces; not from plucking or shaving but because hair did not appear by nature to grow on their faces.

Massasoit launched into a long, slow, grave discourse, speaking in a deep, emphatic voice and belching frequently; during which Mr. Brewster many times looked around the corner of the cabin in the direction of Strawberry Hill, otherwise Cantaugcanteest, where was poor Edward the hostage, alone, unarmed, in the midst of the wild men's camp.

"Kekutto kâunta [let us speak together]," Massasoit pronounced strongly. "Cowauôntam. We tom pátitea. No we tom patimmin!"

"Massasoit pleased man to be friend of wise mens ataús kaw awauog," Squanto interpreted.

The King raised his hand, commanding Squanto to be silent until he had finished all he had to say, and went on, speaking slowly and emphatically for about ten minutes. It all meant, Squanto explained, though they had difficulty in understanding the interpreter's broken and jumbled English, that Massasoit would be their friend—if they entered into certain agreements with him. The Narragansetts, a strong and quarrelsome people, were harrying him. If the men from the ship would always take his side against the Narragansetts, or make it plain to the world that they would do so in the event of trouble, therefore keeping the bad Indians within bounds, he would be forever their man.

The eastern sky was darkening when the settlers at length brought the discussion to the actual points of the treaty. The agreement ruled that neither party should allow hurt to any person or persons of the other, settler or Pokanoket. That the Indians would not steal from the settlers or the settlers from the Indians. That if any unjust war was made against either party to the treaty each would come to the other's aid. That Massasoit should send warning out to all concerned that such a treaty of mutual assistance existed, to all the other peoples on the coast, including the Indians of Cape Cod. That when they entered each other's towns they would leave their bows and arrows outside, in the one instance, and their guns, in the other. And that by virtue of the said treaty Massasoit might consider himself the esteemed friend and ally of the all-powerful King of England. . . .

No sooner was it agreed at last than Standish was all haste to get rid of the visitors—before darkness fell. His suspicions were by then nothing allayed. He marched up the ragged guard pointedly with drum and trumpet, to escort the Indians back to the river ford, as the savages seemed inclined to linger and make sight-seeing tours of the houses, wanting to see inside the Common House and asking questions about the cannon mounted at the top of the hill. With a certain silent determination each insisted on having his turn to try to blow the kuttówonck, the trumpet, before going, pleased to hear it emit any sort of groan at their lips.

Finally the small, fierce-looking Captain, whose bright red beard was a source of stolid wonderment to the savages, marched back up the hill before the twenty warriors and their Sagamore, turned down the bank and conducted them to the river, the leaders bringing up the rear.

Dusk was falling, the evening air full of the smells of wood smoke; from higher on the hill where it was possible to look down over the woods, the smoke of the savages' fires could be seen where they had made their encampment, and here and there their red twinkle.

Squanto said that Massasoit and his people would camp in the woods for the night about half a mile from the settlement. In a few days they would come, as was their yearly practice, to sow corn on the good land near by across the river; and Massasoit's

385

people would henceforth come to the settlement to trade furs and corn.

The Indians splashed across the river, and picked up their bows and arrows. Massasoit raised his arm in farewell, "Yahen wàiyàuw. Saûop," as they all straggled off towards the hill of Cantaugcanteest.

Shortly, Squanto returned, bringing Winslow, well fed, safe and sound, and the Indian hostages were sent back. It fell to old Mr. Carver's lot to have to tell Edward Winslow that his wife was no more amongst them.

Squanto seemed to take it for granted that he was from then onwards their permanent guest. He walked home with them and was lodged with Stephen Hopkins.

The night passed quietly.

26   The Indians began to come into the settlement early the next morning, appearing first on the side of Plymouth Hill overlooking the river, standing in little groups and knots like deer on the alert, then moving down towards the houses until they stood about boldly as if presenting themselves proudly to be observed and admired in exchange for a like privilege from the settlers. They came with bundles of skins on their arms and backs to exchange for the settlers' bracelets, beads, copper chains, eating knives, bits of blue and red cloth, scissors, mirrors, pipes, hatchets, nails, blankets and balls of twine. "Anaqushénto," they said, "anaqushénto"; which was their way of saying "Let us give each other in exchange"; and they brought skins of the beaver, otter, wolf, deer, squirrel and moose.

Isaac Allerton was put in charge of the trade cabin for the meanwhile, with two assistants to help him. By ten o'clock the Indian women had edged their way in, trailing their shy, black-eyed children behind them and bringing fresh deer and dried fish, both as presents and to cook on the spot.

Had the settlers decided that they were being invaded cunningly for the purpose of being attacked in their houses, they would not have been able to break the invasion by any other means than force, as by letting their guns off or trying to push them back physically toward the river. They came in from all points around the hill. If a guard looked at one sternly he disappeared back the way he had come, only to enter the settlement by another way. Quickly they grew bolder, as if having established a right to be there; and the Indian women hurried back and forth over the river ford, bringing their bundles and their earthenware pots.

The Indians, especially their women (the faces of the men and women were confusingly alike), were not immodest; but it was soon apparent that they had, as formerly rumoured, little or no shame of their bodies. It was a mild day, with frequent bursts of sunshine. About their cooking fires, which they set upon Plymouth Hill, the Indian squaws took off their upper garments, which in the first few instances caused the settlers considerable embarrassment. But for the moment they had to ignore the savages' nakedness as best they could. It was impossible also, as well as impolitic at that early and delicate stage of their relationship, to keep the settlers' and Indian children apart; and the latter had even less sense of shame than their parents.

Standish continually roamed back and forth, pistol in belt, or stood and stared at the Indians with his most intimidating glare. Some said that surely the Indians would not bring their women and children to the settlement if the warriors meant to cut the settlers' throats—but who could as yet tell what the habits and customs of savages were? Who knew but that it was a custom of theirs to bring their children to see throats cut and the skin of victims torn off in strips as a pleasant spectacle? . . . But even if that were nothing of their intention it was more than possible that one hot word would set the same childish and changeable savages in a very different mood, and then it would be all pillage and murder. They were not Christians, Standish argued, and therefore had nothing to restrain them from "wanton killing." . . . At any moment it could dawn on them that they might get what they wanted for nothing, by falling upon the strangers tooth and nail.

The military Captain had the cannon reprimed and the guard there was instructed to let it off over the settlement at the first sign of a scuffle. Once the initial onrush of trading was over the savages would have to understand that they could not walk in among the cabins any time they liked and turn Plymouth Hill into a fair ground.

Massasoit himself did not come that morning, but sent word that he would be pleased to receive any of the settlers who wished to visit him in his own camp, following upon which Governor Carver sent two men over the river with a kettleful of dried peas for the King, and these Massasoit entertained with a dish of groundnuts and tobacco to smoke.

Near noontime Gilbert stood in the doorway of the cabin that housed the Winslows, amongst others, looking out across the street. Within Ellen Moore was abed, where she had been for over a week, ill with a coughing, galloping consumption. That morning there was a certain cold, clear-eyed serenity about the child, which Gilbert knew to be a sign that she was in the last stage of her illness. The day before she had seen Edward's wife die on the pallet against the end wall. To humour the child he stood in the doorway and told her what he saw of the Indians. And though he looked out at the still fascinating spectacle of two hundred New World savages squatting, cooking, eating, playing with rattles and wooden balls, he was as conscious of her as if he had eyes in the back of his head; the thin skin of her small cadaverous face was turning a dark muddy colour, out of which her eyes shone wonderfully large and blue.

"What more, Master Gilbert, what's up the hill that way?" she whispered, when he fell silent.

"The sun has burst out again. Here before the door some are doing a dance; that is a sort of rattle they play on that you hear. The most of them are sitting about fires eating, like they were having a feast or celebration."

"What is their dancing, Master Gilbert?"

"With a shuffling of their feet on the ground, and waving their arms up and down. Five of them go about in a closed circle, with antic gestures. They are a thin agile people; in colour from yellow to brown; the men tall, the women shorter and fatter. They are a poor people, flea-bitten in their poverty, know not gold, but well content. More and more go to the dance. You hear their shouting and clapping hands? More circles of dancers farther off. More now dance than not, both the savage men and the savage women. Many have thrown off their clothes but for what they wear about the middle, the which is a sort of apron with a fringe to it. The dancing grows wild, yet it is solemn, and yet it is all happiness for the springtime and the sun shining. Mr. Bradford and old Mr. Carver come up to Squanto to speak with him. You hear their voices? Our men can do nothing for watching this antic dancing. Some of our women go in, bringing their children, and they are shocked. Mr. Bradford is making a great argument with Squanto. Can you hear Squanto's voice? He but laughs, waving his arm."

"Nickómmo!" Squanto said. "Nickómmo. Nippauoc hâumen. They merry mens for you. Ahânuock. Peace—aquène. Happy be for friends—friends of you mens. No stop. Honour for you. Good. Commoco, good, neèn womasu Bladford, neèn womasu Winsnow, all, pineses, powahs, squaws dance to honour you, give food, dance. Pokanokets men's friend, love, brothers—dancee, dancee, dum-dum, dum-dum, dancee-dum-dum."

Suddenly Gilbert was aware of the utter quiet of the cabin, and turned and walked quickly across the earth floor to the bedside of Ellen. She was lying half over the edge of her mattress, as if she had strained up to see out of the door and fainted with the effort. Her head was hanging down, the eyes closed, a gleaming trickle at the corner of her mouth. He turned her back gently and laid her flat, covering her up. She was breathing laboured, faint breaths, and tried to raise her head. Her eyes opened for a few moments as he put his arm under her head, then closed again as her head fell sideways against his breast. He was to her, he knew, the only father she had ever known, and she to him as though she were his own child. He held her close, rocking gently, smoothing the thin hair.

While the Indians danced six men stood between the Common House and the nearby river mouth, in serious converse; Mr.

Jones, with the first mate, Clarke, and the quartermaster, Williamson; Brewster, Carver and Standish.

"It is no justice for them, by heaven it is not," Mr. Jones said, his brow knit in discomfort. "I break the very promise that set them out across these oceans. No sailor would take shipping into the farthest realms, as like to die by storm and starvation as have his throat cut, if this very right of free trade was not held out to him. His entire hope is to truck an old knife for a rock of gold, to return home rich as a king. Now the savages are come. How can I deny them their right? It is as much the sailors' right to truck for the beaver skin as it is yours or mine——"

"There is no gold. These savages know not what it is," Mr. Brewster said, with evident satisfaction. "But, Master Jones, you will endeavour to keep the crew to the ship one more day?"

"Your ruffians shall not be let come on land this day to fleece the savages," Standish declared. "They have already traded the very beaver off their backs as it is. . . . Let the crew ashore now, to find the savages with nothing left to trade that is worth a pin, and God help all here!"

"It is the least of what I want, to let them ashore today," Mr. Jones said, with for him a new helplessness. "You impute it to me!"

"Your treatment of your crew is in no need to be imputed," Standish snapped. "It is plain to be seen. You may say it is none of our business. But whatsoever endangers our continuing here is our business, right until you dock back at London with our letters. We call these here savages—but your sailors are no better. They fear nothing but punishment or the threat of it; and that you have removed or let fall away. I know them, and knew their kind before I met this ship. Since you have about-faced to treat them all as little princes they call you 'Mother Hen' behind your back. I'll lay double they'll hang you yet for your pains, on your own yard, before you're halfway home, and sail your ship into the West Indies."

John, patrolling with musket on shoulder, halted behind Standish to listen; he had come to have a certain amount of admiration for the explosive little military man, got on well with him, and was lodged in the same cabin ashore.

Mr. Jones stepped back from the outjutting red beard and addressed Brewster. "You can tell the savages to go—go back whence they came. Let them at the least keep to the forest round about, out of the way. The crew can then have no proof that there is no beaver skins left for them. . . ."

"God's wrath," Standish snorted, "there's little likelihood of them not knowing it already. They'd tear what remains on the savages from their limbs. Then we'd have war on our hands—which means we would be all murdered! While you talk as if you were no longer Master on your own ship!"

"Our bosun is dead and gone; our leading quartermaster is dead," Mr. Clarke reminded them, "without which the men are hard to keep in the yoke."

"Get the savages away," Mr. Jones persisted, though with no great conviction, "and the men can come ashore as formerly."

They had tried to turn the savages back that morning, Mr. Carver explained, to let in only those that came to trade, but they might as well have been trying to beat rain out of the air with their cloaks. The Indians would have become sullen and warlike at any unfriendly act. If the sailors came ashore, Mr. Brewster continued anxiously, trouble must follow. It was impossible to send the savages away in the middle of their eating and rejoicing over the treaty of peace; the sailors must be kept aboard some way or another, until the savages cleared out that night.

"They want to get ashore for the savage women," Standish exclaimed. "Then we're all cooked! Oh no, by God, not while I'm alive."

"But see here," Brewster said, after a moment of further argument, "there is a solution. Let us make over to the crew one third of all the furs we got in trust . . ."

"The jollyboat comes in," John said, from the back.

They looked harbourwards; the jollyboat was halfway to shore, one man in her, rowing uncertainly. In the deep channel over against the sandspit, separated from the shore by a mile of slime, pools and mud flats, the ship lay like a lifeless toy. On the jollyboat came, sculling laboriously on the winding channel that led up to the river mouth.

"Hello," John said. "He's no expert with the oars."

The man in the rowboat seemed to pause and rest; then waved with some bit of sail or rag. Mr. Clarke turned his spyglass on the boat. "The humpback," he said, after some delay, "no one but the cook. Rowing has hard as he can come."

The six men, followed by John, descended by the path to the landing place in the river's mouth where the shallop lay tied up, and waited for the rowboat. It would take five or six minutes to get in. John noticed that Priscilla and a bunch of the older children had come out onto the bank behind the Common House and were watching a couple of the Indians wading in the mud and fishing with long poles and nets on hoops. He walked up by the riverside, waved to her, and had the unexpected delight of seeing her wave back.

Because of the savages' coming in to trade the day was something of an enforced holiday, with very little work being done except that of keeping muskets freshly primed. Up till that day he had not had many opportunities of seeing her alone; he took that which then offered gladly, and climbed up the bank to her. Aware that she was still bewildered and suffering at the loss of her whole family, he said little for the while, content to be near her. She would be over it soon; already it was a fortnight past. With sidelong glances at her he realized that the young girl's look had gone from her forever; now her face was a little careworn, mournful, but with strength and patience. She was marked with the life there, as he was, hardened, forbearing; her old shoes caked with sandy earth, mud on the hem of her dress; her heavy shawl knotted on her breast, already an old thing, a garment to protect against the winds.

After a while he talked to her a little, and she answered him quietly yes and no. Out of one of their silences he said abruptly, "I would have gone to your father long before, to make up with him—too late it was then. . . ."

"He spoke well of you after you did. It was not too late. He said you were a good man. He forgave every man."

Then all was changed! He felt that he would take her hand and hold it for a few moments; but one of the Indians caught an eel in his net and flung it up at their feet. John stamped on its head and the children carried the writhing slimy knot off in triumph. Their attention was caught by the jollyboat, coming in to the bank in the river mouth. Mr. Jones helped the cook step to land, where Tandy staggered and sat down with his hand to his head.

"There is blood on his face," Priscilla said.

John hurried down the bank and made his way along by the side of the river to Jones and the others, the girl following.

The little humpbacked cook, dabbing Mr. Carver's handkerchief to a bloody lump on his left temple, was holding forth in a shrill voice, distraught, indignant and shaking in a kind of ague. With his pale, bony, birdlike face and black greasy clothes he looked like a wounded crow crouched on the riverbank.

"Cup-shotten roarers, wild rogues, sir, every one. There is this great noise going on in the mess. I pulls up the trap a crack to listen. God's blood, sir, seein's believin'! I look down on men drinking like a band o' rich pirates. Drinking, sirs, drinking spirits, full of bottle courage, shouting out they will do this and they will do that. I'd be feared to repeat what is said there. The Cap'n 'as betrayed them, they cry, by 'is keepin' the ship 'ere in the mud to their death. And now the Cap'n orders them to keep close on the ship, while 'is friends get all the wild men's gold."

"Where is Mr. Coppin?" the Master asked.

"Now what did I say?" Standish shouted.

"Mr. Coppin, by God, sir, is crying, 'Gold! Gold!' louder than any," the cook said. "They seed the savages wot's comed up yonder on the hill. They 'ave it in their heads the meanest 'as gold plates hanging on his neck. So you keep them close on board to get it all yourself. I look down on them scabby ship rats, mad they are with the cry of gold, a-drinking cups o' brandy and gin! They can't get off, I know—but the longboat is coming back from fishing! And then I knows they'll get off to land, to make bloody murder. I shouts down to them that we are due to sail, if they will but have patience. I shouts down to them that they'll be hanged every one. But they curse awful, sir, and come up the stairs at me, till they force the trap though I stand on it. And some throw me down on top of the others. They know me for a sick man, but they pitch me one to t'other like a bale o' straw, till in the end of it my head is stopped by the timbers and I am no more in the world. Then when I will have no drink from them they forget me. There I am, till I crawl out on my knees, and find the deck. So by the mercy o' God I get down the rope to the jollyboat, while they are still at what drink they have left. And I tell you, sir——"

"Where do they get spirits?" Standish demanded of Mr. Jones. "Do you leave spirits on the ship for them to lay hands on?"

"They have had it hid since the spirit store was broke open," Mr. Jones said quietly. "Let this man go lie down in one of the houses."

"How in blazes could you continue to let them have drink hid on the ship?" Standish said.

"What should I do?" Mr. Jones answered. "Myself and Clarke put the whole crew to torture to disclose it? We will go out to them in the shallop."

"Not before I've got my men together," Standish said promptly.

"I go with Clarke and Williamson, no others," the Master said, without raising his voice.

"Wait, wait——" Brewster put his hand on Standish's arm. "He is right. If he cannot command his crew here, alone, he will not do it out on the ocean."

"By all the saints, you'll not go alone," Standish told the Master with ferocity. "If no other man wants it, I want it, that the ship gets home safe and reports Miles Standish is alive in the New World, else we'll be abandoned and forgot for the rest of the world's time."

Carver intervened, to suggest that some at least of the settlers go to the ship with Mr. Jones, if only to guarantee his safety while he dealt with the crew. But Standish, without consulting anyone further, sent John up for certain of the settlers whom he named; and he returned with Hopkins, Bradford, Fuller, Billington, Allerton, Dotey, Tilley, the three hired sailors and many others, all armed to the teeth.

Mr. Jones wanted to wait awhile, to allow the effect of the sailors' stolen brandy to wear off; saying that more than likely if left to themselves it would all blow over. Standish, however, insisted that action be taken immediately. A nice state of affairs if

394

they stood there and waited for the drunken crew to attempt to take the ship out, and run her on a sandbank!

The boarding party was no sooner gathered by the riverside than the longboat was seen putting off from the ship. Standish had no need to argue further; the drunken crew were coming ashore. News of what had happened was by then known in the settlement and many of the remaining settlers, men, women and children, gathered on the outjutting sandy bank where the lower end of Plymouth Hill terminated. The savages, forsaken by their audience, began to abandon their dance and come down the hill to see what was going on.

"Come aboard, Mr. Jones," Standish shouted from the shallop, "if you'd not be left behind!"

"No muskets, no muskets or knives in God's name," Brewster and Carver implored. "Throw back your muskets."

The men handed their muskets to land and they were laid on the bank. John felt a hand on his arm and found Priscilla by him.

"I forbid you to fight," she said in a fierce whisper. "Do not think I can't see it in your foolish looks—you have been waiting your chance to fight with that man."

"What man?" he asked innocently.

"I mean Coppin, as you know very well. Now is your chance—you need not grin at me!"

"Will you bandage me up again?" he mocked hurriedly, with one eye on the boat.

"If you make of this a fight you need never look to me again."

"Fair enough," he whispered, bending over her. "If I don't get killed, will you marry me?"

"I will," she said with desperate seriousness, "if it is your intention not to get killed."

He uttered a boyish whoop that shocked her, pulled her to him and kissed her resoundingly. Grinning and whooping by turn, he jumped aboard the shallop as it was being pushed off. Old Mr. Carver and Mr. Brewster, behind on the riverbank, shouted last-minute advice, imploring them all to settle the matter pacifically, to remember that they would be in full view of the Indians.

The tide was out, the whole vast harbour stretching on either side of the narrow winding inlet, an expanse of mud, sand, sea-weed and pools. With Mr. Jones, Clarke and the quartermaster, they were fifteen all told. The man poled the shallop off and set out six oars to row. She was too heavy and clumsy to do more than keep her way under oars; the swifter longboat would be more than three quarters of the way in before they met her in the channel. Already the shouting and singing of the sailors could be heard.

In less than five minutes they were close enough to see that the longboat was laden with all the fit remaining members of the crew, some fifteen or sixteen men. When the settlers looked back to land they saw the rest of the settlement standing on the high bank, and behind them gathering groups of wondering savages.

Mr. Clarke stood up and shouted to the longboat, "Put about. The Master's order, you to put back to the ship. Are you mad? Do you want the people murdered by the savages? Your fair share has been promised on oath. Coppin, order the boat back."

Coppin and the sailors roared back in answer; they would go ashore and have their fair share of trucking for fur and gold with the savages or be damned for it. They were in high spirits and not too drunk to row well enough to keep them in midstream. The sight of the settlers coming to quell them made them even more determined to have their way.

The longboat came on apace. When fifty yards off the slower-moving shallop it edged into the side of the stream to force a way past. But the shallop bore in upon the longboat, still being rowed full tilt. The distance rapidly diminished between them, with warning shouts and curses from the ship's crew. Attempting to force their way past, their oars fouled the muddy bank and almost in the same instant the shallop ground against the long-boat, breaking her right fore oar and carrying away the rest. A dozen pairs of hands from the higher shallop seized the long-boat's gunwale from end to end and held her fast.

The sailors, led by Coppin, Hinge and Daggot, stood up, argu-ing and shouting curses; a jam of wild, ragged, dirty men with long hair and bearded faces, they had not a whole shirt between them. Hinge, with the end of the broken oar, caught Hopkins a blow on the arm, and in a moment the curse of long inactivity fell from them. Fighting mad and happily drunk, they swarmed at the settlers with their fists, the duckboards and the iron rowlocks.

"Knock the scum down, we'll hang 'em!" Standish roared oaths and threats, scarlet in the face.

Jones, with one leg over the side, shouted at the military Captain to stay out of the longboat, that the affair was none of his. The Master kicked Hinge in the ear, captured the piece of oar, leapt down onto the centre seat of the longboat and began laying about him.

Mr. Brewster and Mr. Carver, on land, and William Bradford, in the stern of the shallop, simultaneously closed their eyes and began praying as hard and as fast as they could. The sailors saw the settlers as old and hated enemies, but their long training at sea made them avoid attacking the Master directly where they could. Mr. Jones rapidly had all who were in the centre of the longboat beaten down, to crouch with their arms over their heads, moaning for pity, or laid out unconscious. He sprang a seat nearer the stern, where Coppin was hitting at the settlers with a rowlock. Hopkins could hold off no longer, though the rest of the settlers contented themselves with aiming blows over the side of the shallop; he leapt into the longboat and grappled with a sailor. John said to himself, "Me for a whack too," and prepared to follow suit.

Coppin, in the stern of the longboat, did not wait for Mr. Jones to reach him with his oar handle. As his cries of, "It is all but in jest, Master!" had no effect on the Master, now apparently returned to full vigour as a Captain of the seas after his lapses, he stepped on the gunwale and sprang for the mud flats.

The sandy mud was not there as firm as it looked, and he sank into it almost up to his knees. John was in the stern of the longboat a moment later and he reached out to catch Coppin by the back of his jacket. The second mate, trying desperately to free himself both from the mud and the clutching hand, and at the same time seeing Mr. Jones preparing to strike him with the oar handle, twisted about, caught John's wrist and with a tug overset him into the water at the longboat's stern. Then, sucking and squelching, he ploughed away from the boats over the mud flats.

John crawled out of the shallow water after him, covered from head to foot in black mud and trails of seaweed.

Mr. Jones by then had the longboat thoroughly subdued. He shouted at Coppin to return and take his beating, with such effort that he lost his voice, his blood so hotly roused that he saw through a film. Coppin found harder ground and managed to run a pace. The Master, his yellow teeth bared, leapt from the longboat and by good chance landed on a hard knoll of sand. Waving his piece of oar, he plunged after the two mud-coated, floundering figures.

Struggling on, getting bogged, escaping, Coppin ran north-wards from the inlet with John close on his heels, both followed at some distance by Mr. Jones. Under the bright northern sky the seaweed glinted and the pools sparkled. Coppin, blindly charging over what looked to be a shallow stretch of water, sud-denly sank up to the waist in black mud and sand; before he could fight free of it John, encased in mud, fell upon him, and they both went down, thumping, slithering, entwined on the slimy seaweed-glinting mud flat, both half blinded and as near smothered. Coppin fought to escape, John to hold him and beat him with his fists at the same time. As they heaved and struggled like creatures of the dark pools risen to the surface in mortal combat, Mr. Jones reached them. Had his rage allowed him pause he would still have had difficulty in distinguishing one from the other; as many of his blows with the oar handle fell upon John as upon Coppin. They broke apart under his be-labouring and Coppin ran around in wide circles, winded and unable to see where he was going. The Master ran at his heels, hitting him blows, the second mate blundering blindly, yelping and pleading. They ran full circle and came back to John, who secured Coppin by the collar.

The three returned to the boats; Coppin firmly held by the young carpenter, Mr. Jones slithering and jumping about them and beating the second mate where he could.

The performance was watched with a still, catlike interest by the savages clustered behind the settlers on the end of Plymouth Hill. So many questions were put to Squanto that he had to come to Mr. Carver for an explanation.

"Oh," the old man began, pulling at his beard in vexation, "it is a . . . well, a game, like dancing . . ."

"A very old custom," Brewster added, "like Indians dancing to be friends, like Commoco. Every spring, when flowers come, we make pretended fight in the mud. For the glory of our God. It is all a game, like you play with balls."

Squanto communicated the information to the Indians, and they seemed to understand perfectly. They were vastly disappointed when both boats got under way again for the ship.

It was, even for the New World, a singularly clear evening. Mr. Jones had restored his command aboard his ship. After sending messages to Massasoit the savages had been persuaded to leave Plymouth Hill and go back to their camp in the woods on the other side of the river. With the wind dropped away and a mist creeping out of the north end of the harbour, the settlers stood about yet another open, newly dug grave.

Edward Winslow's wife, Elizabeth, and her adopted waif, Ellen Moore, lay side by side in the same grave, wrapped in shrouds roughly sewn up out of the dead woman's old skirts. The sandy earth was shovelled into the foot of the shallow trench first. Prayers were said with heads held up, eyes raised to the evening sky; but Edward watched the earth cover the body of Ellen, and then begin to fall about the face of his dead wife. The earth dragged down the shroud on either side of the face and for a moment the features of the dead woman shewed their recognizable shape through the thin stuff; Edward winced and stepped back. Gilbert saw it too, but watched on as if in bitter self-punishment, until the earth had covered both figures.

The grave was filled, and smoothed level.

"Amen," Brewster said. "Amen for all who lie here."

"Who are they that asked only to be let live!" Gilbert said savagely. He stamped the loose earth with his shoe, his sense of desolation and waste brimming over into trembling speech.

Bradford looked at Mr. Jones, felt himself threatened with saying something he also might regret, and moved away.

"What a little thing—to be let live in the world," Gilbert said, jabbing the earth with his heel. Never would she walk up the hill again to take him by the hand. She should have grown into a creature like Dorothy; and he saw it that the world of men had crushed her from the beginning to the end. "Let us have but life and we were ready to slave from dawn to dark, our wives to sweat like the beasts of the field, all without complaint——" He raised his eyes, breathing heavily, and looked into the eyes of Christopher Jones, standing at the other side of the grave. "But you brought them here to die! Of cold, plague and starvation—for what no man knows. When we should have been in the south where the sun is kind and the fruit grows."

"Gilbert, Gilbert," Mr. Brewster whispered, shaking his head vehemently.

Mr. Jones's mouth opened and his round face suddenly puckered as if on the instant of receiving a bullet in the back. He licked his lip, frozen for immeasurable minutes, breathed out with a gasp, turned on his heel and walked unsteadily away. He did not know in what direction he walked, but he kept on walking up the hill with short, quick steps, staring straight before him and washing his hands together.

"How do you dare speak to the man like that?" Brewster reproved Gilbert, and those remaining about the grave agreed with him. "He is more redeemed in God's sight than some there are here! Your brother would not so offend he that we owe so much. It is his wife lies dead, not yours."

Edward shook his head, which might have meant anything, and walked away in the direction of his cabin.

"These are the dead that set out in hope to the New World," Gilbert said, his voice choking. "Chilton, Britteridge, Solomon, Degory, Tinker, White—all, all, how they are removed, man, wife and child, cut away of the world, and its salvation that you so covet. Forty-two poor souls that asked only to live. Who shall answer for them? Who shall say he is not guilty? That man you now cherish is guilty."

"We are all guilty," the old man answered, and he in turn moved away and walked towards the Common House.

After a short conversation with Carver he came out again and turned up the hill in search of Mr. Jones, to offer an apology.

But there was no sign of the Captain on the brow of the hill all the way up to the cannon platform. Tall and straight of back, he strode up by the path overlooking the river, until he had to slow down, puffing. There, halfway up and quite by chance, for he was about to continue, he happened to glance down through a parting in the tangled growth, and saw the Captain's back, half hidden in a thicket of young trees. He descended through the grass of the bank, pulled a branch aside, and stopped.

Mr. Jones was kneeling on the ground, stiffly upright, his hands clasped before him, staring at the limitless distance of the New World. The old man thought to draw back; in the circumstances it was not so strange to find Christopher Jones praying; but on second thoughts he moved around to get a better view of him. Then somehow he knew that the Captain's stiff posture was no part of prayer, that in all probability he was hardly aware that he knelt on the earth. Certainly he was not engaged in prayer as it was commonly known; his hands jerked as in grief, his teeth clenched, his lips moved as though with some intense and convincing argument, but no sound came from him—he could have been a man making a public confession except that he did not utter the words aloud and that there was no one to hear him.

Brewster drew back up the side of the bank a little way, and made a noise breaking twigs and coughing. "Master Jones, sir, Master Jones." He found the Captain standing, where he had before seen him kneeling. "Dear sir, what can I say in the face of such an offence?"

"He spoke the truth," Mr. Jones said after a moment.

"There are truths and truths," the old man hedged gently.

"You are men that have spent your lives to speak the truth, and cared not what you suffered for it—then spare me not, I am the least deserving of men."

"You are the man that toiled in the winter woods to feed us. Without you we would surely have died."

"I carried you here for my own ends. And you have died," Mr. Jones said hoarsely, still looking away into the distant, green landscape, as moved to find how easy it was to speak out the truth at last as by the thing itself and the tide of relief that

401

flooded him. "Why do you think I have lingered, stayed with you? Because I had no courage to tell you I had sold you. I tried to work my sins away in service to you. I sold you for Master Weston's money. He paid to set you here. He is in league with the men that have the patent and rights to this part of the country. He would betray his own merchant friends, to make a greater profit from the other company."

The older man expressed no surprise, despite what he felt, but laid a hand on the Captain's shoulder, speaking gently. "No matter, no matter. You may think it was you who brought us here, but we would rather think it was God. Let us say no more about it either here or in time to come. It has been done; we are come home. What you have done here cancels out all that went before."

Mr. Jones felt the iron bands loosen about his breast; he calmed, breathing more easily, and wiped his forehead with the back of his hand; then he was able to look the old man in the face. And Brewster looked down into the Captain's round, weathered face. It would have been a strong man's face, he felt, but for the pale weak blue eyes that lived there uneasily, betraying that the Master, tough and compact of body, had perhaps the soul of a young woman.

"Consider," the older man continued. "We may be where we have not patented right to be. But what are patents and authorities to merchants and kings but pieces of paper? Here the savages are weak, all but wiped away by what plague it was that fell upon them. Out of all this mighty New World we are in that one place where we would seem to be in least danger from the savages. Where, pray, else would we have found an Indian with English on his lips? The King of this place that was, to welcome us. He is to shew us how to build traps of wicker for the fish that he says will soon be coming into the river. He is to shew us how we must put fish in the ground to manure our corn seed or it will not come up. This evening he has taken men that they may learn by him how to stamp out eels from the mud of the marshy places. That single man will from henceforth be the means of our continuing alive. Here in this place we found him. We would not have found him anywhere else. Here to this place you have brought us. Whatever wrongs you may in the past have worked against us, it is all now in the past. You may explain it further to me if you wish, but whatever, I will speak of it to no man, nor ought you speak of it at home in England. Our great want of you, Mr. Jones, is that you get home safely and there acquaint our friends of where we are and what are our needs."

They climbed slowly back up the bank and stood on the brow of the hill looking out over the harbour. The tide was in, the great stretch of harbour water serene, darkening, splendid.

A fresh breeze blew out of the northwest, smoothing and ruffling by turn the bright water of the harbour, filling out the fore- and topsails of the *Mayflower,* moving out to sea on the full tide. As she cleared the point of the long sandy arm that enclosed the harbour before New Plymouth Hill, the watchers there saw her great square sail creep up the mainmast, assume position, flap, and fill out solidly. The wind for which Mr. Jones had waited fourteen days since the Indians' coming was there, at his back, to carry him home to England.

On the gun platform Miles Standish dabbed at the touchhole of his biggest cannon with the glowing end of a slow match, ducking back and shielding his red face with his hand. From the gush of crimson flame and soot the dull WHOOF and BOOM of the cannon rolled out to sea and inwards over the new and unexplored world. To answer it, half a minute later, a red wink of fire came from the Master's small saluting cannon on the back of the poop and its weaker THUMP sounded in the ears of the settlers. She was on her way out into the vast, pitching ocean; and they must believe at last that she was gone. . . .

They gave her sad cries of farewell that mingled with the forlorn and seeking calls of hovering gulls, and waved their hats and scarves, though there was little chance of being heard from such a distance.

In the early morning light fifty-six souls stood on the end of the hill overlooking the water. With them was a sad-faced Indian in an old red coat and black felt hat, who held one of their children by the hand. Of the fifty-six, twenty-five were children, alive and well. But of the married women only six had survived; of the original nine bondmen only three remained. The thirty-one men and women that remained stood on the edge of a vast continent the terror, beauty, riches and extent of which was known to no man, gamblers with their lives. They had stayed alive. They had won the first round.

Their tear-marked faces were thin, but of a healthy, wind-whipped colour. The Sickness had devoured half their number but those that remained had conquered that too. No single one had accepted Mr. Jones's offer of transportation back to England. Their rough clothes were pitifully worn, patched, and weathered by the elements. There was little food in the store; but it was the spring of the year. They had lived through the voyage and the winter. The summer stretched before them. In England they might be forgotten, but the God of heaven would not forget them. There, in the hard breeze, they sang all together to the God of heaven, in strong, fearless voices.

Edward Winslow's cheeks were hollowed, so that he seemed to be all nose; but his eyes were bright and keen as they glanced back at the forests and the hills, and had Dorothy Bradford lived to see them then, to look upon the upright and proud figure of William Bradford and hear his clear voice singing out, she would have had an answer to her question as to why such men of talent drove themselves forth into the wilderness when they might by suppressing their hunger for the truth have possessed their hearths and homes in comfort.

The women's headcloths flapped and the men's full beards ruffled in the wind, and as always a great strength seemed to flow into them from their singing to God. The young carpenter from Southampton, with his arm around Priscilla Mullins, sang like a young bull, though he knew not half the words. Old John Carver, Brewster, Fuller and Allerton sang forthrightly as if singing to each other in triumph, weathered images, indomitable patriarchs in broken shoes, earth-stained breeches and patched coats.

Then in silence they watched the ship grow smaller, and smaller . . . Gilbert stood behind, not of them, but not apart from them. He saw the ocean as an empty desolate thing that had taken his love and swallowed it up. Next year or the year after he would go back. For the moment there was fresh air, work, work, and the great mystery that lay inland, by which he might learn to forget.

But William Brewster saw the true sea over which they had escaped and that would help them live with harvests of fish. "Look hard," he said, "and see them coming—two sails, three. Then, mark you how short a time, there come fleets of sail to us, with kith and kin."

And though they saw nothing themselves but the declining speck of the *Mayflower*, they did not doubt that the shining eyes of the old man beheld by the power and clarity of his mind's eye a vision of the ships that would one day come, not by ones or twos, but by hundreds, to partake of the life that they, the Firstcomers, had fought for and secured for the world.

APPENDIX

The *Mayflower* arrived safely in London on the sixth of May 1621, and on the following first of June the settlers' agent, Robert Cushman, arranged to have a new Patent or "Form of Authority to Make a Plantation" taken out with the northern or Plymouth Company, which held the rights to New England. The Patent was taken out under the name of "John Pierce and His Associates," to avoid drawing attention to the new settlement and its wanted leader.

Cushman then so far succeeded in arranging transfers of interests between the moneylenders and rival companies that a small relief and produce-collecting vessel was sent out, carrying a further handful of settlers and Cushman as negotiator. This was the ship *Fortune,* which arrived at New Plymouth on the ninth of November 1621, exactly one year after the *Mayflower* sighted Cape Cod.

By this ship, stocked with furs, clapboard and other produce of the New World, Edward Winslow sent a letter home to a friend in England, besides other informative writings and agreements. To spur the merchants at home to greater efforts in sending out ships and help, straightening out the entanglements between Weston, merchant moneylenders and rival companies, his letter was couched in perhaps more hopeful terms than affairs in the New World warranted. It gave, nevertheless, a concise and useful account of some subsequent events, and read, in part:

Loving and old friend. Although I received no letter from you by this ship, yet, as I know you expect the performance of my promise (which was to write to you truly and faithfully of all things), I have therefore, at this time, sent unto you accordingly;

referring you, for further satisfaction, to our more large relations.[1]

You shall understand, that in this little time that a few of us have been here, we have built seven dwelling houses, and four for the use of the Plantation, and made preparation for others.

We set, last Spring, some twenty acres of Indian corn; and sowed some six acres of barley and peas; and, according to the manner of the Indians, we manured our ground with herrings, or rather shads, which we have in great abundance and take with ease at our doors.

Our corn did prove well and, God be praised, we had a good increase of this Indian corn, and our barley indifferently good; but our peas were not worth the gathering, for we feared they were too late sown. They came up very well, and blossomed; but the sun parched them in the blossom.

Our harvest being gotten in, our Governor sent four men on fowling, that so we might after a more special manner rejoice together, after we had gathered the fruit of our labours. They four, in one day, killed as much fowl as, with a little help besides, served the Company (the fifty people at that time left alive) almost a week. At which time, amongst other recreations, we exercised our arms; many of the Indians coming amongst us (in friendly visiting).

And, amongst the rest, their greatest King, Massasoyt, with some ninety men; whom, for three days, we entertained and feasted. And they went out and killed five deer, which they brought to the Plantation and bestowed on our Governor, and upon the Captain [Standish], and others.

And although it be not always so plentiful as it was at this time with us, yet, by the goodness of God, we are so far from want that we often wish you were partakers of our plenty.

We have found the Indians very faithful in their Covenant of Peace with us; very loving and ready to pleasure us. We often go to them; and they come to us. Some of us have been fifty miles by land in the country with them, the occasions and Relations

[1] I.e., *A Relation or Journal of The Proceedings of The Plantation Settled at Plymouth in New England*, written by William Bradford and Edward Winslow and known as *Mourt's Relation*.

whereof you shall understand by our general and more full Declaration [*Mourt's Relation*] of such things as are worth the noting.

Yea, it has pleased God so to possess the Indians with a fear of us and love unto us that not only the greatest King amongst them, Massasoyt, but also all the Princes and peoples round about us have either made suit unto us or been glad of any occasion to make peace with us. . . . So that there is now great peace amongst the Indians themselves, which was not formerly, and neither would have been but for us; and we, for our part, walk as peaceably and safely in the woods as in the highways in England. We entertain them familiarly in our houses; and they, as friendly, bestowing their venison on us.

They are very trusty, quick of apprehension, ripe-witted, just. The men and women go naked, only a skin about their middles.

The temper of the air here agrees well with that of England, and if there be any difference at all this is somewhat hotter in summer. Some think it to be colder in winter, but I cannot, out of experience, so say. The air is very clear; and not foggy, as hath been reported. I never, in my life, remember a more seasonable year than we have here enjoyed, and if we once have but cows, horses and sheep, I make no question but men might live as contented here as in any part of the world.

For fish and fowl, we have great abundance. Fresh cod, in the summer, is but coarse meat with us. Our Bay is full of lobsters all the summer and affords a variety of other fish. In September we can take a hogshead of eels in a night with small labour, and can dig them out of their beds. All the winter we have mussels and clams at our doors. Oysters we have none near, but we can have them brought by the Indians, when we will. All the Spring time the earth sends forth naturally very good salad herbs. Here are grapes, white and red, and very sweet; strawberries, gooseberries, raspberries, &c., plums of three sorts, white, black and red, being almost as good as a damson; abundance of roses, red, white, and damask.

This country wants only industrious men. For it would grieve your hearts if (as I) you had seen so many miles together, by goodly rivers, uninhabited, and withal to consider how those parts of the world where men live are so greatly burdened with people.

These things I thought good to let you know, being the truth of things here as near as I have so far been able to experimentally take knowledge of.

COMING OF *FORTUNE*

Our supply of men from you came the 9th of November, 1621. Putting in at Cape Cod, some eight or ten leagues from us, the Indians that dwell thereabouts (they that were the owners of the corn which we found in graves, for which we have since given them full satisfaction and are now in great friendly league with them), sent us word that there was a ship near.

These [settlers on the *Fortune*] came all in good health, not any being sick by the way otherwise than by sea sickness, and so continue at this time, by the blessing of God. The good wife Ford was delivered of a son the first night she landed, and both of them are very well.

When it pleases God we are settled and fitted for the fishing business and other trading I doubt not but by the blessing of God the gain will give content to all. In the meantime, what we have gotten we have sent by this ship, and though it be not much, yet it will bear witness that we have not been idle, considering the smallness of our number all this summer (32 men only). We hope the Merchants will accept of it, and be encouraged to furnish us with things needful . . . which will also encourage us to put forth ourselves to the uttermost.

Then he went on to give advice on what future would-be settlers should bring as equipment, listing such things as a good store of clothes and bedding, fowling pieces, the juice of lemons for illness, butter, salad oil, paper and linseed oil for windows and cotton yarn for lamp wicks, and ends,

Your loving friend,
E.W.

Plymouth, in New England,
this 11th of December
1621.

NOTES

The settlers found trees on the end of Cape Cod, even upon Long Point; these have long since disappeared, as they have from other areas all over the end and middle of the Cape.

The men and women who crossed on the *Mayflower* did not come to be known as the Pilgrim Fathers until some hundred years later; nor was the word "Puritan" in use amongst them. The true fanatical Puritans began to arrive in Massachusetts in the 1630s, flooding across in their thousands as soon as it was proved that men could live permanently in the New World. Twenty-thousand English men and women emigrated to New England between 1628 and 1640. (Today ten million people live in New England, an area as big as England and Scotland.) But for decades the Plymouth Colony remained separate, self-contained and much more humane and liberal, at least by the narrow tenets of the day, than the other settlements that so quickly sprang up.

All dates given in *The Plymouth Adventure* are Old Style, as used by the settlers at that time, which may for all practical purposes be reckoned as ten days behind our present-day method of reckoning by the Gregorian calendar. For instance, the settlers landed at Plymouth in New England on the eleventh of December, Old Style, which we would write today as the twenty-first of December.

Captain Jones, in the year after his return to England, expressed his desire to settle permanently in New Plymouth with the settlers, and asked for a grant of land; but he was taken ill and died in Rotherhithe, on the side of the Thames, in 1622, probably from consumption contracted with the settlers in that first winter in the New World.

The following is a complete list of all the passengers who set sail on the *Mayflower* for the New World after the *Speedwell* turned back at Plymouth:

JOHN ALDEN, aged twenty-one, a cooper and carpenter engaged at Southampton to work for the settlers for a year. Stayed in the New World and married Priscilla Mullins. Died at Duxbury, New England, 1687, in his eighty-ninth year.

WILLIAM MULLINS, aged forty-two, of Dorking, Surrey. Died aboard *Mayflower,* New Plymouth Harbour, February 21 (Old Style), 1621, of combined scurvy-pneumonia-tuberculosis—termed "the sickness," the cause of death principally of all who died in that first spring. With him went his wife:

MRS. ALICE MULLINS, who died shortly after her husband.

PRISCILLA MULLINS, aged eighteen. Lived to be over eighty years of age.

JOSEPH MULLINS, Priscilla's brother, aged six. Died at the same time as his father and mother.

WILLIAM BRADFORD, aged thirty-one. Born near Austerfield, Yorkshire. Became Governor of the settlement and wrote its history, *Of Plymouth Plantation.* Died after a lifetime of wholly unselfish service to the settlement at the age of sixty-eight.

MRS. DOROTHY BRADFORD, aged twenty-three. Drowned, Cape Cod, December 7, 1620. Born in Wisbeach, Cambridgeshire.

EDWARD WINSLOW, aged between twenty-five and thirty; born in Worcestershire. Supposed author, with Bradford, of *Mourt's Relation,* one of the first accounts of the plantation sent home to England for the purpose of encouraging merchant moneylenders to continue support. Returned to England in later years and never came back. Died of fever in the Caribbean while on a mission for Cromwell, 1655.

MRS. ELIZABETH WINSLOW, his wife. Died of the sickness.

GILBERT WINSLOW, younger brother of Edward; age uncertain. Returned to England eventually, where he died in later life.

WILLIAM BREWSTER, aged fifty-four, born in Scrooby, Nottingham; died in New Plymouth, 1643. Matriculated Peterhouse, Cambridge. Founder and leader of dissenting group around Scrooby which removed to Leyden in Holland and thence to New England.

MRS. MARY BREWSTER, his wife. Died New Plymouth, 1627.

LOVE BREWSTER, their son, a little boy of nine. Died 1650, New Plymouth.

WRASTLE BREWSTER, their son, six years. Died New England, 1635.

SAMUEL FULLER, aged thirty-five, born Redenhall, Norfolk; died New Plymouth, 1633. Deacon and physician.

JOHN CARVER, aged fifty-five to sixty. Died of a stroke while working in the fields during first summer in New Plymouth, 1621. Originally a merchant of Doncaster, Yorkshire.

MRS. CATHERINE CARVER, his wife. Died soon after her husband.

CHRISTOPHER MARTIN, aged forty-six. Born Essex. Died on *Mayflower* of the sickness, Plymouth Harbour, January 8, 1621. Deposed from governorship of *Mayflower* by Brewster's group at start of voyage.

MRS. —— MARTIN, his wife, of whom nothing is known.

CAPTAIN MILES STANDISH, aged thirty-six. Soldier engaged to teach settlers use of guns, et cetera. Died Duxbury, New England, in 1656, when he was seventy-two.

MRS. ROSE STANDISH, his wife. Nothing known of her but her name. Died of the sickness.

STEPHEN HOPKINS, aged thirty-five, of Gloucestershire. Died New Plymouth, 1644, aged fifty-nine.

MRS. ELIZABETH HOPKINS, his wife.

GILES HOPKINS, their child.

CONSTANCE HOPKINS, their child.

DAMARIS HOPKINS, their child.

OCEANUS HOPKINS, their child (born on voyage).

JOHN BILLINGTON, aged thirty, of London. Always made trouble. Hanged for killing one of his fellow settlers, 1630, New Plymouth.

MRS. ELLEN BILLINGTON, his wife. (This family, "one of the profanest," escaped the sickness altogether.)

FRANCIS BILLINGTON, their son, aged eight.

JOHN BILLINGTON, their son, aged six.

ISAAC ALLERTON, aged thirty-four, of London. Died 1659.

MRS. MARY ALLERTON, his wife. Died of sickness first spring.

BARTH ALLERTON, their son. Escaped sickness.

REMEMBER ALLERTON, their daughter. Escaped sickness.

MARY ALLERTON, their daughter. Escaped sickness.

WILLIAM WHITE, aged twenty-eight. Died of the sickness.

MRS. SUSANNA WHITE, his wife, aged twenty-six. Later married Edward Winslow, 1621. Died 1680.

RESOLVED WHITE, their child, aged five. Died 1680.

PEREGRINE WHITE, their child, born on *Mayflower*, Cape Cod. Died 1703.

EDWARD TILLEY, of London. Died of the sickness.

MRS. ANNE TILLEY, his wife. Died of the sickness. They brought two adopted children, "cousins":

HUMILITY COOPER and

HENRY SAMSON, both of whom escaped the sickness and lived on into old age in New Plymouth.

JOHN TILLEY, of London. Died of sickness.

MRS. BRIDGET TILLEY, his wife. Native of Leyden, Holland. Died of the sickness.

ELIZABETH TILLEY, their young daughter. Died 1687.

THOMAS TINKER. Died of the sickness.

MRS. —— TINKER, his wife. Died of the sickness.

—— TINKER, their child, a little boy. Died of the sickness.

DEGORY PRIEST, aged forty-one, hatter, of London. Died of the sickness. The following all died of the sickness:

JOHN CRACKSTON.

—— CRACKSTON, his son.

MOSES FLETCHER.

JOHN GOODMAN.

THOMAS ROGERS.

JOHN TURNER.

—— TURNER, his son.

—— TURNER, his son.

RICHARD BRITTERIDGE.

JAMES CHILTON.

MRS. —— CHILTON, his wife.

RICHARD CLARKE.

MRS. SARAH EATON, Francis Eaton's wife.

EDWARD FULLER.

MRS. ANN FULLER, his wife.

Richard Gardiner.

Edmund Margeson.

Solomon Prower.

John Rigdale.

Thomas Williams.

John Allerton.

Thomas English, the hired sailor.

John Hooke, a boy in bond to Isaac Allerton.

Jasper Moore, a boy in bond to Isaac Allerton.

Roger Wilder, servant of Carver's.

—— Moore, an orphan boy.

William Button, servant boy to Samuel Fuller.

John Langemore, Christopher Martin's bondman.

Robert Carter, William Mullins' bondman.

William Holbeck, William White's bondman.

Edward Thompson, William White's bondman.

Ellen Moore, orphan child brought by Edward Winslow's wife.

Elias Story, Edward Winslow's servant.

The following escaped the sickness:

Desire Minter, a girl of twenty, brought by the Carvers.

Francis Cooke, wool comber.

John Cooke, his son.

Joseph Rogers, twelve-year-old son of Thomas Rogers.

Peter Browne.

Francis Eaton.

Samuel Eaton, his infant son.

Samuel Fuller, four-year-old son of Edward Fuller.

Richard Warren, of London. Born 1580; died 1628.

—— Ellis, a hired sailor.

William Trevore, a hired sailor. (Both returned to England, 1621.)

Richard Moore, orphan boy adopted by Brewsters.

—— ——, a maidservant of Mrs. Carver's; name unknown.

William Latham, a boy brought by the Carvers.

John Howland.

Edward Dotey, a man Hopkins stood bond for.

Edward Leister, a man Hopkins stood bond for.

George Soule, a man Edward Winslow stood bond for.

These were the one hundred and two persons who sailed on the *Mayflower*, besides the crew.

Brewster's exiles from Holland:	17 men
	10 women
	13 children
Those who went directly from England:	17 men
	9 women
	13 children
Hired hands:	5 men
Servants, men in bond, et cetera:	11 men
	1 woman
Orphan children and servants:	6
So that there were	50 adult men
	20 women, and
	32 children
TOTAL	102 set out.

Of the one hundred and two, half died in the first year.

BRIEF BIBLIOGRAPHY

No story is ever the whole story. And the truth of history usually otherwise than as taught in the schoolroom. Those who would know more of the story of their fathers can do no better than read the words of the men themselves; and the first comers to America left many words about themselves. Such healthy appetite, if once whetted, requires food that the man may be whole, but the speed of life today gives few the opportunities that lead to a knowledge of where exactly to look. A very select list of source material is therefore added here, which is of course only a minute fraction, but will give a good round picture both before, during and after the *Mayflower* voyage.

William Bradford, OF PLIMOTH PLANTATION. All other writings. MOURT'S RELATION, supposed by Bradford and Edward Winslow, 1622.

Robert Cushman, Sermons, Tracts, Letters, many if not most of which are to be found in Arber. See Massachusetts Historical Society Collections, et cetera. THE DANGER OF SELF-LOVE, et cetera, London, 1622.

Thomas Nashe, PIERCE PENILESSE, 1592; THE ANATOMIE OF ABSURDITIE, 1589; et cetera.

Captain John Smith, A DESCRIPTION OF NEW ENGLAND, 1616. HISTORIE OF VIRGINIA, 1624. See also his SEA GRAMMAR on ships and shipbuilding, 1630; his ADVERTISEMENTS FOR THE UNEXPERIENCED PLANTERS; NEW ENGLAND'S TRIALS, 1622; et cetera.

Pulsifer, PLYMOUTH COLONY RECORDS, Boston, 1861.

Edward Winslow, HYPOCRISIE UNMASKED, 1646; GOOD NEWS FROM ENGLAND, 1624; et cetera.

Richard Hakluyt, PRINCIPALL NAVIGATIONS, 1589; et cetera.

Thomas Dekker, THE GULLS' HORNE-BOOK, 1609; et cetera.

Fynes Moryson, ITINERARY, 1617.

Edward Arber, THE STORY OF THE PILGRIM FATHERS, 1606–1623, As Told by Themselves, Their Friends and Their Enemies, Edited from the Original Texts by Edward Arber, Boston, 1897.

Roger Williams, A KEY INTO THE LANGUAGE OF AMERICA, 1643.

George F. Willison, SAINTS AND STRANGERS, New York, 1946.

H. M. Dexter, THE ENGLAND AND HOLLAND OF THE PILGRIMS, 1905; and other related works.

Stephen Vincent Benét, WESTERN STAR.

Richard H. Tawney, RELIGION AND THE RISE OF CAPITALISM, New York, 1926.

Alexander Young, CHRONICLES, 1841.

John Robinson, COLLECTED WORKS, London, 1851.

Robert Browne, A TREATISE OF REFORMATION WITHOUT TARYING FOR ANIE, Holland, 1582.